THE GUARDIANS

A.M. Colwell

For Danny J.

Prologue

"You're absolutely certain that what you're telling me is correct?"

Bora Black stood with her back to her Second, darkness curling off her skin. There weren't many windows at the Headquarters of the White Mask Society, as most of the building was subterranean. But she had one of the few offices above ground, granting her a view overlooking the rundown corner of downtown Los Angeles where the building was located.

She saw none of it, however, her mind preoccupied.

Zak Glover responded in a voice too calm given the situation. "Yes. These are the results the investigation turned up."

"A diplomatic response," said Black. She considered his words for a moment. Considered her next actions.

There was a spy in the White Mask Society.

The ultimate betrayal.

A person in whom Black had bestowed so much trust had been responsible for the chaotic events of the last few months. An invasion of Headquarters; the kidnapping of six hyden, of one of her Guardians; the deaths of said Guardian and of one of the hyden…

"I'd like to hear your thoughts," said Black at last, turning to face her Second.

Glover was one of a few people who could stand their ground against her, somehow never intimidated by the unnatural stare of her obsidian eyes or the constant shadows that surrounded her. He straightened to his considerable height before answering. "I believe we could use this to our advantage."

"Explain."

"Let them stay. Find a pariah so they think we're off their trail. Give them—"

"—give them false intel," said Black, finishing his thought.

He nodded.

Black considered him a moment. "Considering Kain is no longer alive, do you suspect they will continue to work against us?"

"Kain may be dead, but his mission lives on. If this spy really believes in the cause, it's likely they will find a way to resurrect the project."

"The Omega Project?"

Glover nodded again.

Black closed her eyes for a moment. She cursed herself for ever having approved of the Omega Project. Nothing good had come of it. "I want the situation monitored closely," said Black. "From now on, I want your first priority to be to keep a close watch on Xaili Williams."

CHAPTER ONE

One Year Later

Sweat dripped down Yara Rivers's forehead. She wiped it away impatiently, focusing instead on her crouched opponent. They circled each other slowly. Her muscles were aching with exhaustion and every part of her body was screaming at her to stop. But she could not stop. She shook her head trying to knock such thoughts from her mind. She was keenly aware of all the eyes watching her, not least of all those of the man in front of her.

His blonde curls, normally voluminous on his head, hung limp over his eyes, just as sweaty as Yara. He shook them out of his face, and, in that moment, Yara charged at him. He was fast, but she was faster. She managed to catch him at the exact moment he was off guard with a swift kick to the stomach, before tackling him and sending them both crashing to the floor. The onlookers cheered loudly. He quickly managed to regain control however, and used her own inertia to throw her off of him, leaping back to his feet as though nothing had happened. He laughed.

"This is pointless," said Yara, collapsing at last on the floor, her back throbbing from the impact against the ground.

"Are you OK?" said the man, hurrying over to her, the laugh fading from his face.

The cheering and jeering crowd flickered out of existence and the room around them evaporated, leaving nothing but the black glass walls and silver grid of the simulators, a virtual reality environment that enabled White Masks to train.

It was also fun to just play around in.

Yara blinked her eyes open to see Robin Green leaning over her, looking concerned.

"I'm fine," she said, grabbing his extended hand and letting him pull her up. She groaned in pain, clutching her backside. Blood was pounding in her face, making her feel both hot and cold at the same time. She was exhausted. "I don't know if I can do this, Robin."

"You can. When you're on form, you're better than any of us," he said, wiping the sweat from his face with the bottom of his shirt. Given how much experience he had, it was hard to remember that he was only a year older than Yara. She couldn't imagine anyone her age being as confident or self-assured as he was. "And you can't call me 'Robin' anymore, remember? From now on, it's 'R.'"

"You see what I mean?" said Yara exasperatedly. "I can't even remember that stupid rule. I'm really just not cut out for this."

Robin frowned at her. It had been nearly six months since Yara had decided she wanted to join the White Mask Society, an operation whose *raison d'être* was keeping a peaceful coexistence between humans and Deviants while ideally hiding it all from the humans as they did. "Deviant" was the name given to any humanoid beings who weren't quite… human. Yara was a Deviant. Specifically, she was a hydan, one of the last. Hyden were a rare race of people who had unique abilities. In Yara's case, she could see glimpses of the future.

Robin already occupied the job title at the Society that Yara was after: Guardian.

The training to become a Guardian at the White Mask Society was grueling and unforgiving. For the last six months, Yara had been up from dawn until well after midnight, spending all of her waking hours studying and training for the upcoming evaluation all Guardian initiates had to pass before being inducted. In that time, she had broken three bones, cracked a rib, dislocated her shoulder, and suffered one relatively serious concussion. Fortunately for her, the Medics at the White Mask Society were the best in the world. Their research on both humans and Deviants had enabled them to discover effective and fast-acting treatments. So no matter how badly Yara's leg was broken, she could be back to her usual schedule in no time at all.

She was happy not to have any down time, however, even though it meant getting back to training so soon after any injuries. The events of a year prior had taken their toll on Yara, and whenever she was alone or she closed her eyes, her mind would replay it all as though determined to drive her mad.

"You can do anything you put your mind to, kid," said Robin. He pressed his finger between her eyebrows, smoothing out her frown. "Unclench, will ya? There's a reason you're here."

"Yeah, yeah, I know," said Yara impatiently. "I'm special, exceptions were made, blah blah blah."

Robin chuckled.

She'd heard it all too many times and was reminded of her special treatment whenever she was with the other Guardian trainees. Initiates applied young. Trained young. Yara had just turned 19, making her nearly three years older than the average Guardian initiate. She would have felt more awkward about it all if it weren't for the fact that, due to her small stature, she blended in well enough with all of the pubescent initiates.

"Black wouldn't have let you join the initiate program if she didn't think ya had it in you."

Yara rolled her eyes. "No pressure, right, *R?*" she said, putting an extra emphasis on the letter. "I think… I think this was just a mistake. You know, maybe I can still join the Society, but be like… a consultant or something. Maybe the resident oracle."

Robin ran a hand through his hair. "Look. Bottom line. Is this really what you want to do?"

Yara bit her lip. Not long ago, she had been sure that this was where she wanted to be. It was that certainty and a feeling of purpose she had never had before that kept her getting up with the sun and working as hard as she had been. Recently though, doubt had been creeping in. A crippling fear that she wasn't good enough. Would never be good enough.

But she wasn't about to tell Robin that.

Bora Black, the Head of the White Mask Society, had made an exception that had never been made in Society history when she let Yara become an initiate. Yara had joined training late in the game. Her Guardians had gone to bat for her, promising to train her themselves rather than take the attention of the other trainers away from the chosen initiates in the already ongoing class. Robin said he'd take full responsibility if she wasn't ready in time for the test she'd have to pass to get the assignment. He used the argument that she had started her training already, which was mostly true. She had practiced and trained with him and her other two Guardians in the height of the crisis last year, and she had been capable enough that she'd orchestrated the rescue of not only herself but six other prisoners. Not to mention, her parents' histories as Guardians themselves indicated she may have a natural born talent for the job.

"Maybe we should go grab some lunch," said Robin. "C said they would wait for us in the commissary."

C was Carter Knox. The second of Yara's three Guardians. They'd been assigned to Yara when she was under the threat of Ramsey Kain, a brilliant but evil man who had stolen Yara's and several other hyden's abilities. Carter was also a Deviant, though not a hydan like Yara. They were a shape shifter.

"Yeah, OK," said Yara. She and Robin left the sims, wiping the sweat from their faces as they walked.

"Hey, can I ask you something?" said Robin. He wasn't looking at her.

"What's up?" said Yara, scrubbing the towel along the back of her neck and trying to smell her armpits as discreetly as possible to make sure she didn't smell too bad to eat before showering.

Robin was silent for so long that Yara turned to look at him. He kept staring at the floor in front of them as they walked, evidently deep in thought.

"Y'know what," he said, screwing up his face and laughing. "Never mind."

Yara furrowed her brow, but smiled. "What?" she said, nudging him playfully with her elbow. "What was that?"

Robin waved his hand, brushing away the subject. "No, it was nothing."

"C'mon," said Yara, poking him with her pointer fingers and grinning, "you have to tell me!"

He gave a huge sigh and said, "I was gonna ask you if I could use your deodorant. I left mine in my quarters and I don't want to assault C with my pungent, manly, yet irresistible smell."

"Oh," said Yara. She may have had the supernatural gift of seeing the future, but she also had one not-so-supernatural gift: she could tell when people were lying. And Robin was lying now. She just didn't know why. She decided not to press the subject and said instead, "I didn't bring mine, either. Maybe my cucumber-melon scented lady sweat will cancel yours out and C won't notice."

"Let's just hope they don't shift into a bloodhound."

Robin and Yara made their way to the commissary, got a couple of sandwiches, and joined Carter, who was sitting by themself at a table reading something on a tablet.

"Hey, C," said Robin. "Is that the new edition of Guardians Monthly?"

"Does that exist?" said Yara, astonished.

Carter looked up, their glasses halfway down their nose, and shook their head, half a smile on their lips. "No, it doesn't."

Yara blushed, feeling stupid. She shoved Robin playfully. He nearly fell from his chair, off-balance from laughing, and recovered with a small "whoa!" before saying, "Right, sorry. So, what are you reading, C?"

Carter pushed their glasses up to the bridge of their nose and sighed. They looked tired. "New assignment from Black."

Just like that, boiling liquid filled Yara's stomach. She could feel heat rising in her face. She tried to stay cool, but feigning calm when she was anxious had never been her strong suit. She had known that this would happen. Dreaded it for the last six months. Carter and Robin couldn't possibly be her Guardians forever. The Society's purpose was not to give Yara friends; it was to help people. But a part of her had hoped that things would never change. That Carter and Robin would always be there. She had wanted Erik, her third and final Guardian, to always be there too, but…

Her thoughts trailed away and she stared down at her sandwich.

Thinking about Erik was painful.

"Red, you OK?" said Carter, noticing Yara's sudden change in demeanor. Despite Yara being an initiate, and the rules stating that she thereby was supposed to go by "Y," Carter had never gotten out of the habit of calling her "Red." It didn't bother Yara, though. She hated being called "Y." It always made her question herself, like people were always asking her, "Why? Why? Why?"

"Hmm?" she said, looking up. "Oh! Yeah. Fine." She took a large bite out of her sandwich and said, her mouth full, "So, you guys have a new assignment, huh? That's cool."

There was a little too much knowing in the look that Robin was giving her, but Yara ignored him.

"No," said Carter. "*We* don't have a new assignment. You do."

Yara blanched. "What? How is that possible? I'm not even officially a Guardian."

"Yet," said Robin.

Carter laughed. "You're a Guardian *short*. Black's finally found someone to replace—well, to fill in."

They had been on the verge of mentioning Erik. It had been hard for

Carter and Robin, too, when Erik died. They had known him longer than she had, worked with him more closely, and while the whole point of avoiding using names among the Guardian division of the Society was to avoid becoming emotionally attached to someone in case they were lost in the line of duty, it was impossible not to. They had all loved Erik.

"Took her long enough," said Robin. "It's been a year."

"She trusted we could handle it, clearly," said Carter.

"Can we not handle it anymore?"

"You know the deal, R. Three Guardians is standard."

"So," said Yara, interrupting them, "you mean, you're still my Guardians?"

"I was actually thinking about requesting a change of assignment myself," said Robin with a heavy sigh. "You've just become too boring."

"Cut it out!" she said, looking from Robin to Carter. Hope filled her belly at the thought of Carter and Robin continuing to be her Guardians, but she was too nervous to trust it completely, and too embarrassed to ask for reassurance. Clearing her throat and trying to appear as casual as possible, she continued, "So, I'm gonna have a third Guardian again? What for? I mean, Kain's dead. It's not exactly like I still need protection."

"Why, you wanna get rid of us?" said Robin. He turned to Carter. "Can you believe this? She gets trained as a Guardian and all of a sudden, she's too good for us."

"You're still a hydan," said Carter, ignoring Robin. "There's not many of you left, and Black thinks it's a good idea to keep Guardians assigned to you, just in case. Obviously, it's not nearly as serious as it was before, but—"

"Cut to the chase, C. Who's the new guy?" said Robin, fitting the rest of his sandwich into his mouth and chewing the sizable chunk slowly, bits of lettuce sticking from between his lips.

"That would be me," said a voice from behind Yara. The three of them looked up to see a girl with a mischievous grin looking down at them.

"Red, R, this is Ash."

CHAPTER TWO

Ash With an A

Yara's first impression of Ash was that she was absolutely beautiful. Her second was just how young she looked. She was barely taller than Yara, which admittedly wasn't saying much, but Ash looked like she couldn't have been older than 18, maybe even younger. Her eyes were a shocking shade of yellow, much more striking than Carter's amber-hued shape shifter eyes. Ash's resembled the dying embers in a fire and flickered with the same quality of flame. Her long, black hair fell to her waist, streaked with red. Not the same red as Yara's hair, who was a natural ginger, but a bright red, made even more striking by the contrast of her dark skin.

"Hello," said Yara, suddenly painfully aware of her own short hair and rather plain face, still sweaty from training. She reached out to shake Ash's hand nonetheless. Ash didn't seem to notice and had already wrapped her arms around Yara in a quick but genuine hug. Ash's skin was hot against Yara's and smelled vaguely of smoke. Yara, who did not like being touched, froze until Ash pulled away.

"Hello, Yara Rivers," she said, beaming.

"A is a Vurwari. Fire nymph," said Carter to Yara as Ash hugged Robin, "in case you hadn't guessed." Yara barely heard them, watching as Robin grinned at Ash, introducing himself.

"What does that mean, exactly?" said Yara under her breath to Carter, hoping Ash wouldn't hear.

"It means I can do this," said Ash. Yara watched as, before her very eyes, a bright ball of crackling fire appeared in Ash's palm. She twiddled her fingers playfully and the fire, moving like a living thing, snaked its way between her fingers before licking her arm and flickering out of existence, leaving not even a trace of smoke.

"That was... I mean, that's..."

"But enough about me," said Ash, taking a seat next to Robin, her bright, fiery eyes fixed on Yara. "You're the Ward, here, right?" She laughed. A clear, infectious laugh. Yara gaped, feeling more and more self-conscious by the second. "A hydan! And you're thinking about joining the Society to boot?"

"Yup," said Robin, looking at Yara fondly. "She's training to be a Guardian. Initiation is tomorrow." He squeezed her hand, looking excited and proud. It made Yara's stomach feel queasy, and she pushed the rest of her sandwich away.

"Well, it was really nice to meet you, Ash, but I think I'm gonna go study before tomorrow."

"I'll come with you," said Robin, getting up to join her, but Yara shook her head.

"No, really. It's fine. I think I'll work better if I'm on my own tonight."

Robin sat back down, looking slightly crestfallen.

Yara walked out of the commissary, feeling bitter and jealous. They were feelings she wasn't altogether unfamiliar with, although she wasn't sure why she was feeling this way. The last time she had felt jealous was watching Robin interact with his ex-girlfriend, another Guardian named Nayla. But that had been a small twinge of jealousy, easily remedied by the fact that Robin spent almost all of his time with Yara. In any case, Yara had no claim over Robin. No right to feel jealous. After all, Yara had fallen in love with someone else. Someone who had loved her in kind.

Now with that someone gone, Robin had been filling a hole in her heart with his crooked face and easy laugh. She didn't want to share him with anyone else.

And Ash... she was so full of life. Ever since the events of last year, Yara had been too busy recovering, physically and emotionally, to have much joy. Yara didn't even know it was possible to have as much energy as Ash had already displayed in the last few minutes. Even more intimidating, she could control fire and probably do all sorts of other impressive nymph things.

Yara couldn't understand where these feelings were coming from. Why did it matter that Ash was more beautiful and more vibrant and probably more talented than Yara?

Because, said a little voice in Yara's head, *because what if Robin falls in love with her and not you?* Yara brushed the thought away, hating herself. Robin was his own person, and he had the right to love anyone he wanted. Nothing had ever happened between them. Yara wasn't even sure she wanted anything to happen. She still felt a painful ache in her heart every time she thought of Erik. She still loved him. And it wouldn't be fair to herself or to Robin if she started a relationship with him or anyone else. Besides, relationships were near impossible in the Society, as people kept reminding her.

There were just too many reasons it was a bad idea.

She found herself back in her quarters. She had meant to walk to the library, but her feet had subconsciously brought her here.

In the time she had lived at Headquarters, she had personalized her room by papering the walls with photographs, taken from her old room at her aunt's apartment. But now, in addition to the photos of her and Aunt Catherine that she had cut and pasted over picturesque calendar pages, she now had pictures of her new life.

There was only one with Erik. Guardians weren't much for taking selfies. She loved that picture the most of any in her whole room. It was the four of them in the training cubicles, back when her Guardians had first started teaching her self-defense. Yara was wearing a white workout uniform, and Carter, Robin, and Erik were in black. They looked exhausted but happy. Erik was glancing sideways at her. The Yara in the picture had not noticed he was looking at her, but the Yara staring at the four of them now could see very clearly where his green eyes had been pointed.

Robin and Ash stayed with Carter at the commissary, chatting and getting to know each other. Ash was vibrant, energetic, joyful. Her devil-may-care attitude would certainly be different from Erik, who had been a stickler for the rules. Up until the end, at least.

Carter didn't speak much as Robin and Ash talked. Carter didn't mind. They liked listening just as much as participating. It was a good way to get to know people. Robin mentioned his two brothers, but glossed over some of the uglier history with his family, while Ash told a graphic story about when her entire family got food poisoning. Robin was in stitches by the time Carter had to excuse themself to return to their duties.

They bid their two fellow Guardians goodbye and got up with their mind already on what awaited them tomorrow, when they ran into someone unexpected on their way out.

"Oh," said the man in polite surprise upon noticing Carter.

"Darwin," said Carter.

Darwin Jackson was just as lovely as Carter remembered. He had soft blonde hair, ears that stuck out, giving him a sort of elfish appearance, and the same almond-shaped eyes as his sister, Nayla, who was standing right next to him.

"N," said Carter, turning to her in kind.

Nayla, usually charming and quick to ease the tension, seemed at a loss for words. "I'll meet you inside," she said gently to her brother. She gave Carter a meaningful look and left the two alone.

Darwin was apparently just as caught off guard as Carter. But how could he not expect to see Carter here? The shape shifter, after all, worked at the Society. Darwin did not.

In an attempt to seem calm, Carter forced a smile, trying to appear as though they were pleasantly surprised to see Darwin after such a long time apart.

Their relationship had started on test day for the initiate class the year after Carter graduated. Family for the new initiates had come to see the new recruits take their tests, and there, amongst the cheering family members, had been Darwin, watching his sister become a Guardian. He was as beautiful then as he was now, and the way he looked at Carter was unlike anything they had ever experienced. His gentle eyes made Carter feel like there was no one else in the world except them.

Carter hadn't expected to receive any attention from a civilian, but Darwin had taken to them instantly. He hadn't had any misgivings about Carter's gender identity and, instead, was fascinated with the fact that they were a shape shifter. Expecting him to just be another human wanting to see magic tricks, Carter had been pleasantly surprised when Darwin, instead of asking Carter to demonstrate their ability, started questioning how the Society handled Deviant-human conflicts. Initially somewhat reserved, he turned out to be funny and smart once he became more comfortable amidst the chaos of Headquarters. He could have joined the Society as easily as his sister had, but he had another objective. He was studying law at the University of Southern California, and from the moment he told Carter that his greatest ambition was working for a non-profit law office that fought for animal rights, Carter's heart melted.

The beginning of their courtship had been slow with both of them so busy. But they still found stolen hours throughout the following months to get a cup of coffee, to take a walk, to huddle up together in Darwin's apartment and hide from the world, laughing and talking until the sun came up.

In the year that Carter and Darwin were seeing each other, Nayla was busy with her own paramour, Robin, who had been in her initiate class. Nayla and Robin had fallen fast and hard for each other with none of the reserve that Carter and Darwin shared.

Then a year after that came Erik, who—in turn—fell for Yara.

Carter watched from the outside as their two fellow Guardians were swallowed up by their feelings, for better or for worse. And then Carter started to see in themself behavior reflected by Robin and Erik. Being in love made their jobs matter less. It was becoming too hard to be away from Darwin. Carter loved him and wanted to be with him. It had begun to make Carter resentful for having to work instead.

So Carter had ended the relationship with a breaking heart, hoping that perhaps one day when Darwin had an established job and Carter had graduated from the field they could find each other again.

Darwin had never forgiven them.

"Lunch with the sis?" Carter managed in an attempt at being nonchalant.

Darwin nodded, but couldn't seem to meet Carter's eyes. He had never been good at hiding his feelings. It was impossible not to read every single thought in his eyes. Carter had told him as much back when they were dating. Ever since they stopped seeing each other, Darwin made a concerted effort not to look Carter in the eye, as though determined to hide whatever he was feeling.

"I'm sorry I can't join you," continued Carter, not at all sorry. "I was just on my way out."

"Yeah," said Darwin, speaking for the first time. They were standing so far apart from each other that they were drawing some curious looks from a few passersby. Even though Carter couldn't see his eyes, they knew there was something else he wanted to say.

"How's school?" said Carter in an attempt to fill the silence. Once, it had been so easy to be around each other. Now, it was as though they had forgotten how to speak.

"Good," said Darwin. "Graduating in May."

"Congratulations," said Carter, genuine happiness expanding in their chest.

At the change in their voice, Darwin finally looked up, his innocent eyes locking onto theirs, causing a small jolt of electricity to surge through Carter's gut. "Thanks."

"You must be so excited. You finally get to pursue your dream."

Darwin's eyebrows creased, a small show of sadness. "I'm not sure we're really there. You know, at the place where we can have honest discussions about how we are."

Carter nodded sadly. "Right. Sorry."

"I didn't mean—"

"No, no. It's fine. I understand. I'll, uh…" Carter looked around and shoved their hands into their pockets. "It was good to see you. Take care of yourself."

Carter started to walk away, could feel Darwin's eyes on their back, but they did not turn around. Darwin belonged to another part of Carter's life.

One that no longer existed.

Night had fallen, but sleep did not come to Yara.

More so because she had nothing else to do, she had taken a long, hot shower, then turned the knobs all the way to cold and doused herself in the freezing water for a full minute before stepping into the fogged bathroom.

She stared at herself in the mirror, still dripping water. If someone had taken a picture of her now and showed it to her a year ago, she would not have believed it. She still had the same high forehead and the same pointed nose, but it was a different person staring at her in the mirror. It wasn't just that she now kept her bright red hair short rather than long, or that her face had lost the baby fat in her cheeks making her chin more pointed, but there was a gleam in her eyes that hadn't been there before. A kind of fierceness she could barely believe was in her own face. Her time in Kain's laboratory had hardened her, and if she was being honest with herself, a part of her that had broken on his table had yet to heal.

The loss of Erik still felt painfully fresh, even after a year. She hadn't expected the pain to still be this fresh after so much time. She had been so young when her parents had died that it had never felt like anything more than a distant dream, a missed opportunity, but while she had only known Erik a couple of months, she had loved him.

She felt a twinge in her heart.

She had loved him.

He'd entered her life when she was confused and vulnerable, and while she was only a year older now, looking back she seemed like a child. How could she have understood what she'd felt for him? What she felt for all of her Guardians?

Yet Erik had loved her back. He had made her feel like a normal teenager with a normal crush on a normal boy who also had a crush on her. It was like what high school should have been and never was for the awkward girl who didn't like to be touched. She could never have that normal-ness again. That naivety had died with Erik.

After drying off, Yara lay in bed for an hour before deciding she was still too nervous about initiation to sleep. A few times, she toyed with inducing a vision to see whether or not she passed, but it felt like cheating somehow. And what if she saw a future in which she failed? Would she even go through with taking the test at all? It was dizzying to think about, and the easy solution was simply not to know. Then she wouldn't have to think about paradoxes and fate.

She got out of bed, pulled a graying Society hoodie over one of her father's old t-shirts, soft and worn with age and sporting a logo for a music store in Burbank that now no longer existed, and headed silently out of her room. It was nearly midnight. The halls were empty. She followed her feet until she found herself at the Hall of Memoriam.

It was a small room tucked away in a far corner of Headquarters with walls of white marble. Unlike most aspects of the Society, technology had not infiltrated this room. It was lit by oil lamps, giving the room a warm, yellow glow that flickered on the smooth walls, casting the engravings in shadow and light. Every inch of the walls was carved with the names of those from the Los Angeles branch of the White Mask Society who died in the line of duty. It was weeks of visiting Erik's memorial before it occurred to her to look for her parents'. Aunt Catherine only told Yara when she was 17 the truth about Sierra and Theo Rivers. Yara had looked for their names, not really expecting to find them, but they were there.

SIERRA TANNER RIVERS

THEO RIVERS

Yara had asked for details about their deaths. Glover told her a story of heroics and noble sacrifice.

He'd been lying, but Yara never pressed for the truth. She didn't visit the names now. The lack of emotion she felt at her parents' memorial always made her feel guilty. So instead, she walked toward Erik's name without thinking.

"Hey," she whispered in the silence. Her fingers ran over the grooves of his name.

ERIK CARPENTER

No pomp, no circumstance. He had only been 18, had died to save her, and this was all there was to remember him. No dates, no empty words of comfort to mark him as "brother," "son," "beloved."

Sadness washed over her. She leaned against the cold wall and let herself slide to the floor, her eyes closed.

"I didn't expect to find anyone down here at this hour."

Yara's eyes snapped open with a small cry of surprise to see Carter standing in the doorway. There were deep circles under their amber eyes, which flickered with the light from the lamps.

"Hi," she said as Carter sat next to her on the floor. "What are you doing down here?"

"Same thing as you, probably," said Carter with a smile. Both of them leaned their heads against the marble and fell quiet.

It helped to have Carter there. They were calming, as though they could simply absorb her anxiety. The two of them sat like that for a while.

"Nervous about tomorrow?" they asked eventually.

"I guess so," said Yara. "Can I ask you something?"

"Of course," said Carter.

"What if… what if I'm not sure I want to be a Guardian?"

Carter was quiet for a few moments before turning to look at her. Yara turned her head to meet their eyes. "I would say you'd probably wanna be sure before becoming one."

"I don't want to upset Robin. He vouched for me."

"I'm sure R just wants you to be happy."

Yara bit her lip.

"What's on your mind, Red?"

"It's just… my parents were Guardians and you guys are Guardians, and you're the first friends I ever had, really. I think I just jumped into this because I thought it was expected of me. But if you're being honest with yourself, do I really seem like Guardian material?"

They pushed their glasses up the bridge of their nose. "It doesn't matter what I think. What matters is what you want."

Yara imagined herself dressed in Guardian gear, armor and all, battling unknown enemies, risking her life on someone else's orders. She had never been good at following orders. She was too stubborn, always questioning, and inevitably thought she knew better. Being a Guardian meant being a soldier who would put their faith in their commander and obey blindly, believing that what they were told to do was the right thing just because someone higher-ranking told them so. Was that what she wanted? Was this what she was good at? After all the training, after all the broken bones and hours of grueling exercises… maybe it wasn't.

"It's normal to have doubts," said Carter after a moment. "Sometimes those doubts come from a real place. But sometimes they come from a fear of failure that's simply masquerading as doubt. It's easier to quit than it is to fail at something you care about."

"So what am I feeling, then? Is it real doubt? Or fear-doubt?"

"Bad news, Red. You're the only one who can know the answer to that."

"I was afraid of that."

"Either way, don't let R be a factor in whatever you decide."

"You really don't think it would make Robin mad?"

Carter chuckled. "It's pretty hard to make R mad."

"Yeah," said Yara. "I can't even imagine what that would look like."

"It isn't pretty."

"You've seen it?"

Carter smiled, their eyes out of focus as if they were recalling a memory. "Here and there. E used to get under his skin. The two of them could always rile each other up."

Yara laughed, and the laugh caught in her throat and came out more like a sob. "I just miss him so much," she said eventually, fighting the tears that burned in the corners of her eyes.

"Me too."

"I don't think I can do it, Carter," she said quietly.

Carter squeezed her arm but said nothing.

When they left the memorial for their beds, Carter bade Yara good night as they headed to their quarters and she made her way to hers. Initiation was in less than seven hours, which meant she had until then to figure out how to tell Robin and Bora Black that despite all their efforts in training her, all the exceptions they'd made in her favor, that she would not be taking the test after all.

She hoped Robin would forgive her.

Stifling a huge yawn, she pushed the door of her room open and screamed.

"Please don't scream!" said the man standing in her bedroom, holding his hands out, pleadingly. "I… I didn't know where else to go."

Yara's breath was shallow and rapid. She thought she might hyperventilate from the shock.

"Erik?"

CHAPTER THREE

Erik

"Hi, Yara," said Erik in a small voice.

Yara had not moved. Her mouth was still hanging open, the blood drained from her face, one trembling hand still on the doorknob.

"Look," he said, taking a tentative step toward her, "I know I probably shouldn't be here—"

Yara made a sound, exhaling loudly, still unable to form coherent words. Her legs were about to collapse under her.

Erik looked at her.

It *was* him.

Wasn't it?

Though perhaps his cheeks were slightly more sunken, he had the same straight nose, the same brilliantly green eyes. His mouth still quirked to the side as he watched her, unsure what was coming next. But his hair... His hair had once been a tousled mess of thick, black locks. Now it was completely and blindingly white.

Despite this change in his appearance, Yara could not deny it. The man standing before her was Erik.

With a tremendous effort, Yara took a couple of shaky steps forward so she was standing right in front of him. He looked at her, tears in his eyes, but he did not reach out for her. Unable to look away from his face, Yara reached up to touch his cheek, half expecting her hand to fall through the air and find he was as insubstantial as a ghost.

But he was real.

His skin was rough with stubble and reassuringly warm. She moved her hand to rest over his heart. It was there. Beating into the palm of her hand as if it had never stopped. It seemed to call her name with each pump. *Ya-ra. Ya-ra. Ya-ra.*

"It's you…" she said, her voice breaking.

Erik nodded, his eyes locked on hers. How had she forgotten how very green they were? She would never forget again.

"How…" but she couldn't phrase the question. Erik had died a year ago. His body had been carried back in a black bag with an embroidered white mask over his face like a shroud, and he had been cremated, his ashes entombed in the memorial she had just come from with Carter. How, then, could he be standing here, in front of her, solid and breathing and warm?

"I don't know. The last thing I remember is going to get you after your crazy suicide mission, and fighting with Kain, and then…"

And then dying.

"I woke up in front of the library and I just came here. Without even thinking about it. I thought you'd died from the virus. But I just needed to see you. And I came to your room and it's still yours so I figured you must have survived somehow and, well, here you are…" His voice trailed away, and his heart beat faster under Yara's hand. Only then did she realize it was still resting on his chest. She wanted to pull it back, but couldn't bring herself to.

"This all happened today?" she said, shock still making her hands tremble.

Erik nodded.

"You don't remember anything since—I mean, before—"

"Please can I kiss you?" said Erik, the words spilling from his mouth as though he simply could not contain them for another second.

Yara's breath caught in her throat. "Yes," she said. Or tried to say. The only sound that escaped her was a breath. The next thing she knew, Erik was kissing her and the world faded around them and the only thing that existed was Erik and his lips on hers and his hands on her back and in her hair. The pain and guilt of the last year faded away with each breath and she let herself sink into his body. Into oblivion.

CHAPTER FOUR

Late

Yara woke up the next morning feeling happier and more well rested than she had in a long time. She couldn't remember why at first, but as she stretched, she found warm and solid arms wrapped around her and the events of last night came flooding back. She carefully turned around, almost afraid of what she would find.

Erik was still there, fast asleep. His once-black-now-silver hair was impossibly mussed, giving him the impression of having just been shocked with electricity. His eyebrows were furrowed as though he were deep in thought. A muscle was twitching in his neck. Yara smiled, unable to help herself. She didn't want to think about what this meant. What it was to have Erik here, suddenly. The thing she wanted most in the world, and it had just shown up on her doorstep. It didn't matter. Nothing mattered. Just that Erik was with her, and he was breathing. She couldn't let herself think about how little sense it all made, or what sort of questions they would face once everyone knew.

She softly trailed her finger down his neck, along his collarbone, down his shoulder and arm. She couldn't stop herself from touching him, reassuring herself that he was real and that last night had really happened.

Biting her lip to stop from smiling so wide that her mouth might slide right off the sides of her face, she turned around, pushing her body into his and relishing the heat emanating off of him, when her eyes caught sight of the alarm clock.

"Oh my god," she whispered, feeling suddenly panicked. It was nearly 0815. She had overslept and was a quarter of an hour late for initiation. The arrival of Erik had pushed everything out of her mind, including the Guardian initiation she was supposed to formally withdraw from. She extricated herself as carefully as possible from Erik's arms, trying not to wake him, and dressed as quickly as she could, her bare skin shivering as soon as it touched the morning air.

Unfortunately, in her haste, she fell over while pulling her pants on, collapsing into her desk with a loud succession of cursing and banging.

Erik woke with a start, looking confused and groggy. "Wha—?" he said blearily, trying to regain his bearings. "Yara?"

She groaned, pulling herself up gingerly. "I'm sorry. I didn't want to wake you up."

He rubbed the sleep from his eyes. "It's OK. Where are you going?"

Yara hesitated. "Well, a lot's happened… I'm running late." She looked at Erik who looked irresistibly disheveled. "You should come with me."

"Come?" said Erik.

"Yeah," said Yara. "I have a feeling I'm about to get in a lot of trouble, but if you're with me, they won't yell at me as much. Or maybe they'll yell at me more," she added to herself as an afterthought. "They can be unpredictable in that way."

Erik laughed and it was a wonderful sound. Bright and unexpected and joyful. She tried to remember if she had ever heard him laugh with such abandon. He got up and started to get dressed. Yara pointedly looked away from his nakedness, feeling embarrassed even after having become intimately familiar with his body just a few glorious hours ago. He didn't have anything different to wear from what he had arrived in yesterday, which was a ragged long-sleeved shirt and dusty jeans torn in several places.

"So, where are we going?" said Erik as he followed Yara out of her room. "What kind of trouble have you gotten yourself into?"

"You mean besides bedding a ghost?" she said with a dry laugh. She stopped laughing immediately. What had she done? She squeezed his hand to remind herself that he was real.

"You mean the hair?" said Erik, tugging at a lock of silver hair.

"No I mean—" She cut herself off.

"What is it?" said Erik, looking politely confused.

Yara stopped in her tracks, and Erik stopped too, still with that look of friendly curiosity.

"Erik," she said, finding herself unable to look in his eyes. "Last night... I mean, when you—" She cut herself off when a couple of Guardians, holding white masks, hurried past them, talking excitedly. No doubt they, too, were running to initiation to watch as the new class of Guardians took their tests. They barely noticed Erik and Yara standing against the wall.

"I'm sorry if you felt pressured," said Erik, his expression suddenly turning to concern, misreading Yara's discomfort.

"No!" she said hurriedly. "No, not at all, that's not what I—Last night was amazing. But there's something you should know."

His brow furrowed.

Words were swimming around her head. She was torn between wanting to bury herself in his arms and forget the world, and running to Robin and Carter to just let them make all the decisions for her so she wouldn't have to think. Erik clearly didn't remember dying. Did he even know how much time had passed? That it had been twelve long months and the world had kept turning and his friends and family had gone on without him, mourning his loss and trying to heal? Was she the person to tell him? Was now the time or place?

"I missed you so much," she said finally. "And when I saw you last night, I couldn't... I still can't believe it. And I was so happy, and—Last night was my first time," she spat, the words spilling from her mouth. She could feel her cheeks reddening as heat climbed up her face. She expected him to laugh, only to find that he looked as sheepish as she felt.

"Me too," he said in a small voice, a hint of a smile playing at his lips.

"Really?" said Yara. "I figured, I mean since you were so... It's just—" She struggled to find the right words, before saying, "You're just so hot."

Erik laughed, that same bright sound as before. "So are you," he said, his green eyes twinkling.

Yara laughed and snorted loudly. "Yeah, right."

Erik stopped her from berating herself further by grabbing her face and kissing it fiercely. When he pulled away, Yara found herself breathless, her mind wiped blank.

"Aren't you late for something?" he said after a moment.

"What?" said Yara. Words were traveling very slowly to her brain. "Oh! Crap, yeah. Let's go."

And they ran hand in hand down the corridor toward the training rooms.

* * *

"Where is she? She should have been here almost an hour ago!" Robin wasn't used to feeling anxious. He was particularly well-suited for the role of Guardian because he was adept at staying calm in the face of danger. For some reason, though, today was a different story.

After their final training session the previous day, Robin had come so close to bringing up a subject he had been sitting on for months. Him and Yara. But it was not the time. Aside from the fact that relationships as a Guardian in the field were near impossible—moreover forbidden if they involved a Ward—Yara had a lot on her plate. The last thing she needed was Robin complicating her life. Mostly, though, if Robin was being honest with himself, his true reason for avoiding pursuing Yara in such a way was Erik.

Robin had known how Erik felt about her right off the bat. Erik had never been good at hiding his true feelings. Carter and Robin had taken it upon themselves to help the new Guardian shield his love for Yara from Black or anyone else who would reassign him if they ever found out. Then it had become apparent that Yara felt things for Erik, too.

Now, however, Erik was gone. A year had passed, and Robin had almost worked up the courage to talk to Yara about how he felt. He needed to know if there was even a chance. Because if there wasn't…

He just needed to know.

Perhaps today, initiation day, in the thrill of her passing the test—which he knew she would—it would be the time to bring it up, when emotions were riding high, and the future felt clear and exciting.

But she wasn't here.

Of all the worst case scenarios he had considered about today, in none of them did he ever imagine that she wouldn't show up. Everyone came out to watch initiation; all of the Guardians and the heads of every branch of the Society. Robin had even coordinated with Yara's aunt, Catherine, for her to come surprise Yara by watching the initiation. Black had made a historic exception in letting Yara train at all. Who knew what the consequences would be for Yara if she bailed. Or for Robin, who had promised to take full responsibility should she fail, such was his confidence in her success.

Now, Catherine stood awkwardly by him and asked, "Is this normal?"

Before Robin could answer her, Carter put their hand on his shoulder. Robin looked at them suspiciously.

"You know where she is," he said.

Carter took their glasses off and wiped them against their tunic. They opened their mouth to reply, but right at that moment, Ash came bounding over.

"There you are!" she said cheerfully, her hair bouncing with every step. "Where's the girl of the hour? Hi!" she added to Catherine. "I'm Ash! I'm Yara's new Guardian."

"Pleasure," said Catherine politely, followed by a surprised, "Oh!" as Ash wrapped her arms around her in a warm hug.

"This must be the first one you've been to since yours," said Carter to the fire nymph, discretely nudging Robin in the ribs, reminding him to stay collected.

"Yup. And I saw that," she added. "Where's Yara? I haven't seen her. Isn't she supposed to be here?" She peered around the door at the group of a dozen initiates all waiting their turn for the physical evaluation.

"That's what I was thinking," said Catherine.

"Yes!" said Robin, the word exploding out of him, unable to contain himself. "Sorry," he added upon seeing Ash's shocked expression. "Yes, she is," he said.

Out of the corner of his eye, he saw the other three exchange awkward glances.

Initiation was an all day event. There were four stages, and the first one—hand to hand combat—had already begun. The sounds of fighting were muted behind the closed door of the training room. Initiates took it in turn to battle a simulated fighter, and they did so before a crowd of nearly everyone in the division, including Black, her Second, Zak Glover, and the Head Guardian, a shape shifter named Xaili Williams. The amount of time each stage took depended on how long each initiate took to pass the test. If they failed to do so within the allotted time, they failed and were either asked to train for another position in the Society or expelled from the Society entirely, but that almost never happened. Initiates were hand selected by Glover and Williams, and it wasn't often that they chose someone who was unable to pass these tests. That didn't mean the tests weren't difficult. Just that training was worse. Robin had worked tirelessly to get Yara up to par, and he wasn't about to let her sleep through initiation day.

Just as Robin turned to go to Yara's quarters and look for her there, she pelted into the room, winded.

"Yara!" said Robin, a confusing jumble of emotions squeezing his stomach.

"Annie?" said Yara in surprise, addressing Catherine. "Annie" was Yara's nickname for her aunt, a long ago habit evolved over the years from—as Robin understood it—"auntie." "You're here!"

"And you're late," said Catherine with a smile.

"Well…" said Yara, looking sheepish. She turned to the person behind her, and—

The air was gone from the room. Robin couldn't breathe, his reprimand frozen in his throat. His hands started to shake, and his knees almost gave out beneath him. He tried gulping down breaths a few times, tried regaining the feeling in his arms, and managed, "E?"

It was him. Somehow, miraculously, back from the dead, standing in front of them. He had the same unnatural green eyes and pointed chin, but now with a shock of white hair and a hollowness in his cheeks that hadn't been there before. Robin could feel his heart beating in his stomach and throat.

This simply wasn't possible.

Erik smiled tentatively, apparently confused by Robin's reaction, and ruffled his hair. The same way he always had.

"Oh my," said Catherine weakly.

"This… this is impossible," said Carter, sounding a thousand miles away.

Robin fought to find his way back to Earth, to understand what was going on. "Who are you?" he said at last, his voice raspy.

Erik looked questioningly at Yara, who was biting her lip and avoiding everyone's gaze.

"I know my hair looks a little different, but do you really not recognize me?" said Erik, bringing his eyes back to Robin's face. He gave a small smile, but it faded quickly when neither Robin nor Carter returned it.

Ash looked awkwardly between the five of them. "Maybe I should go get Black," she said, her gaze lingering on Erik, and without waiting for anyone to respond, she bounded out of sight.

Carter turned to Yara. "How is this possible?"

"What's going on?" asked Erik, now looking at all of them in turn. "What happened?"

"You mean," said Carter slowly. "You mean, you don't remember?"

"Remember what?"

At that moment, the sounds of fighting had stopped completely. Robin turned around to find the door to the training room blocked by the crowd of people gaping at them, all eyes on Erik. Black stood at the forefront, darkness rippling off of her in agitated waves, her depthless eyes fixed so hard on Erik's face that Robin was impressed despite himself that Erik didn't cower.

The world held its breath for several tense moments, before Black's soft voice said, "Initiation is postponed. Initiates, find your trainers. Guardians Level 3 and up, please wait for me in the forum. You four... come with me."

Yara's heart was pounding wildly. This was what she had been afraid of. What she hadn't wanted to face. The look on Robin's face when he saw Erik...

What would this mean? Would they take him away from her? They couldn't possibly. She had just gotten him back.

And her poor Aunt Catherine had come all the way here just to have the whole thing be postponed. Why had she come? Had Robin invited her? Just another person to disappoint when she would announce she didn't want to do this anymore.

She tried not to think about it, instead squeezing Erik's hand and ignoring Robin's burning eyes, as she, her Guardians, and Zak Glover followed Black into the elevator, all the way to the top. In the impenetrable silence, Yara was left to run through each and every worst case scenario in her head in the minutes it took to get to Black's office.

She hated being in here. It was too dim, the lack of light amplified by Black's presence as a Tenebrae, a nymph of darkness. Yara clutched Erik's hand harder. He seemed just as confused as she was nervous.

Black took a seat behind her desk and steepled her fingers in front of her. Glover stood behind her, his eyes not leaving Erik. Everyone else was left standing in front of Black's desk like children about to be told off by the principal.

After what felt like an eternity, Black lifted her head and fixed them with her stare. It was like looking into a void. Here eyes were pure black, like a shark's, balls of obsidian.

"I find myself," she said slowly, in that same soft voice she could somehow command a room with, "at a loss for words."

No one spoke. No one could help her. They, too, didn't know what to say.

"Erik, perhaps you should start. Tell us how you've come to be here."

Erik shifted his weight and looked to his fellow Guardians, begging for some kind of help. "Honestly, sir, I don't know what the problem —"

"Please," said Black, cutting him off with her long-fingered hand. "Erik, just tell us what you remember."

Erik took a deep, shuddering breath. He looked nervously at Yara. She hoped the look in her eyes offered him some comfort, though she didn't feel like she had much comfort to give. "I remember," Erik started, "going with R and C to get Yara. She was using herself as bait and had gotten kidnapped by Kain after infecting herself with a virus developed in the Omega Project. There was a fight... I got hit in the head. Knocked unconscious, I think, because I don't remember anything after that. I woke up yesterday at the library and... and came here."

"Yesterday?" said Black, looking between Erik and Yara. "Why are we only hearing of this now?"

Erik was shaking his head. Yara had never seen him look so brittle. "I didn't know where to go," he said. "I went... I went..."

"I found him," said Yara, her voice sounding stronger than she had intended. "I couldn't sleep. I was nervous about the test today, and I found him heading toward your office, and I was—" Her voice cracked. "I asked him to stay with me, to try to explain what was going on. I was just so happy to see him." She said the last sentence to Robin and Carter, begging them to understand. She didn't want Erik to get into trouble, and it wasn't altogether a lie that she had kept him to herself, postponing the time when this would happen. When she would have to give him up to Black and the Society to find out what the hell was going on.

Carter collapsed into a chair, their face buried in their hands. Robin wouldn't meet her eyes. Ash, for all the world, looked like she was watching a riveting movie.

"What's going on?" Erik asked. "What happened?"

"Erik," said Black finally. "I think we're all just as confused as you are. Because, you see, the events you described happened one year ago. The night you died."

CHAPTER FIVE

Coming Back

At first, Erik laughed. He looked around at everyone in the room, expecting someone else to laugh too, though he had never known Bora Black to make a joke.

"What are you talking about?" he asked. He shook his hand out of Yara's grasp. He did not want her to feel it as he started to tremble.

"You died during Ms. Rivers's rescue operation last year. A solenoidal star…" Black hesitated. "A solenoid was lodged in—"

"That's enough," said Robin, his eyes on Yara. Then, evidently remembering himself, he added to Black, "Respectfully, sir."

"That's impossible," said Erik. But the grin on his lips was evaporating as each moment passed, and no one else smiled.

"We can show you the report the Medics submitted of your body, the images taken of the damage. We can show you the ashes from your cremation, if it would help. Now we need—"

"What?" said Erik, all hint of a laugh gone from his voice. "Cremated?" The trembling had moved from his hands to his arms to his whole body as he backed away from all of them. "This is insane. I can't have been cremated. I'm standing right here!"

"The fact remains, Erik," said Black, her voice lowering as Erik's got louder, "that our interpretation of what happened is very different from yours."

"No shit!" yelled Erik. "But you're obviously lying! I can't be cremated! Do I look cremated to you?" He looked to Robin and Carter, begging for help.

Black did not respond.

Erik's mind was racing. This was all impossible. Dead. *Dead?* Ashes? A solenoid? He ran his hand through his hair, trying to find any wound, any scar that would indicate he had indeed been killed by a sharp blade. There was nothing there.

"This is a trick. How the hell do you explain that I'm standing here if you burned my goddamn body!"

"Erik, please." But it was not Black's voice this time. It was Yara's. Erik looked at her to find her wide eyes glazed with tears. She looked frightened. He had never been able to stomach when she looked liked that. Worse, what she was frightened of was him. His job was to protect her, not to scare her. He staggered back and crouched in the corner, trying to empty the contents of his stomach, but there was nothing there. He hadn't eaten since he had woken up. He retched, his gut convulsing painfully, coughing up bile.

A hand was on his back. A soft, warm hand. Another on his arm.

Yara again.

She was pulling him up, but he could not look at her. Would not. But those same hands were now on his face, turning his head so that his eyes met hers.

She was still so beautiful. No longer the girl he had fallen in love with, but now a woman who had endured so much. There were tears lining her eyes, but she was not letting them fall. Erik took two breaths, drinking up the sight of her before nodding. She let go of his face, taking his hand instead, and led him back to Black's desk where they took a seat together.

"Erik." Black this time. "I can't imagine how this must sound. I can't imagine what it is you're going through. But we are here to help you. And trust me when I say that we want answers just as much as you do. And goddammit, Erik, we will find them."

Robin, Carter, and Ash had been asked to leave Erik and Yara in Black's office. Ash excused herself, but Carter and Robin stayed in the hallway just outside Black's door, waiting. Carter sat stock still on one of the benches lining the walls. Robin paced.

Erik was back.

Somehow, miraculously, Robin's brother, his friend, his rival had returned. To think, Robin had been about to tell Yara he was in love with her. Thank god he hadn't.

Whatever they were talking about in Black's office took a long time. Yara was sent away first. She left Black's office, muttered something unintelligible, and disappeared downstairs.

Another half hour later, Erik emerged, escorted by Glover, who said, "Five minutes," and left them alone.

Erik stood before Robin and Carter, looking lost. All at once the three of them embraced.

"It's so good to see you, E," said Carter, their voice hoarse.

"We thought we'd lost you, man," said Robin, fighting the quavering in his throat. Of course, they *had* lost him. Whatever this was, this second chance, it couldn't be real. But it was nice to imagine that it was, at least for the moment.

When they pulled away, Erik rubbed his eyes. "It's weird. It doesn't feel like it's been long. I remember being with you guys like it was yesterday. But everyone is looking at me like I'm a ghost."

"You really don't remember anything?" said Carter.

Erik shook his head. "But I guess it's been a year…"

Robin slapped Erik on the back. "You haven't missed much."

"I'm not sure that's true."

The three of them took a seat on the benches. Glover would be back for Erik soon. They didn't have much time.

"Yara's becoming a Guardian?" Erik asked.

Robin nodded. "She's good, too. You'd be proud of her."

"I am. I'm sorry I missed all that. Is she…"

"She's OK," said Carter. "She took it really hard when you—" The words caught in their throat.

"She missed ya," supplied Robin. "We all did. But I think it was hardest on her. She blamed herself."

Erik shook his head. "I didn't want that for her. I just wanted her to be safe. I still do."

"She's safe."

"Is she happy?" asked Erik.

"She is now," said Carter. "Or she will be."

Erik smiled softly to himself and reached for Carter's and Robin's hands, squeezing them. "I'm glad you're both here."

"So are we, brother," said Carter. "It hasn't been the same without you."

"Yeah," said Robin. "Who're we supposed to tease when you're not calling in updates every hour?"

The three of them laughed and it was an easy thing. They had been a unit who had worked seamlessly together for so long. While Erik may have been the only one who was truly unaware of the passage of time, it felt for just a moment to Robin as though he had never left. But then he remembered where they were and the reality of the situation. Death was the one certainty in life, and it was irrevocable. At least, it was supposed to be. It always had been before.

And Erik had died. So whomever this was, this man standing in front of him, it could not be Erik. Not really. No matter how much Robin or any of them wanted to believe that it was.

Glover popped his head out of his office and cleared his throat.

"Quick. Give me the highlights. Ten words or less," said Erik.

"Carter got bit by twelve mosquitos in one night."

"It's true," said Carter.

"You went a word over," said Robin.

Carter shrugged.

Erik laughed.

"Mr. Carpenter," said Glover, and the moment was over. "You two are excused. Go make yourselves useful."

As she knew they would, the powers that be had taken Erik away from Yara. He had to be examined by the Medics and the Researchers and questioned and debriefed and scrutinized.

"Just for now," they kept saying, but she knew they were lying. They would never let her have him again.

A solenoid… he had been killed by a solenoidal star. She had no idea. They hadn't let her see the body before covering it with their shroud and burning it to nothing.

Now she found herself sitting in the commissary with Robin, Carter, and Ash. Carter had been patiently filling in Ash who, while she had known of Erik's death insomuch as she knew whom she was replacing, didn't know many details.

Yara wasn't listening. The food in front of her sat untouched. She could hardly believe that it was already lunch time. She could feel the eyes of almost everyone in the commissary on her and her Guardians. Initiation had never been postponed before. Another historic barrier that Yara had somehow managed to breach without trying. She supposed she would be the only person to withdraw from the tests after training as well. The thought made her stomach squirm. She hadn't told Robin, yet.

Erik's reappearance had changed everything. Everything and nothing.

It was a few moments before Yara realized that it was silent. Carter had stopped talking. She looked up to find them looking at her.

"What?" she said.

"Black's instructions are to act as though nothing has changed," said Robin. "Initiation has been moved to tomorrow, so you have an extra day to train, and after that, you'll get your assignment."

Yara looked at Carter who raised their eyebrows at her. *Tell him,* they said silently.

She took a deep, shuddering breath. "I've decided not to take the test," she said.

Robin set his fork down and looked at her, his eyes piercing. "Nah."

"Excuse me?" said Yara.

"You're taking the test."

She hadn't been expecting his reaction to be good, but she certainly didn't expect this. His face was without a hint of a smile, his knuckles were white, and a muscle was feathering in his jaw. "What the hell does that mean?" she snapped.

"It means you made a commitment, kid, and you're gonna honor it."

Yara chewed her lip, trying to decide what to say. She was fuming. Everything had gone to shit in the last few hours, and now this. She had never seen Robin in this state. Robin, who had always been vibrant, full of life, ever the jokester, laughing and making comments to ease the tension. Now, he was the one who needed the easing.

"Well, that's not your decision," she said finally.

"You can't do this, Yara!" yelled Robin so loudly that it gave an excuse for everyone around them to stare openly. "You can't just decide randomly to quit after everything—after—" He struggled with words for a few moments. "People have spent time and energy and resources on training you," he said, his voice a controlled calm. "Just because E—just because something happens, it doesn't give you the right to turn your back on everything like this. The world doesn't work like that!"

"R," said Ash, reaching for Robin's arm, but he yanked it away from her and stormed away.

Yara stared after him, livid.

"Hard to make angry, huh?" said Yara. "I guess I have the magic touch."

Carter looked at her for a few moments before saying, "He's confused."

"Yeah, well, we all are." She so wanted to storm away, too. To flip the table over and start a fight, but she had nowhere to go and no one to blame. She wanted answers. She wouldn't find them by running away.

She looked at Ash, suddenly embarrassed.

"I'm sorry," said Yara, trying to meet those flickering eyes. She rubbed her face in her hands. "I met you like 12 hours ago and all of a sudden we're in the middle of some soap opera where people are storming out and coming back from the dead..." Her voice caught in her throat, but Ash reached over and hugged Yara. Yara stiffened but didn't pull away. From the few times she had interacted with the nymph, it seemed that avoiding hugs was out of the question.

"Thanks," said Yara awkwardly.

"Here's the thing," said Ash, unaware of, or simply ignoring, Yara's discomfort. "Erik died. Now he's back. The elephant in the room, right?" She started counting off on her fingers: "What happened. How the hell did he get into HQ. Why now." She shrugged. "Best way to find out is using the few clues we have. What do we know? He woke up at the library. That's Kain's last known base of operations."

"Last known?" said Yara, frowning. "Kain is dead. His lab was destroyed. The library's just a library now."

Ash raised an eyebrow and stuffed pasta into her mouth. How could she be hungry at a time like this? "Kain is dead," she said through a mouthful of food. "Erik is dead. Is it just me who doesn't think 'dead' means what it used to mean anymore?"

Yara looked at Carter and it was clear that they were just as unsettled by these words as she was.

"You think Kain might still be alive?"

Ash chewed pensively. "I'm not sure if 'still' would be the word I would use. Maybe 'again' would be more appropriate. But we don't know what's going on. That much is true. And the library is the first place to look."

"That's not our job," said Carter at once. "The Eyes—"

"The Eyes are the ones who investigate, yeah, yeah," said Ash, waving around her fork and taking a big sip of water. She seemed supremely unconcerned by the whole situation. Were all fire nymphs this flippant or was it just her? "But who's to say that what they find out will come back to us? Lotta rules, lotta red tape in the Society. If you really want to know what happened..." she shrugged and didn't finish her sentence. She didn't need to.

Yara looked at Carter.

"We have to," said Yara.

"No," said Carter.

"We *have* to," she repeated.

Carter frowned. "It's too dangerous."

Yara waved her hand. "That's absurd. You're both Guardians, and I'm..." She trailed away. What was she? Two days ago, she was so confident she was on the right track. Now, she found herself in the middle of the woods with no paths to choose from.

"I have to take the test, don't I?" she said, staring at the table.

"I didn't say that," said Carter.

The shape shifter looked sad. Yara replayed Robin's reaction when she told him she wanted to quit. Her Guardians were on edge.

Erik's face swam in and out of focus. There had to be an explanation for his return, and while she was determined to find it, she had been so preoccupied with having him back that she had selfishly ignored how it might affect Carter and Robin.

"Are you OK?" she asked Carter.

"I'll be fine, Red. Go find R. He needs you more right now."

"You're sure this is the right call?" said Glover, walking two paces behind Black as she headed back up to her office.

"Not in the least," said Black. She hadn't been sure of much at all lately. Not since Glover had told her that the Head of her Guardians had been a spy for Ramsey Kain, which, admittedly, had been a year ago.

It had been a hard year.

"Need I remind you, sir," Glover continued, "that you had decided to expel E entirely after his insubordination during the events that took place last December."

"You need not remind me." They reached the elevator and waited a moment before it arrived to take them up to the top floor. "But the alternative to keeping him here is sending him out into the civilian world. And I don't intend to do that with a nymph who's supposed to be dead. Better to keep him here. Where I can keep an eye on him." The elevator arrived with a soft *ding* and they stepped inside, the darkness that curled off of Black's skin filling the small space as the doors closed. "And Mx. Williams?"

"Nothing to report," said Glover. "They've been following protocols, as far as we can tell. No unusual assignments, activities outside of Headquarters, nor any contact to anyone outside the Society."

"You're monitoring their ConvOrb?" said Black.

"Yes, sir. Here's a list of the people they've communicated with. All Guardians who are on assignment."

"Good. And what has their response been to the return of Erik Carpenter?"

"Nothing yet."

"I want special attention given to that," said Black. "I don't know how that boy is back. But I have a feeling it can't mean anything good."

It didn't take long for Yara to find Robin. He was in the sims. Robin and Yara had spent most of their hours training together there.

He didn't notice her at first. He was running his favorite simulation. A simple one in which he robbed from the rich and gave to the poor. Robin Hood. It took place in Sherwood Forest, of course, and he was running the program at the highest possible level and fighting four giant guards at once. Three others lay unconscious on the ground beside him.

Yara walked up behind him and said, "Robin?"

She surprised him, causing him to turn around and swing wildly for her head. She managed to duck out of the way and instinctively parried with a swift uppercut to his jaw, causing her hand to bark in pain. "I'm so sorry!" she cried, rubbing her knuckles. Her hit wasn't enough to knock him to the ground, but he was so caught off guard that he was booted in the side by one of the simulated guards, then swiftly attacked from the other side by the remaining two.

Not thinking to turn the simulation off, Yara kicked the first guard in the knees, sending him crashing to the floor with a cry of pain before she pulled the dagger from his belt and hurled it at one of the others. It didn't land in his heart, where she'd aimed, but rather in his right shoulder, giving Robin the opportunity he needed to escape from their onslaught, knock the other guard to the ground, and grab the knife from the last one's shoulder before plunging it back into him, this time striking true. Yara backed away into a tree, breathing heavily and slid to the ground. Six months of fighting, of training with weapons and simulated enemies whom she could kill with an empty conscience, and it still made her shake with adrenaline.

Robin looked over at her, panting, his hands still on the hilt of the dagger protruding from the guard's chest.

They locked eyes, breathing hard, and the simulation quit. The tree

Yara had been leaning on vanished and she fell backward. They were alone in a gridded black box with no weapons and no enemies.

"What are you doing here?" he asked, collapsing on the floor next to her and staring up at the ceiling.

"I came to talk," she said, fighting to resist the urge to leave and bury her face in a pillow so she wouldn't have to face the world.

"So talk," he said.

Yara had never seen Robin like this. She hated the harshness in his voice.

"Can't you be happy?" she said. "We lost Erik, and now he's back! We have a second chance with him. But everyone's acting like something horrible has happened."

"First of all," said Robin, sitting up and glaring at her. She set her jaw and did not look away. "We didn't lose E. He was killed. He was brutally murdered by Kain and his Shadow Men a year ago. This isn't a second chance. This is a trick. A trap. And whoever that is," he pointed out of the room, supposedly toward wherever Erik was, "it isn't E. It isn't Erik. I saw Erik's body, I watched it be burned to dust and that dust was locked away in a marble box."

"How can this possibly be a trap?" said Yara. "What, you think someone found Erik's identical twin and they're using him to infiltrate the Society?"

"Of course not! I—"

"Or better yet! He's from an alternate universe! Some other dimension where Erik didn't die, and where—"

"Enough!"

"He's not a shape shifter," said Yara, her voice strong. "His eyes are green, not amber. And he knows who he is. He remembers everything until he was—he remembers everything until that night. How could that be possible unless it really is *him*?" If only because she herself could not believe it fully unless Robin did, she needed him to understand. Needed to hear him say that it was possible. That somehow, miraculously, Erik had come back. And the question wasn't "why" but "how."

Robin looked at Yara. The anger was gone from his face, replaced with hopelessness. "It isn't him, Yara."

Yara glared at him. "Fine," she spat. She pushed herself up and made toward the exit. "You and the rest of the Society can wallow all you want. But Ash and I are going to figure this out with or without you."

"Wait!" Faster than she could have believed, Robin's hand was gripping her wrist, holding her back. "Please, Yara. Reconsider."

"Ash thinks we can find answers at Kain's old lab, and I think she's right."

"Not that," said Robin, his blue eyes flicking back and forth between hers. He was standing so close. "Reconsider the test tomorrow."

"Oh," said Yara, looking away. "Why?"

"Because I know you. Because I know that not only would you be an amazing Guardian, but what's holding you back isn't that you don't want to do it. You're afraid. You're afraid you won't be good enough. And you owe it to yourself to prove that you are."

CHAPTER SIX

Shattered

Yara had never had any female friends. She had never really had friends at all until she'd met her Guardians. But Ash was something entirely different. Yara barely had time to find Ash leaving the commissary, eating a pastry and licking her fingers, and tell her that Yara wanted to go to the Los Angeles Public Library downtown to look for clues before Ash grabbed her hand and swept her out onto the streets.

They hadn't taken a Society car, as they technically weren't authorized to make the trip, but Ash was perfectly unbothered by breaking the rules.

"We'll get a black mark on our record, blah blah blah, and then they'll forget all about it and ask us what we found. That's what's important, anyway. And I would have thought that you would know all this already, after your stunt with Kain and the Omega Project."

"What do you mean?" said Yara, already feeling better due to Ash's infectious *joie de vivre*.

"Well, you ran away, didn't you? Took matters into your own hands when no one would agree to let you carry out your plan."

"You mean when I almost died?" *And got Erik killed?* "Maybe this isn't a good idea…"

Ash laughed. "Don't back out on me now, lady. I'm all hyped up."

"I didn't realize Black would exactly broadcast that I broke the rules," said Yara.

"Oh, believe me. She didn't. But we nymphs stick together in the Society, you know," said Ash, grinning at her. They reached the bus stop just as one was approaching.

"Thuja?" said Yara. Thuja had been the nymph who helped Yara, had given her the tools she needed to take down Kain when no one else believed she could do it.

Ash winked, and they climbed on to the bus.

"So, tell me about this power you have," said Ash in a voice that was not exactly a whisper.

"Um," said Yara, looking around, worried of being overheard. No one was paying attention.

"Can you really see the future? How far into it?"

"Well," said Yara, in a much quieter voice, "it depends. I'm still learning to control it. Usually I can only see a little ways ahead. Things get foggier the further away they are in time. And it all depends on what decisions people make, otherwise the future isn't set. Does that make sense?"

Ash's eyes were wide. While she watched Yara with undivided attention, she was absentmindedly twisting a line of flame in between her fingers in the same way someone might flip a coin.

"Aren't you worried someone will see?" said Yara, throwing a look around the bus.

"Hmm?" said Ash, and then, "Oh!" She laughed and flexed her fingers, the flames disappearing in a wisp of smoke. "Nah. Even if someone was watching, they wouldn't believe it. Trust me."

Yara looked around skeptically, but sure enough, no one was paying them any mind. Then she flinched when Ash grabbed her hands and squeezed.

"Lighten up, will you? You look so tense."

Yara laughed nervously. She tried pulling her hands away from Ash, but the nymph didn't let go.

"What's the matter? Afraid I'm going to burn you?"

"Oh no, it's not that," said Yara, feeling awkward. "I just... don't really like being touched."

Ash frowned, then looked down at their hands as though it were taking her a moment to understand. "Oh!" She let go immediately.

"Sorry," said Yara.

"Don't be!" said Ash. "We've all got our stuff. I go crazy when I see people tearing up grass."

"Really?"

"Oh yeah! You know, like when people are having picnics, and they just grab handfuls of grass and tug it up for no reason? Drives me insane. Anyway, here we are."

Just down the street from their stop stood the library, a gloriously classic building amidst the modern skyscrapers of downtown LA. Yara followed Ash into the park that led up to the front entrance of the central branch.

The last time she was here, she had been escaping with the rest of the hyden from Kain and his ruthless Shadow Men. It was surreal to see so many people sitting at the park, walking into and out of the library as though nothing special had happened here, completely oblivious to the war that had been waged beneath them.

The White Mask Society was nothing if not good at covering their tracks.

"I read the report," said Ash, leading Yara not to the front door, but rather toward the back of the building. "They never found the entrance Kain used. So they built one in the back here. Unless you want to go through the vents again." She winked and Yara snorted.

"Hard pass."

Yara wondered what they must look like as they walked confidently toward the back of the library; Ash, with her free flowing locks of black and red hair bouncing merrily against her traditional Guardian uniform: a close-fitting black tunic that wrapped around her petite waist, blending perfectly into her matching slacks and boots. Yara wore the same outfit in a forest green, identifying her as an initiate, with brown boots. Both had the emblem for the White Mask Society stitched on the collar, a half mask barely the size of a quarter. The uniform made Yara feel powerful—if not a little rebellious given the circumstances—and it gave her courage.

Ash had had the good sense to sneak some weapons out, but it would have looked too suspicious to walk out of Headquarters in full armor or properly equipped with solenoids and gauntlets, the standard weapons for Guardians. Instead, tucked into the hidden pockets of their uniforms were a few small blades, though they didn't expect to use them.

Yara was grateful not to have to go through the library. She didn't need to be reminded of the dizzying atrium filled with the screams of dozens of Guardians and Shadow Men, solenoids crashing through the air, slicing through flesh and metal, the pain of her bare feet against the ridges of the escalators, the cold biting her skin, the pounding in the back of her head where Kain had drilled into her skull...

"Yara? You OK?" Ash's voice brought Yara back.

She shook her head and nodded. "Yeah," she said. "Sorry."

"I got you, lady," said Ash. They approached a utility box large enough to accommodate an adult and Ash tried opening it. Locked.

Yara's shoulders fell. "Dammit."

But Ash had already placed a hand flat against the lock and the metal started to glow red with heat from Ash's palm. After a moment, the door simply fell open. Yara looked around nervously, her mouth hanging open, but no one paid them any mind. Two people in uniform working on the electrical system. Nothing to see here.

Of course, there was no electrical system to work on. No utility of any kind. Instead, it was an unfinished tunnel that led down into the bowels of what had once been the laboratory of Ramsey Kain.

One at a time, they stepped inside and closed the door behind them.

Erik sat perfectly still on the exam table. The White Mask Society Medics had poked and prodded him, withdrawn blood, scanned him from head to toe, swabbed his cheek, clipped his hair, and performed all manner of invasive examinations before leaving him in the room to fetch Bora Black so they might report their findings to both her and Erik at the same time.

He felt numb.

One word kept clanging around his skull.

Dead.

He couldn't have died. He would have remembered. Remembered the pain of being cut open by a solenoid…

The thought was too awful to dwell on. Perhaps it was a blessing he couldn't remember. That is, if it had ever even happened at all. The fact remained, here he was. Alive. Breathing. His heart beating. Certainly not burned to ash as everyone here kept insisting he should be.

He didn't have too much time alone to think about how such a thing could be possible before the door to the medical ward opened and Black came in, followed by Frankie Sweet, the Head Medic, a short woman with untamed brown hair and amber eyes that marked her as a shape shifter. Unlike most shifters, including Carter, who did not subscribe to a specific gender or sex, Frankie preferred to occupy the shape of a woman and almost always presented as female.

Erik didn't waste any energy in trying to interpret the expressions on the women's faces, and instead waited for one of them to talk.

Frankie made a good show of taking a seat, turning on classical music, which she always did when she was working, and reading through her notes, absently gesturing for Black to take a seat as well. Erik just stared, letting the gentle sounds of Tchaikovsky chase the silence away.

"Honestly," said Frankie with a heavy sigh, "I have never seen anything so inexplicable." She looked up to find Erik's expression blank, and Black looking as she always did, stone faced and so dark that the light around her seemed to evaporate. "I've done every test I can think of, and I have two dozen of my top Medics and Researchers doing every test I *couldn't* think of. So far, we can't find any answers. As far as we can tell, this is Erik Carpenter."

A slight crease appeared between Black's eyebrows. "What does this mean?"

"I'm afraid that's not all," said Frankie, pulling a folder closer to her and offering it to Black. So far, neither of them had shown any awareness that Erik was even in the room. He wasn't even sure why he was there. If only they would let him leave, he could go find Yara and let them worry about all this nonsense.

"There's no genetic differences whatsoever between the man sitting in this room and the Erik we cremated a year ago, *but* there are several noticeable *physical* differences."

"The hair?" said Black, flipping through the folder until she turned to a photograph. A shadow crossed her face. Erik craned his neck to see what was on the picture, and managed to make out enough blood to know that it wasn't anything he wanted to see.

"Not just the hair," said Frankie, eyeing Erik's mop of silver. "We pride ourselves with keeping excellent records here in the Research and Medical Division. Every injury for every member who has walked through those doors has been catalogued and included in their file. Naturally, since you were working on a high profile case as a Guardian to one of the hyden," she continued, finally addressing Erik directly, "we were very careful to include extensive notes on your injuries."

"Where are you going with this?" said Black, her eyes still on the picture of what could only be Erik's mutilated body.

"They're all gone."

"The injuries?"

"Yes. Every single one. All the scar tissue, all the bones that had ever been broken show no signs of ever having been damaged at all. To say nothing of the injury that killed him—that killed you," she added, looking into Erik's eyes, "doesn't exist. Like none of them ever happened."

"But they did," said Erik, frowning. "I remember them." *All except one, at least.*

"That may be," said Frankie, "but there is no medical evidence to suggest that they ever really happened. This body, it's as if it's brand new."

Erik shook his head. "That doesn't make any sense. If it was brand new, how come I still look 18? How come I can remember my life?"

Frankie looked at him sadly, but said nothing. Black finally closed the file and handed it back to Frankie, still without looking at Erik.

"I don't have to tell you, Ms. Sweet, that these answers are unsatisfactory."

"No," said Frankie, sounding irritated, "you don't. I have people working 'round the clock trying to find every possible solution, and so far there are none. We have entertained every possibility, examined them from every angle, and the fact remains. People don't just come back from the dead, but as far as we can tell, he has."

"The ashes—" said Black.

"They're still there. Untouched. That was the first thing we checked. No sign of tampering whatsoever in the memorial."

Black stood up abruptly and paced wildly in the room. The lights flickered. Erik knew that she was a nymph of darkness, but she had always kept her powers contained. Tenebrae had a reputation for being bad luck. Silly superstitious fears. Erik had never put much weight in the notion that she was more dangerous than any other kind of nymph, but now, watching her, he wasn't so sure. Her hair crackled with black electricity and her skin was crawling with tendrils of night.

"Bora," said Frankie in a low voice.

Black stopped pacing, and eventually, the lights stopped flickering, her hair stopped buzzing, her skin slowly changing back to normal. When she looked at Erik, none of the wildness was left in her face.

"Erik, I'm at a complete loss," she said. "The Society has existed for centuries. And never have we had a situation like this." She fell silent for another moment, looking down at her hands, folded in front of her. If Erik hadn't felt so horrible himself, he may have been inclined to try to comfort her. "We," she continued slowly, "will do everything we can to find out how this has happened. In the meantime, how would you like to proceed?"

Erik frowned, looking from Black to Frankie. They were both staring at him.

"Uh..." he said, uncomfortably aware of their gazes. "You mean, like, in life?"

Black nodded. "Would you prefer to continue your work with the Society? Perhaps a different post would suit you better, or an early retirement—"

"No!" said Erik. "I want to stay. I want to keep being Yara's Guardian."

Black raised an eyebrow. "I'm afraid that won't be possible."

"What?" said Erik, his stomach clenching.

"Yara has three Guardians already. We can find another assignment if that's the position you prefer—"

"Who?" said Erik, an angry fire burning inside of him. "How? Why?"

"Erik, I'm sure you understand," said Black in as soft a voice as he had ever heard her use, "the last anyone knew of you, you were dead. Yara Rivers spent too much time with only two Guardians while we tried to find a suitable replacement. Once we did, we had no choice but to appoint them, as I'm sure you know is standard procedure after the loss of a Guardian."

"Who is it?" said Erik, breathing heavily, trying to calm himself down, yet still unable to look Black or Frankie in the eyes.

"Her name is Ash. A Vurwari."

Breathing was becoming harder and harder. It felt as though the walls were closing in. Erik's hands started to tremble. He had to calm down. What was happening to him? He had never felt this angry before in his life. He couldn't control it, and suddenly, the rage was rising to the surface and he thought he might die from the pain of it. He screamed, a horrible, piercing roar, burying his face in his hands as he fell from the exam table, landing painfully on his knees. His roar reverberated in his body so much it felt as though the world were shaking around him.

When it finally felt as though he had unleashed the bubbling anger within him enough that he could breathe normally, gulping down buckets of fresh air, he slowly lifted his head out of his hands.

The music had stopped. Frankie and Black were against the opposite walls, staring aghast at Erik and the chaos that had erupted around him.

Large cracks in the polished white floor spread from his knees around him like an erratic spiderweb, beakers and equipment from the counters had fallen and lay shattered on the floor, and one of the lights from the ceiling was hanging at a strange angle. Spreading from the eye of his storm was an untamed overgrowth of leafy vines, climbing up the walls and equipment. Nearly every inch of the ward was green and rustling.

"What happened?" he managed after a moment, his voice hoarse.

Frankie fought through the growth to get to him and started to count his pulse. Her firm hand felt frigid against his burning skin. He couldn't stop shaking. Black, however, did not move. Her obsidian eyes were fixed on Erik, a dark crease between her eyebrows.

"I thought you said he was genetically identical to Erik Carpenter," she said quietly.

"He is!" said Frankie, still counting Erik's pulse. "This is impossible —"

Their voices disappeared in a haze as Erik focused his attention inward.

He inhaled. How had this happened? He had always kept a strong control over his ability and had never come close to being able to produce this much growth. He was, after all, only half nymph. His mother had been human.

He exhaled. Perhaps more concerning, he had never been able to shake a room, let alone split the floor like this.

He inhaled again. Yara had another Guardian. He was no longer assigned to her.

He exhaled. Had Carter and Robin so easily forgotten him? Had Yara?

CHAPTER SEVEN

In the Wreckage

Yara and Ash made their way carefully down the dark tunnel that led into the old lab. The only light was a hot ball of fire summoned by Ash, hovering in the air, crackling happily ahead of them. It wasn't until Ash's soft, warm hand wrapped around Yara's that she realized she was shaking. Yara instinctively withdrew her hand, but looked at Ash. While she was no longer smiling, her glowing eyes were friendly.

"We don't have to do this right now," she said.

Yara stared at her, thinking. Erik had come back somehow. He had found her. And Robin and Carter and Black and everyone at the Society would take too long to figure out how this had happened. If it weren't for her making decisions like this, breaking the rules, Kain would still be alive. *And so would Erik,* said a small voice in her head. But who else might Kain have killed in that time? What other damage might he have done? Yara had to do this. She shook her head.

"I want to do it now."

So they continued.

Unfounded fear was gripping Yara as they descended. She didn't want Ash to think her weak. Surely, there was no reason to be afraid. There was no way that the Shadow Men were still using the lab. So why was she so scared?

She toyed with trying to see into the future, to prove to herself that there was nothing to fear. Yara had learned to control her ability under duress during her incarceration with Kain, but had barely used it since then. There weren't many occasions when she needed to have visions while living at Headquarters or while training with Robin and Carter, nor had the Society taken it upon themselves to ask her to use her powers to help them with any of their missions. Not that Yara didn't want to help, but she wasn't about to offer that particular skill. Not when every time she thought about using it, she felt like she was back in Kain's laboratory, in those cold and winding hallways, deep underground, barely clinging to life.

Most of her young life had been plagued by devastatingly painful headaches which accompanied visions—before she knew what they were and how to control them. While they no longer engulfed her as they once had, she hadn't forgotten all those years of prescription pain medication, doctors' appointments, and crippling migraines. None of that compared to what she had endured in learning to master her ability.

The tunnel widened into a hallway where a passage had been blasted open. Rubble still sat in messy piles all around them, but the dirt had settled into a fine powder that coated everything. It had clearly been a while since anyone had been here. Any footsteps the Society might have left after their initial raid were barely visible under a new coating of dust.

"Where do we start?" said Ash. Yara flinched. Ash's cheerful voice felt loud and wrong in the stillness.

"This way, I guess," she said, heading toward a nearby room. She swallowed as they stood in the threshold. It was in disarray and chaos. An exam table lay in the center of the room, bent so severely that the middle of it touched the floor. More debris littered the ground, casting long shadows from Ash's fireball, as if being in a mad scientist's abandoned underground lab needed to be any creepier. All the cabinet doors were either open or hanging at strange angles, the few contents left strewn about as though by a tornado. Yara took a few steps forward, stepping carefully through the wreckage. Ash followed close behind, her fire staying alongside them.

"What the hell happened here?" said Ash, her voice the only sound save for the crackling fire and scraping metal and crunching glass beneath their feet.

"I guess the fight between the Shadow Men and the Society?" said Yara.

"Looks like Black had the place sacked. You know, to make sure all the research was lost."

"Maybe."

"Is this where it happened?" said Ash in a small voice.

"It's so different than I remember," said Yara.

"That's normal," said Ash. "Things tend to change in your memory, especially when they're connected to a traumatic event."

Yara stared at Ash. No words could possibly express the gratitude she felt for everything she had done for her in the few hours they had known each other. Where Carter and Robin had been preoccupied with following protocol, Ash had been the opposite. The only one of her Guardians who cared enough to help her find out what might have brought Erik back. She opened her mouth to say something, but Ash just gave her a quick wink and looked around.

As soundlessly as they could, they continued down the corridors that Yara had become painfully familiar with when she had been imprisoned there. The cement walls looked just as terrifying in the warm glow of Ash's fire as they had in the harsh fluorescent lights that had once illuminated them. Yara closed her eyes a moment and took several deep breaths. She hadn't considered how being back here might affect her. She had given no thought as to what revisiting this part of her life might mean.

Ash's hand found her way back into Yara's and squeezed.

"You're doing amazing," Ash said, and then, remembering what Yara had said about being touched, withdrew her hand.

After a few more shaky breaths, Yara nodded.

They pressed on. Left turn, right, right again.

"So," said Ash into the suffocating quiet. "What exactly are we looking for?"

"I'm not sure," said Yara. "Maybe we'll know when we see it?"

They kept exploring, finding more empty rooms until at last they came to a massive steel door.

"Well, we *have* to see what's in there," said Ash with glee.

"Yeah…" said Yara.

The door was ajar, but it took both of their combined efforts to heave it open wide enough to fit through.

"What the devil was Kain keeping in here?" Ash grunted through her teeth from the strain of pushing the door.

Yara didn't answer, focusing instead on her breathing.

Once they were able to slip inside, they stood at the threshold of the colossal room and gaped. This room, unlike the others, did not seem to have been ransacked. Instead, it had been meticulously emptied, every inch of it scrubbed down. The room was vast. Yara almost got dizzy just standing at the entrance. It was so enormous that Ash's singular ball of fire didn't completely illuminate it, and the three far walls were cast in shadow so completely that the room felt endless. Without Yara having to ask, Ash summoned four more fireballs and sent them to each corner of the room. The light, having nothing to reflect upon, was swallowed up by the darkness, but it was enough to give Yara and Ash the confidence to take a few more steps into the room.

"What is this place?" said Ash, her voice echoing.

Yara shook her head. She was starting to feel slightly lightheaded, the first sign of an oncoming headache. It had been a while since she'd had a migraine, and she had forgotten how much they could disable her.

"You OK?" said Ash, looking at her with concern.

Yara forced a nod, squeezing her eyes shut in an effort to regain control. She took several rapid breaths, trying to push the migraine away, knowing it could only mean that a vision was coming. *This can't be happening…* thought Yara. She had learned to control her visions, learned to control her mind, and since then, a premonition had never come unbidden.

She could feel Ash's hand reach out to her shoulder, but Yara shrank away from her impatiently, shaking her head as though trying to rattle her brain and force the headache out. She tried to sink into her mind and let the vision come, but nothing happened. The pain was only getting worse. She clapped her hands over her ears.

"Yara!"

Yara fell to the ground, catching herself with her hands. The moment she made contact with the floor, the room transformed around her.

Unlike most of her visions, however, in which everything around her disappeared and was replaced with a completely different scene, this one was shaped by the world around her. The vast, empty room was suddenly filled with rows upon rows of enormous glass pods, lined in aisles as far as the eye could see. Yara gasped, looking around. It felt so real. Ash was gone. Instead, Shadow Men were walking around, like drones. Yara felt a visceral surge of fear before she noticed that no one in the room was taking any notice of her. The drones moved from pod to pod, checking things on the bright screens at the foot of each one. Forcing her shaky legs to step forward, Yara's breath came out shallow when she saw what was within the sickly light emanating from each pod.

Stay calm, she thought to herself. *It's not real.* She tried to focus on her breathing, a visualization exercise from a long-ago therapist that had helped her cope with anxiety. *Inhale a calming liquid gold. Exhale the anxious red smoke.*

But Yara's hands did not stop sweating. Because in each pod was a person. Hundreds. Suspended in a viscous pink liquid, floating in virtual stillness, fleshy tubes attached to their bellybuttons. She moved through the room—or rather the room moved around her—past dozens of pods, all filled. The people inside were getting smaller. Younger. Until no longer were adults floating in the pods beside her, but teenagers, children, infants—

Yara cried out in horror, and the room emptied, the pods vanishing, replaced instead with a dark vacuum. Suddenly, Ash was there, her hot hands holding on to Yara. But Ash's touch made Yara's head pound even harder and the present started to disappear again, threatening another vision, so, panting heavily, Yara pushed Ash away.

"What's wrong?" said Ash.

"I saw... something..." said Yara, her breath still coming out in ragged gasps.

"A vision? Is it always that dramatic when you see the future?"

Yara looked at her, taking a few moments to comprehend what Ash had said, only then realizing that she had fallen on the ground and was staring up at the nymph's wide, fiery eyes.

"No," she managed finally. "I don't... I don't understand."

"What don't you understand?" said Ash, kneeling next to her, keeping her distance. Yara could barely focus from the pain in her head. It was squeezing her so tightly she thought her eyes might burst out of her skull. She took a few deep breaths, trying to calm her mind the way she had learned. The pressure was somewhat alleviated, but still there.

"I can control my visions. I learned to control them. But this..." She paused, trying to sort out what she wanted to say. This vision had been unlike any she had experienced. She couldn't explain it, just that she knew it was different somehow.

"What did you see?" said Ash eventually.

Yara met her eyes, more to have something to focus on than anything else. "This room..." she began. "It was filled with... with giant pods. And Shadow Men were walking around, and the pods were filled... They were filled with people."

CHAPTER EIGHT
Growing Things

Yara was shaking. The walls felt like they were closing in on her when Ash abruptly shushed her.

"What?" Yara managed.

"Did you hear that?"

They strained to hear in the stillness of the old lab, but Ash was right. It was a distant sound on the other side of the steel door.

"I think someone else is here," Ash whispered.

The fear that Yara had felt from her vision was replaced with a different, visceral terror.

It must have been clear on her face because Ash gave her a reassuring smile. "It's fine. We'll be fine. Just follow me."

Yara managed a nod and trailed behind Ash, who stood at the door, listening, waiting. Yara tried to pick up any of the distant sounds. They were nothing more than echos, and it was still impossible to tell much about the cause.

"Who is it, do you think?" said Yara, her voice so low it was barely audible.

"I'm not sure," said Ash. "Let's get out of here."

Just as Ash was about to sneak around the door, Yara grabbed her arm and gestured for her to wait.

"What?" said Ash.

"Wait. Trust me."

Just like last time, Rivers. You've done this before. Yara took a deep breath, trying to calm her racing heart, and sank into her mind. It was like riding a bike, falling back into the familiar routine of letting the present drift away from her, finding the future in her mind's eye, and rewinding until she found what she wanted to see.

"It's the Society," said Yara, a wave of relief falling over her. It wasn't Shadow Men. They were safe.

"If they see us, we'll get in a lot of trouble," said Ash, but she didn't sound particularly worried.

"No, it's OK. I can get us out without getting caught."

In the same way she had escaped Kain a year ago, Yara let herself decide what route to take in order to see what lay ahead, making different choices any time they came to an obstacle, until she had a clear and unimpeded view of the way out. She led Ash back toward the exit. It was slow going, with a lot of doubling back and ducking around corners to avoid being spotted. A few times, they got close enough to overhear some hushed conversation between the interlopers.

"...don't know what they expect us to find," said a disgruntled male voice. "We did all this already before. This place has been cleaned out."

"I dunno," replied a woman, "I mean I guess I kinda get it. That whole story about the dude coming back is pretty nuts."

"Yeah, what exactly is that story?"

"No one knows, I guess. Guy died and now he's back? It sounds crazy, honestly. Meyer didn't really go into detail. Just that Black gave the order to comb through the whole area. The lab, the library, the block..."

The man groaned. "Gonna be a long week."

Their voices faded away as they moved off.

"Eyes," Ash whispered to Yara, identifying what division the White Masks were from. "Seekers, probably. Probably looking for clues since Erik woke up around here. Just like us."

"Now, go. Down the hall, then right," said Yara.

The closer the two of them got to the tunnel through which they had come, the harder it became to avoid detection by the half dozen or so Society members who had come to investigate, just as Yara and Ash had.

Yara could not get out of the library fast enough. Ash used her flame to light the way again, and after confirming there were no more White Masks in the tunnel back to the surface, Yara sprinted back up until they were out in the cool afternoon air.

Ash bounded along the street cheerfully beside Yara, unconcerned with the questions that plagued Yara's mind.

"That was awesome. A solid lead!" she exclaimed as they made their way back to the bus stop. "And we didn't even get caught. Good to see Black is sending people in to investigate though, right? I wonder if they'll find anything. Not like you did, though. That was so cool how you did that!"

Ash kept up a steady stream of excited chatter all the way onto the bus, but Yara had more questions than answers. Did her vision mean that the Shadow Men, leaderless, would return to the lab? They had never seemed capable of commanding an operation like what she had just seen. The fact remained, however, that Yara saw that room filled to the brim with Shadow Men doing...

Doing what?

"Why aren't you happier about this?"

Yara chewed her lip. "I just don't understand what those things were..." she said. Or rather, she didn't want to believe what she suspected.

"Tell me again."

Yara did her best to describe the scene to Ash once they got on the bus, going so far as to sketch one of the pods roughly with her finger on her phone, complete with an unconscious stick figure inside. "They almost look like... cryo-chambers or something."

"What're those?"

"I'm not a Researcher or anything," said Yara, ignoring Ash's question, staring instead at her crude drawing. She was not an artist, either. Perhaps Carter would be able to draw it more accurately if she described what she'd seen. Like a sketch artist. "But these are definitely meant to hold people."

Ash frowned. "What for?"

"That's just it. I don't—"

"Were they all full?"

Yara closed her eyes, trying to hold on to what she had seen. "Yes." She was afraid of telling Ash everything she had seen. The children... But Ash had to know. They had to stop this—whatever this was—from happening.

"And the room was full of them?"

"Hundreds."

"Yara," Ash whispered, the *joie de vivre* now gone. Yara opened her eyes to look at her. "What're you not telling me?"

"I think," said Yara, afraid of sounding crazy, "I think... they're going to grow people."

* * *

It was nearly three in the afternoon, and Robin had not heard anything more about Erik, nor had he seen Yara or Ash in hours. And just to add to his growing list of concerns, he'd missed two calls that morning from someone he had no interest in hearing from. Choosing to ignore the messages, he and Carter had locked themselves in one of the training cubicles at the gym and spent the time discussing what to do while Robin let out his pent up energy against a punching bag.

He had worked up such a sweat that his tunic lay discarded in a corner of the room, and his hands were wrapped in fraying tape as he worked the bag. Carter, who had experienced a lot of Robin's energetic way of dealing with nerves last year when Yara had been in so much danger, sat in a corner, fiddling with their gauntlet and throwing a training solenoid—one with no blades—around the room.

"Aren't you tired?" said Carter. "You've been alternating between beating up sims and bags all day."

Robin shrugged but said nothing. Carter knew well enough how Robin coped. This was it.

"If Red and A did go to the library—" Carter said, returning to the subject at hand and sending their solenoid straight up before bringing it back down into the palm of their hand, testing its balance.

"You know they did," interrupted Robin between jabs.

"They probably did," conceded Carter, "but we don't know for sure. We need to decide if we tell Black."

Either they told Black, getting Yara and Ash into unknowable trouble and risking losing Yara's trust forever, or they kept it from the higher-ups, in which case they would be equally implicated if Black ever found out, which was very likely. Their conversation went round and round for what felt like forever before they agreed to confront Yara before deciding anything else.

"I gotta say," said Carter, "I agree with her."

Robin stopped hitting the bag, holding it to prevent it from swinging wildly, and looked at Carter. He laughed, despite himself. "Yeah," he said, shaking his head, his hair falling over his eyes. "Me too. Honestly, I'm almost proud of her."

Carter raised an amused eyebrow. "You and E always did admire the part of her that's most likely to get her killed."

"You mean her infuriating stubbornness?" said Robin, hitting the bag again. "Or her disregard for her own well-being?"

Carter chuckled.

"I still think we should have gone with her," said Robin.

"A is with her. If we had all gone, we'd be more likely to get caught. She's safe."

Silence fell and Robin stared at his fellow Guardian. Though the words had never been said outright, Robin was sure that Carter knew how he felt about Yara. Erik had always made it easy for Robin's feelings to be ignored because Erik had never been as good about hiding his own. After Erik died, Robin had been near the breaking point. More than once, he'd been on the verge of telling Yara, but the fear of losing her as a friend and as a Ward always stopped him. Now, looking into Carter's eyes, Robin could tell that Carter knew everything he was thinking.

"Why won't they let us talk to E?" said Carter, and Robin was grateful for the subject change.

"I don't know," he said. "Is there any hope in asking what's going on? You think they'll tell us?"

"Did you only just start working here?" said Carter and Robin gave a short laugh. Information was on a strict need-to-know basis at the White Mask Society.

At that moment, Ash and Yara came running into the cubicle Robin and Carter had hidden themselves in.

"There you are!" said Yara. "We've been looking everywhere for you!" Her eyes raked over Robin's sweaty, naked torso and she averted her eyes, looking instead at Carter, her cheeks pink. Robin bit his lip, smiling crookedly despite himself.

"Does 'everywhere' include the abandoned laboratory of one Ramsey Kain?" said Carter, putting their solenoid away.

Robin put all of his energy into trying to look just as reproachful, trying to wipe the grin from his face. He looked at Ash. She winked at him, also evidently appreciative of his state of dress... or rather, of undress. He suddenly felt much more exposed.

"Spare us your words of reprimand and disapproving looks," said Yara. "We found something."

Carter stood up swiftly, their amber eyes fixed on Yara.

"We can't know for sure that we're right," said Ash, "but it looks like the Shadow Men are gonna grow..." She trailed off, looking to Yara for support.

Robin could feel the blood drain from his extremities. He clenched his numb fingers in a tight fist and tried to control the urge to reach out to Yara and hold her—anything he could do to get that look off her face—before he started to process what Ash said. Shadow Men? Back? Without Kain?

"Grow what?" said Carter slowly.

"People," finished Yara, her eyes locking onto Robin's.

A heavy silence followed these words.

"How can you know?" Carter's voice felt very far away.

"I saw what looked like gestation pods," said Yara. "Hundreds of them. All sizes."

"You *saw*? They were there?"

Yara shook her head. "It was a vision."

Robin ran a wrapped hand through his sweaty hair. "My god."

"We just narrowly avoided getting caught by a bunch of Seekers on our way out, too. All thanks to this lady," said Ash, nudging Yara.

"What?" said Robin.

"It wasn't a big deal," said Yara dismissively.

"Apparently Black sent a bunch of people down to investigate," said Ash. "Same idea as us. Great minds, and all that."

"Wait," said Carter, "how do you know that what you saw were gestation pods?"

"They were filled with people." Yara struggled to get the words out. "Carter, I saw people inside. Children. Babies."

"That doesn't sound like enough to be sure," said Carter slowly.

"I know what I saw. They were growing in these pods. With umbilical cords and everything." She turned to Robin and he could see the desperation in her eyes.

"Wait," he said. "You don't think—"

"—his Shadow Men," said Carter.

"That's what we were thinking," said Ash. "I've never seen any, but I've read all the case files, obviously, and from what I can tell, he had an endless supply of them."

"If he was growing them in a laboratory, they would be completely dispensable," said Yara.

"Exactly," continued Ash.

"And who knows what else he was doing to them," said Yara, her face contorted with disgust. "If he could take our abilities, all the abilities of the hyden, and use them on himself, who's to say he couldn't alter a fetus? He might have been growing Shadow Men with the abilities of the hyden. And maybe they're going to continue his work now even with him gone."

"Holy shit," said Robin, as the weight of these words sank in. A potentially invincible, infinite army. With super powers.

"Well," said Carter, trying to take the situation by the reins. "We have neither seen nor heard a hint of Shadow Men in a year. Maybe they can't survive without Kain."

"Or maybe," said Yara, "they're just reorganizing." Clearly, she and Ash had had the opportunity to discuss the possibilities already. "I *saw* it happening. I saw it."

"But Kain is dead," said Robin, attempting a smile, hoping to reassure everyone—mostly Yara—that things weren't as bad as they seemed. "How could they possibly be able to do all this without him? He was the brains; they were the muscle. Even with the abilities of the hyden, they couldn't figure out how to *grow people*. And we know Kain's dead. His body was destroyed. In January after the battle. We watched his body get burned from the inside out by the virus Yara injected into him."

Ash's eyes flashed. "Erik's body was burned, too."

To this, Robin had no response.

"I hardly think we have enough evidence to think that Kain might still be a threat," said Carter in a quiet voice. "E's return proves nothing." They looked at Robin for support, their forehead wrinkled with doubt.

"It proves that 'dead' doesn't mean anything," said Yara, her voice stern. "It proves that we know nothing."

"You said yourself that Black sent Seekers in to look things over," Carter continued. "If there's any evidence that's cause for concern, they'll find it."

"I don't think they'll find anything," said Yara.

"Yeah. I mean, the only reason we found anything was because of Yara's vision," said Ash.

"Wait a second," said Carter. "He grows his Shadow Men…"

Robin could see a thought forming in Carter's mind, but it had yet to take shape.

Yara was the one who got there first. She gasped.

"What?" said Ash.

"Clones," said Carter and Yara at the same time. Except Carter's had been a question, Yara's a statement.

Robin cursed.

"I can't believe I didn't see it before," said Yara. "So many twins, so many identical Shadow Men."

"That's why he branded them," said Robin.

"Hold on," said Carter, holding their hands up, trying to encourage everyone to slow down. "This is quite an assumption."

"Is it?" said Robin. "He's a goddamn biologist, C, you think it's beyond him to perfect cloning?"

"Oh my god," Yara breathed.

"Is anyone else thinking what I'm thinking?" said Ash. They all turned to her. "E? Erik?"

"Oh my god," Yara said again, this time sounding sick. Robin's stomach dropped. "No. No no no," said Yara. "He can't be. If the Shadow Men are clones, Erik can't be. The Shadow Men are nothing. There's no one there. I mean, they're like drones. Not like Erik. How could Erik be himself? How could he remember… everything if he's a clone?"

Everyone was quiet for a long moment before Carter broke the silence. "We have to give this information to the Society."

Robin could anticipate that this would not go over well with Yara. Sure enough, her face paled at Carter's words and her lips thinned. A telltale sign that she was angry. Robin tried not to smile. Despite himself, he loved how fired up she got when she was angry and that he knew her well enough to know when it was coming.

"No," she said.

"It's not your decision, Red," said Carter, reaching out to touch her shoulder, but she shrugged them away impatiently, starring daggers at them.

"Their first priority will never be to find out what happened to Erik. To keep him safe. And if they even *suspect* him of being a… a…"

"But that's not your decision," said Carter.

"Like hell it isn't!" Yara looked between the two of them. "You spent all that time trying to protect me and it cost Erik his life." She choked on the words, but kept going, her eyes shining. "If we tell Black or Glover or anyone else, this whole thing is gonna be about finding Shadow Men. They won't care about helping Erik."

"Finding Shadow Men, finding out about what you saw can *help* us find out what happened to him," said Carter as gently as they could.

"Yeah, it can," said Yara. "And it will. But not if this gets to Black. Erik's well-being isn't her priority. But it is mine. And I owe it to him."

Carter bowed their head.

"OK," said Robin.

Carter's head snapped up to look at Robin, incredulous. "What?"

"Yara's right. Black, Williams, all of them will turn it into an investigation about Shadow Men, and E will fall through the cracks. Or worse."

"You don't know that."

"I know that saving Guardians isn't the prime concern for the Society. Our entire purpose is to protect people. Right now, E is people. Erik is people." Saying the name still felt foreign and strange on his tongue, but the situation had changed. And Erik deserved a name.

All eyes were on Carter as they looked between the three of them, obviously struggling, before they caved and said, "Fine. We don't tell Black. *Yet.*"

Yara was radiant as she leapt into Carter's arms, hugging them tightly. Robin swallowed the twinge of jealousy, occupying himself by starting to take the tape off his hands, but Yara ran over and hugged him, too.

For someone so small, she came at him with a lot of force, squeezing him so tightly that she forced the air out of his lungs. He gave himself a moment to enjoy the feel of her in his arms, her lithe body small enough that he could grab his own elbows around her, her hands gripping his sweaty back. His muscles tensed under her touch. He breathed her in—citrus—but she was gone just as fast, beaming at Ash, that same pink tinge back in her cheeks.

This day had really gotten way from him.

And to think that this morning he had been waiting to tell Yara that he loved her.

CHAPTER NINE

Whole Lives

Erik was still in the same room of the medical wing. Much of the growth that had exploded from him after his outburst had been removed and taken away for study. Black was gone all afternoon filling in everyone who was deemed "need to know." Frankie had gone with Black, but her assistant, a Medic named Paul Chun, was monitoring him.

"This is all a gross overreaction," said Erik, who was sitting, not on the exam table as was expected, but on a nearby chair, his arms crossed, being unapologetically uncooperative. If they wouldn't give him what he wanted and let him see Yara, he wouldn't give them what they wanted either.

"You caused a small earthquake and turned this room into a forest. I hardly think we're overreacting."

Erik had always liked Chun, insomuch as he ever liked any members of the Society with whom he had little to no interactions. Chun had helped Yara several times when she collapsed from her vision-induced migraines last year. But now, the spiky-haired man was just another obstacle between him and Yara. "Was it actually an earthquake?"

"Do you mean did anyone outside of this building feel it? The answer to that is 'yes.' It was registered as a 5.7 on the Richter Scale. Regardless, however, it cannot be ignored that whether or not it was a 'real' earthquake, you caused damage to the building. In a very 'real' way."

Erik looked down, but didn't respond for a while. "I don't know what happened."

"We didn't think you would," said Chun. "But maybe now you can see why we're treating this situation seriously."

"What I don't understand is why you won't let me see Yara."

"When we know that you can't harm anyone—"

"I would never hurt her!" said Erik, leaping to his feet, fury firing up within him at the insinuation. But when he saw the fear in Chun's eyes and how his hands subtly moved toward the sedative Erik was sure was in his pocket, Erik focused on regaining his breath and calming this foreign, unfamiliar anger which now constantly felt so close to the surface. "I would never hurt her. I don't want to hurt anyone. I just want things to go back—" His voice cracked. He cleared his throat and continued. "All I want is for things to go back to normal."

Chun said nothing.

"How do I even know you're telling me the truth?" said Erik, sitting back down and crossing his arms again.

"About what?"

"Me. Dying. I don't remember it."

"Well, Mr. Carpenter, there seems to be a lot you don't remember."

"Like what?"

"Like how your hair turned white. How you ended up alone in the middle of downtown Los Angeles in the middle of January in clothes you've never worn. How you're suddenly able to shatter the earth beneath your feet. How—"

"OK," said Erik, holding up his hand. "OK. I get it."

More silent minutes passed. Chun seemed perfectly content to sit without speaking, occasionally making a note on his tablet. Then, the door opened and Black came in, followed by Williams, Glover, Frankie, and—Erik's breath caught in his throat—Yara along with Robin, Carter, and the young woman he knew to be Yara's new Guardian.

Yara's face lit up in a way that made the world around him disappear. He hardly noticed that he'd gotten to his feet and started drifting toward her when she broke eye contact with him, and he suddenly realized that Black was talking.

"—decided to let Erik Carpenter reenter the Guardian division. However, until we can determine what events led to his reappearance, as well as the cause of his changes, physical and otherwise, he will not be permitted in the field."

"What?" said Erik. "What am I supposed to do, then?"

"There is work with the Level 2 Guardians that can be done—"

"No!" Everyone's heads turned to Yara, whose face was red, either from embarrassment or frustration. "He deserves to be able to find out what happened to him."

"Ms. Rivers," said Glover in his deep voice. There was no hint of friendliness behind his eyes. Yara recoiled under his warning gaze, but didn't back down.

"Is this how things work here?" she said, looking at everyone. "A group of people in a room make a decision and we all follow it even though we know it's bullshit?"

"Red," said Carter, putting their hand on Yara's shoulder but leaving their eyes on Erik.

"Yes, Yara, that is how things work here," said Black. "I'm surprised that after all the resources and time we have spent training you to join our ranks, you still seem confused about it." Black's eyes flashed at Yara as she spoke, and it seemed enough to stifle her. Yara looked at her three Guardians then back at Erik. He beamed at her. He couldn't help it. It was a completely involuntary reaction. To his enormous surprise, her face melted into a warm smile as well. Erik wasn't any happier than she was about this decision to keep him behind a desk, but Yara was what was most important. Black could stick him anywhere in the Society as long as Yara was safe and close. Very close. Close enough to hold. Black was talking again but Erik could barely hear her. Even now, the little distance between him and Yara was agony.

From far away, Black's voice said, "We'll give you a little time to catch up. Erik, please report to Mx. Williams when you're ready and they'll give you all the information you need."

Erik nodded without taking his eyes from Yara's. Everyone but her and her Guardians filed quietly out of the ward.

"E," said Carter, hugging him and clapping him on the back. Erik hugged them back, smiling. He laughed as tears came out of the corners of his own eyes. When Carter let go, it was Robin's turn to hug him.

"It's good to have you back, buddy," murmured Robin.

Erik gave him a quick squeeze and looked into his blue eyes, grinning. Then, before turning his attention to Yara, he held out his hand to the third Guardian. She was very obviously a Vurwari, identifiable primarily by her burning orange eyes. She looked to be no older than he was.

"Hi, I'm E," he said.

She beamed at him, her teeth bright against her brown skin. Ignoring his outstretched hand completely, she wrapped him in another embrace, her skin hot against his. "Hello, E. I'm A. A for Ash. Nice to officially meet you!"

"Likewise," he said, raising his eyebrows at Carter who shrugged.

When Ash let go, Erik looked at Yara, his heart pounding in his throat, unable to stop the wide smile on his face.

"They won't tell us anything," she said, but she didn't move toward him. Unsure of what was holding her back, Erik didn't reach out. His stomach clenched, but he tried to ignore it.

"They're trying to figure out what's going on," said Erik. He made a conscious effort to look at everyone in turn, and not just at Yara.

"So are we," said Robin.

"Yara and I found something," said Ash. "At the library. And we think we can find out what happened to you."

"That's great! What was it? Did you tell Black?"

Robin and Carter exchanged exasperated looks.

"Well," said Carter, "we decided not to."

Erik laughed. "What? Really?"

Robin cocked an eyebrow, giving Erik his trademark crooked smile, exaggerated now under an equally crooked nose. It had broken since Erik last saw him. A sign of the missing twelve months, he supposed. "See how we've changed," said Robin.

Erik laughed again, more out of shock than anything else. He ran his hand through his hair.

"We want to find out what happened, and we think we could be more effective if we… did it alone," said Yara. "Without Black." She was looking at Erik tentatively, as though unsure of what he was thinking. "We want you to help us."

At this, both Robin and Carter looked at Yara, their mouths open. Evidently, this decision had not been made with them. Ash started laughing.

"This girl," she said, gesturing with her thumb at Yara. "She knows what she wants, I'll give her that."

"Red, you just heard Black say it. Erik isn't allowed in the field."

"I don't care. I want him with us."

Robin was shaking his head and looking up at the ceiling, with an exasperated smile on his face. "Let it go, C," he said. "It's not like she's suggesting we storm any more castles any time soon."

"I would prefer it," said Yara, looking at Robin pointedly, "if you didn't talk about me as if I weren't here."

Robin held up his hands acquiescently. "Pardon me, your grace," he said. "But right now, what we have to worry about is getting you through initiation."

"Oh yeah," said Erik. "I heard something along those lines. What's this about our Yara becoming a Guardian?" The smile slid from his face when he noticed that Yara did not altogether look excited about this prospect.

There was a tense moment before the silence was broken by Ash saying loudly, "Well, things just got awkward real fast."

"Alright!" said Yara. "Alright." She looked pointedly at Robin, her eyebrows raised. "I'll do it. I'll take the tests. I'll even… pass them, if you want." She gave him a coy smile. "Can you come to dinner with us?" she added, looking at Erik.

"Uh," he said. "Honestly, I don't know. I'd guess probably not. I have to report to Williams and get my… new assignment." The words felt like poison on his tongue.

"Oh," said Yara, looking crestfallen.

"We'll give you two a minute," said Carter to Yara and Erik, as the rest of them left the ward. They gave Erik warm smiles and comforting words of parting, such as, "See you soon," or, "Great to have you back."

After the door closed, Erik and Yara looked at each other for a full minute without speaking. Finally, Yara opened her mouth to say something, but Erik had already closed the distance between them and crushed his lips to hers, cutting her off. She responded in part by kissing him back. Her hands were on his back as he clutched her face, holding her to him, kissing her fervently. Her lips, her cheeks, her nose, her eyes and forehead, every part of her that he could, he kissed. When he finally pulled back to look at her, there were tears in her eyes, but she was smiling.

He couldn't speak just yet. His throat was tight from emotions that were welling up inside of him, fighting to get out, but he knew that if he let them out, bottling it back up would be a lot harder, and he didn't know how much time he had with her.

They laughed as they stared at each other, lost for words.

"So," he finally managed, "you're going to be a Guardian, huh?"

"I don't know if it's what I want."

"What do you want?" he asked her, brushing a strand of her hair out of her eyes.

"Right now?" she said. "You. Do I have to decide more than that?"

He smiled. "Let's pretend like you don't."

"OK." Her eyes drifted up to his hair and he was suddenly self conscious of how different he looked. "I like it," she said, evidently sensing his insecurity.

"You do?" he said, tugging at a lock, as though he could turn it back to the jet black it once was.

She smiled and ran her hands through it. He suppressed a shiver of delight. "Yeah. It's sexy."

He purred at this, melting his body back into hers and placing a light kiss on her lips. "I'm glad you think so."

She sighed as she rested her head against his, and he inhaled deeply, having missed the scent of citrus that he had come to associate with her. "I think I have to leave," she said in a voice so quiet it was clear she didn't want to be saying the words at all.

Erik bit his lip to stop himself from replying, because he knew he would only have words of protest. But she was right. They both had things to do. And if all went well, they would have their whole lives ahead of them for more of this.

CHAPTER TEN

Initiation

The spy knocked twice on the gates at the entrance to the mansion. The buzzer made a loud sound and the gates groaned open, scraping against the unkempt driveway. The forcefield that normally protected the grounds powered down long enough for the spy to pass the threshold, then a faint hum indicated the field had been turned back on. The mansion had been long abandoned, and purchased by the mass of wealth the Necromancer had somehow acquired. The spy didn't question it, sure the Necromancer wouldn't respond well to idle curiosity about something so gauche as money. In any case, it wasn't anything the spy had to concern themself with.

They made their way up the long, overgrown gravel path to the double doors leading to the grand hall. The doors were opened by two identical Shadow Men, both with the same dead look in their eyes. They made no acknowledgement of the spy's presence, simply closing the doors once the spy passed through the threshold. Then, the Shadow Men stood there, still as posts, waiting for another order.

A shiver ran down the spy's back. It was undeniable that the Shadow Men made them uncomfortable. They had no idea why all Shadow Men had that same dead quality, but again, it was not their job to know.

The spy went up the stairs, down the hallway on the left, through the third door on the right, and into the sitting room where the Necromancer was always waiting for them.

"You have news?" said the Necromancer. She stood at the window, looking out into the overgrown garden, hands clasped delicately behind her.

The spy did not move far into the room. The Necromancer had never shown any signs of violence, but there was a quality about her that kept the spy well away every time they met.

"Yes. It has arrived—"

"'He,'" said the Necromancer.

The spy hesitated. "I'm sorry?"

"'He.' Not 'it.'"

"Of course. Forgive me," said the spy. "He has arrived at Headquarters and successfully made contact."

"And?" said the Necromancer, turning her head slightly so that the spy could see the outline of her cheek.

"They are nowhere near discovering how it—how he's alive, or what he is."

"Good." The Necromancer looked back over the garden.

The spy hesitated, unsure of whether they should speak without prompting. "Apparently, he has… already had an outburst. Revealing his enhancements."

At this, the Necromancer turned around and stared directly into the spy's eyes. Like the Shadow Men, the Necromancer's eyes were impassive and unfeeling, but there was something more dangerous beneath them that the spy had never seen in any Shadow Man. The spy shifted uncomfortably.

"What do they think of that?"

"No one knows," said the spy. "I believe the Researchers and Medics are working on it."

"You will alert me if they ever find out."

"Of course," said the spy, bowing their head respectfully.

"Anything else?"

"Yes," said the spy, still looking down, unable to maintain eye contact with the Necromancer, who seemed unbothered by this show of weakness. "A Guardian and one of the hyden found the former Incubation Room in the old lab."

Silence.

The spy chanced a look at the Necromancer to see her reaction to this statement. If the Necromancer could feel fury, the spy was sure this was what it looked like. Her lips were pursed in a thin line and her dangerous, blank eyes were fixated on a point behind the spy, presumably seeing nothing.

"Which hydan?"

"Yara Rivers."

"That room was meant to be dismantled and relocated," said the Necromancer in a quiet, dangerous voice.

"It was. Seekers were sent in as well. They found nothing. The hydan… apparently had some sort of vision."

"But she only sees the future."

The spy had assumed the vision indicated the Incubation Room would be reinstalled, but the Necromancer's confusion made that seem unlikely. The spy remained quiet, unsure if they were expected to respond.

"You may leave," said the Necromancer eventually. "The Shadow Men will handle it."

The spy gave one last respectful nod before backing out of the sitting room as quickly as possible without running. They kept their head down, avoiding looking at any of the Shadow Men who were now marching in droves to the sitting room. Somehow, the Necromancer had already silently called for them. To give orders, to punish, to do whatever it was the Necromancer had planned. The spy didn't think it would be a good idea to hang around to find out.

Out the front door, down the gravel drive, and past the gates, the spy leaned against one of the brick pillars and took a deep, shaky breath. It was done. It was over. Hopefully, they wouldn't have to be back here for a few weeks.

"Bad news, I'm afraid, sir," said Glover in his deep voice.

Black bowed her head. She knew it had been coming. Had anticipated that their luck would run out. "Mr. Carpenter?" she said.

"Xaili Williams."

Worse than she'd hoped. But what she'd expected.

"They left the compound. Left their ConvOrb. Disabled their tracker."

Black turned to face her Second. "When?"

"Last night." Glover gave her a moment before he continued. "Shall I have them brought here?"

"No," said the Tenebrae, trying to keep her anger under control, to stop the darkness from consuming the room, at least until she was alone when she could drop her human form and rest as shadow. "Not before initiation. I don't want the initiates distracted." She looked at the man before her, the one she had chosen to be her successor because of his demeanor, his instinct, his diplomatic nature. "I will want this handled with the utmost discretion," she said.

"Of course."

"No one is to know that we have been compromised. I don't want trust in the Society to be lost over this."

Glover nodded and left her office.

This, her home, the White Mask Society, was at a breaking point. A spy. A traitor… And not even the only one in the whole of the organization. She had heard of the events in Paris last summer. The founding branch had had their own breach in security. Another shape shifter, as well. What were the implications, then, if she had a shape shifter in her own branch who wanted to betray them? It could lead to a dangerous precedent, another form of persecution, the very thing the Society existed to prevent.

Black let herself collapse, shedding her human skin as she melted into her natural form, nothing more than the night itself.

Yara's uniform today was white. Her green initiate training tunic, slacks and brown boots had been replaced by a sleek, blinding uniform of the same design. White, she supposed, was intended to represent the youth and inexperience of the initiates, a clean slate.

Often during her sparing sessions with Robin, she had shed the long-sleeved tunic in exchange for a sleeveless tank top, which made her feel less constricted. Robin had warned her that getting used to fighting in different gear would only come to "bite her in the ass," as he put it, come test day. He hadn't been wrong. The long sleeves felt unnaturally tight and hot, though she couldn't deny that the extra protection the reinforced fabric offered could come in handy during combat.

Trying to take deep breaths, Yara made her way to the initiate training grounds where testing took place. With every step, her mind vibrated with a thousand things she shouldn't be thinking about, distracting her from what she was about to face.

Left foot. Erik.

Right foot. All those containment pods from her vision.

Left. What if she failed? Robin might never forgive her. Would he really be angry about that?

Right. Bora Black had changed history by letting her train.

Left. Maybe this was all just a huge mistake.

Right. Erik was back. He was home. He was alive.

What did that mean?

Did it matter?

Before she knew it, she was facing her three Guardians. Ash was beaming. She flicked her fingers, and a burst of flame in the shape of a thumbs up hovered in front of Yara for a moment before vanishing with a puff of smoke. Yara nodded appreciatively. Carter gave her a wink over their glasses, and Robin, who was dressed in the same white as her—as did all trainers on test day—smiled crookedly.

No Aunt Catherine today, however. Robin had been planning her surprise attendance yesterday long enough ahead of time for her to have gotten the day off of work. As a nurse, Aunt Catherine had not been able to swing another day off with no notice, so she had texted Yara good luck, demanding promises of updates throughout the day.

Yara let her eyes flit among the spectators quietly standing around the room murmuring to each other. Many of them were holding their white masks, some were already wearing them. Silly tradition.

No shock of white hair stood out in the crowd.

"Sorry, kid," said Robin, reading her thoughts. "Apparently they sent him up to Research to run a few more tests. He really wanted to be here, though."

"Oh," said Yara, trying to act like she wasn't disappointed. "No, it's fine."

"He said to wish you luck."

She forced a smile and tried to focus her attention on the matter at hand.

"Good luck today, Yara," said a female voice from behind her. Yara spun around to see Nayla Jackson's beautiful blonde head walking away to join the rest of the crowd. Nayla was another Guardian and Robin's ex.

Yara barely had time to choke out a soft "thanks" before her attention was turned back to the center of the room.

"Welcome back, initiates," said Black's cool, collected voice. She was standing amid all the nervous initiates, her black uniform and matching hair an impressive sight amidst the sea of white. "Thank you for your patience, I know many of you were hoping to have this behind you by now. Hopefully, you took advantage of the extra time for more preparation. Or rest, whichever was most valuable to each of you."

There were a few chortles from the initiates. Yara was sure that each and every one of them had been training even harder. Though she certainly hadn't been. She had been galavanting across the city on a wild goose chase and hadn't spared initiation a second thought. She bit her lip and clenched her fists to stop them from shaking.

"As I'm sure you all know, today will pass in four stages, the first of which is hand-to-hand combat. Your names will be chosen at random and you'll take it in turns to fight the simulator. Those of you who passed this test yesterday will not have to fight again. Our next initiate is..." Black turned to Xaili Williams, who was standing beside her looking proudly at their potential new Guardians.

Williams pressed a button on the tablet they were holding and said in a loud voice, "Axle Jones."

A boy with neatly parted hair stepped forward. His jaw was set, but Yara could tell he was nervous. He nodded respectfully to Black, Williams, and Glover, who was standing nearby, before moving past them and heading into the arena.

For the purposes of test day, a small simulator had been set up at the end of the room with a screen on the outside so the spectators could see the initiates at work. Axle would have no more than ten minutes to beat his opponent, a faceless fighter who waited immobile within the confines of the sim. Not a real fighter, of course, but for all intents and purposes, as real as it needed to be.

Yara couldn't help but be impressed by the coolness with which Axle approached this fighter. Axle was tall, not quite six feet, but almost, and the simulated fighter who awaited him still looked enormous by comparison.

So this is how it'll go, she thought, as Axle started to battle the simulation. *One by one, we get called up, and perform in front of every Guardian in the Society. Like trained monkeys.* Axle was an incredible fighter, though she was sure that was true of every one of the people standing next to her. You were more likely to not make it past training than to get this far and fail here. In the six months since Yara had joined the initiates, two candidates had already washed out.

Axle only took six and a half minutes to knock out his opponent. The simulation flickered out of life and there was applause from the onlooking Guardians as Black, Williams, and Glover made notes on their tablets. A couple of Level 3 Guardians in the crowd were jotting things down as well. Yara swallowed.

Next up was a girl named Olive Quigley. She was about Yara's height and had tied back her hair in braided ponytails. Despite this juvenile style, she cracked her neck as she approached the simulation. She fought the same fighter, almost twice her size, and took 6 minutes and 47 seconds to defeat it. More applause, more notes.

Yara was starting to get very nervous now. She wished she could just get it over with. She could feel Robin and Carter watching and knew how important it was to Robin that she succeed.

Three more initiates went, all defeating the simulation in under seven minutes. Yara felt on the verge of vomiting when her name was at last called by Williams. Yara stepped forward, conscious of putting one foot in front of the other and trying hard not to think about anything else. About the hundreds of eyes on her and the stillness of the simulation awaiting her. As she passed by Williams, she looked in their direction and saw the same amber eyes Yara associated with Carter looking back at her. For a moment, Yara allowed herself to imagine it was Carter standing there instead, smiling encouragingly.

Then she turned her attention to the simulation, and, in the split second before the fighter lunged at her, time slowed as a ludicrous thought occurred to her.

Yara could see the future. A power she had underutilized because of the fear that gripped her when she thought about some of the things she had seen since learning to control it; her own kidnapping and Erik's torture at the hands of Kain, for instance. But this power she had… it was hers. It did not belong to Kain. And it was not just a result of hours of being tested on in his laboratory. She was stronger than that.

She had power.

What if… What if she could see her opponent's moves before he made them? What if?

Concentrating with all her might, Yara focused. She didn't have time to sink into her body as she had before when she'd triggered visions. She didn't have time to test out all possible scenarios. She only had time to—

She ducked right, moving out of the way of the oncoming attack just in time. Without knowing how she knew it was coming, she managed to parry a blow that the sim was aiming to throw behind her back, and slammed it to the ground with her leg, still clutching the arm it had thrown at her. It didn't scream—it wasn't programmed to—but there was a loud crack from its shoulder.

Yara let go and backed away from it, breathing heavily. What had just happened? She had somehow managed to anticipate its attacks without consciously being aware of it. She looked down at her hands in awe.

The fighter was getting back to its feet, cradling its shoulder, before rolling it around a couple of times, testing the joint. Then it lunged again.

Yara didn't need to think twice this time. She saw the attack coming. It was going to swing upward with its right fist and try to trip her—

It never saw her coming.

She was already behind it by the time it registered she had moved, and kicking it in the back of the knees. It fell with a loud crunch, and she grabbed it around the neck, immobilizing it long enough to chop her hand against a pressure point in its neck, knocking it out completely.

She stood over its limp body, panting, barely able to process what had just happened, when the simulator died and she heard the sound of applause from the Guardians watching just outside, having seen the whole thing projected on the viewing screen. She exited the simulator and looked at the screen displaying her time. It had taken her all of 52 seconds. The judges were all whispering frantically. She smiled to herself, avoiding eye contact with all the other initiates.

It wasn't over. She had three more tests to pass today. She met her Guardians' eyes among the crowd. They were ecstatic. She gave them a nod, and wished that Erik had gotten to see her fight like that.

Everyone had passed the first stage, but no one came close to Yara's time. That didn't stop her nerves from rearing their ugly heads again when she faced stage two: the gauntlet.

Gauntlets were used to control solenoidal stars, the Guardians' weapon of choice, more lethal than guns against certain Deviants and more effective than traditional handheld weapons. Solenoids were large, metallic discs with edges made of a nano-filament carbon fiber, making them impossibly strong and sharp. The only way to safely handle them was with the gauntlet, an intricate metal glove.

Despite her success fighting the simulation in hand-to-hand combat, Yara's palms were sweating. Perhaps her spectacular victory in the first stage had simply been a fluke. She had never been very confident with solenoids, but it was pointless to fixate on that now.

Stage two of the test was the same general pattern as in the first with one terrifying difference. Though the simulator could create a holographic projection of a solenoid, which was how initiates had first learned to use the weapon, they had long ago graduated to using training solenoidal stars, which had no blades, but could still do considerable damage in the hands of an expert. The simulated opponent would be wearing a real gauntlet equipped with an equally real solenoid. Of course, Yara had fought against solenoids before while training with Robin. Over the last six months she had practiced controlling them and defending herself against them, but Robin had never been actively trying to hurt her. For all she knew, this simulated fighter would be just as vicious as the real thing.

Just relax, Rivers, she thought to herself as the gauntlet was fastened onto the opponent. She would be able to gauge the situation by watching whoever was unlucky enough to go first.

"Yara Rivers."

Shit.

Her armor—chain mail made from diamond, the only substance hard enough to protect against the razor sharp blades of a solenoid—was waiting for her by the simulator. Today, the diamond chain mail was less to protect her and more to test her endurance under its weight. She slung it over her white tunic and took deep breaths before walking into the sim, trying to calm down. Her opponent was standing perfectly still when she walked in, its gauntlet-wearing hand outstretched, a solenoid hovering over the palm.

The silence in the room felt heavy. The hundred or so people gathered outside the room to watch were just as interested as Yara to see if she could demonstrate the same skill and speed she'd used in the first round.

Yara took a moment before stepping over the threshold and activating the simulation to take a few more deep breaths and collect her thoughts. The same clarity washed over her, and she took a step forward, leaving her uncertainty behind.

The fighter's solenoid didn't have time to change direction fast enough to follow Yara's attack. She was two steps ahead of every movement it made. The sound of the solenoids clashing filled the air. The fighter couldn't get its weapon anywhere near her. It was completely caught off guard by Yara's speed so she took the opportunity to punch it in the gut with her gauntlet free hand. It doubled over and, its concentration faltering, its solenoid hung limply in the air. Yara quickly shot hers with precision control to within an inch of the fighter's neck and froze it. The fighter didn't move. It was yielding. She wrapped her hand around its gauntlet and yanked it off. Its solenoid clattered to the ground. She had won.

She had no idea how it had happened, but it was just like before.

Somehow, she had been able to intuitively anticipate every movement before it happened. She laughed, more as a release of tension than anything else. It was all so easy. How had she never discovered this before?

The spectators were applauding as she exited the simulation.

"Reset the fighter," said Williams to a nearby Level 2 Guardian who hurried over to the simulation and reaffixed the gauntlet. Williams didn't take their eyes off of Yara, but they were smiling, their amber eyes, so like Carter's, twinkling. Yara nodded and rushed to the back of the group of initiates. Olive Quigley nudged her with her elbow and winked. "Well done," she said. Yara grinned and watched as everyone else took their turns. She barely noticed anything. She was too busy trying not to look too cocky, and ignoring the excited pounding of her heart.

This, she could do.

This, she was good at.

Feeling lighter than she had in a year, she let her mind wonder what else they might throw at her and thought, *bring it.*

Stage three did not offer Yara the same advantage as combat: endurance. Her least favorite. Deliberately placed right before the last stage—which they only knew consisted of some sort of obstacle course —in an effort to tire and weaken the initiates. Over the last six months, she and Carter had gotten up at dawn six days a week to run. The only reason she got a day off from running at all was because the seventh day was used exclusively for fight training. Needless to say, Yara's endurance was better than it had ever been, though that wasn't saying much. For most of her life, all it took to wind her was a long set of stairs. Now she was running seven miles before breakfast. The endurance test was as brutal as it was boring, consisting of two hours on treadmills that changed speed and terrain without notice. This was the one stage no one watched. Not even Black. So as everyone else went to lunch, the twelve initiates mounted their treadmills in the gym and started to run.

Two hours elapsed in what felt like ten. Everyone passed, but all conversation—a few people's feeble attempts at making it less dull— had ceased after the first five minutes when the treadmills started to change under their feet. The silence was indicative of how hard they had to concentrate in order not to fall off their machines.

Sweating, starving, and generally feeling miserable, the thrill of having come out on top in the first two stages gone, Yara moved with the crowd to where the fourth and final stage would take place: the sims. Evidently the small individual simulator set up in the training rooms was insufficient for the last test.

The floor was already filled with spectators; all family members and White Masks who had returned after lunch to watch the new class join the rank of Guardians. There were twelve simulators and twelve initiates. Yara wondered if they would each get their own room. She didn't know what to expect. For all Robin had done to prepare her for becoming a Guardian, he wasn't allowed to tell her anything about the test itself. But in looking around, Yara didn't think all the sims would be used. Only six of them had viewing screens set up on the doors. At the moment, the screens were blank.

"Congratulations, initiates, on having gotten this far," said Black. "Welcome to the final stage of testing."

The excited chatter quieted. Yara searched the crowd for Carter, Robin, and Ash and thought she spotted them in a far corner close to room 6.

"You will be going through the fourth stage with a partner," she continued. "Both of you must complete the course in order for either of you to pass because, as you know, much of the work you'll be doing in the field will require you to work effectively as a team." Yara looked nervously at the other initiates around her. She knew all of them to be exceptional, of course, but relying on someone else was just as daunting as having someone else rely on her.

Inhale liquid gold, she thought.

"You'll be given a time limit. Complete the course—together—within the allotted time, ensuring that neither of you fall behind or are injured. Mx. Williams will be informing you of your partners and assigned rooms."

Black looked over her shoulder to Williams, who started reading off pairs from their tablet, followed by their room assignment.

"Yara Rivers and Wesley Thorne," they called out without looking up, "in room 6."

Yara looked over at Wesley, a Black boy with long dreadlocks he kept tied back. She smiled at him. He looked apprehensive but determined, and gave her a small nod. Wesley was one of six humans in the class.

When everyone had been given their assigned partners and rooms—it seemed that every Deviant had been partnered with one of the humans—Yara and Wesley made their way to room 6 where her Guardians and his family were waiting. No one spoke as the initiates all stepped into their respective sims, but Yara was held back briefly by Williams, who had a soft hand on her shoulder.

Wesley looked back curiously and Williams held up a finger.

"Yara, a quick word before you start."

Yara only had a second to worry that she was in trouble before Williams started speaking.

"Have you looked forward into the future at all regarding this test?" they said.

Yara shook her head, cursing herself. Why hadn't she thought to do that? Being a seer was definitely something she had not taken advantage of enough.

"Good," said Williams. "Please do not. You may not always have that luxury in the field, and we want to be able to assess how you might pass without using your hydan abilities. Understood?"

"Oh. Yes, sir," said Yara.

Williams nodded with a small smile. They ushered Yara after Wesley as the fourth and final stage began.

CHAPTER ELEVEN

Hurdles

Yara and Wesley barely had time to wish each other luck as they stepped through the automatic doors of the simulator directly onto what looked like the bridge of a stealth aircraft. FV-960s were ships used by the Society, affectionately nicknamed Furtives by the Guardians. Part of training had been learning how to fly one. Still, it felt strange to be on the bridge of a Furtive when she had expected to find nothing but the glass walls of the sims. Of course, this wasn't a real Furtive. This was all a simulation. The only difference between this and the bridge of a true Furtive was that this one had a countdown clock suspended outside the windshield. It showed them as having 60 minutes.

Aware that what they were doing was being broadcast to an audience in the hall, Yara took a seat in one of the pilot chairs.

"You run controls," said Wesley, "I'll navigate?"

Yara nodded, thinking idly to herself how strange it was that she felt more comfortable piloting a stealth aircraft than driving a car. *Less traffic in the sky,* she thought to herself with a smile. Her nerves were starting to ease.

"Do we have a destination?" she asked.

Wesley nodded. "It's here. A message." He pressed a button and a small screen popped up with Williams's face.

"Guardians. Your mission is as follows: you are to rescue civilian hostages who have been kidnapped by anti-human extremists. Do not let any civilians die. Getting them out unharmed is your primary responsibility. Failure to do so will result in failure of the test. Disable the extremists only; do not kill. Sending coordinates now. Good luck."

The screen closed.

No casualties, including the bad guys.

"We got this," said Wesley.

Yara smiled at him. "Ready when you are."

As it turned out, the two of them worked well as a team. Wesley was able to navigate efficiently as Yara piloted the Furtive to their destination. There had been some turbulence when they ran into an unexpected storm that hadn't shown up on their radar, but it was a small adjustment that only cost them half a minute.

They still had 53 minutes on the clock when they set down gently at their destination.

One of these days, Yara thought to herself, marveling at the seamless experience of stepping out of their simulated Furtive and onto the rocky surface, *I'm going to have Robin explain to me how these sims work beyond just "nanotech."* While the Furtive was a small location that could be replicated in its entirety within the confines of the simulator, their destination did not attempt to recreate the same level of reality. On either side of them were the gridded walls of the sims, and ahead was a steel wall that rose nearly to the ceiling.

"Climbing," said Wesley. "I hate this part."

Secretly, Yara agreed. The scaling she and Robin had trained on did not involve a steel surface like this. There were usually handholds. Before she could wonder how they were meant to climb without full gear, however, the wall started to shift. Steel plates the size of small bricks began to emerge from the wall before seamlessly receding back into the surface, leaving no sign at all that they had ever existed. They ebbed and flowed ceaselessly with no discernible pattern.

"This looks fun," said Yara.

"We gotta do it," he said, and the two of them leapt at existing handholds which started to sink back into the wall just as soon as they emerged.

Williams had told Yara not to look into the future. But what she had done in her first two stages had not been premonition. It had been a deep seated instinct. True, it was likely fueled by the same powers that made her visions possible, but now Yara couldn't stop it from happening. Without understanding how she knew, she could see the next handholds emerge before they did and she leapt to them just before she started to slide back down the wall. She was concentrating too hard to wonder if this was considered cheating. Either way, there was no stopping it. Yara could not prevent herself from anticipating each move any more than she could stop her heart from beating.

Her fingers ached and her toes were sore. Sweat made it harder the further she climbed, but she made it, hopping from one disappearing hold to the next until she pulled herself over the wall.

Looking down, she saw Wesley was only halfway up, barely managing to stay as far as he'd gained. She could see the next handholds before he could, and called back down to him.

"To your left!"

He didn't hesitate and managed to grab on a split second before falling.

"Up, now! Up!"

With Yara's help, Wesley made it to the top, where she pulled him up, giving them each a moment to breathe while straddling the top of the wall. He had a scrape on his uniform, evidently having fallen at least once back to the rocky surface below during his climb.

"Thank you," he panted.

"Partners," she said. "C'mon, let's keep going."

Turning ahead, however, did not fill Yara with confidence. There was a steep fall down to the same rocky surface, and a tall landing that looked to be about 2 meters away.

Yara cursed. Wesley gaped. But the clock kept counting down.

"We can't even get a running start," said Wesley.

A standing jump. Yara had a feeling they wouldn't be able to climb either down the wall they'd just climbed or up the far one across the chasm. If they fell, it was over. Just as she braced herself to jump, the wall they stood on started to lower.

"Shit," she said, watching the landing get further out of reach.

"Now or never," said Wesley.

"One…" she said, nodding.

"Two…" said Wesley.

Then together, "Three!"

Propelling themselves off the lowering wall, they launched at the landing. Wesley's jump was more powerful than Yara's, and he scrambled up relatively easily, his longer legs giving him an advantage. Yara slammed into the edge of the landing, the breath knocked out of her. White spots filled her vision for a moment as she groped frantically on the landing, trying not to lose her grip and fall. But then Wesley's hands wrapped around her wrists and pulled.

She had no time to recover, though, as the ground beneath them started to crumble.

"Go, go, go!" said Wesley, helping her to her feet. Together they sprinted away from the edge of the landing as it fell and broke apart on the surface below them. They ran headlong into the far wall of the simulator, which flickered and changed into an image of what they had just run from. Turning around, they caught the end of the transition as the next challenge in the course materialized in front of them.

The two initiates found themselves facing a force of half a dozen faceless assailants. Yara's legs were aching, her arms were weak, her ribs were pounding after slamming into the landing. The simulators weren't real, but the nanotech they used to simulate environments still hurt like hell. She wanted to stop, wanted to rest, but there was no time. The clock showed less than forty minutes left.

"I'll take the three on the right," she said to Wesley.

He wasn't looking at her, his eyes fixated on the fighters ahead of them, his body in a stance that said very plainly, "bring it on." He nodded, and that was enough.

Together, they ran at the six assailants with only a few rudimentary weapons at their disposal. It was nowhere near as easy as it had been in the first two stages. Not only were there more attackers, but she and Wesley were tired and slower than they had been. Yara got knocked down. Her head slammed painfully against the ground before she was able to disable one of the attackers with a jab to its thigh from a small knife stashed in her uniform. For a moment, she thought it might be over when the other two much larger attackers overpowered her, but she slipped out of the grip of one and used its body to bowl over the other, giving her just enough time to yank her knife out of the leg of the first attacker and slice into the legs of the remaining two, incapacitating them. She looked up to see if Wesley needed help just in time to see him kick the sixth and final assailant over the edge of the chasm they'd escaped, a rope attached to its waist so it wouldn't fall to a simulated death.

"Nice," said Yara breathlessly, high-fiving Wesley.

"Thanks," he replied, just as winded. "Onward."

"Right."

At a slow jog, they reached the front of the room. Nothing happened. "Is it over?" Wesley asked, looking around the room.

"No," said Yara. "We haven't even gotten to the hostages, yet."

Sure enough, the room flickered again and everything changed around them. The floor where they stood rumbled and rose toward the ceiling, the rest of the ground falling away. At the same time, the walls closed in on either side of them leaving less than five feet of space, until Yara and Wesley were stranded on a small platform far above the ground in a long, narrow tunnel.

"Holy shit!" Wesley exclaimed in surprise.

"What are we supposed to do?"

Wesley squinted in the distance. "I see something on the other side. I think we're supposed to get over there."

Looking across the room, Yara spotted what Wesley had seen. Another platform. "We can't jump that far."

"Do you think we need to scale the walls again?"

"No handholds," said Yara. "I think we have to do a plank traverse."

Wesley nodded. "My favorite."

Yara laughed. "You wanna go first?"

"Not particularly."

Bracing herself, Yara placed her hands on the right wall, trying hard not to look down. A pointless endeavor as she would soon be facing the floor, suspended horizontally above it as she wedged herself between the two walls.

It was a stretch. She could barely reach the left wall with her feet, too short to comfortably cram herself in, only just making it on her tiptoes.

"You good?" asked Wesley as she started inching herself slowly toward the far wall.

Her breaths came out in short, quick gasps, focusing every single part of herself on keeping her toes taut. Her palms were sweaty, working against her on the slick surface of the wall. "Yeah—" she managed between breaths. She heard Wesley climb up and start following her lead.

It was slow going at first but before long started to get easier, and Yara soon realized why.

"Hey, I think the walls are getting closer together!" she called to Wesley. "It's getting easier!"

"Great," he said in a clipped voice, no doubt focusing as much as she was.

But the walls didn't stop closing in. Before long, Yara's knees were uncomfortably bent. "Oh no," she gasped to herself, her arms trembling with effort. Looking under her shoulder, she saw that soon she wouldn't have much space left at all, certainly not in this position. She was only a few meters away from the far side of the room, but she could see the walls narrow in to a point barely a few feet across. "Uh," she called to Wesley, weighing their options. "We're gonna have to reposition here..."

"Yeah," said Wesley, sounding as though he were struggling, too.

"Take it slow, Yara," she said, trying to get control over her breath. *Inhale. Exhale.* She moved one step further down, the walls uncomfortably tight. Her arms were trembling so violently she was sure they would give out at any moment. She straightened her legs until her head was against the wall and slowly started to spin around so she was facing the ceiling, sliding down her back as she did, until she was crouching in midair, feet and back against the walls. She moved a few more feet down and looked over at Wesley, watching him perform the same awkward maneuver. *We got this.*

The walls didn't stop closing in and Yara got more and more vertical, eventually having to use her arms again as her legs stopped being able to extend. She was so close to the platform... just a few more steps... But just as she reached out to pull herself onto it, the wall in front of her so close she could lean her forehead against it, the platform vanished like a light going out.

Yara cursed loudly, startling Wesley.

"What?" he called.

"The platform!" she said. "It's gone!"

"What now?"

"Wait..." said Yara. She looked around, starting to feel uncomfortably claustrophobic, using more energy to stay upright, to prevent sliding down from the sweat on her back and hands. There was no way she would be able to make it back to the other side. Just as she was worried that this was the end, that they would fail, that she had worked this hard and come this far for nothing, something else materialized where the platform had been. A solid beam, less than a foot across, reaching from the opening between the walls to the end of the room.

"Wait, something's here now. Like a bridge. It's small."

"Do it," said Wesley, his voice strained.

Yara managed to get a foot on the beam, and with some difficulty pushed herself onto it. It took a moment to find her balance, not something she was very good at, particularly when her legs were jelly from exhaustion. She inched forward, leaving enough room for Wesley behind her, wishing he had gone first. A grunt told her he made it.

They started to carefully walk forward, gaining confidence as they went. Just as Yara was feeling like they were close to the end, the narrow bridge gave a sudden jerk, as though from an earthquake.

"What the hell?" said Wesley.

Yara had dropped to all fours, gripping the beam. "They don't want to make it easy, do they?"

"Keep going. Let's get this over with."

Yara crawled forward a few more steps when the bridge jerked again. She let out a cry of surprise but held on. "You still good?" she called back to Wesley.

"Yeah," came the reply.

She didn't dare look back, focusing too hard on staying on the beam. The rumbles kept coming at random intervals, trying their best to shake the two initiates off the bridge, but they managed to keep hold, even when pellets started firing at them from the distant walls on either side, stinging with every impact but doing no real damage.

It was a relief to make it to the platform at the true end of the room, shaking off the tension that had gripped them as they clung to the beam and the stings caused by the flying shots.

"We done yet?" asked Wesley, rubbing his arms.

Yara looked at the clock. "Doubt it," she said, when she saw how much time they had left. "Still no hostages."

She was right. Once again, everything disappeared, the floor lowering them back down to ground level, before another room materialized before them.

Wesley groaned.

The dark glass panels of the sims were hidden by the white walls, ceiling, and floor of a sterile room with a hallway that forked off around a corner to the right and another to the left. Yara heard a scream from around the corner closest to her and started to run down the hall after it.

"Wait!" Wesley called behind her. He was looking in the opposite direction. "I heard someone over here."

"No, it was this way," said Yara.

"I'm telling you, I heard someone screaming around that corner," he insisted, pointing away from her.

Yara chewed her lip. Williams had asked her not to use her ability, so she couldn't confirm one way or another who was right. The clock kept ticking down their time. They had to make a decision fast. "You go left," she said. "I'll go right. We'll meet up back here."

Wesley nodded and they both took off, running around opposite corners. The walls were identical, blindingly white. It was impossible to gauge where she was in the room in relation to anything. Another scream. Closer this time. There were doors on either side of her. Yara was afraid of opening doors at random without knowing what might be behind them. Perhaps it was the screamer, perhaps it was another obstacle that would slow her down. She was acutely aware of every passing second as the time ran down. She had less than 15 minutes to find the person screaming, reunite with Wesley, and… and then what? How much of the test was left? For all she knew they were only halfway through with less than a quarter of the time left. If only she could look into the future she would at least know *that*…

She wanted to call out to the hostage they were meant to rescue, but it was just as likely there were more "bad guys"—"anti-human extremists," Williams had called them—who would hear her and come running. As she took a deep breath to call out, she distinctly heard the scream again from a door she had just passed. Doubling back, she went into the small room, a white cube the same size as—her heart froze—the cell in which Kain had held her a year ago. Her hands started to shake, her breath constricting, the world narrowing into a pinprick of light as the walls closed in.

No, she thought. *Get it back, bring it back. Inhale liquid gold, exhale—*

"Hello?" said a small voice.

Yara took several shaky gasps, trying to collect herself, to push away the memory of the cell where Kain had held her long enough to remember why she had come in here. A middle-aged man was huddling in the corner, bruised and bloodied, eyes wide with fear. With him huddled a young girl who appeared unharmed. The hostages. Finally.

"Hi," said Yara. "Can you walk?"

The man nodded. She reached out for him, desperate to leave the room but not wanting to stray far from the door. There was a clock counting down in this room too. Just under twelve minutes.

The man let himself be led out of the room and back into the maze of matching white hallways, supported by Yara, who held the girl's hand.

"Wesley…" she exhaled, trying to decide if she should retrace her steps or go forward, wondering what he would decide. The urge to look forward into the future was overwhelming.

The choice of which way to go was made for her when the girl shouted, "Look out!" pointing behind them.

Yara turned to see two more faceless assailants headed toward them at a full sprint.

"Shit!" Yara cried, starting to run as fast as she could under the man's weight. The hostages ambled along with her, trying their best to keep up. Incredible how a simulated man could be so heavy.

The figures chasing them were gaining, but not before Yara was able to round a corner and find, to her great relief, Wesley.

"Y!" he yelled.

"Help me!" she said, but not before Wesley was already running toward her to help with the weight of the man. Yara had just enough time to turn to see the assailants rounding the corner, but by then it was too late. Still weighed down by the hostage, she wasn't able to stop them from ripping the man from her hands and pinning him to the floor. The girl was screaming. Yara started to raise her hands to fight the bad guys off when she heard Wesley scream from behind her. Over her shoulder, she saw that he had in turn been pursued by three more attackers, who now had Wesley face down on the ground, his arms pinned behind him.

Yara froze, a deer in headlights.

She had to make a decision and fast. One hostage was being choked by an attacker, his fingers grasping uselessly at the grip while the other started running at the girl. But Wesley was trapped on the floor, two assailants holding him down, the third charging at Yara. In a few seconds, the bad guys would be on her, and they would have lost. She couldn't save them all. It would have to be the hostages or her partner. But not both.

If she saved the hostages, Wesley would fail, and by proxy, so would she. If she saved Wesley, she'd be breaking a cardinal rule of the Society by letting civilians, including a child, die in order to save a White Mask.

She couldn't believe it. After her stellar scores on the first and second test, she was going to lose. The cost was either one partner or two hostages.

Taking one last look at Wesley, his eyes watering, his face turning red, she trusted that he wasn't truly in danger and tried to convey her regret in the split second she had before turning away from him.

Yara dodged out of the way of the attacker running at her, grabbing its outstretched arm in the process and using its weight to slam it into the one that was attacking the girl. The other hostage was passing out, his face purple, spluttering as he took his final breaths.

Fortunately, only one assailant was holding him down, and Yara was able to take it down quickly enough to get the man back to his feet.

Maybe there was still time…

She looked over at Wesley and saw his body limp on the ground, being dragged away by the remaining attackers, all of whom had decided to take him and run rather than try to apprehend Yara. Her hands started to shake as she was overcome with doubt. He had to be OK, right? The Society would never risk an initiate's life for a damn test…

How stupid could she be? She had just failed the test for both her and Wesley. He would never forgive her. Robin would be so disappointed. And all for simulated hostages.

She cursed again, angry tears stinging her eyes, wondering if it was even worth continuing. But she had nowhere else to go, so she kept moving forward.

Six minutes left.

Maybe she could get the hostages to a safe place and go back for Wesley. If he was just knocked out, she could carry him to the end. Maybe there was still hope that they could pass.

She opened a door at the end of the hallway and—

The room flickered around her and white turned to black, the sterile environment replaced with glass walls and a silver grid. The man she carried guttered out of existence, his weight vanishing along with him. The girl's small hand fell through Yara's grip as she too disappeared. Straightening up, Yara looked around and gaped.

To her left was Wesley, looking as surprised to see her as she was to see him.

"Did you—" she asked.

"Are you—" he replied.

But before either of them could make sense of it, the door to the sims opened up behind them, filling the room with a cacophony of cheers.

People stormed into the room, jumping up in the air, screaming their names, and Yara was still trying to make sense of things when Robin and Carter and Ash were all surrounding her, pounding her on the back, rumpling her hair, and raising her fists in the air.

CHAPTER TWELVE

Passed

"What... just happened?" Yara asked, her voice barely audible over the sound of cheers in room 6.

Robin was laughing, remembering his own test, the same confusion he shared at this stage. "You passed!" he yelled as Carter grabbed Yara's hands and started spinning her around.

"But Wesley... I mean..."

"The Wesley you saw was a sim!" said Ash, her fiery eyes dancing. "You got separated to see what decision you each would make. Save a civvy, or save a White Mask. It was a test!"

"So he was never in danger?"

Robin and his fellow Guardians shook their heads. "And he made the same decision as you. He saved his hostages over you." Robin watched the realization dawn on Yara's face as she and Wesley met each other's eyes through the crowd.

"Well, that was damn sneaky," she said, a smile finally starting to reach her.

Robin laughed and clapped a hand on her shoulder, refraining from hugging the girl who didn't like to be touched. "Congratulations, kid."

"We're all so proud of you," said Carter.

"I passed..." said Yara, slowly. Her eyes were out of focus. Robin watched as a huge weight came off her shoulders, like she was exhaling for the first time in months.

"Congratulations, lady!" said Ash as she barreled into Yara, hugging her so tightly that Yara stumbled back a few steps, either oblivious or ambivalent of Yara's preference.

"Thanks, Ash," Yara laughed. Robin thought he was the only one who noticed that Ash's hug had brought back some of the tension to Yara's shoulders.

"You were outstanding," said Robin when Ash pulled back, bouncing on her feet with excitement.

"Don't sound so surprised," said Yara.

"I never doubted you for a moment. I told ya you could do it, didn't I? You think I would have wasted all that time training ya if I didn't think so?"

They made their way out of the simulator, a few more people taking it in turn to congratulate Yara and Wesley. Robin saw Yara give Wesley a private acknowledgement as they exited. He was with his parents and trainer, looking just as dazed and pleased.

"You had the best scores," said Carter, looking up at the screen outside the sim. "No one's even come close to you. Most people are still in their tests."

Yara smiled. "All thanks to my trainers," she said. But her eyes were not on the scores. She was looking around the room, no doubt for Erik.

"He's still up in Research," said Carter, noticing Yara's crestfallen face, "but I've been sending him updates." They held up a small, silver sphere: their ConvOrb, what members of the Society used to communicate with each other. "He knows how you did and he couldn't be more proud. And R has been updating your aunt."

Yara gave a feeble smile.

"Well," said Robin, clapping his hands together. "We should celebrate! Newbie's choice. Anywhere you like. It's on me."

"Y-you mean... we can leave Headquarters?"

"Only on the third Sunday of every month, and we have to follow the trajectory of the moon," he said.

Yara blanched. "What?"

Robin and Ash laughed as Carter shook their head, grinning.

"I'm kidding," said Robin. "Man, you're gullible."

Yara punched him playfully in the arm.

"You would think you'd know the rules a little better by now," said Ash as they strolled toward the elevators.

"I studied combat. Don't tell Carter, but I never paid attention to the written crap."

"Hey," said Carter.

"I think they heard you," said Robin.

"Good thing we don't get tested on that. I wonder why," said Ash, absentmindedly fiddling with a lick of fire between her fingers.

Deep down, Robin thought he had a pretty good idea why. All that Level 1 Guardians—Guardians in the field—had to be good for was following orders. While they did study them as part of their training, rules could be learned on the job as the need arose. They didn't really need to know "the written crap" as Yara called it, unless they advanced to Level 2 or 3.

"So, what you in the mood for?" he said. "Mexican? Thai? Italian?" Yara hadn't eaten all day. She had to be hungry.

"I heard that a bunch of the initiates and their trainers are all going out to The Imperial over in Hollywood," said Ash. "That could be fun."

"Ah. American bar food," said Robin. "Even better. I hope everyone likes greasy tater tots."

"What do you say, Red?" said Carter. "Shall we be social? Stretch our legs outside the bubble of the White Mask Society?"

"Brave the great unknown?" said Robin. "Wander valiantly into the wilderness of the greater Los Angeles area, where we may face foes unlike any the Society has ever seen: valet parking, cover charges, and the ever elusive C-list celebrity sighting?"

"When you put it like that," said Yara, "who could resist?"

When most of the initiates and their families had cleared out, Bora Black made her way over to Xaili Williams, who was shaking the hands of the final new Guardian to pass as he headed out of the sims with his parents.

"A word when you have a moment, Mx. Williams," said Black in a low voice.

Williams was beaming when they turned to see Black and Glover waiting for them. "Of course," they said, no hint of knowing on their face. They followed Black and Glover to the back of the room as the elevators took the rest of the crowds to their respective destinations. "Another success, a full class," they continued as the three of them walked. "You must be pleased! I know I am—" But Williams stopped speaking when Black turned around and they saw the expression on her face. "Is everything OK?"

Black was fuming. Was it not enough that Williams had betrayed the Society? They had the audacity now to behave as though they knew nothing at all, suspected nothing, feigning such ignorance.

"Mx. Xaili Williams, you are being arrested for treason against the

White Mask Society," said Glover. Because Black had wanted this done in secrecy, no Guardians had been alerted. It was up to her and her Second to handle the entire situation. No one could know.

"What?" gasped Williams. "*Treason?*"

"The charges against you will be presented in a way you can comprehend," Glover continued by rote. "When such time is seen fit, you will face trial. If your guilt is so determined by a jury of your peers, you will then face punishment at the hands of the White Mask Society. Do you understand what I have just said."

Black's face was contorted with fury as she watched Williams fumble for words, their performance convincing… but not convincing enough.

"Bora, you can't be serious!" they said, looking from Black to Glover. "Zak, what is this…"

"I do not want to march you to holding in cuffs," said Black coldly. "But I will if I have to."

Williams closed their mouth, considering their options. "This is outrageous," they said. But they did not resist. They simply lifted their chin and let themself be led all the way down to the holding cells.

Yara showered and changed into some of the few civilian clothes she had left: a white tank top and a pair of torn jeans. Her jeans used to hang limply on her, but her legs were more muscular now, and she barely managed to get them on. Taking them off would be a whole other story. She slapped a little makeup on and even donned a pair of earrings shaped like lemons before heading up to meet her Guardians in the lobby on the ground floor of the Society Headquarters.

It was shockingly strange to see them out of their Society vestments. It had only been a little over a year since Yara's life had been turned upside down, replaced with one that centered around the White Mask Society, but it was long enough for her to become accustomed to a world of uniformity. She couldn't even remember the last time she had seen Robin in street clothes. Now, he wore a tight black t-shirt with a grey checkered button down undone over it, and a pewter jacket. And jeans. *Jeans.*

He looked… good. Then she noticed that he was looking at her and smiling. She blushed, suddenly feeling incredibly underdressed. But not as underdressed as she felt when she looked at Ash.

Already gorgeous in uniform, she had elevated into a vision of beauty. Her hair had been pulled back into two long braids and she was wearing a flowing red and yellow dress that complimented her in all the right ways. Carter still managed to look just like themself, though they too looked particularly elegant. They were wearing a dark green v-neck, a brown blazer, and a scarf. Carter was accessorizing. Up was down and right was left. Yara grinned at them. They all looked so normal. She tugged self-consciously at the hem of her tank top.

"I guess I didn't get the 'dress like a supermodel' memo."

Ash laughed. "I never get to wear dresses. If we ever leave HQ, you can bet I'm losing the pants."

"Uh oh," said Robin, and Ash winked at him.

"So, are we meeting people there?" Yara asked as the four of them headed out the doors of the perfectly ordinary lobby onto the perfectly ordinary street. The bulk of Headquarters for the White Mask Society was underground, buried under a four story building which they utilized for relations with the human world.

"N said that a bunch of people left not too long ago."

"Nayla?" said Yara.

"Yeah," said Robin.

"I thought it was just, like, initiates tonight."

"Oh, you don't want us coming anymore?" said Robin.

"Initiates and… guests," she amended with a laugh.

"First of all," said Carter, "you're not initiates anymore, Red. You're a Guardian now. And second of all, it's not unusual for a bunch of people to celebrate on test day. You guys are part of the family now. It's a big deal. And we don't typically have a lot of excuses to go out and do stuff."

"Yeah, the Society isn't much for having fun," said Yara. "I've noticed that about you."

"That isn't true," said Robin.

"Yeah!" said Ash "We have a big party once a year for the Fête de Libération." She said these last words with a French flair.

"The what?"

"February 21st," said Robin.

"But… I was here last February 21st. I knew you guys. There wasn't any party."

Robin and Carter shared a look while Ash laughed.

"You… weren't invited," said Carter.

"What?"

"If it's any consolation, kid, I didn't go either," said Robin.

"It was a smaller party. Not that much fun last year, honestly," said

Carter.

"They're lying," said Ash. "It was a rager. But civvies aren't invited, and R was on duty."

Yara raised her eyebrows feeling equal parts guilty for preventing her Guardian from going to a party and jealous that she wasn't invited.

"You'll see this year," said Robin.

"It's like our independence day," said Carter.

"Independence from what?"

"Red, didn't you listen but at all during training?"

Yara took a second to look ashamed before pressing Carter for the answer.

"When the Society was founded in the fourteenth century, Deviants were being hunted, tortured, and executed."

"Yeah, the witch hunts," said Yara. She remembered that much.

"Well, February 21st was when our founder, Elizabeth DuBois, signed a treaty with the king of France which ushered in the first age of peace between humans and Deviants in 400 years," said Carter. "If it wasn't for that treaty, the Society would look very different today."

"Yeah," said Robin. "So would the Renaissance."

"You mean..." said Yara.

"Oh yeah. Bernini, Fouquet, many of the masters were Deviants, and may not have had the opportunities to create such masterpieces if it weren't for the burgeoning peace between Deviants and humans."

"I have so many questions..." said Yara.

"Enough with the history lesson!" said Ash. "Tonight, we celebrate!"

Robin rarely left Headquarters unless he was on duty. Almost all of his free time was spent in the simulators or reading in his quarters... when he ran out of sim credits. While it was traditional for people to leave base and go celebrate after each initiation class, it was never expected for other White Masks to participate. Robin had never felt particularly inclined to join. Now, as Yara's trainer, he was not only expected, but he found he actually wanted to go.

Erik's return, combined with his own feelings for Yara had been weighing heavily on him. An evening of mindless fun in which he could just hang out with her and enjoy her company sounded like exactly what the doctor ordered.

His wardrobe of civilian clothes was limited, but he had tried on three different jackets before deciding on what outfit to wear, and had swallowed a laugh when he saw Yara in her tank top and torn jeans.

She had never been one to care much about her appearance. It was one of the many things he loved about her.

Nope. Can't think like that.

Robin tried to clear his mind of such dangerous thoughts and turned his attention back to his surroundings. It was about a twenty minute car ride from Headquarters to The Imperial, a restaurant slash bar that pretended to be a club in the evenings, though still allowed people under 21 in. Carter was the only one who got a wristband labelling them as old enough to drink.

It was such a strange rule, thought Robin, that you had to be 21 to consume alcohol. Meanwhile 18 year olds were voting and 16 year olds were training to become Guardians. They felt much older than most of the civilians around them.

The Imperial was a dingy little place in North Hollywood with ceilings that felt low due to the hanging light fixtures, mismatched chairs that all creaked or wobbled when you sat in them, and tables so covered with grime that your fingernail could leave a significant dent if you dared to touch it. Nevertheless, the twelve initiates, their trainers, and a few other more sociable Guardians had taken over the entire building. "Welcome to the Jungle" was playing from an old jukebox and a couple people were dancing, including Olive Quigley and—Robin's heart skipped a beat—Nayla. Ash immediately ran over to join them and started dancing ferociously, literal sparks emitting from her fingertips.

Robin, Carter, and Yara took a seat at an unoccupied booth and started perusing the sticky menus that sat by the fake candle.

"I'm not sure I have the stomach for any of this food," said Carter, looking over the options.

"What, shape shifters can't eat onion rings?" said Robin.

"Fortunately, I've never had to find out." Carter put the menu down and said, "I'm going to go get us a couple of glasses of water."

"Woah, C. Isn't water a little strong?"

"Need I remind you that you're both underage at this table?"

"No," said Robin. "No need to remind us. But thanks for doing it anyway."

Yara laughed and Carter even cracked a smile as they left.

Robin took a deep breath and looked at Yara. "So," he said, "Y."

Yara made a face. "Please don't call me that. I beg of you."

Robin laughed. "Honestly, I don't think I'll be able to get used to it with you." She looked at him and he held her gaze for a moment, his hands starting to feel numb. He wanted to tell her how he felt. He wanted to tell her so much that it felt like it was eating him from the inside. Looking into her eyes was like staring into the sun. But then she blinked, and looked away and the feeling ebbed enough for him to collect himself.

"I know that I'm not supposed to be worrying about it right now," she said, "but I can't stop thinking about Erik."

Robin scoffed. "Right."

"What?"

"You're right. Me too."

"Like, what's our first step? I mean… all I've been thinking about was how to pass the test. I haven't really thought about what would happen once I actually became a Guardian."

"By the way," said Robin, seizing upon the opportunity to change the subject, "I've been meaning to ask you. How did you do that?"

"Do what?"

"Pass the test like that? I mean, you were incredible! I've never seen you move like that. Hell, I've never seen *anyone* move like that."

"Oh," said Yara, blushing and looking pleased with herself.

"I was just gonna say the same thing myself," said a voice behind his shoulder. Robin spun around to see Nayla standing behind him, beaming at Yara.

"N. Hey."

"Hello," said Yara.

"You did so amazing," said Nayla, taking a seat next to Robin. "I mean, I know R is a good teacher, but I've never seen anyone move that fast."

Yara gave a shy smile. "Thank you."

At that moment, Carter came back from the bar with three glasses of water. Setting them down on the table, they said, "Hi, N."

"Hey, Specks!" said Nayla enthusiastically, hugging Carter.

"Glad you could join us," said Carter, taking a seat between Yara and Nayla. "Have you seen X? I thought they said they would celebrate with us tonight."

Nayla looked around for Williams and shrugged. "No, I haven't seen them. But," she continued, looking at Yara, "your Ward was just about to tell me how she beat the test with such an amazing score."

Yara opened her mouth, obviously struggling to find the right words. Nayla was a very forward person, and Robin got the impression she intimidated Yara, who hadn't spent enough time with her yet to really understand that Nayla was as much a goofball as any of them.

Before Yara found the words to respond, Robin said, "She's a hydan, N. You can never underestimate the power of a Deviant."

Nayla looked at him, her brown eyes seeing much more than he wanted her to, and grinned widely.

"Of course. A seer." She looked back at Yara, that smile still on her face. "A useful skill when faced with an attacker, to know his moves before he makes them."

Yara shrugged awkwardly.

"Oh, no," said Nayla with a laugh and reaching across to brush Yara's arm with her fingertips. "There's no need to be embarrassed. Deviants are some of the most valued members of the Society. Just look at Specks, here." She winked at Carter who rolled their eyes, but they were smiling. "After all, we've had members try to give all of us that advantage."

Robin frowned. "What are you talking about?"

Nayla's smile faltered and she looked between Robin and Yara. "You know… the Omega Project."

"Uh…" said Carter, suddenly looking worried.

"What about the Omega Project?" said Yara at once. Robin knew enough about the Omega Project to know that it was not something that should be discussed in public. It was one of the Society's greatest failures, and something that Black had tried to bury. A secret venture started by Kain that had hurt a lot of people. Including Kain himself, in the end. Robin glared at Nayla for bringing it up, but she was pointedly ignoring him. Yara was not supposed to know about it, strictly speaking, but Robin had no regrets about telling her what it was. Had it not been for his decision to break the rules and tell her about it last year, she never would have been able to destroy Kain. After all, it was a virus developed from the Omega Project that enabled her to kill him.

"Well," said Nayla with an innocent shrug, "its entire purpose was to give humans the powers of Deviants."

"But it didn't work. At least not with nymphs or shape shifters," said Yara.

Nayla gave another little laugh. "I knew you knew about the Omega Project after your little stunt in January, but I had no idea you knew so much. I'm impressed."

Yara shifted in her seat. "Maybe you shouldn't be," said Yara.

"Doesn't the fact that I know confidential information suggest that the Society isn't doing a very good job at keeping secrets?"

Robin looked away, trying to hide his smirk from Nayla. She, however, did not seem as impressed with Yara's tongue. Her smile faltered.

"I suppose," she said, her eyes penetrating Yara, who stared back, unflinching.

The tension was eased when Ash came crashing back to the table and downed Yara's water in one gulp. "Whoo!" she said, out of breath. "Whoever's working the jukebox is on fire!" She laughed, slumping into the last empty seat at the table, but faltered when she saw the look on everyone's faces. "What the hell did I just walk into?"

"Just conversation that shouldn't be happening on a night like tonight," said Carter.

"Oh, my favorite kind," said Ash, leaning forward. "What did I miss?"

Nayla looked at Robin, her expression much less amused than it had been a moment before. Robin couldn't help but feel proud of Yara for holding her own, but he did his best to arrange his face into what he hoped was a sympathetic mask.

"Seriously," pressed Ash, "someone tell me what you're all talking about before I light this table on fire."

"The Omega Project," said Carter.

"What the devil is that?" said Ash, unimpressed.

Nayla ignored Ash, continuing to address Yara. "In any case, Varma's entire purpose was to give human members of the Society the same advantage as the Deviant members."

"Varma?" asked Yara.

"Zenobia Varma. She was the Director of Research, and the spearhead of the Omega Project."

Yara frowned. "That name sounds familiar…"

"That's because Janya Varma," said Nayla, "one of the hyden you rescued last year, is her daughter." Janya Varma had the ability to heal herself, and it was the serum that Kain had made using her santocin—the hormone that gave Janya her gift—that enabled the Society to bring Yara back from the edge of death.

"Oh," said Yara. "I didn't realize."

There was an awkward moment before Nayla said, "Well, in any case, congratulations, Yara. Or should I say, Y. You did great today." She gave a smile which Yara did not return, hugged Carter one last time, and squeezed Robin's arm, letting her hand linger, before leaving them to return to the dance floor.

For a few moments, the four of them sat in silence before Ash downed Carter's water as well. "Well, I was hoping that conversation was going to be more about fun drama. So, as much fun as this has been, I'm gonna go dance some more." In a flash of sparks, she was back on the floor, gyrating so ferociously that she created a wide berth around her.

Robin looked back at Yara and Carter expectantly. "You guys want anything to eat? C's buying."

Carter snorted. "I thought you said it was on you."

"Did I say that?"

But Yara didn't seem to be listening to a word they said.

Yara's mind was racing. Zenobia Varma had been the Director of Research. She had created the Omega Project and was the mother of a hydan. She was vaguely aware that Carter and Robin were talking. Without hearing a word they were saying, she interrupted, "Was Zenobia Varma a hydan?"

They stopped and turned to her. Clearly, they were debating whether she should be privy to this information. Yara rolled her eyes.

"Are we still on the whole 'Yara isn't supposed to know stuff' brigade? Because I'm a Guardian now. Officially. I should be allowed to know whatever you guys know. Technically." *Right?*

Robin looked at Carter with a look that said, "She has a point."

So Carter sighed, and looking bemused, said, "Yes. Zenobia Varma was a hydan."

"A healer, too?" said Yara.

"Yes."

Yara's mind was racing, trying to remember everything that Robin had told her about the Omega Project what felt like so long ago.

"Look, Red," said Carter, taking a sip of water and standing up. "The Omega Project was abandoned. There's no point in thinking about it right now. Tonight, we're meant to be celebrating your victory. Now, let's go join A on the dance floor. She looks like she could use our company."

Yara and Robin laughed. Ash did not look like she needed any company whatsoever. In fact, she seemed completely unaware of the world around her.

Smiling, the three of them went to join her.

CHAPTER THIRTEEN

Contact

Despite Carter's insistence that the Omega Project and Zenobia Varma were of no importance, Yara couldn't stop thinking about them. They had danced—or, in Yara's case, stood awkwardly to the side, smiling if someone looked in her direction—until well after one in the morning, when the restaurant was empty but for the celebrating Guardians and grumpy staff. The drive back to Headquarters was short at this hour. There weren't many opportunities to drive in Los Angeles without traffic, but the dead of night on a weekday was one of them. Carter drove in silence as Ash kept an unrelenting one-sided conversation going with them. In the backseat, Yara stared past her reflection at the dark streets outside her window. She glanced at Robin. He met her eyes and smiled his familiar, crooked smile.

"You OK?" he mouthed.

She nodded and turned back to the window.

When they got home, everyone bade each other good night and retired to their separate quarters, but Yara lay awake in bed, staring at her ceiling.

She knew there was something Robin had told her about the Omega Project that was important. Something that she needed to remember, but she simply couldn't. Her mind was at a complete standstill, and the harder she tried to remember what it was, the more her brain just drew a blank. She wasn't sure if Robin would tell her more about it. It had been hard enough convincing him the first time.

The clock kept ticking, and no matter how hard Yara tried to sleep, or how much she tried to remember, nothing happened at all. Before she knew it, it was four in the morning. Unable to stand it, she got out of bed. Pulling on the same worn hoodie she always wore, she left her room. The halls were deserted and dimly lit. There was a time when the maze of corridors and endless passages of Headquarters made her head spin, but six months training as a Guardian had finally gotten her comfortable enough to find her way around.

Now that they had officially given Erik back his title as a Guardian, could it be possible that he had his old room back? If it had taken them a year to replace him with Ash, maybe they hadn't assigned his quarters to anyone in that time, either.

She took the chance and padded softly down to where his old quarters were. Taking a deep breath, she knocked before she had time to consider what kind of excuse she would give to whomever she might be waking up at four in the morning on the chance this was no longer Erik's room. Fortunately, she did not have to think of one. Because a few moments later, Erik opened the door, looking bleary eyed and positively adorable, white hair poking in every direction.

"Yara?" he said, his eyes widening when he saw her.

All thoughts left her head at once. She smiled broadly at the sight of him, and he smiled back.

"What are you doing here? It's the middle of the night. Are you OK? What's wrong?"

"Nothing," she said hurriedly. "I just…" … *wanted to see you. Wanted to talk to you. Missed you.*

He understood somehow, and stood aside, letting her come in.

They looked at each other for a moment. He was wearing boxers and a white t-shirt with a torn collar that looked to be about as old as he was. She smiled, unable to help herself. She had not yet become used to seeing him after having spent so much time trying to accept that he was gone.

"What are you grinning at?" he said, wrapping his arms around her waist and holding her close as he looked into her eyes.

"You," she said. "Ugh. Listen to me. I sound like some fool in love."

"Well, aren't you?"

She bit her lip to stop from smiling too much. "I dunno. Are you?"

"Definitely," he said, without hesitation, before kissing her gently.

She closed her eyes and leaned her head against his cheek. "Then I guess it would be bad form for me to deny it."

"I know this started out as a joke, but now it's making me sad."

Yara laughed and kissed him repeatedly.

"Did you come here for any specific reason?" said Erik. "Not that I'm not happy to see you, obviously, but I'm wondering if I need to wake myself up completely or if I can look forward to going back to sleep and curling up with you under the covers." He nuzzled his nose into the nape of her neck.

They sat down on his modest bed, and Yara took a deep breath, looking at their intertwined fingers.

"I do have a question," she said tentatively. Erik waited until she managed to ask, "You know… about the Omega Project?"

"What?"

"The Omega Project. Robin told me about it last year."

Erik stiffened. Yara could see behind his eyes that something of what she'd said had upset him, but she didn't know why. "Oh," he said.

"Well, Nayla brought it up again today, and I just…"

"N?" said Erik, cutting her off. "What were you and N doing together?"

"She came to The Imperial with us tonight."

Erik frowned.

"You know, the traditional acting-stupid-in-a-public-place to celebrate us becoming Guardians."

"Oh yeah!" he said. "Congratulations!" He grabbed her head and kissed her. "How did you do? I want to hear all about it. C only said that you passed."

"Maybe in the morning," she said, not wanting to lose track of what she wanted to ask. "But I did pass top of the class," she added, grinning sheepishly.

Erik gaped.

"Don't look so surprised!" she said, slapping him playfully on the arm.

"Sorry," said Erik, ruffling his hair, still looking shell-shocked. "From my perspective, you're still… untrained," he finished lamely.

"Ha," said Yara. "Fair."

"But really, that's amazing, Yara. I'm so proud of you."

"Thanks," she said, feeling awkward. Distantly, her head was starting to hurt. She wanted to dismiss it. Perhaps this was nothing. It was the middle of the night, and she had just had a big day. Maybe it was simply the effects of exhaustion. She rubbed her eyes and pressed on.

"Anyway," she said, "Nayla mentioned the Omega Project, and I feel like there's something I'm missing."

"What do you mean?"

"Well, I remember about the virus, obviously."

Erik shifted in his seat. Yara knew that he had hated her decision to sacrifice herself to destroy Kain. She tried hard not to think that it was this decision that led to Erik being killed in the first place.

"And I know that they were trying to turn humans into Deviants…"

"That's kind of all there is to it," said Erik.

"But the Researcher in charge of it all… Janya Varma's mother…"

Erik looked at her. "Janya? The hydan?"

"Yeah," said Yara. "The Researcher in charge of the Omega Project was her mom."

"Uh huh."

"But what happened to her?"

"Janya's mom? She died," said Erik. And the memory was coming back vaguely to Yara as Erik spoke. Her head throbbed even harder and she tried to push it away and focus on what he was saying. "Kain was working on that project, and when he stole whatever it was they had been working on, they found her body in the lab. The whole place was ransacked. Presumably, he killed her and stole their research."

"But Robin said," said Yara, rubbing her eyes harder, trying to push away her headache, "that the research he took had nothing to do with the virus they created."

"Right," said Erik. "But whatever he took, we don't know what it is. The only people who ever knew all the details about the Omega Project were Kain and the Head Researcher. Varma."

"And now Varma is dead, and so is Kain."

"Are you alright?" said Erik. Yara had gotten up and was squeezing her head.

"Something's wrong," said Yara, but her voice sounded far away.

"Let me call a Medic—" said Erik. He sounded far away, too.

She stumbled, and there was Erik, holding her up, but the moment his skin made contact with hers, the world disappeared around her.

She was floating above the room. A room just like the one she had seen with Ash. But it wasn't exactly the same. Smaller. Dark. But still filled with those same enormous glass pods, like the ones she'd seen in her vision at the old lab, lit only by the glow of electronic screens at the head of each pod and the sick, pink light coming from inside them.

There were a few people walking around the pods, lifelessly accomplishing tasks. In the dark it was hard to tell what color their clothes were, but when one of them stood directly in front of a glowing pad at the head of a pod, Yara could see that he was dressed in the crimson uniform of a Shadow Man. She couldn't breathe. She tried to pull away from this strange place, but instead she kept getting pulled closer and closer until she was staring straight into one of the pods. It was filled with a viscous liquid and—

Yara screamed and found herself being handed off to a Medic she recognized as Fatima. More people were around her and there was Erik's worried face, being ushered away from her behind the crowd of white coats. He reached out for her, his face frantic, but the moment he touched her face, the world disappeared again…

… and she was staring again into the gelatinous pink liquid inside the tube and the horrifying sight that was inside it.

Just as quickly, it disappeared and Erik was gone and the world was filled with Medics and needles and the drugs that were pumping into her veins.

CHAPTER FOURTEEN

Visions Again

Nayla had kept a smile on for the duration of the celebration for the newly initiated Guardians, despite the pain she felt at watching Robin with her.

Yara Rivers had been the reason that Nayla was no longer with the man she loved. It had been hard enough when Yara was just a Ward who was far from Headquarters, some abstract persona that Nayla never had to see. Nayla had been so preoccupied with her own Ward during the crisis with Kain that she'd barely had time to notice her ex pining over the girl.

But now, Yara was a Guardian. And there was no escaping her and no escaping the look on Robin's face when he looked at her. Nayla remembered when she had been the one to illicit such reactions from him. When she was the one who made him laugh, who made his eyes twinkle, who took up all of his time.

When the two of them had been initiates, they—like all future Guardians—were warned that while they held field assignments, romance and personal relationships would be all but impossible, and they were strongly discouraged. Perhaps that was one of the reasons Guardians were moved out of the field so early. But that didn't stop Robin and Nayla from finding comfort in each other's arms. Nayla didn't know if she would have been able to survive training if she hadn't had Robin's shoulder to lean on, and while he had never said the same, she knew that she had been instrumental in helping him through it as well. They had bonded quickly, being the only two humans in their entire initiation class.

That was over now. Boring human Nayla had been replaced with the hydan who could see the future. And so Nayla wandered the halls of Headquarters in the early hours of the morning, wide awake, fighting the same urge she'd had for months: the pull to Robin's quarters.

She was tired of being the one who constantly sought Robin out. Though while Nayla felt sure that he still had feelings for her, she had her pride. At least, she wanted to. So when the elevator doors opened up to the Guardians' quarters, Nayla stared down the hallway until the doors closed in front of her. Then she pressed the button to go down three more floors to the simulators.

All in all, there were nine simulators available for recreation or training to members of the Society. Three more were only available to be reserved by those who worked above ground, who most of the White Masks called the "shoots," named for the part of a plant that was above ground. Many of the flora nymphs didn't abide by this nickname, though none of them objected to its use.

At this early hour, all of the simulators were unoccupied, so Nayla went to the panel outside of Room 2 and pulled up the menu of pre-programmed battle scenarios she could run. Her go-to was a French Revolution program in which the player participated as a revolutionary against the monarchy. Nayla's Ward, Emmanuelle had gotten her hooked on it. Emmanuelle was French herself and, as a result, tended to favor all the programs that had to do with French history. One of the most popular programs among Society members was the Deviant Wars of the 14th century in Paris, when the founder of the White Mask Society, Elizabeth DuBois, led the Deviants out of the squalor and fear in which they lived, persecuted and tormented by fearful and superstitious humans. Back then, Deviants used to raid burial sites—abundant at that time due to the plague—and use human skulls as masks to hide their faces. These macabre adornments were the origin of the white masks still used by the Society today. Though, of course, they were no longer made of actual bone.

Before Nayla could make a definitive selection, someone spoke behind her.

"French Revolution?"

She turned around to see Carter approaching from the elevator.

"Hey," said Nayla. "You're up early."

Carter shrugged. "Got a lot on my mind, these days. Makes for short nights."

"I was just hankering for a good fight. Wanna join me?"

They considered her for a moment. "Yeah. Let's do this."

"Any preference?" said Nayla.

Carter walked over to the panel and scrolled through several options. "I'm not much for the historical reenactments," they said. "How about this one?"

Nayla looked at the program pulled up on the screen. Camelot. She smiled, shaking her head. "I should've guessed."

Carter grinned at her and activated the program.

The simulator doors whooshed open onto a beautiful rolling field. Despite being close to dawn in Los Angeles, night was falling here in Camelot. The sun still lit the sky from below the horizon with hues of dark purples and pale blues. The tableau was broken by an enormous medieval castle, flags waving from turrets, and small figures patrolling the battlements.

Often, when running fantastical simulations such as Camelot, people would indulge themselves with costumes. Carter the shape shifter likely did enough pretending to be someone else as it was, and Nayla had never been much for dressing up. She didn't need all that. All she needed were weapons, and the simulators provided.

They both picked their preferred weapons from the selection neatly arranged by the metal door, which looked absurdly out of place, plopped structurally unsupported in the middle of the medieval field. Otherwise, it all looked startlingly lifelike, though when looking closely enough at the forced perspective, it was possible to make out the faint silver lines of the walls against the apparently distant sky.

The weapons automatically provided in programs such as these were often period or story appropriate, robbing Nayla of the opportunity to wield her favorite. There were no solenoidal stars in 6th century England.

"A broadsword, huh?"

Carter shrugged. "I like having something big and heavy to throw around."

Nayla laughed, choosing a bow and arrow for herself.

For over an hour, they exhausted themselves slaughtering simulated Saxon invaders before taking a moment to recuperate, lying on the grass and staring at the now dark sky. The silence was thick, but Nayla could feel Carter itching to break it.

Then, as if on cue, "How's Darwin?"

Nayla chewed her lip for a moment, trying to decide how to answer.

The truth was a dangerous thing. Perhaps a lie would help more in the long run.

"He's doing OK. He's almost done with school. Last semester."

Carter said nothing in response, but took off their glasses and started to clean them with the hem of their uniform. Nayla wondered, her stomach clenched, if the shape shifter could sense the lie. Nayla had never truly forgiven Carter for having broken her brother's heart. She thought about asking how Carter was, but opted not to as she didn't want to linger on the subject.

They were all victims of a broken heart. She and Carter and her brother. The difference was that she could not return to the arms of the man she loved. Carter couldn't say the same. If they still loved her brother, they were the only thing in their way.

Erik couldn't understand what had happened. Yara had collapsed in his arms, her face completely unresponsive. She looked as if she had been having some kind of seizure. If she had been anyone else, perhaps that's what he would have assumed was wrong. But he knew Yara, and he remembered her collapsing the same way before. Back when she couldn't control her ability.

She'd had a vision. He had carried her in his arms all the way to the medical ward and found the first person on duty, a Medic who had experience with Yara's situation.

Fatima had managed to sedate her, which was all she could do. Yara's visions were not an illness. They had determined that the negative effects came when she suppressed them, when she wasn't controlling her ability. So why had she suppressed this vision? She was connected to a monitor as a precaution, and Erik was sitting on a chair, slumped face down at the foot of her bed, breathing in the clinically clean smell of the sterilized sheets and trying to calm down.

Hours passed. It was morning, and soon Robin, Carter, and Yara's new Guardian Ash would come looking for her, wondering what was going on.

The sheets tugged under Erik's face. He leapt up at once to find Yara stirring gently.

"Hey," he said, trying to keep his voice quiet and collected.

She blinked up at him, bleary eyed. He smiled, and to his horror, she burst into tears.

"What's wrong?" he said, brushing hair off her forehead.

She pulled him into her arms and cried into his neck. "I saw something… I don't know what I saw…" she managed between sobs.

Erik was too taken aback to find any words, so he said nothing and simply held her tightly.

"It's not even seven thirty and you've already got her in tears?" said Robin entering the room with Yara's other Guardians. Robin sounded cheerful, but one look at him told Erik that he was faking it. The crooked smile did not reach his eyes, which were locked on Yara's tear-stained face, searching for any signs as to what could be wrong.

"What's going on?" said Carter.

"She had a vision," Erik replied at once. "And collapsed. Last night."

"Last night," said Carter, frowning. "When? She was with us all night. We didn't get back 'til after one in the—" Carter cut themself off, looking between Yara, who was sniffling, and Erik, who averted his guilty gaze. "Oh."

"How bad was it?" said Robin.

"She's fine," said Ash, rolling her eyes and pushing past the two other Guardians to sit next to Yara on the bed. "'What did you see?' is the more important question, I think."

A smile tugged at Yara's mouth, but it was gone as quickly as it had come. She didn't speak right away. A strange, burning curiosity was eating away at Erik's insides competing with a simultaneous dread at whatever she was about to say.

"I saw…" She hesitated and took a deep breath. "I saw Erik. In the lab. Well, *a* lab." She said this to Ash, whose face fell. "I mean, like the one I saw at the *old* lab. But it was a different one. But it had all the same glass pods and they were… All the pods were filled with people, and…" Her eyes darted in his direction. "…Erik was inside one of them."

Erik's heart was beating rapidly. Something was constricting in his chest. "Pods? What are you talking about?"

"Yara had a vision at Kain's old lab," said Robin. "Of some pods. We think the Shadow Men are grown inside them."

Erik's stomach churned.

"You're sure that's what you saw?" said Carter to Yara after a moment.

Yara nodded. She wouldn't meet Erik's eyes.

"But… E is here," said Ash. "How could he end up at a lab that we don't even know where it is? Why would E go there, right? Right?" she added, addressing Erik.

He was too stunned to speak.

"But who even are 'they' anymore?" said Carter, rubbing their eyes under their glasses. "Kain is dead. The Shadow Men are aimless without him. Yara, did you see who was in the lab? Besides E?"

"Shadow Men," said Yara. "There weren't many of them, but they were definitely Shadow Men. I recognized the outfits."

Carter and Robin exchanged confused looks. "Could this mean that the Shadow Men are going to continue Kain's work without him?" said Carter.

"Ugh, *hello!*" said Ash.

Carter and Robin looked at her, still just as flummoxed. "What?" they said in unison.

"You keep fixating on the fact that Kain is 'dead,'" she said, making air quotes with her fingers, "but for all we know, he isn't!"

"We saw his body get burned to dust—" Carter started.

"Yeah, well you saw E's body get burned, too. We've been over this. 'Dead' means squat. For all we know, they clo—" She cut herself off and looked meaningfully at Yara. When she spoke again, it was more deliberately. "The same thing that brought E back could have brought Kain back, too."

Yara bit her lip.

Erik got the distinct feeling there was something they weren't telling him. No one was looking at him.

After Yara's vision of herself being kidnapped by Kain the year before, Erik knew she struggled with the idea of fate and destiny, but none of them had truly discussed it. If he was meant to end up somewhere, would knowing change anything? Did he have any power over his own future? Was there any way to truly find out?

"Is there any way you can see it again?" asked Carter.

"Have the same vision?" Yara asked.

Carter nodded. "To get any additional information. Maybe there's something more you can see that will tell us what to expect."

Yara took a deep breath and closed her eyes. She was quiet for a moment, her brow furrowed, deep in concentration.

She opened her eyes and looked at Carter. "I can't find it," she said desperately.

"At all?" said Robin.

"Do you remember what brought on the vision?" said Carter. "I thought you had them under control. Was anything... unusual happening when you saw all this?" Carter's eyes barely flickered to

Erik as they spoke, and Erik shifted uncomfortably.

"No!" said Yara at once, defensive. "I mean… I had a headache, and then I… I don't know! It just happened. I couldn't help it. This was… different. It felt different than any vision I've ever had before. Except the one I had two days ago. At the old lab."

"How?"

"I can't explain it. But I had no control over it whatsoever. And I've learned to control my visions. I have," she added, staring pointedly at Carter's skeptical expression.

The five of them were silent for a moment, all deep in thought. Erik's mind was racing. He was trying not to let panic overtake him. He wasn't entirely sure why he felt so anxious. Obviously, being a Guardian was a dangerous job and it came with its risks. But the idea of being in a glass pod surrounded by Shadow Men sent a visceral tightness through his body that he could not shake off.

"I think we ought to reconsider telling Black about all this," said Robin.

"What?" said Yara.

"R is right, Red. This is too much for just us."

"Out of the question," said Yara. "I do not want Black finding out about this."

Robin bit his tongue, but Erik could tell it was all he could do not to retort.

Seeing Robin's expression, Yara started, "It wasn't—" She froze, mid sentence.

"What?" said Ash.

Yara looked at Ash, and after a beat was already half out of bed, yanking the wires that connected her to the monitor. She didn't give any of them a chance to protest, before Frankie came strolling into the room, one eye on the tablet in her hand.

"Ms. Rivers, good to see you're awake," said Frankie, her amber eyes roaming over the five people in her ward, as though she were trying to determine what had been happening before she walked in. "How are you feeling?"

"Fine," said Yara, who then proceeded to continue climbing out of bed.

"Allow me," said Frankie, sounding somewhere between amused and impatient. She methodically unhooked Yara from the monitor before turning back to her tablet. "Any headaches? Nausea? Double vision? Loss of hearing?"

"No, no, no, no," said Yara who was now looking around the room for her clothes. Erik pointed to the chair in the corner of the room where he had folded them. She grabbed them with one hand. "I'm completely fine. Thank you, Frankie."

She threw Ash a significant look and the two of them left the room without another word. Yara's abrupt departure left Erik bewildered. All he could do was stand there, stunned and hurt and clenching his shaking fists, alongside Carter and Robin.

Frankie walked to the desk in the corner, turned on music that Erik recognized as Bach, and moved back to the monitor where she started transferring Yara's readings onto her tablet.

Carter moved closer to Robin and Erik and spoke quietly so as not to let Frankie overhear. She was absentmindedly humming along to her music. "Do we have any idea what that was all about?" said Carter.

"I do remember Yara saying that she wanted to run to a craft store so she could start work on a bird house," whispered Robin.

"Do we even bother following them?"

"They'll tell us whatever they need to tell us when they can," whispered Erik, trying to stay calm. "Better we stay here in case Black or someone comes poking around."

Carter nodded. "What have they decided about you?"

Erik sighed heavily. "I'm supposed to be working with the Level 2 Guardians on evaluations."

Erik could tell that both Carter and Robin were making faces that were trying to look politely interested.

"You think I don't know you guys well enough to recognize when you feel sorry for me?" said Erik, punching Robin lightly in the arm.

Frankie looked up and said, "If you gentlemen don't mind."

Robin apologized and the three of them hurried to the door as Frankie pointedly increased the volume on her tablet and skipped forward to the next song.

Robin looked around, noticing that Erik was no longer next to him.

"E?" he said. But Erik's face was completely blank.

"Erik?" tried Carter, backtracking to where Erik had stopped, waving a hand in front of his face. His eyes were empty as he stared straight ahead, unblinking, unmoving.

"Uh, Frankie?" said Robin, starting to feel nervous.

The Medic moved over to them, her eyebrows raised. Her wild hair was pulled back and knotted into a bun with a tongue compressor.

"What happened?" she said.

"I have no idea," said Robin. "We were just leaving and all of a sudden he just… stopped…"

Frankie pulled a light out of her white coat pocket and flashed it in Erik's eyes. They were completely unresponsive. She frowned.

"Erik?" she said in a loud voice. "Mr. Carpenter!"

He still didn't move.

"You better leave him with me," she said in a wavering voice.

"What?" said Carter.

"Leave him with me, and please fetch Paul."

"But we—"

"Now." Frankie's voice was harsher than Robin had ever heard it.

Robin and Carter reluctantly left the room, watching Erik as they moved. They kept their eyes on the room through the door as it closed. Erik looked like a statue. Stock still. Frankie was taking his pulse and looking nervous.

"I'll go get Chun," said Carter. Robin met their eyes. Carter looked terrified. More terrified than Robin had seen them in a long time.

"I'll come with you."

CHAPTER FIFTEEN

Trance

"What's going on?" said Ash, hurrying to keep up with Yara.

Yara was walking with no real destination, her only goal to move, to get away from the medical wards, where she had already spent too much of her life.

"That vision was different, Ash," she said, weaving through the early morning Medics and Researchers heading to their various posts. "It felt different, and I can't get back to it. I tried looking into the future, and I didn't see it. I didn't see anything around Erik at all."

"What does that mean?" Ash was smiling, looking excited.

"You could at least feign some concern, no?" said Yara, one eyebrow raised.

Ash laughed. "This is just too exciting. I love my job!"

"I think…" She didn't finish her sentence, unable to understand why or how she had come to the conclusion, afraid of sounding crazy, afraid of being wrong. "I think I'm seeing the past…"

Ash squealed. "Yes! I love it. Why?"

Yara shook her head. "I don't know, it's hard to explain. But I have a feeling… it's just like if you see the world one way and then something small changes, but you can't define it. Like… the colors are slightly off. Or everything looks a little smaller. I don't know!" She rubbed her face, frustrated. "But the vision I had at the library, and the one I had last night… Those weren't visions of the future. Think about it. They know we know about that location. It would be insane for them to move all that equipment out and then move it all back."

"So then…" said Ash, "the vision you had at the old lab was from

114

before?"

Yara nodded.

Ash squealed. "Wait, this is so cool!"

"What?"

"You can see the future *and* you can see the past? Aren't you even a little excited by this? I'd be freaking out if I were you."

"You *are* freaking out," said Yara.

"Look, I know a lot is going on right now, but just let yourself be happy about at least one little thing, right? This has to be one of the coolest abilities of all time."

"I guess."

Ash's smile faded when she saw the look on Yara's face. "Oh," she said. "So the vision you had of Erik in one of those pods?"

"Was the past, too," said Yara.

"Well shit," said Ash.

Yara's insides churned.

"So Erik really is a… a…"

"I think I'm gonna be sick."

Erik blinked his eyes open to find himself still in the medical ward. There were many hushed voices, all speaking rapidly and sounding concerned. Something else must have happened to Yara.

Without sparing a thought as to what he was doing on a hospital bed or how he had gotten there, Erik pushed himself up and found that he had wires taped to his head and chest. He was naked, covered only by a white sheet.

He started removing all the wires, but at his first sign of activity, the crowd turned to him. Frankie, Chun, Black, and Glover, as well as several other Medics were all huddled around a monitor, evidently reading whatever activity the wires had been recording.

"What the—What's going on? What happened?"

No one spoke. They stared at him, eyes wide, looking completely dumbstruck.

"Erik," said Black, stepping forward, her obsidian eyes revealing nothing, "how are you feeling?"

"What's going on?" Erik asked again, getting angrier. "What am I doing here? Where did C and R go?"

"Do you remember what happened, Erik?" said Black.

"Yes!" said Erik, fighting to regain his temper, feeling that dangerous heat rising in his chest. He squeezed his chest. *Don't lose it…*

Don't have another episode. Can't give them more to worry about. "R, C, and I were leaving, and—" He stopped, realizing that he did not, in fact, remember what happened after that. Between deciding to leave this room and somehow winding up on one of the beds.

"You… how shall I put this?" Black said, turning to Frankie.

"You entered a fugue state, of sorts," said Frankie.

"What?" said Erik. "Is everything OK?"

"Everything's fine, Erik," said Black. "At the moment, we're just worried about you."

"But I'm *fine!*" said Erik, continuing to peel the wires off his face and chest. "I've told you a hundred times. I'm fine. I'm fine!" The heat in his chest was rising.

"You were completely unresponsive, Erik," said Frankie, stepping closer to him and laying a hand on his arm. "We couldn't even move you. Eventually, we had no choice but to sedate you, and—"

"Sedate me?" said Erik. "What—what are you talking about? You asked us to leave and—and… and I woke up here…" He looked down at his hands. They were shaking.

"Something happened, Erik. Something we can't explain. And you disappeared."

"Disappeared?" asked Erik.

"It was like your mind was turned off. You were still physically here, but there wasn't anything we could do to illicit any reaction from you. At all."

Erik met Frankie's eyes. Everything felt numb and distant.

Something was wrong with him, and they didn't know what it was. They couldn't do anything to help except sedate him. He had been denying this fear since he returned. Since he woke up three days ago in front of the library with white hair and the power to cause earthquakes and his nymph abilities amplified. But if he had blacked out, if he had no memory of what had happened…

He was broken. Dangerous. Unsafe.

He thought of Yara. So beautiful and smart and funny. So special. So very important to him. If something truly was wrong with him, could he really afford to be with her? Even to be around her could be too dangerous. What if he lost his temper and caused another earthquake? What if he entered another fugue state and something happened? He couldn't risk hurting her. He wouldn't.

He was shaking. He couldn't breathe. He looked up at Frankie, who was observing him quite objectively, but not unkindly.

"Erik?" she said gently.

He stared into her amber eyes, his mind racing.

"Can you fix me?"

Things were getting out of control. Yara and her Guardians were in her quarters. Ash was sitting cross-legged next to Carter and Robin on the bed, her eyes burning dangerously. Carter was watching Yara pace relentlessly back and forth, but Robin's head was in his hands.

"Let me get this straight," said Yara. Robin had told her about what happened to Erik gently, as though expecting her to break into tears. Far from it. She was manic. "I see a vision of Erik. In one of those gestation pod things. Then Erik turns into a statue. And when he snaps out of it, he decides that he doesn't want to see me and locks himself in the medical ward. Does that sound like I hit all the major bullet points?" She stared at them all in turn.

Carter said in a tired voice, "Remarkably succinct."

"So, what the hell?" she said, exasperatedly. "Are you really telling me that somehow we don't have the resources to find out *what the hell*?"

No one spoke.

"I'm actually asking!" said Yara, feeling frantic. "No one knows what happened to Erik, no one knows what the vision I had is, and no one goddamn knows what the hell that laboratory is!"

"Listen, kid, you're the one who doesn't want to ask for help from the Society," said Robin. "How exactly do you expect us to have the resources to figure this shit out?"

"Well," said Ash suggestively. "We do have an idea."

"We do?" said Robin.

Yara crossed her arms. She hadn't wanted to share her new theory about seeing the past until she knew for sure that it was true. She did want her Guardians to know. They deserved to know. Eventually. But the thought of being wrong was frightening. Yara liked this new status she had found as a Guardian. Graduating at the top of her class, being a hydan; it made her feel a way she had never felt before: capable and strong. If she dangled some new superpower in front of her best friends and then it turned out to be false, she wasn't fond of the crash of self-esteem that could accompany that. "Maybe. I don't know yet."

Robin raised an eyebrow but didn't press the issue.

After a moment, Carter broke the silence. "I have an idea. But you're not gonna like it."

"What is it?" said Ash.

"We have a tool at our disposal that can enable us to get information." Carter took a deep breath, staring at the floor. "Me."

Yara blanched.

"What?"

"We know there are still Shadow Men from Yara's vision," they said, looking at the ceiling now. "And no one within the Society has any of the answers we're looking for."

"Again," said Robin, "I just want to reiterate that we can't know that for sure since we're not actually asking for help in finding these answers."

"I can shift into a Shadow Man, and find out as much as possible that way."

Yara was shaking her head frantically. "No."

Robin stared at Carter, frowning.

"C," said Ash, standing up next to Yara, "how would you even know where to go? We haven't seen a sign of Shadow Men in a year."

"Plus we don't even know who they're reporting to," added Robin, his voice raw. "This whole thing with E may have nothing to do with them at all."

"Yara has seen Shadow Men in her vision," said Carter, still avoiding everyone's eyes by wiping their glasses on the hem of their uniform. "In a laboratory that once belonged to Kain. We don't know who they're reporting to, but they're reporting to someone. They're organizing. And this is the only way to find out who."

"Carter," said Yara desperately. "Don't."

"Red, you said yourself, we don't know anything. The Society has no idea where to turn, and you don't want to give them the little information we have. Without using the Society's full resources, I don't see that we have much of a choice beyond this."

She stared at them as they finally met her eyes, amber drilling into hazel. She understood in that moment, as much as she hated to admit it, that this was Carter's battle as much as it was hers. And were she standing in their shoes, she would be making the same argument. She nodded mutely.

"Really?" said Ash, looking between the two of them, her eyebrows raised in disbelief. "This is where we're going with this? We have no smarter plans than C turning into a Shadow Man? What if you're found out?" she said, turning to Carter.

They looked at her and sighed. "It's not as dangerous as what Yara did last year. And that worked out." Carter gave Yara a weak smile.

"And she almost died, by the way," Robin mumbled.

"Yara, you have to tell them," said Ash.

"Am I here? Can you guys hear me?" said Robin.

"Tell us what?" said Carter.

"I'll take that as a 'no,'" said Robin.

"Listen to what C is talking about doing," said Ash, ignoring them both, her eyes still on Yara. "They deserve to know what you said."

"But I don't know if it's true. It can't be true. It doesn't make any sense."

"Are you seriously not gonna tell us what the hell you're talking about?" said Robin.

Yara turned to meet his eyes. "I don't think I'm having visions of the future."

"What are they, then?" said Carter.

"The past," said Robin softly. "You're having visions of the past..."

"I know, it doesn't make any sense," said Yara dismissively.

"No," said Robin, still quiet. "It makes perfect sense."

"What?"

"It's less about seeing in only one direction in time..." said Robin, "as it is about seeing through *all* of time."

"What?" said Carter.

"It's just a theory," said Yara.

"What does this mean?" asked Carter.

"It means," said Ash, "that what Yara saw in the old lab was what *used* to be in there. Those pods, those people, that's all from *before*."

"And when you saw E?" said Robin.

"Where was that?" said Carter.

"We don't know," said Ash.

"But it was definitely E? He was there? In those pods?" said Robin.

"This means that after that room in the old lab was dismantled, they reassembled the equipment somewhere else," said Carter.

"And wherever that somewhere else is, E was there. *New* E. *Our* E. Silver Fox E," said Ash.

"And that's why I couldn't see anything when I tried looking into the future," said Yara. "Because it wasn't *in* the future."

Yara looked at Robin. He looked fervent, excited. He nodded.

"How do we test this?" said Carter. "How do we make sure that this is right?"

"Try to see something in the past," said Robin. "Anything.

Yesterday, maybe, or…" He trailed off.

Yara nodded and took a deep breath. She closed her eyes and sank into her mind. But trying to see the past felt like trudging in mud that pulled her back, sucking on her feet, preventing her from going where she wanted to go. She struggled to find Erik, to hold on to his face, the feel of him. Everything was completely murky. There was no sense of clarity, nothing like when she looked forward in time. But she could sense that what she was looking at—whatever it was, as indecipherable as it was through the fog—was definitely not the future.

She opened her eyes to find her Guardians staring at her, mouths agape.

"Well?" said Ash impatiently.

"I couldn't see anything," said Yara, and their faces fell, "but I know that I was trying to look into the past. I know it's there. I can tell."

Robin raised his eyebrows. "Are you sure?"

She nodded.

"How could you have seen what you saw before?" said Carter.

Yara thought back to what had happened. She had been close to Erik when the headache started. And he had touched her at the peak of the pain and that's when it had happened. "I was with Erik," she said. "When I saw it. Maybe it had something to do with that?"

"With E?" said Robin. "You think he helps you see into the past?"

Yara shook her head. "Not necessarily, but maybe into *his* past."

"This is exciting," said Ash. "Am I the only one who's excited?"

"C," said Robin. "Go sit next to her. Try to see something in their past," he added to Yara as Carter joined her on the bed.

Yara looked into their eyes, focusing on the amber hue, seeing the rivulets of gold spreading from their pupil like a corona. Then, she closed her eyes once more, taking a deep breath, and willed herself into Carter's past. *Show me something,* she thought. *Anything.*

Again, that horrible sensation of squelching through sucking mud held her back as she fought to see. She was close. She could feel it. Without realizing what she was doing, she leaned forward, closer to Carter. The closer she got, the more the mud let up. Then, as though some hidden impulse drew her to them, she reached out and grabbed their arms, holding them tightly. Light and color burst open in her mind as hundreds of scenes became available to her.

She zoomed toward one at random.

Carter was sitting on the bench outside Black's office. They looked several years younger, but terribly sad. They closed their eyes, leaning their head back against the wall, but after a few moments, Robin walked out of the elevator, his nose still straight, unbroken. Carter sprang to their feet.

Robin cheerfully greeted Carter. "Hey!" he said, his voice sounding far away, muted, but it was clear he was happy to see his friend. "Have ya heard anything about the new guy?"

Carter nodded. "Half nymph, I think. Graduated early."

Robin lifted his eyebrows in surprise. "Oh, it's *him*. Wow."

"Yeah, this case is no joke. They're handpicking the best candidates."

"You think he'll be another stick in the mud?"

Before Carter could answer, the elevator doors opened again and out walked Erik, whole and black-haired. He looked nervous, but excited.

"Hi," said Robin, shaking Erik's hand. "I'm R."

"E," said Erik—

—when Yara was jostled back to reality by Robin's voice quietly asking, "Do you see anything?"

Yara was laughing. She was still holding on to Carter's arms, and instead of letting them go, she hugged them. "It's the past! I saw it!" Carter hesitantly put their arms around her.

"What did you see?" said Ash.

Yara looked at Robin, noticing as she pulled away from Carter that the shape shifter's face looked slightly wary. "I saw the three of you outside Black's office. You, Carter, and Erik. The first time you met him, I think," she said, still feeling giddy at this new and exciting discovery.

Carter exhaled, and Yara couldn't be sure, but she thought it looked like they were relieved.

"This is amazing," said Robin, who started to laugh with Yara.

"Yeah, this is good, right?" said Ash. "I mean… Couldn't Yara theoretically be able to see into E's past? It could tell us everything we need to know! And we don't need to worry about any of this… going undercover stuff."

"Well, no," said Carter. "We have to find out where and *how* it happened. If anything, this just makes it even more urgent for me to go in as a Shadow Man to find out where it is he came from. We still have so many unanswered questions."

Yara could feel Robin's eyes on her. Neither of them said anything as

Ash and Carter spoke.

"Your eyes, C. They are kind of obviously not Shadow Man eyes. In fact, they're pretty recognizable." It was common knowledge that while shape shifters could transform into any mammal, they couldn't change the color of their eyes. Shifters could always be recognized from the golden hue of their eyes, no matter their form, which were so unlike the dead and lifeless eyes of a Shadow Man.

"Believe it or not," said Carter. "I have colored contacts for just this occasion."

There was a long moment of silence and Yara wanted to scream at Robin to stop looking at her. Her skin was crawling and she didn't know why.

"It's a risk," said Yara finally, closing her eyes to avoid facing her Guardians, "but Carter's right. It's our only chance of finding anything out."

"I'm just gonna pitch one last time that we report this to Black," said Robin.

"We do that and she may never let us see Erik again," said Yara. "She'll assume he's a clone, and that it makes him unsafe. Who knows what she'd do to him."

In the silence that followed these words, Yara chanced a look at Robin. His normally joyful face was dark. He was looking at her as though he had never seen her before. She turned away, unable to stomach it, and Carter gave her a small nod.

"When do we start?"

CHAPTER SIXTEEN

Stuck

Robin sent another call to voicemail and threw his ConvOrb on the bed, hoping no one noticed.

He, Yara, and the rest of her Guardians spent the rest of the day planning how Carter would infiltrate the Shadow Men. Robin was starving and completely exhausted, but he was nowhere close to as tired as Yara looked. She had spent hours searching into the future for any signs or hints as to what Carter should do, where they should go, and how they should appear.

But her ability to see the future was not without its limitations. No matter what they did, what they talked about, or what decisions they made, Yara could not see past Carter being taken by the Shadow Men. Once they put their hands on the shape shifter, time simply froze.

"There's just no way I can see a future without specific decisions being made," she said, her frustration palpable. "I can see Carter's future, and it changes anytime you make a different decision," she said, turning to the shape shifter, "but then whenever I try to see the future of any Shadow Men, I see nothing. It's like… they're not even there. They don't exist. No images, no feelings, nothing. Just… a solid wall in my mind where the future should be." It was the same as it had been when she'd infected herself with the Omega Project virus. What could possibly be inhibiting her ability to see the future when it came to Kain and his men?

"But we know they exist," said Robin. "Because you *did* see them. Right?"

"Right," Yara sighed.

"If the Shadow Men are still active, the Eyes will know about it!" said Ash for the third time.

"The Eyes are useless," said Robin, remembering their ineffectiveness when Yara had been kidnapped by Kain the year before. The only way they'd found her was thanks to Erik breaking protocol and looking for her himself.

"Maybe some of the Seekers who went down to the old lab on Black's orders are monitoring it. Just in case," said Carter.

"Why would they?" said Yara.

Robin waved their words off. "If the Eyes found anything when they were down there, Black would know."

"If Black knows," said Carter, "she wouldn't share that intel."

"Wouldn't she?" said Ash. "Do you seriously think the Eyes aren't trying to keep tabs on the Shadow Men? I mean, where do mindless drones like that even go when their leader dies?"

"I just don't see how we could get access to that information," said Yara. "If it even exists."

"C wants to shift into a Shadow Man? Let them shift into a Tracker and find out."

"The Society has measures in place to prevent shifters from assuming the identity of another member," said Carter.

After hours of bickering and trying not to scream and pulling at their hair, they had determined there was only one way for Carter to find the Shadow Men.

"We already know the easiest solution," said Carter. "It's what Yara's already done. We draw the Shadow Men to me."

"How would we even go about doing that?" said Robin. "They want to stay hidden."

"Think about it," said Carter. "The Society is a secret organization. And it's not always easy keeping it a secret, so we have to be careful when a Deviant starts causing trouble somewhere. We monitor all that kind of activity, so that if there's a crisis, we can handle it before any civilians gets wind of what's going on."

"And Kain was the same," said Yara.

"Right. That's how he found the hyden."

"You think there's someone in a room somewhere, looking for rogue Shadow Men, waiting to round them up if they get lost?" said Robin, skeptically.

"Maybe not in so many words, but if there's a noticeable enough disturbance involving someone who is... obviously..."

"A Shadow Man," supplied Ash.

Carter nodded. "If Kain was growing Shadow Men, if he was cloning them, he wouldn't have wanted them to get into the wrong hands. It would open up a lot of questions. So, it stands to reason that if anyone is left of his whole operation they would do anything to get any lost individuals back in their possession. They can't risk being found out. Especially not if they're still regrouping."

"So, what?" said Robin. "You're going to make a big, weird scene, then get yourself arrested?"

"That's exactly what they're gonna do," said Yara, her eyes locked on Carter, knowing that's where their mind had been going.

The look Carter gave her reinforced that notion.

Robin laughed in exasperation. "Just when I thought this whole plan couldn't get any crazier."

"If they don't come for me, if I'm wrong, then I'll break myself out. It won't be hard."

"How?" said Yara. "Turn into a mouse and crawl between the bars? I thought shape shifters couldn't change their mass."

"Not a mouse. Something long and skinny. I wouldn't have to change my mass. As long as I can get thin enough to get between those bars."

Ash burst into laughter. "I'm sorry," she said at the expression everyone gave her, wiping tears from her eyes, "it's just, that's a hilarious image."

Yara lay in the dark, staring up at the ceiling. As was often the case these days, sleep eluded her. She wondered if this was simply what life was now. Lying in bed, tired but awake.

Thoughts raced through her mind so fast she felt dizzy, but she kept coming back to the same question.

Had her father been able to see the past, too?

She had inherited her hydan abilities from Theo Rivers, a fellow seer. He, too, had worked as a White Mask and the Society had known about his capability and had studied it, though not extensively. What little they had learned was just enough to have a basic understanding of how Yara's power worked. It was this research conducted on her own family that gave the Medics the information they needed to treat her back when she'd been having migraines. So if her father had been able to see the past, as she now suspected she could, wouldn't they know about it?

The fact that no one within the organization seemed to have any inkling that such a thing was possible indicated that—even if her father could see the past—the Society didn't know about it. If Theo had seen more than the future, he'd kept it secret. And Yara couldn't think of any reason why he might keep something like that secret, which suggested he hadn't had that particular skill.

However, Yara had to admit that she really didn't know anything about her father. She couldn't make the assumption that he'd want to keep something secret or not because he was as much a stranger to her as anyone else long dead. As far as she knew, the only things they had in common were a name and genes.

If only she'd had anything of her parents' left. Letters, notebooks, papers. Her closest connection to them was Aunt Catherine, who had already told Yara everything she knew. Besides, Aunt Catherine was the sister of Yara's mother, not her father. Aunt Catherine knew more about Sierra than Theo. Theo had always been the man who took Aunt Catherine's sister away to work a dangerous job that ultimately got her killed. White Masks didn't have much in the ways of personal effects, but Yara couldn't believe that there wasn't more left behind for her to inherit. She had a few trinkets here and there—an old t-shirt, a simple necklace, two photographs, a worn book—but nothing that really left a mark. No footprints that definitively proved that Sierra and Theo Rivers had well and truly lived.

Yara was the closest thing to that.

She hated asking about her parents. After a few lackluster attempts, she had gotten everything she could from Aunt Catherine, and the Society was infuriatingly cagey about the history of their members. After she'd joined as an initiate, it hadn't taken long for Yara to give up trying to learn more about her parents. The frustration wasn't worth it.

But now she wondered. There was so much more to know about the people who made her. Did anyone have the answers to her questions?

Learning how to live was already hard enough. She burned with resentment that she was having to do it all without the help of someone who had perhaps gone through the exact same thing. For the first time in her life, Yara hated her parents for leaving her without a roadmap. They must have known that there was a possibility of her growing up an orphan. After all, they had dangerous jobs. And her father was a hydan. Didn't he want to impart any wisdom on a daughter who would likely have the same powers that he did? Had her parents really been so arrogant as to believe that they were immune from harm? Or had they just not cared about leaving her behind?

Records were held within the Cleaning division of the Society, who did most of the administrative heavy lifting. Being a shape shifter had its advantages when it came to duplicity, but since the Society had their ways of preventing that, it was fortunate that most of the administrative information was available to all Society members. Carter hadn't needed to employ any shape shifting tactics to get what they were looking for: a picture. A simple picture of one of the Shadow Men.

All the Shadow Men they had ever captured had died suddenly in captivity from suicide pellets. Perhaps this one… hadn't.

As they walked back out of Records, Carter tried to ignore the feeling of betrayal against the organization that had given them so much. Tried to think instead of Erik, the implication of his return, what it could mean to the entire Deviant community if Kain could indeed come back as Erik had. The Society had to get a head start on stopping him, and this was the best way to do it. Even if it meant skirting a few rules.

Or every rule.

Carter was moving slowly. Perhaps they were just looking for excuses to postpone the inevitable.

But it had to happen eventually, and there was only one place to start…

The old lab.

Robin, Ash, and Yara had all agreed to try to get a bit of sleep, but when they met up in the commissary at 0700 hours that morning, it was clear that Robin and Yara's attempts had been fruitless. Ash, however, looked well rested.

Carter's empty chair next to Robin was so loud, he was surprised no one else in the commissary took any notice.

The plan was for Robin and Ash to cover for Carter's absence; buy as much time for Carter as possible while they were gone and hope that they would be able to get home, unharmed, before their absence was noticed. If they were gone longer than Robin and Ash could excuse, Yara insisted that she go rogue so Carter's alibi would be that they went after her. If this happened, it meant that she could face expulsion from the Society. Hopefully, it wouldn't come to that, and the shoots would all be too preoccupied with whatever the hell was happening with Erik to notice Carter's absence. Robin could not stomach the thought of losing Yara in such a way, but she was determined not to place anyone else's position at the Society at risk.

And if worst came to worst, if it looked like Carter was in real trouble, Robin would go behind Yara's back and report it all to Black. Whatever it took to get Carter back safely.

"So, X is giving you your first assignment," said Ash, trying to break the silence they all sat in. "You nervous?"

Yara looked at Ash with an air of just having realized where she was. "Hmm? Oh. Uh, I guess so..."

Robin chuckled. "Haven't thought about it much, have you?" he said.

Yara raised her eyebrow, and said sardonically, "No. I haven't." She shoved a giant piece of toast in her mouth and said, "What should I expect?"

"No idea," said Robin, pushing the dregs of watermelon around his plate. "Things have been quiet lately."

"Well," said Ash, whose appetite appeared unchanged, wiping crumbs off her face as she pushed away from the table, "I'm gonna head to the training rooms and work off my breakfast. Make room for second breakfast. Yara, I'll see you in a bit? You can fill me in on what your assignment is." She hugged Robin and waved at Yara before skipping out of the commissary, trails of bright flame dancing around her hair.

Robin watched her leave, painfully aware that he was alone with Yara for the first time in what felt like forever. Truthfully, it had only been a few days since their last training session together, but so much had happened since then.

Erik had happened since then.

When he looked at her, she was leaning so far over her plate that he thought she might be sick.

"You OK?" he said, reaching for her, only to find that she had been morosely tearing up another piece of toast.

"Hmm?" she said again, looking up at him.

"Oh," he said, feeling awkward.

"Oh..." she repeated. "No, I'm fine." She kept tearing up her toast and her eyes glazed over as she stared over his shoulder, evidently deep in thought. "Yeah... so fine. I feel really good about the direction everything in my life is taking right now."

"Yara," said Robin, unsure of what he was going to say.

"No, Robin, it's fine. You know, my boyfriend is back from the dead, he might be a clone, he's voluntarily locking himself up in the medical ward and refusing to see me, one of my best friends is running head first into the lion's den, and this morning I'm starting a new job that I'm totally unprepared for and may even get fired from before the end of the week!"

In her panic, she had stood up and started walking out of the commissary, forcing Robin to run after her, leaving their uneaten food on the table.

"Hey! Where're you going?"

"To Williams. To X," she spat. "To get my assignment!"

"That's not for another hour," said Robin, running to catch up to her. She was already in the elevator when he grabbed her arm and spun her around to face him. "Yara, would you just stop for a second?"

She was breathing heavily, her eyes crazed. The doors of the elevator shut behind them and they started to ascend to the main offices when Robin pulled a lever, triggering the emergency stop. The elevator shuddered as it halted abruptly. She looked at him, and once again he had the feeling of getting caught in her gaze like a deer in headlights.

"What?" she hissed.

"Just... stop. For a second. OK? I know you're stressed. We all are. But that's what this is. This job. This whole thing is all just a constant game of feeling helpless and scared." He took a few deep breaths to steady himself as he stared at her. "We're all worried. We all want to know what's going on with E. With Erik. And we're all—"

"No, but—"

"Let me finish!"

She clamped her mouth shut.

Robin continued. "We're all on your side. I know that you and Erik..." the words got lost as he tried to say them. He wanted to be happy for his friends that they had a second chance. But no matter how much he said it to himself, it didn't matter, didn't make it true. The truth was that there was a part of him that wasn't happy at all. It was angry. Angry with himself for never having had the courage to tell Yara, angry with Erik for having showed up when he did, even angry at Yara for not loving Robin back. "I know that..." he tried again, still failing to find the words.

"Look," she said, sighing and shaking her head. "I'm sorry. I know, you're right. It's just... I never thought I would see him again."

Robin looked at her, trying to swallow his feelings, and realized that he was still holding her shoulder. He let go and instead pressed his finger on the space between her eyebrows where her anxiety lived, smoothing out the crease. "I know," he said.

She laughed at this routine of theirs. Of his constant reminders to "unclench." With a heavy sigh, she whispered, "Thank you."

"For what?" he said absentmindedly.

"For being calm and sane while I'm busy losing it."

"Calm-and-Sane is my middle name," he said without thinking.

She snorted. "What actually *is* your middle name?"

"It's Daniel."

"Do you think he'll be OK?"

"Daniel?" said Robin.

"Erik."

"Oh." Robin tore his gaze away from her, rubbing his neck. "Honestly, kid, I don't know," he sighed.

Yara pressed a button and the elevator jolted back to life as it restarted its ascent. Robin didn't know where they were going. He leaned back against the wall and tried to clear his mind. He felt her small hand slip into his and he jumped slightly at her touch.

"What's wrong?" she asked, frowning at his reaction.

He looked down where she was reaching for his hand, which he had shoved into his pocket. "Nothing!" he said a little too fast. He slapped a crooked smile on his face and tried laughing it off. Thankfully, at that moment the doors opened and a woman in Tracker garb joined them. Robin had no idea what floor they were on, but he barreled out of the elevator into the hallway beyond, desperate to get away from Yara and the temptation to tell her everything.

Wearing the skin of the Shadow Man from the picture, armed with a gauntlet on their hand and a solenoid strapped to their back, Carter stood outside the library.

The stillness of the pale morning was oppressive. They didn't expect to find any other Shadow Men there, but they wanted to see where the heart of Kain's operation had been. And it was as good a place as any to do what they needed to do.

Out of curiosity, they wandered around the library, taking advantage of the opportunity to get used to their new body. It was much more solidly built than Carter's usual form, so they had become shorter than they were used to. A shape shifter could not change their mass, so if a new form was bigger in one direction, that mass had to come from somewhere else. The hardest thing to replicate was the mark on the Shadow Man's neck. A brand in the shape of the letters "Re." It had taken quite a bit of concentration before they managed to copy it.

Carter circled the building once, twice, three times. It looked perfectly ordinary. People sat outside, passed by on the sidewalk, entered and exited the building with bags and books. The last time Carter had been here was when Emmanuelle Moreau's tracker had been activated, and the White Masks were dispatched to collect Yara and the other prisoners during their daring escape.

Carter hoped their own collection would go more smoothly than that one had. They knew they had a limited amount of time before the Society would start to question where they were, and that time was already running short. So, with butterflies in their stomach, they began.

Robin was sure that if any Shadow Men were out there, they had seen the news. It was all anyone at the Society was talking about that morning. A Shadow Man, arrested at the downtown branch of the Los Angeles Public Library for destroying the art installations suspended from the ceiling four stories up with a solenoid. The massive sculptures had fallen and shattered, rendering the escalators below unusable and injuring five civilians. Fortunately, no one sustained anything more serious than a concussion.

Shaky cell phone footage showed the Shadow Man confused and unresponsive as he was apprehended by the police. Robin had to admit that Carter's performance was very convincing. They had believably replicated the vacant, emotionless attitude of every Shadow Man Robin had ever encountered.

Robin had been unable to look anyone in the eye since news of this strange occurrence came out. The Society's contingency team was already working on retrieving the Shadow Man through diplomatic channels via their connection with one of the few civilian government officials who knew of the Society's existence.

Yara had assured Robin that she would continually try to see Carter's future and let him know right away if she found anything. For the moment, no news was good news.

Robin needed to distract himself from everything that was going on. From Carter, in peril in a place where Robin could not help. From Yara and how desperately he wanted to be with her. How being around her had become almost painful. How she had gone on and on about Erik, calling him her boyfriend. How she had reached for Robin's hand…

So he went to clear his head the way he always did. In the simulator, running his favorite program where he got to rob the rich and beat the crap out of them too. He fought until his shoulders ached, his legs trembled, and his eyes stung from the sweat.

He was grappling with two enormous goons when he heard the simulator doors whoosh open behind him. He grabbed one of the assailants in a headlock and used its body to propel himself off the ground to kick the other assailant in the face, causing the second goon to stumble back. With a swift movement, Robin broke the simulated neck of the one he had in a headlock and watched the lifeless body crumple to the ground. The second assailant came lumbering back, but now freed from the other, Robin swiped its feet from under it and slammed it down hard enough to knock it out. The limp forms of the attackers all flickered out of existence, and a menu popped up, asking if he wanted to start another level.

Robin stalked over to his discarded tunic on the floor and used it to wipe the sweat from his face as he turned the simulation off with a lazy push of a button. Only once the menu and the forest around him disappeared did he turn to the person standing in the doorway.

It was Yara.

He forced a smile on his face. "Hey, kid. We have to stop meeting like this."

"Sorry," she said. Her eyes were darting nervously around his naked torso.

"How's your first day on the job?" he asked, slinging his tunic around his neck and grabbing a drink of water from his canteen.

"Enlightening," said Yara. She was staring at the ceiling.

"Yeah? Where did X assign you? Patrol?"

"Not even," said Yara, evidently grumpy. "Headquarters security."

Robin laughed. Widely considered to be the worst posting, Headquarters security was a job so boring Robin had a sneaking suspicion it only existed when Black felt the need to keep a Guardian out of the field, safe and out of the way.

"And it wasn't X. They weren't there. Told me they were out or something, I dunno. Wouldn't tell me."

"Huh," said Robin. "That's weird."

"Yeah. But I got to meet G. I guess she's standing in for the moment."

"What'd you think of her?" said Robin, smiling. Gale Trumbull was an intimidating woman in an organization full of intimidating people. It was hard to forget a face like hers. Robin still remembered the first time he met her, and how he'd tried so hard not to look at the thick scar from when she'd allegedly had her throat slit in Phuket.

"She's… hardcore."

Robin laughed.

"I saw Carter."

Robin swallowed another gulp of water. "And?" he said, trying to act calm.

"And they're coming for them. More Shadow Men are, I mean."

"Well, that's good, isn't it?"

Yara sighed heavily. "Shadow Men aren't known for their… tact."

"What are you getting at?"

"Several police officers are going to die."

The room was quiet save for a faint humming that always filled the sims. Robin nodded and took another swig from his canteen. "I'm sorry, Yara," he said.

She looked as though she might throw up. "This is all my fault."

Robin rolled his eyes and walked over to her. "Hey," he said, forcing her to meet his eyes. "This is not your fault. Do you understand?"

Her hazel eyes flitted back and forth between his own. "How can you live knowing that we are responsible for the deaths of three people?"

"Because this is how life works. It's not always pretty. People die. And police officers, Guardians—we're the fighters. We all know that when we sign up for the job."

"That's easy for you to say," said Yara. "You don't have to watch it happen."

"I'm sorry that you had to see that, kid," he said, smoothing out the crease between her eyebrows for the second time that day. "But we're saving more lives by doing this. It will help us find the Shadow Men and get to the bottom of this whole thing."

She nodded absently.

"Maybe you should get back to your post," he said, throwing his tunic back in a corner to prepare for another bout. "Your shift can't possibly be over already."

But Yara did not move, standing instead in the middle of the room and looking lost.

"Yara? What's wrong?"

"This," she said. "This whole thing is wrong. I mean, what am I even doing here?"

"Well, based on the way you're dressed, I'd say you're here to make balloon animals for the birthday party on the third floor."

"I didn't realize I was talking to 'funny' Robin," she said.

"Is there any other Robin?" He quirked an eyebrow.

"Sometimes there's funny Robin, and then sometimes there's 'funny' Robin." She made air quotes with her fingers.

Robin choked back a laugh.

"I mean," she continued, still looking morose, "what am I doing as a Guardian? Following orders? I mean, Black is probably so scared that I'm gonna get hurt because I'm a hydan, that all I'm ever gonna be is a glorified mall cop—"

"Yara, I'm in love with you."

CHAPTER SEVENTEEN

Tension

For a moment, Robin wasn't sure that Yara heard him. He couldn't know why or how it came out. He knew he shouldn't have said it, yet he couldn't have stopped himself if he wanted to. It had been eating away at him. At every part of him. He heard the words come out of his mouth before he even registered that he had been speaking them.

It became evident a few moments later that Yara had heard him when she turned her wide, unblinking eyes toward him. Her lips were parted, her head slightly cocked to the side.

It was a mistake. He shouldn't have said anything. He had to take it back.

He tried smiling, but it felt unnatural, so he stopped.

"Wha—uh…" She cleared her throat. "What?"

"I don't suppose you'd believe me if I said I was joking."

"Are you?"

"No."

Dammit.

The silence was pressing in on him. He watched her for what felt like ages as she stood in front of him, completely speechless. He so wanted to beg her to say something. Anything. Was afraid of what she might say. But more than that, he regretted his own weakness. After all this time, after years of being her Guardian, after resigning himself that nothing would ever come of it, after training her and spending nearly every waking minute with her, he had succumbed to the urge to tell her now, with everything going on, when she was already guilty and sad and confused, all because of the callow hope that she would say, "I love you, too, Robin. Let's run away together and forget the world."

Instead, he said, "I know that I shouldn't. And I know that this... definitely isn't the time. But I, uh... I couldn't keep it from you anymore. I think I just needed to tell you and see..."

She still said nothing.

"Look, Yara, I know what the deal is. With being Guardians, with you being my Ward and with... with E. I know. I just... uh, I guess I need to hear you say it." *Say that you love me or that you don't. I can't live in this limbo.*

More silence.

"I'm sorry," he said, unable to handle the quiet. "I shouldn't have said anything."

She looked at him, her eyes glazed with a silver sheen, her cheeks pink. "No," she said, her look hardening. "You shouldn't have."

Robin's breath hitched and he stared at her, breathing heavily for a few moments. She was right. The words hurt like knives to the gut, but she was right. He nodded, never taking his eyes away from hers.

"Carter is going to be broken out of civilian jail this evening by the Shadow Men. I'll monitor the situation. Meet me and Ash in my room at midnight so we can discuss our next move."

And without another word, she walked out of the simulator and disappeared.

Yara stood in the hallway, staring at the closed door of the sims, fuming. Robin was still inside. How dare he? Six months. He'd had *six months* since she had started training to be a Guardian. Six months during which they had spent nearly every day together, nights spent crying on his shoulder, grueling sessions in the sims and the gym. Six months spent side by side when he could have told her how he felt. The injustice of it made her want to punch him in the face, something she was now quite capable of doing.

But a little voice deep inside her kept saying, *Why are you so angry?* Could it possibly be because she wanted him to have told her when she could have done something about it? Did she resent the fact that she didn't have six months under her belt of being with Robin?

If she had, what would she have done when Erik returned? She loved Erik.

Didn't she?

Yes. But... she also loved Robin.

Well, of course she loved Robin! He was her Guardian and one of her closest friends. She loved Carter, too! And Ash. But she had never gotten flustered by Carter or Ash, never reached for their hands or let her eyes drift over their exposed skin. And despite her dislike of being touched, she never seemed to mind when it was Robin. She leaned into the feel of his finger on her forehead and looked forward to their wrestling matches during training.

She felt sick. Her stomach was so tight she thought she might vomit from the pain. She clenched her fists, mostly to stop her from opening the door and charging at Robin. Whether she wanted to hit him or kiss him, she couldn't tell. But the one thing she knew was that she would never be able to forgive herself if she did either. Regardless of how she felt about Robin, she loved Erik. And she was with Erik. He was hers and she was his and that was that.

The longer she stayed there, the more likely it became that Robin would open the door and find her standing there, as though waiting for him. That couldn't happen.

With great effort, she forced her feet to carry her away.

Carter had not even been properly processed by the civilian police when the Shadow Men came for them. They were waiting in the interrogation room, hands cuffed to the table, when they heard the alarm.

Becoming a Shadow Man meant fighting every instinct they had. Not much was known about Kain's goons, but what they did know showed that they were unresponsive and inscrutable. So Carter did not so much as turn their head when the sounds of commotion started rumbling outside the room. It wasn't until someone unlocked the door that they turned to look, trying to keep their face as impassive as possible.

Another Shadow Man had a police officer in a chokehold, a solenoid hovering in the air next to him. The cop had unlocked the door and dropped the keys, her hands shaking as she raised them in the air as a show of compliance.

"P—please," she stuttered, tears streaming down her face.

The Shadow Man released her carelessly and the officer barely had time to sigh with relief when the crimson clad man flung his gauntleted wrist, sending the solenoid cleanly through the cop's neck.

Her head hit the floor with a sickening thud as her body fell to its knees and eventually crumpled to the floor in a pool of blood. The room was filled with a sharp, metallic tang that Carter could almost taste.

Two more Shadow Men came into the room and stepped over the decapitated body without a second thought. One of them picked the keys up and rapidly unlocked Carter from the table. The other pulled a needle and syringe out from their uniform. It took a concerted effort for Carter not to shy away as the Shadow Man plunged the needle into Carter's neck without hesitation.

Could they know that Carter was an imposter? Had they just let themself be killed without putting up a fight?

But Carter felt no pain, no sedation, nothing different at all. There was no time to wonder what had been done to them. Without a word, mimicking their careless attitude, Carter followed them out of the room, keeping their eyes forward. As they stepped over the fallen officer's body, they sent a silent plea for forgiveness to her and to her family, hoping against hope that she was the only casualty.

This was likely a futile hope given the state the rest of the police station was in. A few Shadow Men were stationed around the chaos, solenoids hovering threateningly around them all. The computers had been destroyed, light fixtures and surveillance cameras were dangling from wires in the ceiling, the only illumination coming from the feeble evening light leaking in through the windows. A couple of people were whimpering, but it was mostly silent.

Once Carter and the Shadow Men exited the precinct, one of them sent his solenoid crashing from wall to wall, just to keep people ducking for cover and buying them a few more moments to escape.

All together, Carter counted a dozen Shadow Men. It was hard to get a good gauge of the situation without breaking their charade of apathy, but they knew enough to see that things were in shambles.

Hopefully, they would get enough intel for it to have been worth it. Destroying what was left of Kain's work, they told themself grimly, was worth a few lives if it meant saving thousands more.

Carter couldn't make themself believe that, but there was no going back now.

They all piled into a black van in silence and sped away. Carter couldn't see where they were going, but hopefully, Robin had managed to acquire a tracepad from a Tracker and would be able to find out where they were using the implant embedded in Carter's forearm.

It was a little while before they arrived at their destination. The entire drive passed in complete silence. Carter could tell from their peripherals that none of the other Shadow Men showed any interest in speaking, nor any signs of discomfort. They all simply sat completely still, staring straight ahead. So Carter followed suit.

Their body aching, the car finally stopped.

They followed the Shadow Men in a strict line out of the van and chanced a glance at their surroundings.

Robin wasn't having a good day.

And he didn't particularly want to leave Headquarters. Normally, he would have made any excuse to avoid what lay ahead of him if he'd had any available to him. But after what had happened in the sims, he was grateful for a distraction. Even this one.

The messages had been coming in a lot the last few days. So when he responded that afternoon, acquiescing, he was sent the address of a nice restaurant downtown. The dinner reservations were under the name of the woman he was meeting. She usually asked to meet on the west side, so the fact that she had chosen a locale so close to Headquarters made Robin nervous. If she was conceding on something this early, it was because she wanted something.

He opted to walk rather than checking out any of the vehicles the Society had on hand. It wasn't far. Twenty minutes or so on foot, and the weather was crisp and cool this time of year, the streets well-lit by the numerous street lamps and high-rises that kept their lights on all night.

Robin had exchanged his uniform for civilian clothes. He walked with his hands tucked into his jeans, his gray coat buttoned up, and his curls blown about by an errant wind.

His mind played over various possible outcomes of the dinner he was heading toward. It was hard to know what she would want to discuss. Not to say that they never spoke, but in-person rendezvous were rare. Most conversations happened electronically, and Robin was perfectly content with that arrangement. The fact that she had asked to meet in person led Robin to feel trepidatious about what lay ahead. So when the restaurant came into view, he could feel himself starting to walk slower, trying to delay the inevitable.

But his treacherous feet continued to carry him forward until he was inside, the brisk breeze replaced with the fragrant warmth of the restaurant. It was dimly lit, with candles on every table, a pianist playing quietly in the corner, and the murmured chatter of the clientele typical of such an establishment. The host smiled flirtatiously as she led him to the table where the other member of his party was already waiting for him.

The woman's face was hidden behind her menu, but there was no mistaking her. Perfectly manicured nails, golden curls coiffed elegantly back, spotless leather heels on her delicately crossed feet.

She put the menu down when Robin arrived and smiled lightly at him, dismissing the host with a small wave of her bejeweled hand. "Robin, darling. It's good to see you. Have a seat."

"Hello, Mother."

CHAPTER EIGHTEEN

Family History

"Well, don't just stand there. Have a seat."

Robin pulled the chair out across from his mother and sat.

Theresa Green was not a particularly warm mother. Growing up, Robin had thought of her as more of an etiquette coach than a source of comfort. He loved her as he knew she loved him and his two brothers, but the way the Greens showed love was by demanding excellence in all things and ensuring their sons had the best when it came to the quality of care and the education they received. There were no kisses on boo-boos. Just lessons on how to ensure it never happened again.

Now she stared at him atop her clasped hands, inspecting his every mannerism as he made a show of looking over the menu.

"Glad you picked a place where I could find something to eat," said Robin lightly. His family knew of the White Mask Society. Knew that the organization encouraged their members not to partake of animal products as a show of respect to the numerous non-humans who were part of the Deviant community. That didn't stop the Greens from giving him grief about it at every opportunity.

"Oh, hush," said his mother, waving his sarcastic words aside as she picked her menu back up. "You're not even there. You can call this your cheat day. Why do you think I asked you to meet here instead of there?"

"Because you would never be caught dead eating in a commissary."

She pursed her lips but did not look up. A sign of disapproval.

A waiter dressed in nicer clothes than Robin had worn since joining the Society came to take their order.

"A second martini, please," said Robin's mother as she handed her menu to the server. "A little dryer, this time, if you could. And I'll have the scallops."

"For you?" said the server.

"Just the house salad. Hold the chicken," said Robin.

"That's hardly enough food for you," said Theresa as the server left to put in their order.

"What's this about, Mother?"

Her lips pursed again. Twice in as many minutes. That had to be a record. "It's about your father."

"OK?" Robin's mother had always had an annoying habit of not offering information unless exactly the right question was asked. "What, he sent you to do his dirty work for him? He didn't want to come meet me himself?"

"Don't be silly, you know how busy he gets."

"I'm busy too, Ma."

Another pursed lips. He had aimed for that one. "You know I don't like it when you call me that, darling."

Robin laughed and leaned forward. "Can you just cut to the chase? Tell me what's going on. What's wrong with Dad?"

"Nothing is wrong with your father, of course," she said. "We've just been discussing it. He thinks—and I agree with him—that it's time you stop with this silly little side project of yours and come back to join the family business."

Robin coughed into his water. "This again?"

"We've given you plenty of time to play around, but now it's time you stop and follow in your father's footsteps."

Robin smiled and looked down at his fork, fiddling with with the tongs as he considered how to respond. "I'm not doin' this again with you, Mother."

"Your brother has more than enough on his hands as it is, and—"

"Then get Evan to help."

"Don't be ridiculous, he's just a child."

"Big deal," said Robin. "You started grooming me and Tristan to take over the company when we were younger than Evan is now."

"Will you please keep your voice down?" said Theresa sternly. Her demeanor never changed. An onlooker would barely have noticed her frustration, but Robin knew her better. "He's still a little boy. And of course we trust that when he's old enough, he'll do what's expected of him. What's best for his family."

"Right," said Robin. "That's what that firm needs. More nepotism. Another spoiled rich kid who's never worked a day in his life—"

"Tristan needs your help, Robin."

Robin leaned back, chewing on his lip as he inspected his mother. The server dropped off her second martini, clearing away the glass Theresa had emptied before Robin had even arrived. She took a small sip and set the glass down delicately. After a moment, she continued.

"The company is growing. We have assets spread throughout the globe, and your father and brother are no longer able to handle it on their own."

"Sounds like the company's too big, then."

"Don't be ridiculous."

"Or maybe you can bring in outside hires. People with actual experience. People who actually give a shit about what you're doing —"

"Robin, please—" his mother cut in, interrupting him.

He didn't even take a breath before changing course. "Are you seriously asking me to give up the only thing that's ever made me happy to come work for a morally bankrupt company just so that you can have deeper coffers? Is that really what you want?"

She didn't respond.

"I'm fulfilled, Mother. I love what I do, and I'm good at it. I'm making a real difference. I'm helping people. Which is more than I can say for you or for Dad or Tristan. Or—god forbid—Evan when it comes time for him, too."

"Oh please," said Theresa. "You're playing dress-up with some made-up organization that pretends to fight demons."

Robin shook his head with a sardonic laugh. "No demons, Ma. And it's not made up. I don't know how to prove it to ya any more than I already tried." That had been a fun afternoon. Bringing his family to Headquarters for his initiation to introduce them to the world of Deviants had ended with the most awkward family dinner of Robin's life. And that was saying something. Robin's little brother Evan had been the only one to show excitement, and it had been stifled quickly by the horror of his mother and the envy of his older brother, Tristan. Whatever his father had made of it, Robin never knew. James Green hadn't said a single word all that evening and had barely spoke to Robin since then.

"I just think it would be easier for you to find a nice girl and settle down once you come home to work with us."

"*That's* what you want?" said Robin. "For me to cash in and settle down with a 'nice girl'?"

"Well, there was that one. What was her name? We liked her."

"Nayla."

"Yes. Such a shame when that ended. She was lovely."

"She *is* lovely. And we're friends."

"Please, Robin. We don't even know what to tell people when they ask about you."

"Tell them whatever you want," said Robin. "I'm not coming home because *you* feel awkward about having me as your son."

Another lip purse. "You know that's not what I meant."

"I think it is." Robin pushed his chair away from the table and stood. "A pleasure as always, Mother," he said, just as the server brought their plates of food. "Don't bother calling again if this is all you have to say to me."

That night, Robin's head was filled with white noise as he deliberately tried to think of anything other than the conversation he'd had with Yara earlier or his mother's words over dinner or what Carter might be facing.

He needed a distraction, and he was out of sims credits.

He was in the elevator at Headquarters, heading back to his quarters. He stared at Carter's unchanging location on a tracepad, his feet carrying him mindlessly, when he found himself in front of a door that was not his own. Without hesitation, he knocked. It only took a few moments for it to open.

"Hey," he said.

"Hey. What are you doing here?"

"Can I come in?" said Robin.

Dark eyes roamed over his face for a few moments, head cocked to the side as though trying to decipher him. But eventually, Nayla Jackson smiled and stood aside to let him in, closing the door behind him.

CHAPTER NINETEEN

Wisdom

Yara and Ash waited in Yara's bedroom. It was nearly a quarter after midnight, and Robin had not yet joined them. Yara wondered idly if it had anything to do with how she had reacted to what he'd said to her in the sims and was about to suggest that he might not be coming when there was a knock on the door. Not waiting for Yara to open it, Robin came in, looking disheveled.

"Hey," he said to Ash, avoiding looking at Yara. "Sorry I'm late."

"No problem," said Ash, smiling. "We were just talking. Yara can't see anything. She kept trying to see where they were going, but no dice."

"No problem," said Robin, feeling around in his tunic for a moment, then pulling a pad out of a hidden pocket. "Tracepad. Called in a favor with a Tracker who gave me this, no questions asked. Provided C's tracker hasn't stopped transmitting, we should be able to monitor them from here. They haven't moved in a while, so that's probably their destination."

Yara ignored her racing heart and reached for the tracepad. Robin handed it to her and they all crowded around to look at it. Something tight in her chest eased at the sight of the little red dot on the map. Carter was alive. They were OK.

"Where is this?" she said.

"Near Kagel Canyon," said Robin, zooming out on the map. "It's north of here, quite a ways."

"Is there even a building here? Where is this? Are they in the woods?"

"There are some nice houses up there," said Ash. "Pretty secluded."

"Looks like we found their new base," said Robin. Yara's heart was still pounding, even as he moved away, leaving the tracepad in her hands. He still had not looked at her. Perhaps it was better that way. Give them both time to forget what he had said. "Now we just gotta sit back and wait for C to learn what they can and… come home."

Robin started to leave and Yara watched, open mouthed, incredulous. But she had no words to stop him. As much as she wanted to call out to him, to yell, he was gone with a murmured "good night."

Yara turned to look at Ash, who was very nonchalantly picking at her nails. A little *too* nonchalantly.

"What?" said Ash, not quite innocently, when she saw that Yara was looking at her with a raised eyebrow.

"You have something to say?"

"Who? Me?" said Ash, keeping up the feigned innocence as she looked around the room. Yara threw a pillow at her. Ash started laughing as she caught it and used it to sit on the floor against the wall. "What the hell was that?" she said, still laughing.

Despite herself, Yara felt the tension in her gut ease up a bit as she, too, dared to crack a smile. "The most awkward situation I've ever been in, that's what," she said.

"Let me guess," said Ash, twirling a piece of her hair between her fingers and watching it turn into flame. "He is allergic to tomatoes, and you made tomato muffins for him, without telling him what was in it."

Yara laughed.

"No wait!" said Ash, sitting forward. "He was doing naked yoga in his quarters, and you walked in on him! Ah, who am I kidding?" she continued, without letting Yara say anything. "If that had happened, you'd be too busy having sex in his bedroom."

Yara choked. "What?"

"Oh, come on. Do you think we're all blind?"

Yara gaped at Ash.

"Everyone in the Society has seen you guys. You were training together for half a year. Word is, Black even talked to C about it a few months ago."

"What?" Yara could feel her face burning.

"Yeah. Wanted to know if anything was happening between you two that hadn't been reported."

There were a lot of rules regarding Guardian relationships, not the least of which included no romantic attachments between Guardians and Wards.

Yara's jaw was still dropped as she scoffed in disbelief, unable to believe that anyone thought something was going on between her and Robin.

"Are you serious?" she said, her mouth very dry.

Ash nodded, watching flames dance around her folded legs.

"Wait wait wait," said Yara, shaking her head and hands, trying to clear the air. "Are you telling me… that everyone thought Robin and I were… together?"

Ash sighed and gave Yara a very exasperated look. "Yes, Yara. That's what I'm saying."

Yara frowned.

"But anyway," Ash continued, "what happened to change the chemistry? He was acting like you killed his sister."

"Does he have a sister?"

Ash shrugged, and Yara kicked herself inwardly that she knew so little about Robin whom, in many ways, she considered to be her best friend.

"So, what happened?"

"He…" she said, hesitating about whether or not she should tell Ash. Perhaps it was the kind of thing Robin would appreciate she kept secret. But if she couldn't talk to Robin, who else could she talk to besides Ash? She couldn't tell Carter, assuming they made it home. Carter was a stickler for the rules. They had been the one who warned Yara against a relationship with Erik in the first place. And Erik… Of course she couldn't tell Erik. Who knew what that might do to his friendship with Robin. What it might do to his relationship with *her*. Since Erik's reappearance, Ash had been the most supportive person in Yara's life. Ash hadn't hesitated to help when Yara wanted to inspect the old lab, had never presumed to hide information from her, and here she was, offering to talk about boys. Something Yara had never done before. It felt strangely… normal. Despite everything, it was, of all things, boy drama. And now she had a girlfriend to gossip with.

She took a deep breath. "He told me he was in love with me."

Ash raised her eyebrows. "And?"

"What do you mean, 'and?'"

"Did you really not see that coming?"

"I mean… no. No, I didn't."

"Really?" said Ash, getting up to join Yara on the bed.

"I'm not the kind of girl boys fall in love with. I'm the kind of girl they tease to get the attention of the girls they actually want to be with."

"Well, we both know that's not true," said Ash, rolling her eyes. "You've got two boys in love with you right now."

It was hard for Yara to believe. She had barely believed it when Erik had fallen for her. That someone as capable and smart and talented as Erik would want someone like her would had seemed unfathomable. Now Robin made even less sense. He was so relaxed and easy going and *cool*. In many ways, he was Yara's opposite. What on earth could he possibly see in her?

"I just don't get it," she said.

"Ugh, don't do this," said Ash.

"Don't do what?"

"Don't go fishing for compliments."

"Is that what I'm doing?" said Yara, legitimately confused. She hadn't meant to.

"You're smart, you're talented, you're cute, and you're funny when you want to be. Blah blah blah. Are we done with this now?" Ash spoke so quickly Yara didn't have time to interrupt. "I am so tired of women not seeing when they're amazing. You're amazing, and Robin knows it. Moving on."

Yara wrapped her arms around herself, trying not to contradict every compliment Ash had just given her. "Thank you," she said in a small voice. "But, why now? Why is he telling me this now? I mean, it's not like he didn't have opportunities before, you know," she said, starting to speak more quickly. "It's not like we haven't had the time. We were hanging out, training together every single day since this summer. I mean, he had a million opportunities to say something, and instead, he decides to do it after Erik comes back from the dead and while Carter is literally in the most dangerous place in the world." She inhaled deeply, out of breath, not realizing how much she had been holding on to. She looked at Ash, who was smiling sympathetically.

"He didn't really have a million opportunities to say something though, did he?" she said.

"What do you mean? We were together all the time—"

"But it wasn't about whether or not you were together," said Ash. "You weren't really *with* him all the time."

"What the hell is that supposed to mean?" said Yara, forcing a laugh to hide her discomfort.

"It means that you were broken. You both were. A lot happened last year, and it's not easy to come back from that. I mean, when do you really imagine would have been a good time for him to tell you?"

Yara opened her mouth to respond when she realized she didn't have an answer. "Yeah, but… this wasn't a good time either!"

"It's not always easy to hold on to stuff like that," said Ash simply. She looked at Yara for a while, smiling gently. "I remember once. Back when *I* was an initiate. There was this person in my class. Myra Stevens. Man, were they beautiful. A shape shifter, so I don't even know if that was the face they were born with or if they just made themself look like that. Either way, it was working for me." Ash laughed. "I had the biggest crush on them and wanted to say something but kept getting nervous that they would turn me down."

"You? Nervous?"

Ash shrugged. "I'm the worst with keeping secrets. My *own* secrets," she amended. "So naturally, I ended up blurting it out to them on the night before we tested. Talk about bad timing. They laughed and said they thought I hated them, that they had a crush on me, too." Ash looked into the distance, smiling serenely to herself before adding, "That was a good night."

"Is… is that the whole story?"

"Hmm?"

"How is that the same?"

"It isn't," said Ash. "Just that sometimes stuff comes out when you don't expect it to."

"What happened between you guys?"

"They transferred to Atlanta. They always said they wanted to end up at the Paris branch one day, so they were trying to inch closer to that side of the globe, I think."

"I'm sorry," said Yara.

"Don't be! We had a great fling. I have nothing but fond memories of my time with M. And I hope you won't let this get in the way of your friendship with R."

"Aren't you younger than me?" said Yara, feeling stupid.

Ash let out a bubbling laugh. "What does that have to do with anything?"

"Something about wisdom, I guess," said Yara, burying her face in her sheets. "Ugh! What am I supposed to do about this?"

"Uh… talk to him?" She said it like it was the most obvious thing in the world.

Yara shook her head.

"You're right," said Ash. "Don't talk to him. Let it fester and rot until you guys can't stand to be in the same room as each other."

Carter had expected the new Shadow Men base would be something more like the old lab. They were certainly not expecting anything like this: a run-down secluded mansion in the mountains an hour or so north of downtown.

The Shadow Men had all unloaded and occupied the house, leaving Carter on their own to deduce what they were supposed to do without being given specific instructions. Much to Carter's dismay, however, there was another Shadow Man identical to them waiting at the entrance to the decrepit house. And then another. The first had a simple "W" branded onto his neck, the second, "Os".

It was becoming harder for Carter to deny the clone theory. There didn't seem to be any other explanation for Kain's identical sets of Shadow Men.

Carter didn't want to stand too close to W and Os, lest someone notice that they were slightly smaller than the two real Shadow Men, but the two clones seemed to be waiting for Carter to join them. Trying to keep their face as bland as possible, Carter marched after them.

As much as the outside of the mansion didn't look like it would be used by Shadow Men, the inside was even further from what Carter expected. There were no high-tech equipment installations, no indications that it was used as anything other than sparse housing, and significantly fewer people than Carter would have guessed.

They were led toward a room filled with bunk beds on the ground floor where even more identical Shadow Men, all with different brands on their necks, sat in complete stillness.

It wasn't clear what exactly they were waiting for, but Carter followed suit, trying their best to imitate the stoicism and apathy exhibited by the rest of the Shadow Men. Yara was right. If the Shadow Men were clones, there was something exceptional about Erik. Not just the change in his appearance, but he was clearly a different breed from these mindless drones. The Erik who had come back to them was himself, with all the memories and personality of the man who had died a year prior. Erik couldn't be a clone if being a clone meant being dispassionate and empty.

It felt like hours before anything happened. Carter wanted to go home desperately, but they had barely learned anything, aside from the Shadow Men's location. While Carter was here, they had to collect as much intel as possible. Too much had been risked for this operation for them to go home with so little.

"Through here, sir," said an unfamiliar voice from down the hall.

A moment later, a slender blonde Shadow Man stepped into the room and moved aside to make space for people behind her.

Carter looked toward the door, following the lead of the other Shadow Men, but it was with some effort that they masked their fear and surprise at what they saw.

There were two people behind the blonde Shadow Man. One of them, Carter recognized instantly, their heart dropping into their stomach.

Ramsey Kain.

Just like Erik, miraculously back from the dead. Unlike his clones, he was fully realized, with the same manic gleam in his eyes that Carter remembered. Much to Carter's dismay, his gaze was focused solely on the shape shifter. Carter fought the urge to shuffle. It was as hard as convincing themself to take a deep breath underwater.

"Thank you, Astatine," Kain said to the blonde without taking his eyes off Carter. "Rhenium, is it?"

"Sir," said Carter.

Kain smirked, an eyebrow raised. "Welcome back. I look forward to your debriefing and hearing about where you've been all this time. Come look, my darling," said Kain, gesturing behind him.

It was the first time Carter had the chance to see the second person who had entered the room. She came forward to stand next to Kain. A beautiful woman with the same vacant eyes as the Shadow Men. Another clone then. But she was not a Shadow Man. At least not in the same way that the rest of them were. She didn't wear the crimson uniform and was being treated by Kain with more reverence than he had ever shown any of his other cronies.

She looked down her curved nose at Carter with complete indifference and said nothing.

Kain turned his eyes from Carter and stared at her hungrily. "What do you think, Zenobia?" he said.

Zenobia... It couldn't be. Could it? Zenobia Varma, the deceased Head Researcher killed by Kain years and years ago. But Ash was right. "Dead" had different rules under Kain. If Kain was back, if Erik was back, why not Zenobia, too? The rumor had been that Kain had been in love with her when they'd both been working at the Society.

That he had killed her in a jealous rage when she spurned his advances. But if he could somehow bring people back from the dead, why then did she have the same vacuity as the Shadow Men? Why was she not more like the resurrected Erik or Kain?

After a moment, Zenobia turned to look at Kain. She opened her mouth to speak but he put one of his long fingers up to her mouth, silencing her.

"Not here, my love," he said. Kain gave Carter another appraising look, something sinister in his smile. "Come, *Rhenium*." He roughly grabbed Zenobia by the arm and led her out of the room.

Carter followed Kain and Zenobia as steadily as they could, hoping that their pounding heart wasn't giving them away.

Kain led them down a narrow set of stairs into the basement. The door at the bottom of the stairs was the only thing that resembled anything Carter had expected to find. It was a reinforced metal door with an electronic lock. Carter faltered for a moment, wondering what awaited them behind the door. Were they letting themself be walked directly into a prison? Did Kain know they were an imposter?

Kain stood aside and gestured for Zenobia to unlock the door. "If you would, darling."

Carter watched as she placed her hand on a pad by the door. A small clicking came from the pad, and then a loud unbolting as the door unlocked. Evidently, Zenobia Varma was the only one with a key to the basement.

Carter had less than a second to decide what to do. Whatever was inside the basement was the most valuable thing Kain held in his new base. Carter was desperate to know what was inside. But it was not without risk. If Zenobia was the only way in or out, Carter could be taking the chance that they would never get out, never be able to recount any of this to the Society. On the other hand, if they turned and ran, there was a possibility that they wouldn't make it out before being recaptured, guaranteeing that they were found out.

They couldn't turn around now. There was a chance they could still escape even if they followed Kain into this mysterious locked room. And at the very least, their tracking implant was still active. Robin would come after them if they weren't back before a certain time.

So when Kain stepped aside to let Carter through the door, they went in without looking back.

It was a full day later when Robin was woken up in the small hours of the morning by the sound of an insistent and steady knocking on his door.

Carter was standing in the doorway, hunched over, wearing nothing but the torn and dirtied pants of a Shadow Man and colored contacts.

"A Necromancer," they said, panting. "He has a Necromancer."

Robin's eyes raked over Carter's anguished face. "What are you talking about?"

"He's back," said Carter. "Kain's back."

CHAPTER TWENTY

Clones

Robin let Carter change into some of his clothes as he paced wildly in his room. They had summoned Ash to join them, and she was now sitting with her legs crossed in the armchair of the living area of Robin's quarters.

"A Necromancer," said Robin. "How is this even possible..."

"This is like... the coolest thing," said Ash, smiling. "I mean, a *Necromancer*. With a capital *N*."

Carter couldn't seem to catch their breath. Once dressed, they sat on Robin's bed and pinched the colored contacts out before rubbing their eyes. They'd had to leave their glasses behind during the mission.

"You can watch the footage," they said, extending the contacts on the tips of their fingers toward Robin.

Robin carefully took the small discs and placed them on the reader he had "borrowed" from the Eyes for just this purpose. The contacts Carter wore had two purposes: hide their amber eyes and record everything they saw. Robin pulled up the footage and the three of them huddled around his tablet to sort through everything the optic had chronicled.

"Skip through all this," said Carter, and Robin fast forwarded through hours of footage, starting with Carter destroying the art installations at the library, getting arrested and detained by the civilian police, their rescue at the hands of the Shadow Men, and the long drive in the back of the van.

"The camera loves you," said Ash.

"I'm not in it," said Carter.

"Still."

Carter ignored this and pointed at the screen. "He's got a forcefield around the house. You can see they turned it off for us here."

"Huh," said Robin.

"How does a biologist know how to erect a forcefield?" said Ash.

"Exactly what I was going to ask," Robin seconded.

"It makes sense he would want one," said Carter. "Makes it a hell of a lot harder to get in or out."

"Great," said Robin.

"This really doesn't look like… Kain," said Ash.

"What do you mean?" said Robin.

"I mean, he's got a vibe, you know?" she continued. "Like, mad scientist vibe. This is different. More like a Dracula aesthetic."

"I had the same thought," said Carter.

"You did?" said Robin.

"In so many words, yes," said Carter.

"It looks temporary," said Ash. "There's no way this is where Kain is planning to stay long term. There's not even that much equipment. Way less than what Yara described in her vision."

"That could pose a problem," said Robin. "If you're right, it means we have to act fast, or we could lose our chance to do anything before he relocates and we have to start from scratch."

"There," said Carter.

Robin let the video play at normal speed and saw a blonde Shadow Man, Kain, and a dark woman approach the camera. They were looking directly at the lens, having been staring at Carter's eyes at the time.

"Jesus," said Robin. "This is off-putting."

"No kidding," said Carter. "There." They pointed at the screen, and Robin paused it. "That's her. The Necromancer."

Robin tilted his head.

Once again, Ash said what he was thinking before he had the chance. "She looks familiar."

"She should," said Carter. "That's Zenobia Varma."

"The Researcher?" said Robin.

Carter nodded.

"The dead one?" said Ash.

"Yes."

Robin sagged forward and cursed. "How… I mean, what—"

"Here's what I figure. He clones people for his Shadow Men. But then the Necromancer does…" Carter trailed off, gesturing vaguely in front of them. "You know."

"No," said Ash. "We don't."

"He uses the Necromancer to bring people back, I guess. He's got clones and he's got—what would we call them? Zombies? What do you call someone who's been resurrected?"

"I like 'zombie,'" said Ash.

Robin waved the words away. "This makes no sense. How could he have brought Erik back from the dead when his body was cremated? When *Kain's* body was burned? And who even knows what happened to Varma!"

"Cremated, too, probably," said Ash.

"Needless to say, there's a lot we still don't know. But I'm guessing —"

Ash cut Carter off. "Obviously, Kain and Erik both started out as clones. Then the Necromancer does her thing and brings them back."

"Well, yes. That's my guess. Kain and Erik are different from the rest of the Shadow Men. It's clear he can still make more. Clones, I mean. So they must have moved the lab. The basement is where they set everything up." Carter took control of the reader and fast-forwarded the footage until it showed the basement where Kain had led them. "He uses Zenobia's blood to open the biometric lock to get inside." They watched the recording of the door unlocking. As the footage continued into the new lab, Carter said, "There's all this equipment there."

Carter froze the footage again so Robin and Ash could see the pods in the basement.

"That looks just like what Yara described from her vision," said Ash.

"I didn't get a very close look at all of this," said Carter. "I didn't want them to know I wasn't a Shadow Man, so it limited how much I could investigate. But this is evidently where he's growing his Shadow Men. Where the Necromancer works. She did something to me here…"

Robin watched with horror as Zenobia Varma approached the camera and raised her hands toward it. There was a faint blue glow outside of view.

"What is she doing?" Ash asked.

"I'm not sure."

"Could they have been…" Robin trailed off, unsure how to ask if Carter had been somehow altered or affected or tracked by whatever the Necromancer had done to them.

Carter seemed to know what he meant. "Whatever it was, it didn't feel like anything. I feel completely normal. Kain yammered on for a few minutes, called her his Necromancer, and then they dismissed me. I didn't hang around after this. I didn't want to risk getting caught, so I came back as soon as I was left alone."

Robin stared at the paused tape, considering. "We have to tell Black," he said eventually, running both of his hands through his hair, staring up at the ceiling. "About E. About all of it. We have to tell her. This is a big deal. We can't keep this from the Society anymore. I mean… This is what Yara wanted to find out, right? She wanted to find out what happened to E. Well, now we know."

"Not exactly," said Carter.

"What do you mean? Kain has a Necromancer. That's how E's back."

"R," said Carter, standing up and facing Robin head on. "The cloning explains why there's a body that looks and sounds like E. But it doesn't explain why they let him go, why they fully resurrected him, much less about the earthquake, the fugue state, or *why* they'd want to do all this in the first place."

Robin swore under his breath. "This is insane."

"So," said Ash, looking between the two of them. "Who wants to be the one who tells Yara that we want to go to Black and tell her we broke every rule in the Society?"

"Ah. That." said Robin. Ash was smiling at him, and there was a little too much knowing in that smile.

Carter raised an eyebrow at them both. "What's going on?"

Robin met Carter's eyes, trying to appear innocent. "Huh?"

"What are you not telling me, R?"

"Nothing."

The shape shifter was scrutinizing Robin to a point of discomfort, giving him the feeling of having his mind read. Ash had gone back to her armchair and was still grinning at Robin. He frowned at her. "What?"

"I didn't say anything," she said innocently.

"What's going on?" Carter repeated, more forcefully this time.

Ash and Robin stared at each other. Did she know?

"You didn't…" said Carter.

"No! Of course not! Wait…" said Robin, turning to Carter. "What do you think I did?"

"You told Yara."

"I would never."

"You didn't tell her you're in love with her?"

"Oh, that. Well, yes."

Ash cackled from her seat.

"Would you stop?" Robin threw in her direction. She did not stop.

"R!" said Carter.

"I know! I know," said Robin, tugging at the hem of his tunic.

"I guess my offer of turning into Yara for therapeutic purposes wasn't appealing enough?"

"Don't take this the wrong way, C, but getting turned down by a tall Yara with yellow eyes isn't exactly my idea of a fun evening."

"Oh, I would have paid to watch that," said Ash.

Robin chuckled despite himself.

"You knew about this?" Carter asked Ash.

"Yara told me," said Ash.

"She did?" said Robin, his stomach clenching.

"No need to be embarrassed, R," said Ash, still looking a little more cheerful than the situation called for.

"Yeah, sure. Nothing embarrassing about getting shot down by someone you're hopelessly in love with then having her talk about it behind your back with your coworker."

"Oh, c'mon. It's not like I didn't already know how you felt."

"You did?"

"Was it supposed to be a secret?" said Ash.

"Well, yeah, kinda," said Robin. "I thought I did a good job hiding it. Didn't I?" He looked to Carter for confirmation.

Carter sealed their lips and looked away.

"Great," said Robin.

"Whatever it's worth, I'm pretty sure the shoots don't know or anything like that," said Ash. "And Yara certainly didn't," she added, laughing.

After a moment, Carter said, "What did she say?"

"She yelled at me and stormed away," said Robin.

"Not exactly the ideal reaction," said Carter.

Robin snorted. "Not exactly, no."

"What about E?"

Robin sighed. "I haven't seen him." Carter was silent and Robin tried to laugh. "Now's not really the time for us to be thinking about this, anyway," he said. "How did you get out?"

"Mole," said Carter. "Dug my way out under the forcefield."

"Ha. Ironic," said Ash.

"Do you think it'll arouse any suspicion?" said Robin. "Anything we need to worry about?"

"Possibly," said Carter. "There were a lot of them, though. Whatever model I was imitating, they kept calling me Rhenium. I guess that was the name of the one we captured last year who tried to apprehend Yara on the bus. Remember?"

Robin nodded.

"I saw a few more who looked just like me, only with different brands on their necks. I think that's how they tell the different ones apart. It was hard to get a very good look at things. I had to keep my head forward. But they also called me a… Transition. Whatever that means."

"Rhenium," said Robin, thinking. "Transition… Rhenium is an element. On the periodic table." He hadn't studied science in a long time, but back in high school before he dropped out and joined the Society, chemistry had been his strongest subject.

"All of the clones had names like that," said Carter. "Lithium, Magnesium, Silicon. There was one who looked just like me. He had a big W branded onto his neck. Another one had a big O and a small S. They called him Osmund or something."

"Osmium?"

"Maybe," said Carter. "I don't remember them all."

"Yeah. Those are all elements."

"And Transition?"

"I can't be sure without checking, but… I think maybe that's a reference to Transition metals."

"So they clone slaves, basically," said Ash, back to her usual habit of twirling a flame around her fingers, "and name them after elements."

Robin did a quick search on his tablet for the periodic table of elements. "Yep," he said. "Rhenium is a Transition metal. So is Osmium. And Tungsten. That's the W. And those two were identical to you?" he asked Carter.

They nodded.

"So they name them by category, then," said Robin, feeling the excitement that accompanied a new discovery. "All the Transition metals come from the same batch. Identical. They're all based on the same… original… body? Is that the right terminology?" He chanced a nervous laugh, feeling shaky.

"Right," said Carter. "But this also begs the question, how many

Kains are there?"

"Or how many Eriks?" said Ash.

The smile slid off Robin's face as this prospect hit him. "Oh shit."

"Yes," said Carter. They were all thinking the same thing, that as many questions as they had answered, a million more had come up. "'Oh shit' is right."

The top floor was off limits to his Shadow Men. It was to be Kain's only refuge with his beloved Necromancer.

She sat next to him now, looking out the window at the faint shimmer of the forcefield erected around the mansion, her hand limp in his. He stroked her fingers, tracing the curve of her nails and tugging at the folds of skin on each knuckle. She did not react when he accidentally tore the skin, drawing a small drop of blood. It healed within seconds, leaving only a trace of red, which he wiped away.

He gazed at her, seeing only her profile, before following her gaze out the window.

Kain smiled.

Everything was going according to plan.

Yara was woken up by her three Guardians who all came to fill her in on what Carter had learned.

She sat in silence, letting all the information get spewed at her by Carter while Ash lay akimbo on the floor and Robin sat in the chair by the door, watching the shape shifter speak and chancing a few glances in her direction. She had not spoken to Robin since he had left Carter's tracepad with her twenty-nine hours ago.

"A Necromancer," she rasped. "And Kain is back."

Carter nodded.

"And Erik..."

No one spoke. No one moved. They didn't even breathe.

"So I was right," Yara said eventually. "I saw the past. I saw them growing..." She couldn't finish the thought. *Growing Erik.* Up until now she thought perhaps there was a chance she'd been wrong, but it was the only thing that made any kind of sense.

"But we still don't know how he's different. Obviously he's not an exact clone," said Carter. They weren't wearing their glasses, and it made their face look strangely unfamiliar. "Red, is there any way you can try to find that vision again? Maybe... identify what they did to bring him back the way he was?"

"I have no clue." This power was still so new, she had no idea what the rules were. She still didn't know why she hadn't been able to see Carter when they had been a Shadow Man. Anything after they got broken out of jail was completely blank.

"Can you try to see it again?" said Ash.

But Yara wasn't listening. She was already closing her eyes and trying to find the same vision of Erik in the pod, sinking into her mind.

"Are we sure this is safe?" said Robin's voice from very far away. "Last time she had that vision, she ended up in medical."

Yara opened her eyes, returning to her body and her eyes locked onto Robin's. He held her gaze for a few tense moments before she said, "I know my limits," and looked away. She immediately hated herself for saying it. Throwing fuel on the flames, making things worse. She wanted to apologize, but before she could work up the strength to form the words, Carter spoke.

"They did something to me when they broke me out. Injected me with something."

"What?" said Robin, Yara, and Ash together. Yara locked eyes with Robin again for a moment, and she opened her mouth but her unspoken apology to Robin died before it reached her lips when Carter spoke again.

"I forgot about it until now because it didn't seem like it did anything, but I just remembered. Maybe..."

"Maybe what?" said Robin, ignoring Yara.

"A tracker?" said Ash.

"But they wouldn't need to track them, not if they believed Carter was a Shadow Man," said Robin.

"Not even if they didn't," said Yara. "They know where Headquarters is. No need to track them."

"Not a tracker, but," said Carter, "they know Yara can see into the future. I can't imagine Kain would be happy that she could see his every move before he made it. So maybe he's found a way to block it. To block you."

Yara frowned. "Could he do that?"

"Who knows," said Carter.

"I mean, he can make clones, he can come back from the dead," said Ash. "Who's to say he couldn't inhibit you from seeing the future, too?"

Carter actually made a strangled sound of frustration. "Try to look at my future," they said to Yara.

She closed her eyes again, but met that same wall as before when she tried to look into Carter's future. "I can't."

"Look at mine," said Robin. He shifted uneasily, but looked resolved.

Yara braced herself, but did as he asked. Through the familiar fog she saw Robin knocking on a door in the Guardian quarters. Yara didn't recognize where it was, exactly, and no one answered the door. But as he started walking away, he was stopped by someone approaching from behind him. He turned to greet them and Yara was able to discern a face out of the mist. Nayla.

Yara snapped her eyes open.

"Well?" asked Carter.

"Yeah, uh," Yara stammered. "It worked. I can see it."

"Still so cool," said Ash quietly.

"Nothing too bad, I hope," said Robin with a nervous laugh.

"Nope," said Yara shortly, offering nothing more.

"That supports my theory, then," said Carter.

"How long do we think it lasts?" said Robin.

"Yara can keep checking for the next few hours," said Ash. "Give us an idea if it's permanent or if it will wear off."

Yara nodded, hardly noticing what she was agreeing to.

"If it's permanent they might have done it to E, too," said Robin. "Can you see into his future?"

"She already saw his past," said Carter.

"But Kain doesn't know she can see the past, only the future," said Ash. "Maybe he's only made a block for seeing *forward* in time."

"Yara, we can't keep this to ourselves," said Carter, "We need the help of the full Society behind us."

"And what is Black going to say when she finds out that you've been gone for two days, galavanting as a Shadow Man?" said Yara. Carter furrowed their brow, and Yara looked frantically between Ash and Robin. "You're not on their side here, are you?"

"Listen, kid," said Robin, avoiding her eyes, "this is starting to get too big for just us."

"If we tell Black that you can see into the past," said Carter, "it means we can tell her what we know without telling her that I went undercover without permission."

Yara looked to Ash for support. Ash was staring at the ceiling. She didn't speak.

"Yara," said Carter, "think about how much more serious this is than we thought."

"We can't do this without the help of the Society," said Robin.

"Yes, we can!" said Yara stubbornly.

"No! We can't!" said Robin, his blue eyes flashing dangerously. He looked away and took several deep breaths. "Listen," he said, and this time when he spoke, his voice was much quieter. "The Society is designed to handle these kinds of situations. They are *equipped* for it. And *staffed* for it. This is beyond just finding out what happened to Erik, Yara. Kain is back. They're cloning Shadow Men, and they're going to come back for you."

"You don't know that."

"We know that Kain spent countless resources to capture you and the hyden last year to steal your powers. We know that his Shadow Men brought him back, and the only reason they would do that is for him to continue his work! Especially now that he knows he can take your powers! For fuck's sake, Yara! He probably only brought Erik back to get closer to *you!*"

The words chilled Yara's blood. Ash sat up straight as Robin snapped his mouth shut and looked at Carter, who looked equally stunned. With those words, the four of them had come to a simultaneous realization.

Robin was right. Erik's return could only mean one thing: he was being used to infiltrate the Society.

"Shit," said Carter. They turned to run down the hall, shouting at Robin and Ash over their shoulder, "Stay with her!"

Robin, who was halfway down the hall himself, stopped at Carter's words and looked back at Yara, but she was already running in the opposite direction.

"Yara!" he called after her.

Ash echoed him from Yara's quarters.

But Yara didn't listen. She didn't stop. She knew where Carter was going. They were going to see Black. She wanted to stop them, but she knew she couldn't outrun the shape shifter. Furthermore, she knew deep down that they were right.

For now, she didn't care about that. In that moment, all she cared about was getting to Erik.

CHAPTER TWENTY-ONE

Betrayal

Yara's mind was racing as she sprinted to the medical ward. She was vaguely aware of Ash on her heels. Yara was still wearing her pajamas, a faded tee and striped pants so slouchy that she had to hoist them up as she ran to avoid tripping over them with her bare feet.

When she burst through the door to the room where Erik was held, he jolted awake. Yara let out a strangled cry at the sight of him. He was strapped to the table, and she had a sudden image of herself in the same position back in Kain's laboratory.

"What? What?" he said, blinking his eyes open and looking around the room. "Yara? What time is it? A?" he said, noticing Ash. "What's wrong?" He tried to get to Yara and was reminded by the restraints that he couldn't move.

Without hesitation, she rushed to him and started to unbuckle them. Unlike the metal claws that had held her down at the old lab, these were easy to remove. At least, they would have been had her hands not been shaking. Ash didn't waste any time and came to help Yara.

"We have to get out of here," said Yara, her voice trembling just as much as her hands.

"Yara, what the hell is going on?" They finished unstrapping his chest and arms and he sat up to help them with the ones holding his legs.

"What did they do to you?" said Yara, tears streaming down her face. Not tears of sadness. She was angry. Desperate. Anxious.

"Is it Shadow Men? Are they here?"

Yara shook her head. "You need to come with me," she said. The straps were finally undone, and she pulled Erik off the table. He stumbled slightly but held onto her hand firmly.

"Where is everyone?"

"Asleep," she said.

"Yara! Stop," said Erik. He tightened his grip on her hand and pulled her back, preventing her from storming back out of the room with him. She spun around to look at him. His green eyes were wide as they searched her face. "You need to tell me what's going on."

"Carter… They're going to tell Black."

"Tell her what?"

"That you're a clone," said Ash. Unlike Yara, she was a picture of calm. "And that Kain is alive, and—"

Erik's face paled. "What?" he said. He looked from Ash to Yara. "A clone?"

Yara grabbed his face and held it, looking into his eyes. "Yes, but it doesn't matter. You're still you. You're alive and you're here and nothing else matters."

Erik fell backward, ripping his face out of her hands.

"Please, Erik," she said, moving toward him, but he held a hand out to stop her. She stopped, and it was agony to be apart from him, to see him in such pain and not be able to touch him, to hold him, help him, fix him. "Please, we have to go now. They're going to tell her, and she's going to take you away from me."

Erik didn't seem to hear her. He had collapsed onto a rolling stool, his skin as white as his hair. His hands had balled up into fists. There was a distant sound, a rumble in the distance.

"Erik?" said Yara.

He didn't respond. It looked like he was fighting something, his eyes distant, his body taught.

"Please…" said Yara one last time.

The floor beneath her feet shook. She and Ash fell sideways, off balance from the small quake.

"What was that?" said Ash, sounding concerned for the first time since Yara had known her. "What the—"

Yara followed Ash's gaze and saw that branches had sprung from Erik, wrapping themselves around the stool he was sitting on.

Before Yara could speak, the door behind her opened and Black's voice filled the room.

"Am I correct in assuming that was you, Mr. Carpenter?"

If Erik heard her, he showed no signs of it.

"And Ms. Rivers." She turned to Yara. "Why am I not surprised to find you here?"

Yara slowly turned to face the assembly. Bora Black was standing in the doorway, plumes of darkness peeling away from her in her silent fury. Her obsidian eyes were boring into Yara. It was hard not to shrink from such anger. Yara was trapped, standing alone in the middle of the room.

Behind Black were Robin, Carter, and Glover, who looked like he had just been woken up. How her Guardians had managed to get Black and Glover up to speed, as well as getting them down here so quickly, Yara didn't know. She supposed it didn't matter.

"Ms. Silino, however, you are a surprise." Black's eyes flashed at Ash. She turned back to Yara. "I see two possible reasons why you are here, Ms. Rivers. One of these reasons is that, despite your training and experience with us, you've failed to understand the chain of command here at the White Mask Society. That you've decided that more important than our cardinal directive of maintaining a peaceful coexistence between humans and Deviants, you'd rather go behind our backs to save one person who poses a significant threat to that directive. Or," she continued, "perhaps you do in fact understand all that and have decided that your judgement is superior to the system we have been successfully implementing for centuries."

Yara's face reddened with anger and embarrassment.

"Which of these two reasons is it going to be, Ms. Rivers?"

"What are you going to do to him?" said Yara.

"I'm afraid that is no longer your concern," said Black. "You are hereby suspended from field duty, and grounded from the Guardian division until they can determine if they want to keep you on their team at all."

A lead weight sank to the bottom of Yara's gut at these words. It was not her suspension that affected her as much as not knowing what was going to happen to Erik. If she was ever going to be allowed to see him again. Clone or no, it *was* him. Miraculously, they had been given a second chance at being together, and it was all going to be ruined because of the woman standing in front of her.

"Ms. Silino, you'll come see me privately concerning *your* punishment."

Ash hung her head.

"It wasn't Ash's fault. It was mine," said Yara, trying to at least spare Ash from being penalized for Yara's actions.

"That's enough from you, Ms. Rivers," said Black.

Yara backed up toward Erik. He was still immobile from the shock of hearing what he was. Yara couldn't even be sure that he was aware of what was going on.

"Mr. Green, please escort your Ward back to her quarters."

Robin hesitated for a split second. For a few short moments, Yara wasn't sure that he would obey. Maybe he would stay on her side, he would support her, even after his blatant betrayal of her trust by going to Black with this information.

But then he took a step toward her.

"Robin..." she pled.

"I'm sorry," he said, holding out his hand. "Please just... don't make this any harder."

Thoughts were flying through her mind. She tried sinking into her mind, looking forward in time, just a little, trying to keep one eye on the present, but nothing came to her. Focus was impossible, her mind too frantic. And there was no future that she could see, because she didn't know what she was going to do. Everything was uncertain.

"Robin," she said again, buying time as she backed into Erik, still feeling lost.

His blue eyes were wracked with guilt, but he kept walking toward her. Before she knew it, his hand was on her arm and he was pulling her away. She could not tear her gaze away from his face. She couldn't believe he was doing this. He had sentenced Erik. Who knew what they would do to him? Would they let him stay? Would they even consider him a human, give him the same rights he deserved, knowing he had been grown in a lab?

Her feet moved without thinking as Robin took her back to her quarters in complete silence. The soft glow of lights illuminating the halls at night, which had often felt romantic and mysterious, now felt empty and threatening. He didn't open the door to her room, instead, waiting for Yara to do it herself.

She didn't want to go in. Wondered if she just stood in the hall if he would eventually leave and she could go back after Erik. But Robin waited. Waited for her to close herself in like a prisoner. She was trembling from head to toe. There were so many things she wanted to say to him. She wanted to yell at him for his blind obedience. She wanted to pound against him for having sold her and Erik out to Black. She wanted to refuse to go into her room like a complacent child being punished for drawing on the sofa.

But no words found her. Her throat was closed. She barely had enough breath to inhale, let alone speak.

"Please, Yara," said Robin in a quiet voice.

Still, she did not move. She could not. Her hands felt impossibly heavy, the doorknob unreachably far.

Eventually, Robin leaned around her to open the door. The lights were still on in her quarters. Yara had not bothered to turn them off in her hurry to run to Erik.

Her eyes were unfocused, and she stayed stock still.

"Yara," said Robin, and his voice broke.

She did not look at him, but suddenly, his face was in front of hers, looking desperate, and his hands were painfully gripping her shoulders.

"Please don't hate me," he said.

She twitched her gaze to meet his eyes, and still said nothing.

"I don't have any choice," he said.

Lies. Empty words. He had a choice. They all did. And his choices had led them here, with Erik's future uncertain and her place with the Society in limbo.

"Can you at least say something?" His eyes were laced with molten silver as tears threatened to fall down his face.

Yara clenched her teeth, and pushed past him, walking into her room and closing the door behind her, locking herself in, locking Robin out.

The spy had never walked toward the mansion which held the Necromancer with such high spirits. It was certainly not the prospect of facing those dead eyes that left the spy feeling sanguine, but things had been going in the direction they wanted. If all continued the way it was headed, these horrible visits soon would no longer be required.

Through the forcefield, up the winding gravel path, past the brick pillars, through the enormous double doors held open by Shadow Men, the spy made the familiar journey up to the room where the Necromancer waited. But the room was empty.

Frowning, the spy looked at their ConvOrb to confirm that this was the right day and the right time. Indeed it was. Yet still, no Necromancer awaiting a report.

The spy poked their head around the door and looked down either end of the hall, too wary to call out. It was unlikely that the Necromancer had forgotten their meeting. The spy sat down in a moth-eaten chair by the dusty window, careful not to make themself too comfortable, not in the least due to the questionable condition of the seat.

They waited for what felt like a long time, silent, ears straining to pick up any sounds or hints of life in the mansion beyond. Aside from the occasional Shadow Man hulking around downstairs, there was nothing.

Just as they started to wonder if it wouldn't be better to simply leave a message with a Shadow Man, someone moved in the doorway.

"It has been a while," said the enormous silhouette framed in the entrance. He took a few steps closer and the spy recognized him immediately.

"Mr. Kain. Hello."

"Oh please. I think we can forgo the formalities. Why don't you call me Ramsey."

The spy nodded but did not speak. Perhaps Kain felt formalities were unnecessary, but calling him "Ramsey" felt like a level of familiarity that the spy was simply not comfortable with.

"The Necromancer has sent me here in her stead. She is otherwise… preoccupied."

A chill ran down the spy's spine, but they focused on remaining as still as possible.

"Well?" said Kain. "Proceed."

"They… know," said the spy, trying to collect their thoughts in the aftermath of such a shock at seeing Kain standing before them. "They know about the cloning."

Something flashed in Kain's murky green eyes. "The shifter?"

"Yes. Sent in as a Shadow Man. They know about the Necromancer, too."

Kain's jaw tightened and he forced his mouth into a broad smile that did not reach his wide eyes. "Fortunately for you, I immediately identified them. What I'd like to know is why I was not alerted ahead of time that this would be happening."

The spy swallowed their fear. "They went rogue. It was done without the Society's permission or knowledge."

"What are they doing with the nymph now they know he's a clone?"

"Right now, he's in solitary confinement over in Research. They're trying to determine—"

"And you say he's already displayed some of his abilities."

The spy nodded.

"Do they know the details of that?"

"No, sir."

Kain's nostrils flared as his eyes glazed over, staring in the direction of the window over their shoulder. Slowly, he brought his gaze back to the spy. "We must be warned if anything like this happens again."

The spy did not respond, having no answer to give. They waited for Kain to speak again.

"Do what must be done to ensure that nothing else happens without my knowledge. I don't like being caught off guard."

The spy nodded.

Kain inspected them, searching for a lie. "Very well. You're dismissed."

The spy hurried out of the room, sidling past Kain, down to the front door, trying to walk as calmly as possible, head held high. When they chanced a glance back at the house, Kain was still standing in the window, watching.

CHAPTER TWENTY-TWO

Growing

For the tenth day in a row, Robin woke up sore.

Erik was now being held in a room in the Research and Medical wing that was under 24-hour surveillance by two Guardians from Yara's class. Black, along with every member of the White Mask Society who was Level 3 or up, had determined that it was highly likely that Erik had been cloned with the intent of using him to gain information about the Society and, more specifically, about Yara.

Robin secretly agreed, which was why he had gone through with enforcing Yara's suspension nearly two weeks ago. She had not spoken to him, or even agreed to be in the same room as him, since then. Carter had not had any more luck than Robin. This meant that Ash had been forced to be on duty pretty much nonstop since then because Yara simply refused to speak to or address either Robin or Carter.

While over the last year, Robin had been able to work the occasional low-profile assignment to fill his time, Yara's case and the threat to the hyden had been elevated due to Erik and Kain's return. As a result, Robin had been unable to take on any other assignments. Combined with daily calls from his mother begging him to leave the Society and join his father's firm, Robin was desperate for distractions. So he spent his hours taking out his frustration either in the sims against the economic elite of Sherwood Forest or in the rec room against every surface imaginable, or else with Nayla.

After Yara's less-than-ideal response to him telling her that he loved her, Robin had returned to his old flame, seeking comfort in the familiar. And Nayla had been receptive to him. Consoling.

Affectionate.

His feet carried him to her quarters nearly every night, knowing that she wouldn't ask questions, craving the closeness she offered him.

He hadn't told Carter that a relationship with Nayla was starting to redevelop. It wasn't that he wanted it kept secret—at least not consciously—but there was a part of him that knew Carter wouldn't be very impressed to hear that Robin's first impulse after being turned down by Yara was to run back to his ex-paramour. There was a heavy guilt in Robin's gut as he lay in Nayla's bed, the sound of her soft breathing next to him as she slept. Guilt for being with Nayla when his heart and his mind wanted to be somewhere else. Guilt for lying to Carter. Most of all, guilt when he thought back to Yara's face when he had come with Black for Erik. How she had refused to look at him, speak to him, how he hadn't even seen Erik since it all happened.

The next morning he would punch the bag harder. Then wake up even more sore than he was before.

As a result, he wound up in medical twice with strained muscles. Both times, Chun, Frankie's Second, had taken care of him. And both times, Robin had casually attempted to learn information about Erik. To no avail. Apparently, his case was now confidential and above Robin's pay grade.

Wanting to share his frustration with Carter, Robin went looking in the library, where the shape shifter had been spending most of their time.

"Still here?" said Robin in a hushed voice, weaving his way around the bookshelves to where they were sitting.

Carter looked up just long enough to see that it was Robin approaching and turned back to the books in front of them.

Robin took a seat at the same table and sighed heavily. Carter did not look up, evidently engrossed in whatever it was they were reading. Robin took a peek at the books and raised an eyebrow.

"Still reading up on the Omega Project, huh?" he said.

Carter grunted, their glasses so far down their nose they were in danger of sliding off.

Robin collapsed on the table. He had sought out Carter as an alternative to finding Nayla, but Carter did not seem interested in offering him any satisfactory distractions. Robin slid his hands over the table and placed them on the book, ruffling the pages.

"Will you cut it out?"

Robin looked up to see Carter's annoyed face, trying to pull the book out of Robin's reach. "C'mon, I'm bored."

"Go back to the simulator, then."

"I've beaten all the games," said Robin. "And I'm out of credits. Can I have some of yours?"

"No."

"So I'm back to you for entertainment," said Robin.

"Then call your mother."

"Is that a joke? Because if it is, it's not funny."

Carter was one of the few people who knew about Robin's family, but they didn't respond to Robin's jab, already re-immersed in the text.

"Whatcha readin'?"

"You already know. I'm reading about the Omega Project."

"Why?"

Carter put the book down with an exasperated sigh and looked at Robin, pushing their glasses up the bridge of their nose. "What do you want, R?"

"There's nothing for us to do. Our Ward won't let us near her, and Black won't give us any other assignments because we're supposed to be focusing on—" He stopped himself right before saying Yara's name, unsure that he could get his mouth around it. "I honestly can't believe you've managed to keep yourself busy all this time."

"You could read, too," said Carter, looking slightly amused, if a bit tired. Their eyes were rimmed with red and their skin was papery.

"What are you even reading about the Omega Project for?"

"I feel like there's something useful that we missed."

"Like what?"

Carter shook their head with an exhausted sigh. "I don't know. If only we knew… what Kain and Varma were studying. The research that got lost."

"You think it's connected?" said Robin, pulling Carter's book toward him and staring at the pages.

"I don't see how it couldn't be," said Carter. "Why would Kain have taken it when he left? It could provide answers about Erik's new… abilities."

Robin frowned. He had honestly never given much thought to Kain's time at the Society. It was easy to forget that such a maniac had ever walked within those walls. "Is there any indication about what research he took?"

"No. Nothing."

"Hey," said Robin, a thought just occurring to him. "Has anyone told Janya Varma that her mother has been cloned and brought back from the dead?"

Carter looked up for a moment, thinking. "Good question. You should go find her Guardians and ask them."

"You trying to get rid of me?"

"Don't be silly."

"Well that wasn't an answer."

"I'm just trying to figure out what our plan has to be," said Carter. "I keep thinking about what you and Ash said. That the house doesn't really feel like Kain."

"Why is that important right now?"

"Well, it's been almost two weeks, and you're both right. It doesn't feel like a permanent installation. I'm worried he's going to relocate his entire operation, and we'll lose any headway we have."

"What are you saying?"

Carter chewed on their lip.

Robin knew that look. "What?" he said.

Carter averted their gaze, reinforcing Robin's hunch that Carter was forming a dangerous thought.

"C..." said Robin.

Carter slowly raised their eyes to look at him.

"Oh no..." he said, shaking his head.

"We don't have many good options."

"Sending in a different team might be a good place to start," said Robin.

"I'm the only one who's been there. I know the layout."

"That's what the optic is for. You can show them the tape."

"It's not the same, and you know it," said Carter.

"Have you suggested this to Black already?"

Carter shook their head. "I was going to wait until I had a full plan. Then take it to Trumbull first."

"They won't let us do it," said Robin. "Not with Yara being such a high target for Kain. They'll want us protecting her."

"Not *us*," said Carter. "*Me*. And a team of other Guardians. People who aren't assigned to any of the hyden."

"Are you crazy?" said Robin.

"I have to," said Carter.

"Yara will kill you. Hell, forget you, she'll kill me!"

"Would you keep it down?" said Carter in a hushed voice, looking around.

"What're you expecting to get outta this?"

"Same thing as you, R," hissed Carter, leaning in and speaking even more quietly, as though they could force Robin to lower his voice by proxy. "I want this done. I want Kain in the ground. And I want to make sure he can never come back."

"Yara would be a Guardian short if you left."

Carter chuckled dryly. "Hell of a lot of difference that will make. She won't let us get near her anyway. Besides, I think she's proved she can take pretty good care of herself."

Robin fumbled for a few moments, struggling to find the right words. Instead, all he found himself saying was, "Please, Carter..."

Carter met his eyes, each of them waiting for the other to back down. "It'll help them to have a shifter on the team. There aren't many Guardian shifters to begin with."

"What about Williams? Williams is a shifter."

Carter actually laughed at this. "Do you really think Black would send her Head Guardian out on field duty? As a *spy*? Besides, I'm sure you've noticed Williams has been MIA, lately. They're probably working on something else."

Robin frowned. It was true. Come to think of it, the last time he saw Williams might have been at initiation. But he didn't say anything. Carter was right. There was no way that Black would send Xaili Williams into the field, particularly for such a dangerous mission. Of the few Guardian shifters, Carter was by far the most experienced, and they had already infiltrated the Shadow Men once, so they were far and away the best candidate to go on this mission. There was still a part of him that wanted to convince Carter to stay, that there had to be another way, but—as he had told a begrudging Yara many times in the past—such was the life of a Guardian. They didn't always get to put their friend's safety first, especially when that friend was also a Guardian.

"Well," said Robin finally, "if anyone can do it... it's you."

Carter gave him an appreciative nod, but did not look away. Robin tried to look as though he wasn't sure why Carter was inspecting him in such a manner, but he had a feeling that the attention was now going to turn to *his* extracurriculars.

"What?" he said, slapping on his trademark crooked smirk.

"Is there anything you want to talk about?"

"Talk about?"

"Any reason why you came looking for me?"

Robin shrugged. "I missed ya."

Carter raised an eyebrow. "And it has nothing to do with all those nights you're not in your room?"

Robin shrugged again, trying to act clueless.

"I see." Carter paused and turned back to their book, letting Robin think he had won, that the subject had been successfully avoided. But then... "I've noticed N seems to be sitting with us at lunch more now that Yara has shut us out. Am I imagining things?"

"You are," said Robin. He was relatively adept at lying, but Carter knew him well. "Besides, how do you know I'm not in my room?"

"The number of times I've come over, hoping to talk to you about what's going on. You're not the only one who's struggling, you know."

At this, Robin felt a new surge of guilt. Too preoccupied with thinking about himself, he had never thought about the effect that Yara's cold shoulder would have on Carter. They had never been in love with Yara, not the way Robin and Erik had, but Carter loved her still. In a different, no less meaningful way.

"I'm sorry," said Robin, not knowing what else he could say.

"In any case," said Carter, "I'm not imagining things, am I? Between you and N?"

"No," said Robin heavily, "you're not."

"That feels like a healthy solution."

"Gee, thanks. For that... stunningly astute observation."

"You have to end it. Before it turns into anything more."

"Why?" said Robin. "We were together for two years. Things only started getting complicated when we started working the hyden cases. Now things have calmed down—"

"But they haven't calmed down," interjected Carter. "Things are looking to be much worse than they were before. And you and I both know that things weren't only complicated because we were busy."

"This is a pointless discussion," said Robin. "I don't even know why you're so upset. You and N used to be really close."

"And now you and I are really close. And I'm trying to look out for your best interests if you would just know what's good for you."

Robin picked at his thumbnail, ashamed.

"Yara doesn't love you. And now you feel like shit, and N makes you feel better. But in the long run, you're making things worse for yourself. And for N. It's not fair to her."

After a few moments, Robin said, "So what am I supposed to do now?"

"I think you already know the answer to that."

Yara stood in the lobby of the White Mask Society Headquarters, zoning out and hating everything. It had been two full weeks since she had last spoken to Carter or Robin, two full weeks since she had last seen Erik, two full weeks in which Ash had been her only companion. After the first week of being suspended, Yara had been assigned back to her menial mall cop duties guarding the lobby with the understanding that another transgression would get her terminated from the Society. Yara would have preferred to just stay in her room. It was hard not to second guess every decision she had ever made in her life that had led to her being here.

She talked with Ash about running away, trying to take Kain down again, but Ash correctly pointed out that the last time she had done that, it not only resulted in Erik's death, but nearly caused her own. Besides, if the Shadow Men and the Necromancer brought Kain back once, they would do it again.

It felt like Yara and Erik's sacrifices had done nothing. Kain was back, possibly even more dangerous than before.

And as much as Yara didn't want to admit it to herself—much less to anyone else—she wasn't keen on doing anything that might get her expelled from the Society. She had worked hard for her position as a Guardian. She had no idea what else she wanted to do with her life and no interest in finding out without the friends she had made there.

So Yara kept her mouth shut, her head down, and followed instructions. Just as she was supposed to, just as she loathed to.

She was grateful to Ash who did not seem to mind having to cover for Robin and Carter after Yara had insisted they stay away from her. The Vurwari never complained about being on call 24 hours a day. Yara couldn't be sure without asking her, but she didn't think Ash ever slept. Maybe nymphs didn't require as much rest as a human, and despite everything they had been through together so far, Yara was still too afraid to ask.

"Kidney beans or lima beans?" said Ash to Yara's left.

"Kidney beans," said Yara. This had become their new game. In spending day after day together, they had run out of things to talk about. Particularly since neither of them were really doing much of anything besides standing in the lobby as glorified security guards and occasionally playing in the sims.

"Me too," said Ash. She shot a fire arrow from the tip of her pointer finger toward the fern by the glass front doors. The fern leapt out of the way and shot an angry look in Ash's direction before climbing back into their pot, sulking. Ash cackled with joy as she toyed with the fire in her hand. "Sorry!" she called out when the fern threw her a rude gesture, indicated by a creative arrangement of leaves.

"Space or ocean?" said Yara, feeling bad for the fern, but smiling despite herself.

"Hmm…" said Ash, her eyes dancing in the firelight.

"Hey!" said the receptionist behind the desk, pointing at Ash. "Put that out! No powers in the lobby!" It was the weekend receptionist. Not Larry, with whom they had a good relationship.

Ash sighed dramatically and extinguished the fire in her hand before leaning against the wall again, looking as bored as Yara felt. "Ocean, I guess," she said. "Fire can't burn in space. No oxygen."

"It can't burn under water," said Yara.

"No, but it can make the water damn hot."

Yara chuckled. "Well, stars burn in space."

"Say what you will about how amazing and powerful I am," said Ash, "but I ain't no star."

"Mm."

"So I guess space for you?"

"Yeah," said Yara. "No boys in space."

"That we know of."

"Even better. Then there's the possibility of mysterious alien boys who will come and sweep me off my feet."

"I know a couple of boys down here who would do that," said Ash in an offhand voice.

"Any who aren't in captivity by my employers, or who didn't put said boy in captivity?"

Ash's face had become very serious, something Yara didn't see often. "It's been two weeks, lady," she said. "I think your other Guardians have suffered enough."

Yara didn't say anything. The prospect of facing Robin and Carter felt insurmountable. Would she apologize? Would they? And then what? Could she even forgive them for having sold out Erik?

"What happened to you, lady?" said Ash.

"What do you mean?"

"Everything in your file before I met you said you were this awkward girl who was scared of her own shadow. And now it's like you're overcompensating. Trying to make up for it by becoming recklessly entitled."

"Entitled?" said Yara, her jaw dropped.

"I like you a lot, Yara, you know that."

"Well, I *thought* I knew that, but—"

"But you're becoming impulsive and domineering," said Ash, not letting Yara continue. "You were so vulnerable before. And, listen. What you went through no one should ever have to go through. And you did something incredible. You got out. That doesn't mean you always know best. And it doesn't mean you get to treat the people who love you like they're out to get you just because you disagree with them."

Yara's face was burning as Ash's words sunk in. She stared down at her hands, feeling angry and… yes. Ashamed. That was shame she was feeling. She said nothing. Glancing back at Ash, she searched for any indication that Ash was lying, maybe just trying to provoke Yara into forgiving Robin and Carter, but Yara could tell it was the truth.

"Listen," said Ash gently. "I know they wouldn't want me to tell you this, but C is going back in. And I know that you wouldn't want to risk anything happening to them without having the chance to smooth things over between you two."

"Wait, what?" said Yara, pushing herself off the wall. "They're going back in? What does that mean?"

"A team is getting ready to infiltrate Kain's new base and C is leading it. Since they made it in once as a Shadow Man, came back with all that intel, they believe—and I agree with them—that they're the best option to lead the team."

"When is this happening?"

"Soon, I think. I dunno. It's pretty secret. R only told me like yesterday. I don't think I'm even supposed to know about it."

A kind of angry buzzing was filling Yara's head. "Why is it happening so soon?"

"They're worried Kain is gonna move or we might lose control of the situation or something." Ash shrugged.

"Isn't there anyone else who can do it? Another shifter?"

"Evidently not."

"But… what if they get hurt?" said Yara.

"Part of the job, lady. You know that."

Yara cursed under her breath. "Well, this is just great. Apparently, I'm an asshole and Carter is going to risk their neck for me. Again."

"Get over yourself," said Ash with a smile, tossing a fireball into the air before getting yelled at again by the receptionist. "No one said 'asshole.'"

"Right," said Yara, feeling nauseous. "Just entitled and domineering, right?"

"Exactly." Ash gave Yara a side-eye, lips quirked in a smile, and nudged her.

"So what am I supposed to do, then? I can't talk to Carter, I'm still on duty."

"We're only here for a couple more hours," said Ash, once again fiddling with flames, unable to help herself. "Just go talk to them when we're done. And it wouldn't hurt to talk to R, either."

Yara closed her eyes and breathed deeply.

Talk to Carter.

Talk to Robin.

The only person she really wanted to talk to was Erik, but of course he was off limits. Too dangerous, too unpredictable, too much of an unknown.

Yara understood the concerns. And if she was really honest with herself, she agreed. It was true that Erik very likely had been resurrected and sent there to get information on Yara and the hyden and the Society.

The difference between her and the rest of them was that she simply didn't care.

There's that entitlement, I guess.

Robin and Carter had worked together on a proposal for Black, which she had accepted. With one caveat. She wanted to take the time to consult with Glover and Trumbull, who had taken over as the Head Guardian during Xaili Williams's mysterious absence that had yet to be explained to the rest of the Guardians. Black wanted to ensure that Carter and their team would have everything they needed. They would likely not get a second chance to take Kain down, and it would not be easy. It wasn't just one man who needed to be stopped this time, but the entire operation. They had to destroy all of his cloning equipment, and the Necromancer had to be removed. There was no room for failure.

There was also the matter of the rapidly approaching Fête de Libération. The atmosphere always changed as they neared the Society's one and only holiday. So the decision was made to send in Carter and two dozen other Guardians after the Fête, which was less than a week away.

Robin and Carter had a quiet, late dinner in the commissary to toast the upcoming mission, during which the shape shifter reiterated their advice to Robin to end things with Nayla. It would be worse to wait until after the Fête. Better to do it sooner than later. Robin begrudgingly agreed, and after dinner, he headed for her room with the intention of doing just that.

She wasn't there when he knocked. Strangely relieved, he started walking away when her voice stopped him in his tracks.

"Hey, you," she said, her smile palpable from her tone.

Robin spun around. "Hey!"

"You coming to see me? Where you off to?" she said, slipping her hands around his waist as they met in front of her door.

"You weren't here, so I was just gonna…" But he trailed off as she pressed her lips lightly to his.

"Come inside for a minute," she said, pulling him into her quarters. Robin followed mutely.

The moment the door was closed, she started to undo her tunic, rolling her neck. "What a day," she said, casting it on the bed, revealing a white tank top underneath and rubbing her shoulders. She looked good. Her slender arms led to sculpted shoulders which flexed smoothly as she brushed back a few strands of blonde hair that had come loose from her braid.

"What?" she said coyly, noticing him watching.

"Nothing," he said, smiling. "Hard day?"

"You have no idea," she said, leaning back on the bed and kicking off her boots. She patted the bed and he joined her. "I was sent after this shifter who was taking it upon themself to pretend to be different celebrities to get closer to some movie star." Nayla's previous post had been to one of the hydan, but her Ward, Emmanuelle Moreau, had left LA after the events with Kain the year prior and gone back to Paris, where she had been assigned a new team of Guardians. As a result, Nayla was back to more traditional cases.

"Really," said Robin, barely listening. She had placed her hand on his knee and was running her fingers in lazy circles along his thigh.

"Mm," she said. "Apparently, it's leading to all sorts of lawsuits with these celebrities that they're impersonating. And god knows it's impossible to tell a human security guard how to prevent a shape shifter from approaching someone. Human restraining orders just won't hold, since they can always just pretend to be someone else."

Nayla gave a dry laugh as she turned to look at Robin.

"They sent you out alone?" he said, trying not to think about her hand, which was now trailing up his chest, lazily unbuttoning his tunic.

"Mm hmm," she said, her almond eyes blinking slowly.

"Weird," said Robin. "Things have been kind of slow for the rest of us. What with the whole hydan thing escalating with Kain, they're not giving us other assignments. Haven't had a lot to do. I'm jealous."

"What about you?" said Nayla. "Tell me about your day."

"Well," said Robin, grabbing her hand, stopping it from sliding under his now unbuttoned tunic and stroking his chest. "It's been a little stressful, too, I guess."

"Oh?"

"Yeah. C is leading a team in to try to take down Kain, and Yara still won't talk to me. I feel kinda bad for A—"

"C's going back?" said Nayla, sitting up, suddenly frowning.

Robin sighed heavily. "Yeah… We're scared Kain's new setup is temporary, and we have an opportunity to go in now. Before they move everything and we're back to square one. I tried to get assigned to the team, but they don't want to use two of Yara's Guardians, so…" He trailed off, his eyes closed.

Nayla didn't say anything at first, and Robin turned to look at her. Her hand had gone slack in his grip and she was staring at nothing, evidently deep in thought.

"Look, I was worried about them, too," said Robin. "But C knows what they're doing. And they're right. If we move fast this could all be over soon."

Nayla made a sound of agreement.

"Hey," said Robin. "Listen, I know you and C used to be close. They're gonna be fine. I promise."

Nayla turned to look at him. She was so close he could feel the warm breath from her nose against his. "You can't know that."

Robin didn't have time to speak before she had placed her forehead against his lips and he kissed her.

"I'm glad you're here," she said in a soft voice. She raised her eyes to meet his and kissed him. Again and again. Softly at first and then with more fervor. Her lips were on his, on his cheeks, on his neck; her hands on his chest, sliding under his tunic and pulling it off.

Hardly knowing how it happened, forgetting why he had come looking for her, he let himself be swept away into her touch.

CHAPTER TWENTY-THREE
Reconciliation

"I wish it didn't have to be you."

Yara had gone to find Carter first thing after her shift. They weren't in their room, but Yara found them in the second place she looked: the library.

They smiled serenely at her in response to her words. "It's all part and parcel, Red," they said.

"People keep saying that. In so many words. I wish they would stop."

Carter chuckled. "Sorry. But if we pull this off, it'll be done. All this nonsense with Kain, we'll never have to worry about it again."

"Will you still be my Guardians?" said Yara.

"Do you want us to be? I'd imagine you'd be kind of tired of having people breathing down your neck all the time."

Yara shrugged and looked down at her hands. The truth was that she had never really had friends until her Guardians had come along. She couldn't help but feel that there was the possibility that without being assigned to her, they wouldn't want to spend time with her.

Carter seemed to know what kinds of thoughts she was having. "We'll always be your friends, Red. You don't have to worry about that."

"Sometimes I think about what life would look like if I weren't a hydan. If I were just an ordinary girl with nothing to offer, nothing special."

"I'm not sure you would ever have been ordinary."

Yara rolled her eyes. "Right."

"Do you really think that the only thing you have to offer is your ability to see the future?"

"And the past."

"And the past," Carter amended with a dry laugh.

"I mean, yeah. Kinda. I had nothing before you guys came along."

"Well, I hope your aunt never hears you say that."

"No, that's not what I mean," said Yara quickly. "I just mean, I didn't know what I wanted to do with my life. I didn't really know who I was. And now I have you guys and I feel like I have purpose. But it's always on the verge of disappearing, you know? Everything I care about, every*one*. What if... what if you don't come back?"

Carter took their glasses off and wiped them on the hem of their uniform before speaking. "When you went after Kain last year, did you think you were coming back?"

"No," said Yara in a small voice.

"But you went anyway."

"I thought it was the only way to help."

"And you wanted to help, didn't you?" said Carter. "Your family, your friends, the people you cared about?"

Yara nodded.

"There are some things that are worth risking everything for, Yara. Even if it's scary. Even if it hurts."

"Yara?" Robin's soft voice startled Yara awake.

"Huh? Oh. Hi," she said, blinking the sleep away from her eyes, feeling completely disoriented. It took her a few moments to realize where she was. She had fallen asleep against the door to Robin's quarters after deciding to wait for him there when she found his room empty after her shift. Having resigned herself to talking to him, she was determined to stay until he came back, lest she lose her confidence by putting it off.

"What are you doing here?" he said. Given how quietly he spoke, she imagined it was the middle of the night. She must have been waiting for hours. He helped her to her feet and let go of her the moment she was standing. He stood far away from her, his hands in his pockets.

"Oh, uh..." she said, trying to regain her surroundings. "I was... looking for you."

"I kinda figured," said Robin. "Finally decided to end the silent crusade?"

Yara looked at her feet and said nothing. Shame burned her face again, just as it had after Ash called her out that afternoon.

"Look, I'm sorry," he said eventually, breaking the awkward silence. "I know you don't understand why we did what we did—"

"I do," said Yara. "That doesn't mean I have to like it, though."

"I suppose that's true."

She forced herself to look at him and instantly regretted it. "Ash told me what's going on."

Robin said nothing.

"I don't want Carter to do it," she said.

"You've got some time," he said.

"Not enough."

"They're gonna be fine."

"You have to say that."

"No, I don't. But I know C. They're good at what they do."

"Anyway... I'm..." She couldn't bring herself to say "sorry." Was she even sorry? She was sorry that this whole thing had happened. But she wasn't sorry for being mad at him. She *was* mad at him, even now. Though perhaps she had no real right to be. It was just so easy to blame him for the fact that Erik was locked away instead of with her. But she wanted to be sorry.

She heard Ash's words in her head. *Recklessly entitled. Impulsive and domineering.* Had she really become those things? She didn't want to be.

"You wanna come inside for a sec?"

Yara barely had time to nod when someone called Robin's name. She looked around him as he spun to see who it was. Nayla was walking confidently toward them. She was barefoot and dressed in a white tank top and matching shorts that showed off her powerful, long legs. Her hair was undone and hung elegantly in effortless curls around her shoulders. She was carrying a ConvOrb.

"Oh!" said Nayla in surprise, seeing Yara. "Hey, Y."

Yara nodded in greeting, trying not to stand too close to her, afraid it would throw into even sharper focus the striking differences between the two of them.

"Robin, you left your orb in my room. Thought you might miss it."

"I did?" said Robin in disbelief. He felt in all of his pockets before taking the orb from Nayla. "Weird. I never even took it out. Thanks."

"Yeah, your mom called. That's how I found it. She left a message." Nayla smiled and looked at Yara. Yara averted her eyes almost instantly, and Nayla got the hint. "Well, I'll leave you to it, I guess. Night, Robin. Y."

Yara raised a hand in farewell, noting with displeasure that Nayla had used Robin's full name. She swallowed any jealousy. She had no right to feel that way. *Just because he said he loves me doesn't mean I have any claim to him*, she thought. Besides, Robin and Nayla made more sense. And Yara loved Erik.

"You guys back together?" said Yara, avoiding meeting Robin's eyes.

"I guess. Kinda," said Robin.

Yara pursed her lips.

Robin scoffed at her reaction. "Is that OK?" His voice was laced with sarcasm.

"Why wouldn't it be?" said Yara. Nayla was beautiful and so was Robin, and no doubt they would have beautiful babies with incredibly strong arms and blonde hair and they could be a Guardian power couple. Good for them.

"Right," said Robin.

There was a pregnant pause.

"So..." said Robin, tossing his ConvOrb in the air and waiting for Yara to speak.

"I should probably go," said Yara.

She was already half way down the hall when Robin started laughing loudly. "Yup! Good solution, Y. Let's not talk about this. Or better yet!" he called after her. "Let's not talk at all for another two weeks. Make it three! What do I care?"

Yara kept walking, fuming. She made it to the end of the hall, heard the door to his quarters close, and changed her mind. Beelining back to his room, she opened the door without knocking and said, "What is your problem?"

"*My* problem?" said Robin incredulously. "My problem is that I told you I was in love with you, and you decided that the right way to react to that was to run away. You realize you've barely looked me in the eye since then? You've been freezing me out for two weeks! Now you finally decide to come and break the silence, then N shows up and you're running away again? Are ya jealous? Is that it?" He waited for her to respond, and when she said nothing, he shouted, "What is it you want, Yara Rivers?"

"I wanted nothing to change!" she screamed back at him. "I wanted you and Carter to trust me! To trust that we could do this without

Black and without the Society!"

"Just because we asked for help doesn't mean we don't trust you!" said Robin. "When are *you* going to start trusting the Society? This is literally what they're here for."

"Oh yeah, they're doing a great job! Now, Erik is locked up in a cell because of you. They won't even let me *talk* to him because of you! And now Carter is going off to galavant with the bad guys and they may *die* and it's all because of *you*!" She shoved him on the last word.

"Hey!" said Robin, his eyes wide with surprise. "Watch it."

"What am I even doing here?" she continued.

"You were the one who wanted to become a Guardian, kid."

"Because! Because I was scared! My life had been completely torn away from me. I'd spent a month being tortured like a goddamn lab rat. I had my skull drilled into by a madman and—"

"Yara," he said, his voice barely registering through the rising anxiety that was building inside her, with no thoughts of breathing exercises or trying to stay calm. He reached for her shoulder but she slapped his hand away and shoved him again. "*Hey!* What are you doing?"

She didn't know what she wanted, but the sight of him standing in front of her, a quiet sea as she raged on, fueled her. "Fight me!" she yelled.

"What? Yara, what is going on with you?"

She didn't know. Couldn't understand the frantic energy that was bubbling inside her, the desire to rip off her skin and to scream and to fight. "Fight back!"

"Yara, I'm not going to fight you," said Robin, his eyes wide with concern.

She tried shoving him again, but he grabbed her wrists this time.

"Let me go!" she said.

"Are you going to keep hitting me?"

She thought back to her very first lessons, training with her Guardians what felt like so long ago, when they taught her how to break a basic handhold. His grip was a vice, but she kicked him, forcing him to release her.

"What is *wrong* with you?" he yelled as she went to shove him again, but he blocked her, holding her at arms length. "Stop it! YARA!"

Finally, she relented, breathing heavily, and stared at him. Her eyes flashed. "You don't understand what I went through."

Robin stared at her, breathing heavily, his eyes wide with confusion and fear. "You're right," he said finally. "I don't. We don't."

"And you're my best friend and I... I see you with her..." She hated herself for the tears that filled her eyes and threatened to fall, but she managed to keep them from spilling onto her cheeks. "I feel like I've lost you."

She couldn't bear to look at him as she continued to fight back her tears, biting her bottom lip to stop it from trembling. He didn't say anything for a long time. He simply let go of her. Her arms fell limply to her side as shame once again burned in her cheeks.

Recklessly entitled.

"Ya haven't lost me," he said finally in a soft voice. "If... if you want me in your life, kid, I'll be there. Whatever you want that to look like." She looked at him. There was no smile on his face, no crooked grin, no gleam in his eyes. "I promise."

And the tears started to fall in earnest, and she was in his arms, crying into his chest, and his hands were cradling her gently as she wept. "I'm sorry," she said through the tears. "I'm sorry. I'm sorry. I'm sorry."

CHAPTER TWENTY-FOUR

Fête de Libération

Yara woke up in Robin's bed. He had talked with her well into the night until she fell asleep. He was still sleeping on the floor, looking surprisingly comfortable, given the fact that he had no pillow and no mattress; only a blanket which had been mostly cast off. Yara tried to avert her eyes from his golden skin, laced with battle scars.

Guilt burned in Yara's gut. She couldn't help but feel like she had been unfaithful to Erik. More than a physical betrayal, it had been an emotional one.

Her eyes were caked with sleep, but she didn't bother trying to wipe it away before slipping as silently as possible out of his bed. She carefully stepped around him, moving on her tiptoes, and headed toward the door when—

"Leaving already?"

She froze, her hand on the doorknob, and looked over her shoulder. "I didn't want to wake you," she said.

"You don't need to whisper," said Robin, the corner of his lip pulled up as he sat forward, rolling his stiff shoulders.

She paused. Then, "I should probably go."

"OK," said Robin.

She opened the door and hesitated in the hallway before leaving. "I'm sorry," she said, finally meeting his eyes. "For how I've been acting. And… thank you. For last night."

He nodded. "Thanks for talkin' to me again." He smiled, but Yara could not bring herself to return it before she closed the door behind her.

* * *

The Fête de Libération was fast approaching. It was the only holiday celebrated Society wide every year. February 21st marked the anniversary of the signing of a treaty between the king of France and the founder of the Society, Elizabeth DuBois, in 1375. The Traité Valois-Déviant outlawed the hunting of Deviants as witches and the burning of them at the stake. Yara had been involved with the Society for over a year, but this was the first celebration she would attend. She had been a civilian the year before, and civilians weren't invited.

As a result, the whole experience was new and exciting for Yara. Though it would have been more exciting if she could celebrate with Erik. Or if she weren't so wrought with anxiety over Carter's upcoming mission.

In light of the upcoming celebration, Yara had begged Glover to let her see Erik. He had begrudgingly agreed to let Yara talk to Erik for an hour two days before the Fête, but only under close supervision.

During the weeks he had been under lockdown, Chun had been coordinating all aspects of Erik's observation. By correlating test results, interrogation responses, and observation notes from every White Mask involved, Chun had become most familiar with Erik's condition, making him Glover's choice to supervise Yara's visit. He would be able to identify signs of trouble before anything had the chance to get out of hand.

When Chun accompanied Yara to Erik's ward, she was happy to see that it looked more like any private hospital room rather than some kind of prison cell—although there were two Guardians from Yara's initiate class guarding the room. They nodded at her in recognition before Chun waved them aside and took Yara into the room.

Erik was on the floor doing push-ups, his chest bare. He looked around at the sound of the door opening and jumped to his feet when he saw Yara, his bright green eyes wide with surprise.

"Yara!" he said.

It was everything Yara could do not to run into his arms. With great difficulty, she stayed where she was. That was one of the stipulations of seeing him: no touching.

"I'll be right over here," said Chun, taking a tablet and getting to work—or at least, pretending to. Yara didn't care. She only had eyes for Erik.

He was staring at her as though he had never truly seen her before. The sight of him all sweaty and panting brought back memories that made Yara's face burn. He looked down at himself and laughed sheepishly. "I'm naked," he said. "I didn't expect to see you."

Yara grinned, unable to help herself. She let her eyes roam over his body. His chest and arms and back had once been scarred and marked by battle, but now he was smooth and unblemished, so unlike the pale scars she had seen strewn on Robin's chest during their training and, more recently, last night as he slept. The cloning process had not replicated Erik's imperfections. It had, however, made an exact copy of his sharp jaw, sculpted shoulders, and toned chest.

Erik cleared his throat and Yara's eyes snapped back to him. He was laughing. "It's good to see you," he said walking toward her, his arms outstretched. "I miss you."

"I miss you, too," said Yara, taking a step out of his reach.

He frowned and looked at Chun, as though concerned it was his presence that made Yara back away.

"We're… not allowed to touch," she said in a quiet voice.

Erik snorted. "Yeah. I didn't think they would be quite so strict about it, but makes sense, I guess."

"What?" said Yara.

"Well, I'm a clone. It makes sense that Kain would want to use me as a weapon. I'm… dangerous."

"You're not dangerous!" said Yara immediately.

"Yara," said Erik sadly, looking so deep into her eyes that she thought she might drown in his. "I'm not me. I'm not Erik."

"Yes, you are," said Yara in a weak voice. "I see you. I know you. It is you. You remember everything, and you act the same and speak the same and look the same. Mostly." She looked at his white hair and grinned.

He smiled back at her, his face lighting up and melting the world around her.

"How long do we have?" he said, gesturing toward Chun with his head.

"An hour," said Yara.

"Let's make the most of it," he said. He walked over to a chair in the corner of the room and pulled another one to face it, sitting down as he pulled on a white undershirt. Yara sat across from him. "So, tell me what's been going on. They don't tell me anything around here."

"Well," said Yara, tucking her legs in to her chest. And she started talking. She told him about how she didn't speak to Carter or Robin for weeks after they had turned him in to Black, how she had been waking up in sweats in the middle of the night from anxiety, that when she finally did speak to Robin she discovered he was back with Nayla. This news about Robin made Erik smile. She decided to leave out Robin's declaration of love for her. Instead, she started on the plan for Carter to lead a team to take Kain's operation down. "...And now everyone is just getting ready for the masquerade party thing, and it just... doesn't feel right."

"It'll never feel right," said Erik. "Not really. There's always something."

"I guess so."

"I remember when I was an initiate, the Society was dealing with a crisis—some gang in San Diego was going on a nymph hunting rampage—and the Fête still happened. I remember thinking how insensitive it felt to have a big party when there were Deviants being killed and we could stop it. But you have to remember, Yara, we're all human."

"Well..." said Yara.

Erik laughed. "OK. Maybe not *all* human. But you know what I mean. We're the same, really. No matter if we're human or Deviant. And there's only so much we can do without blowing off a little steam now and then. I mean look at you," he said, gesturing to her.

"What?" she said defensively.

"You look tired, Yara."

"Gee, thanks."

"I mean you look weary."

"I look *weary*?" said Yara, raising an eyebrow.

"You need a break, is what I'm saying. You've got too much on your shoulders. It's too much for one person to handle."

Yara was silent as she looked at him. "What about you? What have you been up to? You must be so..." *Bored. Unhappy. Frustrated.*

Erik took a deep breath. "Well, I've been busy, actually."

"You have?" said Yara, unable to keep the surprise from her voice.

"Turns out that whatever Kain and the Necromancer did to me, there's some sort of..." He paused, searching for the right word. "Uh, 'brainwashing' I guess you'd call it. 'Conditioning' is what Research is saying."

"What?" said Yara, panic fluttering in her chest.

"Yeah," said Erik with a sardonic laugh. "Not great, I know."

"What does that mean?"

"It's these fugue states. Apparently, Kain did something to me that makes it so he can control me. It's what happened before in the medical ward, I guess. So Chun and everyone, they've been down here trying to figure out what causes it, how to stop it, all that fun stuff."

"Have they figured it out?" said Yara.

"It seems to be triggered auditorily. Some song I've heard way too much of now triggers it."

"Music?" said Yara.

Erik nodded. "Beethoven. Which is why I was triggered accidentally by Frankie before. She always has music playing."

"That's it?" said Yara. "That feels too easy."

"Simple. Not easy, though. Triggering it may be straightforward, but the whole process of conditioning me to respond to the trigger is the hard part. Frankie calls it 'installing the switch.' I guess Kain did all that to me before I woke up outside the library. From there, 'flipping the switch'—triggering me—is pretty straightforward. So anyway, they can get me into it and out of it, but getting rid of the conditioning so I can't be controlled by the trigger, well, that's been… complicated."

"What does that mean?"

He sighed heavily. "It means they'll flip the switch—play some Beethoven song to put me under the trance—and try stuff to put me back in charge of myself so that Kain won't be able to control me if he tries."

"And?"

Erik looked at her with a sad smile. That told her everything. It wasn't working.

"What about the earthquakes? And all the…" she gestured vaguely around him, "the leafy stuff. Do they know what's causing that?"

Erik chuckled. "Me, apparently. I don't know. I just always feel like I'm on the verge of exploding. And I guess I kind of am. Whatever Kain did to me, it seems to have made my powers just a little… heightened."

"Your nymph powers?"

He nodded.

"That's cool, though, isn't it?"

"It would be," said Erik. "If I could control them. I'm working on it."

"I wish you could come with me to the party," said Yara as quietly as she could, feeling self-conscious about Chun sitting across the room.

Erik gave her a small smile.

"Any chance they'll let you escape for the night?" she said. "If we just make sure that song doesn't get played." She laughed at her weak attempt to make light of the situation. "Let us 'blow off some steam' together?"

"I usually like to buy a girl dinner before she starts talking about blowing off steam."

"That's not what I meant!" said Yara, her cheeks reddening.

Erik was too busy laughing to hear anything.

"Ugh!" said Yara, unable to stop a smile from creeping onto her face as well.

"I'm afraid I'll be here," he said. He scooted his chair closer to Yara and tried to graze her hand with his fingers as subtly as possible so that Chun wouldn't see. It sent tingles along her skin, and she suppressed a shiver.

She wanted to ask if he thought they would ever let him out, but she wasn't sure she would like the answer.

Chun intentionally cleared his throat in the corner.

Erik gave Yara a sardonic look. "I guess our hour is up."

Yara's heart began to ache as she looked into his eyes. "So fast…"

"Thank you for coming down here."

"It wasn't enough," said Yara, tearing her eyes away from him and trying to smile, "but now I owe Zak Glover a kidney. So you owe me."

"Deal."

They stood up, giving Chun the excuse he needed to stop pretending like he was working.

"Maybe I'll bust you out for the Fête," said Yara as Chun accompanied her to the door.

"Bring me an outfit."

Erik stood still in the middle of the room. When she turned away from him, he was still smiling.

The day before the Fête the Society had effectively shut down and, for the first time, Yara had gotten to enjoy what it meant to have money. White Masks were all comfortably paid, something she discovered when she and Ash took the morning to go buy outfits for the masquerade. They had even invited Aunt Catherine to join the shopping spree, despite her not being invited to the party itself. Aside from not having seen her aunt in a while, Yara wanted the chance to spoil her with a gift.

It was difficult for Yara to stop looking at the price tags and give herself permission to splurge along with Ash, trying on a million dresses before picking the prettiest one instead of just the cheapest one. Not only that, but they got to shop at an actual boutique, not a thrift store, which meant that Yara kept hearing Aunt Catherine mutter under her breath, "Who would spend this much? Honestly," every time she looked at a dress.

Yara had never had much interest in clothes, and the three of them had drawn a lot of strange looks entering those shops. Yara with her pixie cut and torn jeans, Aunt Catherine in her work scrubs, exhausted after a fourteen hour shift, and Ash with her unnatural eyes and red-streaked hair. Fortunately, Ash had a keen sense of fashion, and she helped Yara in more ways than one. Clerks were less likely to kick Yara out of the shops when she was with Ash, who had the confidence of a Bel Air influencer with daddy's credit card. She seemed genuinely excited to instruct the women in the shops on what colors to pull for both Yara and Aunt Catherine, informing them what "silhouettes" would suite them best, whatever that meant.

In the end, they each walked out with a new dress. Aunt Catherine insisted she would never wear the pink gown Yara had bought her before hugging her fiercely, which Yara patiently endured after such a long absence from her only family, and bidding them goodbye, desperate for a nap.

The first thing Yara did when they got back to Headquarters was to arrange for half of her salary to go straight to her aunt.

The second half of the day was long. Her shift with Ash dragged as they stood in the lobby, counting the seconds until they were relieved. Ash had no interested in dinner, however, bouncing away to presumably prepare for tomorrow, leaving Yara to head to the commissary by herself.

Perhaps it was nerves about having to dress up for the first time since her freshman year homecoming dance, but Yara found that she, too, had little appetite. Still, she got a wrap and looked around the commissary for a place to sit.

"Apparently, I'm stalking you," she said, joining Robin. His plate was empty and he was fiddling with his fork, staring at nothing.

He laughed and looked up as she sat, but it did not reach his eyes.

"I would say from the looks of it that we both are super excited about the party tomorrow."

"Oh. Right," said Robin. "Yeah."

Yara didn't say anything. He looked tired. Weary, in the same way that Erik had described her. She wanted to ask him if he was OK, but her voice was having a hard time finding the words. She had nothing to offer him, really. And she had the feeling that he would dismiss any efforts she made, insisting that he was fine.

"It'll be my first time," she said instead.

Robin didn't seem to hear her. He was looking at his fork, his eyes glazed over.

She tried taking a bite of her wrap, but it felt like cardboard in her dry mouth. She was acutely aware of Robin at her side, unbidden memories of the other night coming back to her in a wave of discomfort. Robin smiling at her, eyes bleary with tiredness. Robin sleeping shirtless on the floor. Robin telling her he would always be there for her. Robin handing her tissues while she talked and talked about her fears, about what might happen to Erik, about what Kain's return meant, about whether or not Carter would be OK. She had told him things she hadn't spoken of in a year, reliving experiences she had done her best to suppress. Her body had literally trembled as she spoke, recalling her own torture and what she had seen Kain and his Shadow Men do to the others in captivity. Robin had let her talk well into the night, talk herself to sleep, her eyes red and puffy from tears and exhaustion.

But now they were back to an uncomfortably icy silence, as though the other night had never happened.

"I hope..." she said, desperate to end the tense silence. "I hope that we still manage to have fun tomorrow. Despite everything that's going on. And I hope that soon—soonish, at least... that you can look at me."

That got his attention, but she did not meet his eyes.

"*You're* not looking at me."

"Well, I've always been awkward. This is a new color on you."

He chuckled, and that was when she finally felt strong enough to look up. After a few moments, he said, "We're getting better at it."

She nodded. "Well, brace yourself for tomorrow," she said as she stood up and headed to the door, her uneaten wrap in hand, "because I'm going to blow your mind with the dress that Ash picked for me."

"Oh boy," he said bemusedly.

"Night, Robin."

"Yeah, night."

"You look so beautiful!" Ash was bouncing on her toes, squealing and looking excitedly at Yara.

"Me? Look at you!" she managed.

Ash let out a loud laugh. Her long hair was pulled back in a mess of elegant curls, several gold pins shaped like flames holding it up. She'd made herself up with a shimmering gold powder which, against her dark skin, made her look iridescent, matching the bright yellow dress which hugged her chest. The neckline was cut down to her waist, where a gold belt cinched her, leaving the dress to billow out from under it in rippling waves, streaks of orange and red climbing up the skirt from the hem. She was absolutely breathtaking.

Somehow, Ash had managed to make Yara look halfway decent as well. Her hair was too short to style, but Ash had lent her a jeweled headband with flowers made of white gemstones. Her midnight blue dress, unlike Ash's, had a high neck, inset with jewels which tapered into the sleeveless, chiffon bodice. It curved gently over her chest and was unforgiving in how it clung to her body, but Yara's Guardian regimen wasn't for nothing. It was hard not to stare at her reflection. She had never looked like this in her life. Not once. Hadn't even known it was possible.

"Do all nymphs know how to apply makeup this well?" said Yara, turning her head and observing herself from every angle.

"Only the ones as vain as me," said Ash, winking playfully, evidently delighted at Yara's reaction. "Which you're on your way to if you don't stop looking at yourself, lady."

Yara laughed and turned to Ash. "Thank you."

"You look like a queen!"

"A princess, maybe," said Yara. "*You're* the queen here, I think."

Ash handed Yara a delicate Venetian mask. It was the same blue as her dress with delicate silver swirls. Yara slipped it on and looked at Ash, who was putting on a similar mask of red and gold to match her own dress.

"We look hot," said Yara, feeling giddy.

"Maybe I'll distract the guards so you can go say hi to Erik before changing out of this outfit."

They giggled, and Yara felt wonderfully normal. They made their way out of her quarters and headed to where the masquerade was taking place.

Yara's jaw dropped. The commissary was unrecognizable. It had been gutted and redecorated from the ground up.

"Hey," said Ash with a shrug in response to Yara's expression. "We only party once a year. You think we're not gonna make a big deal out of it?"

Sheets of fabric were artfully draped from the ceiling, the walls hidden behind long curtains of emerald and gold, with variations of the masks that were part of their uniform used as decor. Yara had never seen any room in Headquarters so full, either. It seemed that everyone was here, whether they were with the Guardians, Research, the Cleaners, or the Eyes. Deviants and humans alike were dressed extravagantly in every color, some wearing delicate masks that barely covered their faces at all, others wearing some so lavish that they extended into full headdresses. Yara spotted a cluster of flora nymphs in the corner who were not actually wearing any clothes at all, but had draped themselves in various flowered garlands of their own creation.

Velvet covered tables lined the room, all covered with different foods and drinks.

"Is that champagne?" said Yara, pointing to a table behind a shape shifter who was amusing their date by transforming into her.

"No," said Ash, laughing. "The alcohol is behind the bar." She pointed to a door in the far corner of the room.

"That's the bar?" said Yara. "Why is it… somewhere else?"

"They just set up a little sim back there so there's a simulated bartender," said Ash. "It serves drinks to people who are, you know… allowed."

Looking more closely, Yara saw that the door was part of a small, square box that wasn't usually there. A temporary simulator, just like the ones they had used for the first two tests in initiation. Yara had to admit it was a relatively ingenious way to have someone serving drinks without actually having someone serving drinks.

"Why?" said Ash. "You want some champagne?"

"I'm underage."

"Please," said Ash. "You can be sent out to fight and die for the cause, but you're telling me you're too immature to have a couple of glasses of bubbly?"

Yara laughed and snorted loudly. "But it won't serve me, right?"

Ash dismissed her with a wave of her hand. "It'll serve me. Nymphs have different rules."

Yara barely had enough time to notice anything else before Ash was back with two glasses of champagne.

"If anyone asks," she said, "it's sparkling cider."

They clinked and looked over the dance floor. The room was already packed. Yara hated crowds. And she couldn't see how she could possibly find Carter or Robin in all this mess. *Though Robin's probably here with his girlfriend,* Yara reminded herself. *He might not want to be found.*

She took a small sip of her champagne. She had never had alcohol before. It was surprisingly crisp, with only a hint of sweetness that was replaced with a tart bite she quite liked. She went to take another sip but coughed slightly when Ash, who had already downed hers, took Yara's hand and pulled her to the center of the room, where people were dancing with abandon.

"Oh, no—" Yara started. She was not a dancer. Some of her champagne sloshed out of her glass, which she tried desperately to keep steady as Ash dragged her along into the crowd.

Inhale. Exhale.

The mass of bodies was overwhelming. Yara's mask made it difficult to see. She tried to focus on Ash in front of her, but the Vurwari was wild. Ash had already found a partner to dance with, Olive Quigley, from Yara's initiate class. Beside her was Wesley, looking dapper in a green and silver dashiki, his thick braids pulled back into a ponytail. He waved enthusiastically at her. She raised her hand to say hi, and spilled some more of her drink in the process.

Bopping awkwardly, wondering how long the song was before she could retreat to the safety of the outskirts of the dance floor, Yara took another small sip. The champagne was good. The more she drank, the more she liked the heaviness that came over her.

How she wished Erik were here. She toyed with imagining him in her mind, dressed perhaps in a fancy suit, maybe something with tails and a high collar, just like the leading man in a Jane Austen movie. She made to take another drink, only to find her glass empty. Erik's silver hair looked just as tousled in her imagination of him as she had ever seen it, unable to think what he would look like were it tamed, and his green eyes devoured her hungrily from behind a delicate mask. She could feel his hands on her shoulders... No. Those were real hands on her shoulders.

Panicking, Yara gasped and spun around, grabbing the wrists of whomever it was who had touched her, her glass flying out of her hand. She was about to slam them to the ground when she found herself staring straight into a pair of familiar blue eyes behind a silver mask.

"Woah!" said Robin, wrenching one of his hands out of Yara's grip to catch her flute before it shattered on the floor.

"Oh my gosh," she said, letting him go and stepping back

immediately, bumping into someone behind her. "Sorry," she said to the man who waved her off with a friendly laugh. "Sorry," she said again, this time to Robin. "Hi. Wow," she added, indicating the glass in his hand.

"You guys look…" said Robin, gesturing at her and Ash, but not taking his eyes off of Yara.

He paused a fraction of a second too long when Nayla stepped forward, smiling radiantly at Yara. "What I think he's trying to say is that you look lovely."

Yara could feel her cheeks reddening. Hearing that from Nayla felt like false praise. Nayla, who looked like a Greek goddess. Or at least a model dressed as a Greek goddess in catalogues that always made girls feel terrible about themselves. Her height and slender figure were more pronounced than ever under a flowing white dress that gave her skin a golden hue in the soft light. It criss-crossed over her torso, revealing much of her ample chest, and sat comfortably against her hips before cascading to the floor. When she moved, Yara noticed a long slit along either side of the dress where Nayla's legs peeked through with every step. She wore little in the way of jewelry. A couple of gold bangles on her wrists and long golden earrings that, combined with her blonde hair pulled stylishly back, made her neck look impossibly long.

"You too," said Yara, unable to state just how beautiful Nayla really looked. Yara could feel her shoulders tense with rising insecurity.

"Here," said Robin. "I think you need a refill."

"Oh, no, that's fine," said Yara, snatching her glass out of Robin's hand, feeling lightheaded. She wasn't sure if she would get in trouble for drinking champagne instead of sparkling cider and didn't feel like she needed to be any more inebriated this early in the evening.

Ash was giggling and hugged Robin by way of greeting. When Nayla went in for a hug too, Ash clasped Nayla's hands instead and said in a very loud voice, "You're so tall!"

Nayla smiled uncertainly, but Ash was already back to dancing with Olive, pulling Yara along to join them. Flames were dancing in ringlets around Ash's arms. Yara shrugged apologetically in Robin's direction. It was easy to imagine how stiff and uncomfortable she looked, still holding her empty flute, which did nothing to ease her lack of confidence.

Just one song, she thought. *Then you can leave and get another drink. Maybe some actual cider this time.*

Much to Yara's discomfort, Robin and Nayla started to dance next to them, so every time Ash spun Yara around, she was forced to look at them. Robin was smiling crookedly, his teeth pearly white as he laughed at something Nayla said.

The moment the song was over, Yara excused herself, eager to get away.

Why did it bother her so much? Was it really possible that she had feelings for Robin after all? She had taken advantage of the idea that he would always be there, perhaps waiting for her. Maybe she only wanted to ignore how he felt about her because she knew that facing it would be too complicated.

She did love Erik, and she wanted more than anything for him to be there.

But maybe it was possible that she loved Robin, too.

Carter liked the Fête as much as anyone in the Society, but their enjoyment came more from seeing all their fellow White Masks let loose and less from doing so themself. Rather than a wild masquerade, Carter wished they could have a nice dinner with those they loved most.

But Darwin wasn't there.

Instead, they looked for Yara and Robin. They spotted their Ward first. She was standing by a drink table looking uneasy, her arms wrapped tightly around herself. It reminded Carter of the first time Yara had come to Headquarters what felt like a lifetime ago. Back then, she had been a teenage girl uncomfortable in her own skin. Now, she was a woman who could fight with the best of them. Yet this, a party, was all it took to devolve her into her old self.

"Hello."

Yara turned to see them walking toward her. She took in their outfit, a simple black ensemble under an embroidered jacket. Their black mask was up on their forehead so they could wear their glasses unencumbered.

"Hi!" she said. "You look so nice."

"I was going to say the same."

Yara laughed awkwardly. "Thank you."

"Not much for dancing?" said Carter. While Yara knew that they were going after Kain, she thought it was happening in two days. Not even Robin knew that it was happening before dawn the next morning. Carter didn't want anyone who wasn't involved to know. Couldn't bear to see their friends worry or listen to anyone try to talk them out of it. The shape shifter would just have to make the most of tonight before heading back into the belly of the beast.

"I think you know the answer to that already," said Yara.

"Yeah," they said. "It's just not the same when you don't get to do it with the person you want to do it with."

Yara bit her lip and Carter wondered if Yara was thinking of Erik, locked in holding, or if the direction of her gaze was more telling. She was staring into the crowd of dancing bodies.

Carter found themself watching Nayla. She looked so like her brother.

"Who do you wish you were dancing with, then?" she asked.

But they didn't have time to answer when the music stopped and the crowd turned toward a raised dais at the far end of the room. Bora Black was standing on the platform, a glass of whiskey in her hand, looking graceful as ever. She had not gone to many pains to dress up, wearing little more than a stylized variation of her usual attire, accented only by some sparse silver embroidery. Her mask resembled those worn by members in the field, lightly embellished to reflect the celebratory atmosphere.

The room went silent, waiting for her to speak. She was smiling, her black eyes roaming over the room.

"My dear fellows, Deviants and humans alike, today is a day of great celebration."

A few people cheered and whooped at this, but quieted soon to hear what else she had to say.

"What we do here is some of the most important work there is. And what's more, many of the people we serve don't know that we're doing it. Many of you have given us everything you have, everything you are. We have all lost people. Friends, family... It is a thankless job. But today is your day. Today we remember our roots. It has been over five centuries since our founder signed a treaty that would protect Deviants everywhere, finally beginning to grant them the rights they— the rights *we* deserve."

More cheering and applause.

"We have faced countless enemies and threats, and yet here we still stand, stronger than ever before. And it is thanks to each and every one of you here in this room that we can continue to fight the good fight. So let us drink to those who have fallen, drink to those who have yet to rise, and drink because we are still here."

* * *

After Black's speech, the room exploded into cheers, the music resumed, and the dancing started up again with impressive gusto. Yara clapped along with the rest of them. Black took a moment, observing the revelry with a smile on her face when she saw Yara in the back of the room, still watching her.

Black raised her glass and nodded at Yara. Taken aback, Yara nodded in return and watched as Black took a sip, before climbing off the dais and disappearing into the throng.

"There you two are," said a voice. Carter and Yara turned to see Robin approaching them. "How long does it take to get a drink?"

"I was listening to the speech," said Yara.

"Multitasking was never your strong suit." He turned to Carter and slapped a hand on their shoulder. "Hey, C, lookin' good."

"You clean up pretty well yourself," said Carter.

Robin spread his arms out, a cocky grin on his face. "Born this way."

Carter cleared their throat very pointedly before saying, "I'm going to go say hi to Nayla and Ash."

Robin and Yara watched them go.

"I didn't actually get a chance to say it before, but you look nice," he said.

Yara shifted. "I told you you'd like the dress," she said, trying to brush off his compliment.

"I'll have to tell A she did a good job."

"And you, you know," said Yara, gesturing at Robin. He was wearing a slate suit that matched his silver mask.

"Thanks," he said. "N picked it out for me. Said it would bring out my eyes or something."

"She was right," said Yara.

Just then, the music slowed and the rambunctious dancing eased as people coupled up and started to sway lazily with one another. Yara and Robin watched them for a few moments, before he said, "You wanna dance with me?"

Yara didn't look at him at first, trying to weigh each word before she spoke. "Don't you have a date?"

"She won't mind. Look, she's dancing with C." When Yara didn't answer right away, he added, "C'mon. If I never told you I was in love with ya, you wouldn't hesitate to dance with me for a second."

Yara laughed and snorted before she could stop herself. "Maybe I would for a second. I'd be scared of stepping on your toes."

"You can stand on my feet."

She looked at him and felt heat rising in her body. He was holding his hand out to her, his face mostly hidden under golden hair and a silver mask, but she could still see his wide and coquettish grin. Unable to stop herself from smiling too, she took his hand and let him pull her toward the dance floor. They stayed on the outskirts of the crowd, his arm gently resting against her waist, her hand on his shoulder.

"Is it always a masquerade?" she said, unable to stand the silence.

"Yeah," he said. "Though not officially. It's not like a rule or anything. But people always wear masks. We are the White *Mask* Society, after all."

Yara chuckled. "Right."

They continued to sway and Yara wondered if Robin could hear the pounding of her heart.

"You probably shouldn't look at me like that," she said. Her breath was coming in short, nervous gasps, heat crawling up her neck and into her cheeks. She wanted to blame the champagne, but knew it had nothing to do with that.

"It's hard not to," he said.

She should have told him to stop. Wanted to tell him to look away, to let go of her. But she couldn't. Wouldn't. She tried to form Erik's name on her lips, but it wouldn't come. No words were available to her at all. *Please,* she thought frantically. *I'm too weak for this, please!*

His lips were parted, though the smile was gone from his face. She could feel his chest rise and fall with each labored breath. Was he moving closer? She couldn't tell. Everything was happening so slowly...

But then time sped up, and all hell broke loose.

CHAPTER TWENTY-FIVE

Masquerade

At first, Robin wasn't sure what was actually happening. It felt like a dream, and then it felt like a nightmare, but none of it could be real.

There was a yell from across the room, followed by a couple of people bumping into him and Yara, and then an explosion that rattled the walls.

He ducked over Yara, trying to shield her from debris raining down from the ceiling. His ears were ringing. People were screaming and trying to determine where the eruption had come from. What in the world was going on?

He had to get Yara out of there. Had to get her to safety. He grabbed her wrist and started to run toward the exit, but she was pulling against him and shouting something. He could barely hear…

"We have to find Ash and Carter!" he saw her mouth, the din of the chaos barely audible over the ringing.

"They'll find us!" said Robin, trusting that the other Guardians would take care of themselves.

Yara finally relented and started to follow him, but their path was cut off by another detonation right ahead of them, knocking them on the ground and blocking the exit they were headed toward with billows of thick smoke. Bodies were sprawled on the ground, blood seeping out from under colorful dresses and masks. There was no time to stop and help. He had to get Yara out.

She was already on her feet, pulling him up with her. She had hiked her long dress up to her thighs, holding it impatiently in one hand and Robin with the other, weaving in and out of people expertly, her eyes narrowed under her mask. There was a cut on her cheek, but she didn't seem to notice. She was heading toward the back, where a rarely used emergency escape led to the surface, when she stopped in her tracks.

"Oh no..." she said.

"Why did you stop?" Robin yelled, the ringing in his ears finally starting to die down. The path was blocked behind a cluster of Researchers who were in way over their heads, frozen in shock, staring at something to Robin's left.

And he got the answer to his question.

On the dais from which Black had made her speech stood none other than Ramsey Kain, dressed elegantly in a black suit. Despite the simple white mask he wore, he was immediately recognizable. He slipped off the mask and held his hands out wide, a sneer stretched across his face. He looked different than Robin remembered. The long scar that had once disfigured his face had vanished completely. No doubt a result of his being a clone.

How long had Kain been at the celebration, undetected by the joyful revelers during their one night of festivities? How had he gotten in?

The crowd hushed and a silence overtook the scene. They huddled closer together in the center of the room, and Yara and Robin were jostled together as they got pushed in by the crowd. Robin could see that Shadow Men were pouring into the room from all entrances, standing at attention along the walls, herding them like sheep.

Suddenly, Nayla was behind Robin.

"Let's get out of here," she whispered frantically in his ear. She tugged on his arm, but Robin didn't move.

"How did he get in here?" he said, eyes glued to Kain, his grip on Yara's arm tightening.

"Don't stop the party on my occasion!" said Kain, smiling at them all. "One of yours gate crashed *my* house, I thought it only fair to return the favor!"

People murmured to themselves, unsure of what he meant. Carter's infiltration as a Shadow Man was not widespread knowledge. That Kain knew about it was more than unexpected; it was suspect. Robin peered over the heads of the crowd, searching for the shape shifter. *Where are Carter and Ash...*

"Besides, I brought a date. Come, my love," he said, looking to the right off the platform. A couple of Shadow Men parted to make room for a woman who joined Kain on the platform. She was wearing a lacy black dress to match Kain's suit, her skin a rich brown, with long black hair cascading down her back. Her face was completely obstructed by a full Venetian mask.

"Some of you may recognize her, in fact," said Kain to the crowd. "Where is Ms. Bora Black? I know *you'll* recognize her!"

Black was brought forward, held between two Shadow Men. Her mask had been torn off, but she was staring determinately forward, her jaw set. Under ordinary circumstances, Black was powerful enough to escape if she wanted to. She had the ability to transform herself into shadow and fill the room with darkness, and the grips of two clones would not be enough to stop her. But around her wrists Robin saw NullBonds, a kind of handcuff used on nymphs that trapped them in one form, rendering them powerless. She was stuck as a corporeal human, locked in a stare down with Kain.

"Say hello, darling," said Kain to the woman standing next to him.

The woman turned her face to Kain and stared at him for a moment, before she reached up to take off her mask.

Robin saw Black's eyes widen with shock, her mouth parted. A few other people gasped or screamed in surprise, including the gaggle of Researchers right beside them.

Nayla gave another impatient tug on Robin's arm, and Yara was squeezing his other hand so tightly his fingers were going numb.

"Who is that?" Yara whispered to Robin.

"It's her," he said, recognizing the woman immediately from Carter's optical recording. She was lovely. Her large dark eyes, round and wide and lifeless, met Black's. It was clear from Black's reaction that she recognized the woman, too. Carter and Robin had shown her the tape, explaining everything they had learned.

"You continue to ignore the laws of nature?" said Black in a low voice that nonetheless resonated in the still room.

"Why shouldn't I?" said Kain proudly, laughing. "Do the laws of nature apply when I can change them if I desire? *This* is the research you killed! And look what I have done with it. Ladies and gentle-Deviants of the White Mask, I present to you, Zenobia Varma!"

The name had the desired effect on nearly everyone in the room. By the tightness in Yara's grip, she had put it together.

The Necromancer was here.

"Say hello, darling," said Kain, barely able to conceal his glee.

Zenobia's dark eyes roamed over the faces of the congregation, all staring up at her in disbelief. She said nothing.

"You cloned her," said Black.

"Yes!" said Kain, pointing at Black triumphantly. "I did! But I did more than that. This beauty is a marvel of science. More than just a clone. She is my crowning glory. You see, Zenobia was more than a brilliant scientist. She was more than the smartest, most beautiful woman to walk the earth. She was a hydan. Just like some of my old friends who are with us tonight."

Kain's eyes found Yara. Robin could feel her shaking beside him. He stepped forward instinctively, trying to shield her. He thought back to Yara's recollection of her ordeal with Kain. The man had done unspeakable things to her, and she had yet to recover from the experience.

"My Zenobia could heal herself," Kain continued. "Such a wonderful ability. And she, like me, agreed that such talent should not be restricted to just a select few. We believed that the abilities of the hyden belong to everyone. That's when we created the Omega Project. She wanted to give people her ability. Why was it fair, she thought, for one person to die of cancer, when she could cure herself as easily as breathe? So we set to work.

"Many told us it couldn't be done." He looked pointedly at Black. "People didn't believe that it was possible to take the so-called 'god-given' abilities of a hydan—or any Deviant for that matter—and give them to a simple human. We did not accept this. We worked. Hard and long." The way Kain spoke was exactly as Yara had described. The ravings of a lunatic who loved the sound of his own voice. He took his time. Dragged each word out as though it were a gift to those listening just to hear him speak. "At first, it seemed that shape shifters could not indeed share their powers. So we looked to the hyden and to nymphs. Of course, there were barely any hyden. We had only a handful to choose from. As for the nymphs, of the few—very few—who volunteered to donate samples, we discovered that yes! It could be done! But as you know, the side effects were lethal. A human cell could not, after all, be infused with nymph DNA without dying.

"At your orders, Ms. Black, the Omega Project was abandoned. Or so you thought."

Black bristled but did not take her obsidian eyes away from him as he continued.

"Zenobia believed, like me, that our research was killed too early. So we continued to meet in secret. Then she had the brilliant idea of changing a *replicated* human cell. Don't you see the brilliance of it? If the human cell cannot be altered externally, alter it *internally*. At the source, so to speak. Before it's learned how to be human, teach it to be something else. Something *more*.

"Cloning isn't new. Humans have been trying to do it for decades. With varying degrees of success, of course. But we had something those other humans did not. Her brain." He looked at Zenobia, his eyes soft with adoration, and actually reached up as if to touch her mind, his fingers hovering an inch away from her temple. She did not so much as blink. "We started small. Not trying to alter anything at first. Just duplication. It wasn't long before we were able to do what humans had never done: clone a person.

"When it was clear what we had discovered, Zenobia started to question the ramifications. Suddenly, she started to wonder if you were right, Bora. Asking questions she didn't need to ask. If changing the face of science was really the right thing to do. Such a silly thing to wonder. 'The right thing.'" Kain scoffed. "Who among us really has the right to decide what is or isn't 'right'? What had once been so clear to Zenobia was suddenly murky, all because of a little voice in the back of her head: yours." He pointed to Black.

"We argued. We fought. For days, I insisted that what we were doing would help people. It would *help* people! It would change the world. Technology would advance centuries in the hands of a new race of lab-grown Deviants. Humans would become a thing of the past. She kept reminding me that *I* was human. And I told her that, for the good of all mankind, I would submit myself to be the first human trial with our new research. I would willingly sacrifice myself if it meant that others could heal themselves, or see the future, or read people's minds. But she refused. She took our research... Was on the verge of destroying it.

"I had to stop her, don't you see? I had to! For the future of our people! But she fought me. And there was an accident. My face was cut, my leg mangled, and in my pain, I knocked her to the ground. She fell..." He looked at Zenobia, his gaunt face stretched with horror at the memory, actual tears lining his eyes. "She hit her head and it... it killed her instantly. Her powers, snuffed out like that," he snapped his fingers, "unable to heal herself once she was already dead. I was faced with an unthinkable decision. To run? Or to turn myself in knowing that our research would be destroyed? Everything we had worked so hard for, gone as quickly as her?

"I couldn't let that happen. Not when we had come so far. I took everything we had studied, I took her body, and I ran. I built my own lab, far from your prying eyes. Far from your judgements and assessments of my work. Of *our* work. I perfected our technique of cloning humans so that I could bring back my Zenobia. I could undo the evil I had done.

"When I knew that my research was advanced enough that I could bring her back. I cloned her, but I did more than that. I made her *more* than what she was. The gift she wanted to give to humanity would soon become the gift *I* would give *her*. I made her more powerful. I gave her powers that would set her above the rest, keep her where she deserved to be. At the top."

"What did you do to her, Ramsey?" said Black.

But Robin already knew where the story was going, just as he was sure Black knew as well.

Kain grinned and tutted at her, waggling his finger. "Patience, dear Bora. Patience. Because you see, it really is genius.

"My first true clone I named Phosphorous, after the first element ever discovered in a lab. Because his existence was just as important. And I noticed something strange with dear Phosphorous. Come here, Phosphorous!"

A Shadow Man stepped forward from the crowd of crimson clones and moved next to Kain on the dais. He was identical to Kain in nearly every way. The only differences were in the way he moved and the capital "P" branded onto his neck. Phosphorous stood before them, completely still, his eyes as dead and cold as any other Shadow Man, revealing none of the madness of Kain.

"Look familiar?" Kain laughed again, evidently delighting in the attention he had from the crowd. "I used my own cells to make him. My prototype. My reflection. And see how *different* he is! My own clone, and yet he has none of my pizzaz. Now look at this one. Erik!" he shouted into the crowd.

Robin heard Yara inhale sharply as Erik marched up to the dais. He was wearing a suit of red and black, dressed by Kain for the occasion.

"Erik!" Yara shouted.

Erik did not so much as flinch at the sound of her voice. Robin didn't understand. How was Erik out of isolation? Kain must have known where he was being kept and fetched him. But why was Erik cooperating? It didn't make any sense. Could it be a different Erik? Had Kain grown several? One still in holding, and another of possibly dozens of copies here now?

"Erik!" Yara shrieked again. He still did not show any signs of having heard her. "Oh no," she said, a grim realization dawning on her.

"What's wrong with him?" said Robin.

"Kain is controlling him. Erik told me about this."

Robin opened his mouth to ask more, unable to comprehend what Yara was saying or how she knew it, but he was cut off by the sound of Kain laughing.

"Show them who you are, boy!" Kain held up his hand in which he was holding a small device. He placed it next to Erik's ear for a moment, and at first, it seemed as though nothing happened at all. Then Erik blinked a few times, before realizing where he was and who he was looking at.

He lunged at Kain. "You!" he said, but the Shadow Men had anticipated this and were holding Erik back. Four of them were needed to keep Erik from launching himself at Kain.

Yara shouted his name again, and Erik's head snapped in her direction.

His eyes wide, he seemed to understand perhaps not the full situation, but at least the scope of the problem. Still breathing heavily, he stopped struggling, his eyes locked on Yara.

"You see how different he is from Phosphorous? From any of my Shadow Men? Can anyone tell me why?"

For all the world, it felt as though Kain were a teacher standing at the head of a class and lecturing them. No one responded. The silence in the room was palpable.

Nayla tugged on Robin's arm again, but he jerked it impatiently out of her hand, his eyes locked on the scene ahead of him.

"There's something missing when you make a clone. Some things that cannot be grown in a lab or fabricated by man, no matter how brilliant he may be." Kain gestured to himself with flair. "Call it a soul, call it consciousness, call it whatever you want. But my clones are born without it. Like Phosphorous here. Watch."

In a swift motion, Kain pulled a knife out from within his suit and plunged it into Phosphorous's chest.

The crowd made a collective sound of horror, but otherwise no one moved. They simply watched as Phosphorous silently fell to his knees before slumping to the ground in a pool of blood. Kain looked up, still holding the bloody knife, his hands outstretched.

"Not even so much as a cry for help or a look of betrayal in those eyes.

"Erik, on the other hand," he continued, approaching Erik with the knife. Erik started to struggle, and Yara made to run to the stage, but Robin kept a tight hold on her.

"No!" she yelled.

Erik's jaw was set as he seethed, his eyes locked on Kain, pure loathing etched on every line of his face.

"You see? He doesn't want to die. He's fighting. He has character. He has *life*. All thanks to my Zenobia." Kain looked again at Zenobia, who all this time had barely moved.

"When I brought her back, I amplified her powers. I made her so that she wasn't simply a healer, but a necromancer... *My* necromancer." Kain smiled gleefully, looking at the crowd as though hoping they would share in his joy. "Don't you see? I make the clones. I give them bodies, and she gives them life!"

"You're playing at divinity, Ramsey," said Black, her voice barely controlled. "And you are no god."

"Yes, indeed I am, Bora. And being a god has rewarded me so wonderfully. In fact, I wouldn't even be here today if it weren't for my Necromancer. After all, *she* killed me." He pointed a long finger at Yara.

"I would do it again, you monster," said Yara, her voice trembling.

"I'm not the monster, Yara," said Kain, his brow furrowed, his face concerned. "I'm offering people a more meaningful life. I'm giving back what has been taken away from them!"

"You're creating slaves for you to use and dispose of as you see fit!" Yara shot back, taking a step forward, ripping her hand out of Robin's as he tried to hold her back. "And now you're using Erik against us!"

Kain nodded. "Well, I can't deny that. Erik has proved incredibly useful. All thanks to this handy little device I built into your boyfriend." He held it up again next to Erik's ear. Robin watched as Erik's eyes unfocused and he stood completely still, oblivious once again to the world around him.

"What the hell," Robin breathed.

"He's new and improved, too. Aren't you, Erik?"

Erik did not move at first, and then Kain said, "Show them."

Erik closed his eyes, bowing his head as though he were praying, but Robin—who knew Erik too well—could see that his fists were clenched. Something wasn't right. And then...

The ground started to shake. A few people made sounds of surprise and fear as the walls rattled, the glasses clinked, and people clung to each other. Sprouting from Erik came leafy vines that shot in all directions like fireworks. A hurricane of green spun around the room, clinging to the walls and tripping people. The earthquake didn't stop. It continued to escalate until they were covering their heads with their arms and shrieking in fear. Nayla was pulling again at Robin, desperate to get away, but Robin was trying to get to Yara as she stumbled toward the stage.

"Stop," said Kain's cool voice. Robin barely heard him above the commotion, but almost immediately, the ground stopped shaking, and Erik straightened again, his dead eyes staring straight ahead. The growths fell limp around him, a wreath of vines connecting Erik to every corner of the room.

The screaming calmed, and a fearful hush slowly overtook them, punctuated here and there by a few people pulling leaves out of their hair or untangling the vegetation around their feet.

"Spectacular, isn't it? *This* is the kind of power I want to bring to the world."

"Power isn't meant for everyone," said Black.

"Only someone with power would say that," Kain snarled, his eyes flashing angrily. "What I plan to offer the world will change everything."

"You have nothing to offer, Ramsey!" Black shouted, her skin darkening as black veins crept along her exposed skin, spidering around her hands and neck. It was a sign of how strong she was that she could display this power despite the NullBonds.

"I'm afraid I have much more to offer than you do, Bora Black. I will give the world what they never knew they wanted. I will give them strength. Knowledge. And yes, *power*."

"How?"

"By cloning them all! Bringing them back with the powers of the Deviants. My Zenobia will call their souls into their new bodies where they can experience the joy of being stronger than ever before!"

Black's lips were pursed in a dangerous, thin line. "You're going to kill every person on the planet? Just to bring them back?"

"Bring them back *better*. It's not an easy road ahead of me. But then again, the world is never easily changed."

"You're mad," said Yara, her voice carrying in the quiet of the hall.

"Unfortunately," said Kain, ignoring her, "my Zenobia couldn't bring her own soul back when I remade her body." He looked at the

Necromancer. This time she met his eyes. He looked painfully sad, his eyes scanning over her face as though he wanted nothing more than to sit there and look at her forever. "I can never truly have the woman I loved. But this Zenobia, my precious necromancer, she understands what I'm trying to achieve."

"Chaos?" said Black.

"Justice!" Kain yelled at her, spit flying from his mouth. "A world where Deviants don't hide from humans! Where we can all reach our greatest potential! And you people are the only ones trying to stop me."

"Robin, please," Nayla whispered. "I have a really bad feeling about this…"

"No!" Yara yelled, her eyes on Kain.

A split second later, his knife was flying through the air before it was embedded in Black's heart, darkness unfurling from the wound in great, billowing clouds that filled the room.

CHAPTER TWENTY-SIX

Safe

The room erupted in screams and shouts as the crowd that had been so still only a moment before started to run in every direction, frantically trying to find an exit. Robin was pulling Yara forcefully away as she fought to get to Erik. The world was a blur through her mask, her vision limited, but she didn't have the foresight to take it off.

Robin's grip on her was burning her skin as he tried to pull her away from the ensuing fray. Erik had leapt off the stage and was fighting members of the Society, his face blank. Branches shot from his hands like whips, disabling people as vines slashed across faces and twisted around wrists.

Yara screamed Erik's name again, wrenching her arm out of Robin's hand. Ash materialized next to her, her face livid as she surrounded Yara with fire, shielding her from a violent lash of Erik's boughs which sizzled and burned as it slammed into a wall of flame.

"He's gone, Yara!" shouted Ash through a mouthful of fire.

"No!" Yara screamed.

She continued toward Erik, stepping over the bodies of the fallen, but burning hands were pulling her back.

"Help me!" she heard Ash scream to someone else.

And then another pair of hands and Yara was too weak to fight it. She struggled, but it was no good. Sweat from the shield of fire was stinging her eyes, her skin red-hot.

"Erik!"

But it was pointless. She couldn't even see him anymore through the inferno.

"Yara, we need to suit up." It was Carter's voice, the other pair of hands on her. The Vurwari and the shape shifter pulled the hydan back amidst the chaos of what had once been a celebration, now a massacre.

Too dazed, Yara barely realized when they were out of the commissary. Ash was gone, her human form abandoned as a ball of angry orange and yellow and white flew back to ravage the Shadow Men.

Robin and Nayla were there, diamond armor already over their masquerade attire, white masks in lieu of the ornate veneers, gauntlets on their hands.

"Get her out of here! She's what Kain wants," Carter yelled at Robin, flinging armor over Yara's shoulders.

"I can fight!" said Yara.

"No, kid," said Robin. "C's right. We're not winning this one."

Yara turned to Carter to protest, to insist that she could help. But they were already mid-transformation into a leopard, tearing their clothes off as they did. Their skin was sprouting silken spotted fur, their teeth elongating into fangs, glasses falling off a wide, snarling snout. Before Yara could say a word, the leopard that was once Carter had shot into the fray, Nayla short on their heels, wielding her solenoid with deadly skill.

People were running in every direction. Nymphs were transforming into creatures of ice or conjuring gales of wind, humans were running for weapons, shape shifters were fighting in beastly forms, as the White Masks who weren't fighters fled toward safety. The Shadow Men were no match for the Guardians, but they were outnumbered and unprepared. There was nothing to do now but buy enough time to evacuate as many people as they could. Even as Robin rushed Yara away with a group of Researchers, she could see it was almost over.

But Erik… And Kain.

"Robin, please!" she said, tugging at him to go back. She wanted to fall into her mind, see how this would end, but she couldn't find the stillness she needed and her head resisted with a pounding throb, so she gave up.

"Yara, now is not the time! Ya gotta let me do my job." They reached the emergency stairwell and started taking the stairs up two at a time toward the exit.

"What about *my* job? I'm a Guardian, too—"

"You're a liability," snapped Robin, stopping in his tracks to face her. They were pressed against the wall by the swarm of people, the heat of so many bodies making her sick. "You're not just a Guardian. You're a hydan. *You're* what Kain wants more than anything else. We can't risk it."

It was the fire in his eyes, the severity in his voice, that stopped Yara from resisting.

She followed obediently to the lobby. Night had fallen. Yara realized she didn't know what time it was. Didn't even know where Robin was taking her. She didn't know what the procedure was for something like this. No training had prepared her for Headquarters being abandoned.

Behind the building was a parking lot. Used, Yara had assumed, for civilian visitors. Most White Masks lived on campus, but evidently they had access to a few of the cars because Robin unlocked an unassuming gray sedan.

"Where are we going?" said Yara.

Robin didn't answer.

An hour later, Robin pulled the car into the driveway of a modest house in a neighborhood in Santa Clarita. He turned the car off and the two of them sat in silence for a few moments. Thoughts had long ago stopped racing through Yara's mind. No doubt the fight back at Headquarters was over. She felt numb.

"My aunt," she said, quietly.

"Is safe," said Robin. "Carter got her from work. They're on their way here."

"Carter's OK then? And Ash?"

Robin nodded.

"And..." She couldn't bring herself to ask about the rest. She wanted to know what had happened. If Erik was OK. And she supposed she should ask about Nayla, seeing as how she was Robin's girlfriend. But the curiosity was muted behind a frosted pane of paralysis. She hadn't thought to take her ConvOrb with her to the party. It was back in her quarters.

"Let's go inside."

The street was quiet. Only a few street lamps cast circles of light on the well-maintained sidewalks and manicured lawns.

Robin unlocked the front door with a digital keypad and they stepped into the dark foyer. The house was sparsely decorated. A cookie cutter picture of suburbia with nothing but motel art and fresh carpets.

"Who lives here?" Yara whispered, not wanting to wake anyone up.

"No one," said Robin. "It's a safe house."

Yara caught a glimpse of herself in a small mirror by the front door. She looked absurd in an evening gown underneath her chainmail, the inlaid headband Ash gave her somehow tangled in her short hair.

"Can we change?"

"There should be clothes upstairs."

They walked in silence upstairs and Robin disappeared into one of the three bedrooms. Yara found jeans, a t-shirt, and a hoodie in another, before remembering she couldn't get out of her dress without help. There was a moment in which that one little obstacle nearly broke her. Her muscles threatened to go limp and tears burned her eyes as she tried and failed to pull down the zipper of her dress. But she froze, closed her eyes, and inhaled deeply.

Remember. Inhale the calm: liquid gold. Exhale the panic: red smoke.

"Robin?" she said quietly, knocking on the door to his room. She still spoke like she was afraid of waking some nonexistent occupant of the house.

"What's up?" he called from inside.

"I… can't unzip my dress."

In a moment, he opened the door, already changed out of his Fête attire and into civilian clothes. He said nothing. He simply stood, looking as numb as she felt, waiting for her to turn around. She did.

There was a slight tug on her dress and the sound of the zipper. The tightness around her chest and waist loosened.

"Thank you."

Fifteen minutes later, Robin and Yara sat in the gray living room, Robin's ConvOrb on the coffee table between them.

"You should have let me fight." The sound of her own voice startled Yara. She hadn't meant to say the words out loud. She didn't want to argue.

"You don't get it."

"Don't get what?"

Robin looked up at her, rubbing his hands together, elbows on his knees. "Our job—mine and C's and A's—it's not to protect you, 'Yara Rivers.' It's to protect the hydan who sees the future."

"What does that mean? I *am* the hydan who sees the future."

"No. *You* are a person. The *hydan* is an asset. Our job is to protect the asset. Not the person."

Yara frowned, confused.

"I don't want you to hate me," he said.

"Why would I hate you?"

With a heavy sigh, Robin spoke. "This is not anything you're supposed to know. Ever. But who knows, now… Ya have the right to know. Since you're willing to put your life on the line for the Society. But this thing with Kain…" He struggled for a few moments. "When we found out what he was doing, our mission was to stop him getting his hands on you. On all of the hyden. Any of you. You were all too powerful to risk getting into his hands. And after he had already captured some of the hyden, our orders changed. And obviously we wanted to get you back, to protect you if we could, but if it wasn't possible to do that… we weren't supposed to risk Kain getting you. D'you get what I'm saying?"

Yara was shaking, but she didn't know why. "No."

"We were given orders to kill you, Yara. All of us. Every Guardian. Any of the hyden. You could not be in Kain's hands."

The numbness weighed heavily on her as his words sunk in.

"Remember Anna?"

Anna Karimov. Kain had called her "the puppeteer." She was one of the hydan Yara had been imprisoned with. Yara nodded. "She died during the escape."

"Her power was to control people. She could make them move, make them do things. She… she wasn't killed by Shadow Men."

"No…"

"Her Guardians had to do it, Yara. She was too powerful, and if Kain had kept hold of her, then…"

Yara shook her head.

"It was bad enough when… and for us…" Robin's disjointed speech as he struggled to find the right words had Yara's head spinning, but she tried to follow his meaning. "When Kain broke into HQ last year before he took you, we were supposed to—but we couldn't—"

"Supposed to what?" Her voice was too loud.

Robin didn't answer, but the look on his face said it all.

"Kill me? You were supposed to kill me?"

"It's called the failsafe. But—we couldn't."

Her hands were trembling. It was hard to identify what she felt as anger under everything else that was going through her mind. But when she looked at the man across from her, a strangely comforting weight settled over her. His voice was weak, his cheeks wet. It was looking into his eyes at that moment that she really believed the words

Robin had said to her all those weeks ago.

CHAPTER TWENTY-SEVEN

Whispers and Triggers

Zak Glover stood outside the abandoned Headquarters of the Los Angeles branch of the White Mask Society. It looked nearly the same as it always did, simply without the bustle of life. No movement in the lobby, no water running in the fountain or ferns by the door, no lights on in the offices upstairs. He looked up at Black's window. Though light had never shone from it, the darkness now felt unintentional and wrong.

"May your energy find peace and give life to those who follow," he said quietly, two fingers on his forehead. He pulled them away before letting his hand fall. "You will be remembered." The words and gesture were little more than a meager tribute to the dead, but people —humans and Deviants alike—sought out ritual as a source of comfort in times of loss.

There was not enough time to mourn the loss of Bora Black or any of the other fourteen White Masks who fell during the celebration.

Glover was now in command. His team was scattered and afraid. They would look to him for strength and guidance. He had to make sure they would find it.

Yara was dozing on the couch, a familiar crease between her eyebrows even in sleep. Robin couldn't so much as close his eyes. Carter and Ash were on their way with Yara's aunt and hopefully more information about the madness they had all left behind at Headquarters. It was nearly four in the morning when headlights illuminated the kitchen through the back door. Robin rushed over to watch as the Furtive set down on the brittle grass of the unwatered backyard. The stealth aircrafts were quiet in flight, but their engines still caused windows to rattle and trees to rustle when landing. It was enough of a disturbance to wake Yara. Still bleary eyed from sleep, she joined Robin.

Carter, Ash, Catherine, and—to Robin's great surprise—Nayla climbed out, all with somber expressions. The Guardians were still dressed in their formal wear, contrasting with Catherine who was in her work scrubs. Yara was running outside and into her aunt's arms before Robin had fully opened the sliding door.

"Honey, thank god you're OK!" said Catherine into Yara's shoulder. "They told me what happened. I just can't believe it."

"What's the situation?" Robin asked the other Guardians, giving Yara a moment of privacy with her only family.

"Black is dead," said Carter. "We killed almost all the Shadow Men. It's almost as if Kain didn't care about getting any of them out alive, as long as he and Varma got out."

"Did they?"

Carter nodded.

"And E?"

"We have him," said Nayla.

"What?" Robin exclaimed, accidentally calling Yara's and Catherine's attentions. "He can't be here, he can't know where she—"

"Calm down, R," said Carter. "He's not *here*. He's in custody. Glover has him."

"Where?" asked Yara.

"At HQ?" said Robin.

"No," said Carter. "HQ's been all but abandoned. It isn't safe until Kain is gone. For good. If he got in once, planted bombs, we can't trust he won't do it again."

"Safe houses, then?" said Robin.

"A few," said Nayla. "But mostly the smaller bases here in SoCal. They don't have the resources that HQ had, but the hope is that smaller targets will be less appealing to Kain."

"Easier to protect, too," said Ash.

"How do you figure?" said Robin.

"I'll tell you in a minute," said Carter. They exchanged a small glance with Ash that only Robin noticed.

"What a mess," said Robin, rubbing his eyes. He had never heard of a Society base being deserted.

"Is Erik OK?" said Yara.

It was a moment before anyone answered. "We don't know," said Ash finally.

A safe answer, Robin thought. The truth was that Erik was not OK. Even alive, that clone wasn't Erik. The Necromancer may have brought Erik back from the dead, but given what they had just seen Erik do at the Fête, he was hardly more than Kain's puppet. Somehow, Kain had control of a man who had once given his life for the same people he had attacked mere hours ago. His partner and his friend was really gone.

Nayla's hand slipped into his and gave a gentle squeeze.

"We need to change," said Ash. "And get some sleep."

"I'll show you the bedrooms," said Yara, leading them inside.

But Carter took Robin's arm and led him aside. "I need a word."

"What's going on?" said Robin once they were alone.

"Remember last year when we were all interviewed by Black?"

"Yeah."

"She was looking for a mole. A leak in the Society."

"What? That's not possible."

"Isn't it?" said Carter. "How else could Kain have broken into Headquarters?"

"He used to work in—"

"Twice, R. He broke in twice. I think Black arrested Williams. That's why they've been gone. Something in Black's investigation led her to Williams. So Black thought it was over and done with. But Kain still got in tonight even with Williams in custody."

Robin knew Xaili Williams. They weren't a traitor. They couldn't be. "Is Williams in custody for sure? They didn't escape?"

Carter nodded. "A shifter who works Downstairs told me when we were evacuating. They wanted to go and get Williams out before it was too late."

"Downstairs" was an internal term the Guardians used to describe those among their ranks who worked on the bottommost floor of Headquarters with the undesirable job of hunting the most dangerous and elusive of all Deviants, a species known as haunts. Gale Trumbull, who had taken over the Guardian division after Williams's disappearance, had previously been in charge of the haunt hunting division. "Williams? A mole?" said Robin in disbelief.

"That's what they told me," said Carter seriously. "I know it's hard to believe, but I can't really believe *any* White Mask could be a spy."

Carter had a point. "It had to have been E then, right? Who got them in?" said Robin, lowering his voice even further, ashamed of the words. "I mean, we saw how Kain could control him. Yara mentioned something about brainwashing. I guess E told her he'd been conditioned or something and they were trying to break him of it while he was in holding. I mean it's not like E would have done anything against the Society of his own accord," he added, feeling the need to defend the integrity of a man he had once trusted implicitly.

Carter shook their head. "I don't see how it could have been E. He hasn't had access to anything any more than Williams has. There's no way he could have gotten Kain in."

"And the E—the Erik who was at the Fête—was for sure the same one? I mean, with clones…"

"I was talking about that with N and A on the way here," said Carter, speaking quickly, matching Robin's conspiratorial volume. "We have a theory. Now, obviously it's only a theory, and we don't have a way to prove it. But if the only way the clones have any personality or soul or life force or whatever you want to call it, if the only way for the clones to have that is if the Necromancer imbues them with it, there can't be more than one… 'real' Erik. Right?"

Robin frowned, sorting through Carter's words. "You don't think the Necromancer could duplicate souls like Kain duplicates bodies?"

"I don't know. But I don't think so. Otherwise, wouldn't all the Shadow Men have them?"

"Maybe Kain just wants his goons to be mindless drones. Easier to control them that way."

"Maybe," conceded Carter. "But I don't think so. He seems to be able to control E just fine. I just feel like we would have seen some indication of multiple copies of the same person. Multiple 'sentient' copies," they amended.

Robin brushed his hand over his face.

"Look," Carter pressed on, "even if Kain can somehow resurrect the same soul more than once, the Erik we saw at the Fête seemed to recognize Yara. He knew at least a little bit of what was going on. If it had been a different copy, I don't think he would have reacted that way. And you saw him, R. That was our E. Until—"

"Until Kain started using mind control."

"Right." Carter paused, before pressing on. "The smaller precincts will be easier to protect because if there's a mole, that had to be how Kain got into Headquarters. There can't possibly be a mole at every location. Right?"

"Yeah," said Robin.

They stood without speaking for a few moments under the weight of everything that was happening, the only sound the song of the crickets. The world Robin knew and loved and relied on was crumbling.

"Then who is it?" said Robin. *Who is the spy? Who has betrayed us?*

Nayla had found some clothes that fit in one of the bedrooms. Yara and her aunt had closed themselves in the room across the hall and she could hear whispered conversation through the door. Ash was keeping first watch outside, but Nayla couldn't sleep. All she could think about was the horror of seeing Kain and his Necromancer. The memory of the blood bath that had ensued as the Shadow Men were left behind to be slaughtered just to make room for Kain and Varma alone to escape. The rest were disposable. Replaceable.

Robin had finally fallen asleep on the couch, leaving her and Carter the remaining two bedrooms, but she didn't want to be alone. The first glow of the sun was already peeking above the horizon, the sky lightening to a purple gray. She didn't want to wake Robin, but she had little choice. As much as she wanted to rest, wanted it all to be over, there was still so much to do.

Erik was strapped to a bed in a room that was not at Headquarters. His mind was hazy with drugs, his limbs impossibly heavy. A few branches were sprouting from beneath his restraints. He had no memory of how he got there or what had happened after he woke up at the Fête in front of Kain and Yara. He was informed it had been another fugue state. Somehow, Kain had taken control of him.

The room in which he was kept was somewhere between a medical ward and a holding cell. It was sparsely equipped. Not much more than the bed he was tied to and a large two-way mirror along one wall. Even through the fog of drugs, he was sure he was being observed.

"Hello?" he called in a groggy voice. He didn't bother to struggle. He knew he was with the Society. He recognized the equipment. He just wanted to know what happened. If Yara was safe. If Kain was dead. If Kain *could* die. And the woman who had stood next to him on the dais with the dark eyes. The Necromancer.

"How are you feeling, Erik?" said a voice through speakers from behind the mirror.

"How do you think."

"That's good to hear."

It is?

A moment later, Frankie Sweet walked into the room, followed by another woman Erik didn't know. "Glad to see you're back, Erik," said Frankie, undoing the straps that bound him to the bed.

"Woah, woah, hey! Don't do that, I could be dangerous!" He tried to stop her, but she smiled and touched his hand.

"Thank you for your concern, Erik," she said. "But it isn't necessary. Things seem to be under control for the moment."

"What happened? Where am I?"

"You're at the San Diego branch, Mr. Carpenter," said the woman Erik didn't know.

"Erik, this is Tina Dyson. She's a Researcher here."

"Hello."

Dyson nodded.

Frankie proceeded to fill Erik in on everything that had happened since he first blacked out before the Fête began. That a resurrected Kain had someone working on the inside, that he had infiltrated Headquarters and triggered Erik, used Erik to attack the White Masks during the celebration.

Erik closed his eyes. "Is everyone OK?" he said, feeling nauseous.

There was a moment of silence and Erik's body tightened uncomfortably, dreading what he might have been responsible for. "Most of us managed to evacuate in time," said Frankie. "But it isn't safe to go back to HQ for the time being."

Erik's skin was clammy, his fingers numb. This couldn't be his life. To die only to come back as Kain's puppet, or else live in isolation, held as a prisoner by the Society. He felt useless. Worse than useless, he was a burden. A weakness. A risk to not only Yara's safety, but everyone's.

"What about Yara? Did she make it out?"

"To our knowledge, Ms. Rivers is fine. She's with her Guardians."

Her new *Guardians*, thought Erik. *As in, not me.* "Good," he said, though he didn't feel it. He wanted to help. To fight.

"Do they know how got Kain in?" said Erik.

"Well," Frankie said. "That's where we were hoping you might come in handy."

Erik opened his eyes and looked at the two women. "You mean there's a way I can help?"

"Perhaps," said Frankie.

"This little thing," said Dyson, holding up a small device, not dissimilar to a ConvOrb, "is what Kain used to trigger you. Switching you from yourself back into a drone he can control."

"I thought you already knew how to do that," said Erik.

"We know what song gets you triggered," said Frankie. "But before we could only use sedation to get you back. Not a great long-term solution."

"And certainly not conducive to speedy experimentation to try to break the conditioning," added Dyson.

"But this," said Frankie, "allows us to bring you back more efficiently. 'Für Elise' puts you in," she fingered one of the buttons on the device, "then transposed into a major key," she fingered the other button, "takes you out."

"Quite ingenious, really," said Dyson.

"How is this supposed to help us figure out who helped Kain break into Headquarters?" said Erik.

"Now that we can flip your switch more effectively," said Frankie, "Tina here is confident that we can make some more progress on allowing you to maintain control, even in these fugue states."

"Does that mean... you can fix me? Erase the conditioning altogether?"

"Let's not get ahead of ourselves," said Dyson. "We may know your triggers, but we still don't understand how he was able to condition you in the first place. And as such, we can't begin to undo what's been done. However, if you can maintain some level of awareness when your switch is flipped, to use Frankie's terms, we may be able to learn more about who was helping Kain."

Erik still didn't understand.

"We're hopeful," said Frankie, "that you might be able to provide some insight into Kain's operation."

"Perhaps the... 'drone Erik' knows who is working for Kain," said Dyson.

"You think I might know who the traitor is?"

"It's possible that you contain memories somewhere in that mind of yours that could help us uncover some of what Kain is hiding."

Memories of the missing first year of his new life. "Let's do it," he said.

Frankie and Dyson shared a look. "I want to make sure you understand what trying would entail," said Dyson. "It wouldn't be an easy process. And we can't guarantee success."

"I don't care. There has to be a way for me to fight this. Whatever *this* is." He pointed to his head, where somewhere in the recesses of his mind, Kain held an iron grip.

"We've never attempted anything like this before," said Frankie. "We only have a theory of what might work."

"I understand," said Erik. "I want to try. Whatever it takes."

CHAPTER TWENTY-EIGHT

Scattered

Five Guardians and a civilian sat quietly around a coffee table, taking in the words that had just been spoken. After a moment, the silence was cautiously broken by Robin's measured words.

"I know it sounds like an unnecessary risk..." He trailed off, evidently unsure how to finish the sentence.

Nayla put her hand on his arm and took over. After all, it was her idea. "Right now," she said, "we have the upper hand. I know it doesn't seem like it, but Kain knows we're disorganized. He's probably counting on it. If I were in his shoes, this is when I would strike. That means we have to act before he can."

"But without the full resources of the Society?" said Ash. She alone in the room looked relaxed, leaning back in her seat and tossing a ball of fire from hand to hand.

"We have an advantage," said Nayla, looking at Carter.

They responded with a questioning look.

"You've been there before," she explained. "You know where his whole setup is. And you were already planning to go in with a team. Now it's just a different team."

They all stared at her.

"I thought no one knew about that," said Ash, her lips pursed, the only one brave enough to break the tension.

"R told me," said Nayla.

Everyone turned to Robin who shrugged, avoiding meeting anyone's eyes.

"Be that as it may, I'm not sure this qualifies as much of an advantage," said Carter.

"But she's right," said Yara. "Kain thinks he has time while we lick our wounds."

"C was supposed to lead a team of two dozen Guardians," said Ash. "There's five of us. We can't take them all down alone. And we can't half-ass this, either. Yara killed Kain once already. It didn't take. As long as he has the Necromancer he's too powerful and nothing we do matters. And there's no way that five Guardians can kill Kain, the Necromancer, and destroy all his equipment. It's just not possible."

"The Necromancer is our mission," said Robin. "For now."

"It's just about getting her," said Nayla. "Away from Kain."

"Couldn't he just grow another one?" said Catherine, speaking for the first time since Nayla and Robin had roused them all in the late hours of the morning to present them with their plan. "I mean, if she's already a clone..." There was a hesitation to her voice. The implication that she didn't really believe what she was saying.

"Annie—I mean," said Yara, "Catherine is right. Maybe he already has more than one. Maybe he has like... hundreds of backups. Who's to say she's the only one? Even now? Ash is right. It's all or nothing this time. It's too big a risk to go in without knowing we can take it all out."

"I'd be willing to bet that Kain would only make one copy of Zenobia," said Carter. "Given their history. He would want her to replace the real Zenobia Varma, and if there's more than one, it would just remind him of their past. Cheapen her."

"Yeah, it's like with collectibles," said Ash. "The fewer there are, the more valuable. Right?"

"Are you suggesting his clones are like action figures?" said Robin.

"I dunno, I'm not a nerd."

"We just can't know he only made one Zenobia for sure," said Robin. "We have to get them both. Kain *and* the Necromancer. That's the first step. If we try to do more than that, we'll end up doing nothing. It's been a year since Kain died—the *original* Kain. If we get them then at least it buys us some time, which we desperately need."

"There aren't enough of us to get to her, though," said Carter. "There could be dozens of Shadow Men standing between us and the basement, which is where he keeps everything valuable. And it's locked. We can't even access it without the Necromancer. Only her blood will open it."

"Jeez, blood?" said Ash. "Why not a fingerprint or retinal scan or something normal? I.e. something that doesn't require injuring yourself every time you want to unlock it?"

"If she's still a hydan," said Yara, "then she'd just heal immediately every time anyway."

"Whatever the reason," continued Carter, "I guarantee that everything Kain cares about, everything we want is in there. Behind that door."

"And if Kain cares about her as much as he claims," said Robin, "he'll have her more protected than anything else. She gives him immortality."

"And she's as loyal to him as the rest of his Shadow Men," said Ash.

"I just don't see how we could get past the biometric lock," said Carter. "Short of burning the whole house down."

"Sounds fun," said Ash, her eyes flashing mischievously.

"Out of the question," said Carter. "It's an old house surrounded by dry brush in the valley. We can't risk a fire. It would spread too quickly."

Ash pouted, extinguishing the flame she had conjured in her hand.

"How were you planning on getting in before?" said Nayla.

"Force in numbers," said Carter simply. "And weapons. Of which we have essentially neither."

"Janya," said Yara. Everyone turned to look at her. "Janya. Her daughter. That's how we get in."

"How do you figure?" said Nayla.

"Well, if it's a biometric scanner and the Necromancer has access, Janya should be able to get through it too, right?"

"It could work," said Carter slowly. "It depends on how accurate the scanner is. But they may have enough in common to fool it."

"Kain isn't expecting her daughter," said Robin. "I'd bet the scanner is meant to be enough to keep out his Shadow Men and us."

"Us being just... all of the Society?" said Carter.

Robin shrugged.

"Even if she can't open it, maybe she can help us. She's the Necromancer's daughter," said Yara.

"She's Zenobia Varma's daughter," Carter corrected.

"Same thing," said Ash. "Isn't it?"

"Not if Kain wasn't lying when he said that the Necromancer hasn't been resurrected," said Robin. "We saw what it looked like when Erik was under Kain's control. He didn't recognize Yara or care about her." Yara shifted. "Who's to say the Necromancer would care about Janya given the same circumstances?" Robin finished.

"Does Janya even know what's going on?" said Ash. "That her mother has been resurrected to be used as a puppet by the guy who killed her? Man, can you imagine?" she added as an afterthought. "That would mess me up."

"I'll call her Guardians," said Nayla immediately. "They should be the ones to tell her now that Black—" She didn't finish her thought, and instead excused herself to reach out to Janya's Guardians.

"Is it even appropriate to involve her?" said Ash. "She's a civvy. Can we really ask to put her in that position?"

"I'd want to know," said Catherine. "If it were my sister."

"R," said Carter quietly to Robin. "Can I talk to you in the kitchen?"

Robin followed them, leaving Ash, Yara, and Catherine in the living room. "Look. I know this sounds crazy—" he started, but Carter cut him off.

"Have you noticed anything strange about Nayla? Has she seemed different at all?"

"What?" said Robin, taken aback.

"Nayla. Anything off. Anything at all?"

"What're you talking about?"

Carter paused for a moment, wiping their glasses before continuing. "I need you to hear me out before you… react. This plan is crazy. There are five of us. Against an army. Yara's never even been in the field. And we know Kain has someone working for him in the Society."

"You think Nayla is the mole?" hissed Robin.

"I'm just asking you to entertain the possibility," said Carter calmly. "How much have you told her about everything?"

Robin faltered, thinking back to the many nights he had spent with Nayla in the last few weeks. He had confided in her so much. He hadn't even thought twice about it. Was this all his fault? "I—"

"I'm not trying to blame you," said Carter. "And I don't want you blaming yourself. I just mean, she probably knows a lot, right? About what's been going on?"

"Yeah," said Robin eventually, ashamed. "Yeah, she does."

"It would explain a lot, is all I mean."

Robin cursed and scrubbed his face.

"I know things are complicated right now with you two," said Carter.

"Complicated is not—That's not—"

"Listen, R. If you don't think it's possible, I'll believe you. If you really believe we can trust her, then I trust you."

Orlando Louis stepped away to answer his ConvOrb. He had worked with the same team for years. Together with Elida and Ben they served as the Guardians of Janya Varma, the young hydan whose ability to heal herself had not only made her a target of Kain, but had saved the life of another hydan who had nearly died in an attempt to destroy the madman. At the moment, Elida and Ben were helping Janya pack as the three of them took on the task of getting her to a safe house in the aftermath of Headquarters being evacuated.

The danger that accompanied Kain's return, however, was somehow not the most unexpected complication of being Janya's Guardians. Rather, it was the return of her mother. Her *deceased* mother, Zenobia Varma, a woman who had died many years before at Kain's very hands, leaving Janya an orphan to be raised at the Society before pursuing a civilian life.

They hadn't told Janya about her mother's reappearance. Yet. They were waiting to mention it until Janya was safe, not wanting to muddle her mind with too much all at once. Elida maintained that they should not tell her about it at all.

"This can't possibly be our responsibility," she had insisted on their way to Janya's apartment.

"Who would ever think to include that in our job description?" Ben had rebutted. "'Protect them. Oh, and also be sure to tell them if their dead parent comes back as a mindless cloned necromancer under the control of the mad scientist who used to do experiments on them.'"

Frankly, Orlando agreed with both of them. The three of them had been a team for years, and it usually amounted to this. Elida supporting one decision, Ben another, and Orlando somewhere in the middle.

"If it doesn't come from us," Ben had continued, "then who? Black is dead. Glover has too much on his hands with everything that's happened. I'm sure the last thing on his mind right now is Janya."

"Probably shouldn't be," said Elida under her breath.

"There's a lot going on, is all I'm saying," said Ben.

"Shouldn't it be his call?" insisted Elida.

"All I know is that if it were me, I would think I had the right to know my mother was back."

"But she's not back," said Elida. "Not really. I mean, if Kain was telling the truth, then she's just a mindless drone."

"Wouldn't you want to know? If it was your mom?"

No one had spoken after Ben said those words. Orlando knew, as did Ben, all about Elida's mother. She had been a nymph. Specifically, a fauna nymph, a class of Deviant who were notorious for their dislike of mingling with humanity due to the poor treatment of animals at human hands. Many of them simply opted to exist in the wild, staying almost exclusively in their non-human forms among like communities. Elida's mother, Thera, had been different. She had split her time between her jaguar and her human form. As a human, she had fallen in love with Elida's human father. As a jaguar, she ultimately met her demise at the hands of a poacher when Elida was very young. The irony was not lost on any of them that the love Thera bore for the humans she tried to live amongst had not been enough to save her from being killed by one of them.

Orlando knew his partners, and he could tell that Ben was going to tell Janya about the Necromancer with or without Orlando and Elida's blessing. He tried to savor this brief moment of calm before a potential storm. One thing at a time.

For the moment, Janya seemed remarkably calm about the situation.

Orlando turned his attention to his orb. A small image was projected from it, and it was not a face he was expecting. "N?"

"Hey," said the image of Nayla Jackson. "You got a minute?"

"We're about to move Janya to a safe house."

"She's with you now?" said Nayla.

Orlando nodded.

"Have you told her about… what's going on?"

"Not yet. Wanted to get her settled first."

"Can you bring her here? We have an idea."

"Who's 'we' and where's 'here'?"

Nayla answered.

"I'll take it to the others and let you know what we decide," said Orlando.

"Be convincing," said Nayla. "It's important." With that, her face vanished and Orlando tucked away his orb. If the four of them joined her in that safe house, there would be ten people under one roof, which was a lot. Too many for one house. But Nayla had said it was important. He wished he knew why, but she was a Guardian. And if she said something was important, Orlando believed her. He would trust any White Mask with his life.

* * *

Erik was tired and his cheek was burning, but he didn't know why. He was in the fifth hour of working with Dyson in their attempt to break his conditioning. She would trigger him and the world disappeared, until she eventually set him free after no changes or improvements.

It was significantly more exhausting than the efforts that had been made back at Headquarters, given that Dyson could flip his switch off and on with the click of a button rather than sedating him and waiting for him to come back, so things were moving much more quickly, which was both a blessing and a curse.

"You're completely immovable," she said, showing him a video of her latest attempt. Erik watched the recording in which he saw himself standing stock still, his face blank. The Dyson in the video shoved him, yelled in his face, held up pictures of people and places he knew.

No change.

Erik watched as Dyson eventually slapped his unresponsive face before she released him from his trance, and the real Dyson stopped the video.

"I guess that's why my cheek hurts," said Erik.

"Sorry about that. Wanted to check if pain might get any reaction."

"Right," he replied apathetically. His cheek was sore, but his mind was too preoccupied by how no progress had been made at all. Dyson was evidently losing confidence as well.

"If we're to have any success," she said, typing notes onto her tablet, "it will likely be a solution that comes from a lab. Something we build or make. I just don't see any evidence that we can break the conditioning with this kind of treatment."

His heart felt heavy. He was worse than a prisoner trapped in his own body—which wasn't even really his body at all; it was simply a copy, one that had not lived his life. He was a weapon. Created and tuned to attack the people he loved most, wielded by those he hated. "There has to be a way…"

Dyson sighed heavily. "I can consult with my team. We can try to come up with ideas, maybe do some more scans, run more simulations."

"No," said Erik. "That'll take too long."

"Do you have somewhere to be?"

"The longer it is before we can figure out who sold us out, the more likely it is to happen again," said Erik. "And the longer Kain has control over me, the greater of a risk it is to keep me…" *alive*, he thought to himself, "…here. He outed himself at the Fête. That means he has a plan. Whatever he's going to do, it's going to be soon."

"What do you propose, then?" said Dyson wearily, dropping her hands in frustration.

Erik didn't know.

Evidently, the expression on his face was enough for Dyson to pity him. She placed her tablet on the desk and sat down in front of him. "Let's see if we can try something different. A more personal approach. Tell me about yourself."

"I just heard back from O," said Nayla some time later. "They've got Janya and are on their way here. Hopefully an hour, depending on traffic, but it's still early so they should be OK."

"Great!" said Ash. "Three more Guardians and a civvy to join in our suicide mission."

"What?" said Catherine.

"It isn't," said Robin firmly. He still didn't know if he could trust Nayla, Carter's words still fresh in his mind. The possibility of Nayla being a spy for Kain was too unbelievable to entertain. It was hard to believe it of *any* White Mask. But Nayla? The woman with whom he'd been spending his nights? To whom he had turned for comfort? With whom he'd been sharing so much of himself? It simply couldn't be true.

Carter and Yara came down the stairs. They had locked themselves in one of the bedrooms to try to see possible futures they all might be facing in an attempt to decide on the best course of action. From the looks on both of their faces, Robin guessed it hadn't gone well.

"No luck?" he said.

Yara shook her head, averting her gaze. "It's just like before," she said. "Whatever Kain did to Carter last time, he's done it to that whole mansion. It's shielded. Like it doesn't exist. It's just like when I infected Kain last year."

"What?" said Robin.

"You didn't see the future when you did that?" said Carter. "Are you saying you didn't know it was going to work?"

Yara pursed her lips, ashamed. Evidently she had not meant to admit that.

"Badass," said Ash, impressed.

"Only 'badass' because it *did* work," said Robin. "It's a fine line between that and stupidity."

"Red, you told me you saw it work. You lied to me?"

"I'm sorry, but I—I—" She struggled to find the words and eventually gave up, saying instead, "that's not the point."

"What is it that's preventing you from seeing, do you think?" said Nayla.

"Wait, you said it happened when you infected Kain too?" said Robin, ignoring Nayla's question.

"I think so."

"And C, the Shadow Men injected you with something when you went undercover?"

Carter nodded.

"How far could you see, Yara?" said Robin.

"Up until I infected myself," said Yara.

"Why?"

She shrugged.

"It was probably something in the virus that blocked her future juice," said Ash who was snacking on chips she'd found in the kitchen.

"My future juice?"

"You know, the vida-whatever-it-is that lets you see the future. The stuff Kain took out of your brain."

"Videtonin," Carter supplied as Yara touched the base of her skull, a tick of hers ever since her ordeal with Kain. Robin knew she was touching the scar tissue where Kain had drilled into her head. He had inserted a tube into her brain through which he could steal the hormone her body produced that allowed her to see the future. The Society Medics hadn't been able to remove the tube safely, so it was still there, buried under new skin and bone.

"Right," said Ash. "That stuff. Makes sense that there'd be something that blocks it, right?"

"And you think Kain used the same thing on Carter?" said Yara.

"He must have found a way to do it," said Robin.

"But it's worn off," said Carter. "Whatever they dosed me with isn't still preventing Yara from seeing my future."

"Kain must be using a constant supply of it to inoculate his entire operation."

"Ingenious," said Carter. "And inconvenient."

"Woah!" said Robin, noticing Yara. Blood was dripping from her nose. "You OK?"

Yara touched the blood above her lip and looked at it, as surprised to see it as Robin. "Huh…"

"Is that normal?" Catherine asked, looking worried.

"No…" said Yara pensively. "That's weird…"

"Are you OK?" asked Carter, a gentle hand on her shoulder as they inspected her for other symptoms.

"Fine. Probably just stress." Everyone stared at her for a moment before she insisted, "I'm *fine!*" and crossed her arms, looking uncomfortable.

"So… Kain has found a way to stop Yara from seeing the future?" said Nayla.

"That seems to be the working theory," said Carter.

"And he wouldn't want her to be able to see his next actions," said Ash. "I'd wager escaping her eye—" she pointed to Yara, "—was a pretty high priority when the Necro brought him back. Especially considering Yara's the one who killed him."

"Necro?" said Nayla, with an undertone of, "Really?"

Ash shrugged. "'Necromancer' is too cumbersome."

"That's what we suspect," said Carter.

"See?" said Ash to Nayla.

"No," said Carter, "I mean about Kain prioritizing beating Yara."

Robin resisted the urge to smooth out the deepening crease between Yara's eyebrows, turning his attention to Nayla instead. She looked as concerned as the rest of them—though perhaps not quite as concerned as Catherine, who was slightly green with worry. Could Nayla's behavior really be an act? If Carter's suggestion was right, Nayla would be leading them to a trap. But she didn't seem more keen than any of them at the prospect of going after Kain and his Necromancer.

"If we decide to do this," he said, trying to keep Nayla in the corner of his eye, looking for anything that could tell him what she was thinking, "we'll need a plan. A good one."

"I think I've got one," said Carter.

"Oh yay!" Ash squealed sincerely. "I *love* plans."

CHAPTER TWENTY-NINE

Moving On

"I just can't go through it again, honey," said Aunt Catherine.

Shortly after Janya and her three Guardians arrived, Yara and her aunt excused themselves. Yara wanted a few moments of quiet with Aunt Catherine while the new arrivals were given an overview of the situation, so they disappeared into one of the small rooms and sat opposite each other on the bed. She was clutching Yara's hands. Yara did not pull away, accepting the discomfort for her aunt's sake.

"Like last time, all over again. Not knowing if you're going to be OK… I promised your mother I'd keep you safe."

"You *do* keep me safe," said Yara gently. "You have. I had a great childhood."

Aunt Catherine said nothing, simply shaking her head.

"I thought you'd already made your peace with this when I started training to become a Guardian."

"Well, there's knowing I can't change your mind, and there's expecting you'd actually go through with it."

"You didn't think I'd do it?"

"I guess you're more like your father than I thought. Although," Aunt Catherine added, "I never believed your mother would go through with it, either. I lost her, too."

"What makes you think you're going to lose me?"

Aunt Catherine pressed her lips together and squeezed Yara's hand.

"I'm sorry, Annie," said Yara. She felt guilt clenching her belly like poison. Her only family was this woman who had lost so many already, who had tried to protect Yara from the fate of her parents, who had given Yara everything. And how was Yara repaying her? By running repeatedly headlong into danger.

"Don't be sorry, honey," said Aunt Catherine. "Just promise that you'll be OK. That you'll come back."

An impossible promise. Yara knew she shouldn't make it. That, in fact, she *couldn't* make it. And yet she heard herself saying the words.

"I promise."

"I will take Janya's shape and use a sample of her blood in a capsule on my fingertip to get through the bio-lock. Janya's Guardians," Carter nodded to Orlando, Elida, and Ben, "will accompany me in. The *real* Janya will be staying back, safe on the ship with Y." Carter turned to address Yara directly. "You'll be our getaway driver."

"Flyer," interrupted Ash, who looked positively giddy.

"Right," continued Carter. "You'll keep Janya away from the action."

"I still don't see why Janya has to come at all," said Elida.

"I am *not* staying behind," said Janya, her eyes flashing daggers in Elida's direction.

"We don't need to have this argument again," said Carter. "It's clear it's important to Janya that she be close by, given… Well. The rest of you," they turned to the other three Guardians, "will provide a distraction to get us through the door."

"What kind of distraction?" asked Nayla.

"Take out as many Shadow Men as you possibly can," said Carter simply.

"I like it," said Ash.

"I really think one of *us* should stay with Janya," said Orlando. He didn't like the plan any more than Yara did, though Orlando was more concerned with leaving Janya in Yara's inexperienced hands. Yara's reasons for being bitter had less to do with Janya's safety and more to do with her own resentment at being sidelined.

"She'll be perfectly safe on the Furtive," said Robin. "Y is more than capable of protecting her if it comes to that. It will look more believable to have all three of Janya's Guardians with her."

"Y, on my signal," resumed Carter, "you fly the Furtive over to us and provide air cover while we get out with the Necromancer."

"Remind me why we can't just blow up the whole damn house?" said Ash.

"They might have information on how to save Erik," said Yara.

"I'm confused," said Elida. "This is the same guy who's already alive and in Society hands, right? That's the guy we're trying to 'save'?"

Yara glared.

"He's been conditioned by Kain," offered Robin diplomatically. "If there's any way to help him break that conditioning, what we need is in there."

At this, Janya reached out and squeezed Yara's hand. Yara, surprised, raised an eyebrow. "Erik and I grew up together," Janya whispered in a voice that was only for Yara to hear. "At Headquarters. I want to save him, too."

"Besides," added Carter to the room at large, "we couldn't get the Furtive through the forcefield that shields the house. Anyway, the basement is fortified. If we leveled the house, we wouldn't get the Necromancer. And we need her. She could be an invaluable asset."

"She's not an asset," interjected Janya, pulling her hand away from Yara as though it had never happened. "She's my mother." Janya had taken the news of the return of her mother—or at least, a replica of her mother—surprisingly well. She had, however, demanded to be included in the mission to recover the clone of Zenobia Varma. It had led to more arguing than Yara thought possible, and the concession was ultimately made for her stay on the Furtive, removed from the action. It was more than was usually accorded a civilian, but given her ability to heal unnaturally quickly, the begrudging compromise had been made.

"But we could level it on our way out, right?" said Ash.

"I like *that* idea," said Yara.

"Even if we can get the forcefield down, the Furtive doesn't have the firepower to take down a house the size C described," said Robin.

"*I* have that kind of firepower," said Ash, eyes twinkling mischievously.

"We've talked about this already," said Carter. "You want to light a house on fire? During a drought? In southern California?"

Ash pouted, her arms crossed. "Fine," she said. Fire nymphs had gotten in trouble in the past for involvement in wildfires. There had been a time, before colonization, in which the Vurwari had worked with indigenous populations on controlled burns to clear brush and make space for new growth. Ash's family had a long history with the Chumash tribe doing exactly that. But since western cultures had put a stop to it, it had become much more dangerous and made wildfires more deadly. Ash knew better than to risk a fire spreading to a point where she could not control it.

"I think that's everything," said Carter. Everyone dispersed to prepare themselves for their various assignments when Robin pulled Yara aside.

"Are you sure you're up for this?" he asked quietly.

"Seriously? Why does everyone assume I can't do anything?" she said. "I passed the test. With top scores! I—"

Robin cut her off. "Jesus, kid. That's not what I'm saying. Can you just stop assuming for once that we don't believe in you? I think you've proved that you can handle yourself."

She closed her mouth.

"I just mean you're going back in to fight a man who did unspeakable things to you. He took a lot from ya, and I don't just mean your... future juice." He gave her half of a smile before continuing. "Kain is gonna be there. I just want to make sure you'll be OK."

Yara didn't answer right away. "I think I will be," she said finally. "I've killed him once already, haven't I?" *And almost died in the process.* "No point in you worrying, anyway. I'll be safe and cozy on the Furtive, remember?"

"Right."

"I guess the real fear is if you'll execute me," Yara added with a dry laugh. "If it looks like I'll be captured."

Robin's eyes bore into her. It was impossible to know what he was thinking. Just as Yara opened her mouth to speak—though what she was planning on saying she did not know—he pulled her into a hug. She tensed as she always did when being hugged, until she felt the thudding of his heart against her cheek. *He* was the nervous one. Yara felt so stupid for not having considered it before. Robin was always so confident, it had never occurred to her that he was even capable of being nervous. But if he was still in love with her, she couldn't imagine how hard it must be to watch her endanger her life. It certainly didn't help that he was apparently under orders to kill her if things were to go awry. The "failsafe," he'd called it.

In that moment she realized why it had been so easy for her to learn of that directive, why the news had not scared her. There was not a moment since Robin had told her about the failsafe in which she believed that any of her Guardians would go through with it.

She trusted them. Implicitly.

So she wrapped her arms around his waist and hugged him back.

* * *

Carter clicked off their ConvOrb, frustrated.

"Still nothing?" said Nayla.

Carter shook their head.

"I'm sure he's just busy," she said.

"Yeah, I'm sure he is." Carter had been trying to get a hold of Glover for the last two hours, and still nothing. They didn't even know which precinct he was being housed in. Wherever Glover was would be the new base of operations, the new central location for the White Mask Society in the region. Carter rubbed their eyes under their glasses. "It would just be easier if we could get a few more people to help us."

"Yeah. Maybe more than just a few." Nayla rubbed Carter's back. "How are you, Specks?"

"Been better," said Carter stiffly, not meeting Nayla's eyes. It was hard to think about how close the two of them had once been, especially now, with Carter doubting her loyalty to the Society. *Darwin would never forgive me for this*, they thought. "How're you?" they asked, trying to force a sense of nonchalance into their behavior.

She shrugged.

"We haven't talked much lately," said Carter. They realized that they didn't know what had happened between Nayla and Robin. Carter had suggested that Robin end things with Nayla, but based on how they behaved at the Fête, Carter was pretty sure that had never happened. "You've been spending a lot of time with R."

"I didn't think you'd noticed," said Nayla, tucking a strand of hair behind her ear.

Carter gave an apologetic nod. "Didn't seem like you were trying to hide it at the Fête, to be honest."

She smiled. "It's going well."

Robin definitely hadn't ended it, then.

"I mean..." Nayla tore her eyes away from Carter and looked in the direction of Robin, who was in the living room with Ash and Yara. Carter studied her and saw a tear roll down her cheek which she brushed away impatiently before laughing it off. "I know he's still in love with her."

Carter did not have to ask who "her" was. Robin was in love with Yara. It was a surprise, however, that Nayla knew.

"But I still love him," said Nayla. "Stupid, right?"

Carter frowned. "I'm so sorry, N."

She smiled through a few more tears. "Things used to be so much easier," she said with a laugh, but her voice was weak from the effort not to break. "Remember when we were young and in love and..."

"... And they loved us back?"

Nayla laughed and nodded.

"Yeah," said Carter. "I do remember." What they wouldn't give to go back to that time.

"Ugh," said Nayla. "Sorry." She wiped her face and shook it off, her eyelashes still wet. "There's too much going on right now for this."

"Maybe."

"I can keep trying Glover?" she said. "And you can go work on refining the plan with the others."

Carter shrugged. "I guess you could try. We've been at it for a while. I doubt we'll be able to get a hold of him before we have to leave. Which means we're on our own."

At last, progress.

Erik was sweating, his head was pounding, every muscle was trembling, and he didn't care.

Dyson was on her fourth cup of stale coffee, Erik his fifth of cold tea. They hadn't slept and they'd barely eaten, but it was all worth it. For the first time, Erik had been aware of something during his trances. He had been talking about Yara with Dyson and privately remembering the first time they kissed, when Dyson unexpectedly played *Für Elise*. His trigger. Rather than hearing no more than the first few notes and waking up having lost time, he had faded slowly, like sinking into cloudy water. He still did not have control over his body, but he was there.

"What was different that time?" said Dyson, nearly as excited as Erik about the potential breakthrough.

"I was..." he started, and the words caught in his throat. He was embarrassed by the truth, but Dyson had the right to know. "I was thinking about something. Some*one*."

"That's great. A great place to move forward from. Let's try again."

Erik closed his eyes and there was Yara's face, eyebrows scrunched in concern, mouth pursed. He imagined running his fingers over her lips, easing the tension—

—and the music started. His eyes snapped open of their own volition, but the world was still there. He saw Dyson as though through a pane of frosted glass, her colors muted and edges blurred. Her mouth was moving, but all he could hear was the muffled sound of her voice, her words completely inaudible.

Movement behind her. Frankie had come into the room and was walking toward him.

The edges started to fade. The world was closing in. He panicked. He didn't want to lose the hold he had, however weak. The panic felt strange as he was completely disconnected from his body. His breath and his heart were both steady, but his mind was frantic.

Yara, he thought desperately. *Think of Yara!*

Though he couldn't close his eyes, he pictured her in front of him, standing behind Dyson and Frankie, smiling softly. Things started to get clearer. It was like trying to staunch heavy bleeding. He could slow it, but not as quickly as it drained. His head hurt, but he didn't want to stop. Could not give in. His body was there and he wanted to get back into it.

He imagined reaching out to Yara, to hold her—

—and then he was back, as suddenly as flipping a light switch. The room was loud and it took him a few moments to understand why.

Frankie was laughing.

Dyson was yelling. "—an incredible breakthrough!"

Erik got his bearings and noticed that his hand was outstretched.

It had worked.

CHAPTER THIRTY
Moving In

It took the better part of the day to go over Carter's plan and prepare everything they would need.

By the time the Furtive set down half a mile from Kain's mansion, the sky was darkening, only a sliver of pale purple and burnt orange on the horizon.

They were quiet as the stealth ship powered down into standby mode and the eight Guardians checked and double checked everything they needed. Robin readjusted his gauntlet to ensure it was secure. Nayla tightened her chainmail to make sure it wouldn't rustle. Elida straightened Ben's solenoid.

Every rustle of fabric, every footstep, every breath felt too loud, so when Carter spoke it was jarring. "Everyone ready?"

They all signaled their assent.

Carter nodded. "My turn, I guess." They took off their glasses and popped colored contacts in, blinking them into place before taking a moment to shift. Robin had seen them change shape before—though infrequently—but it never got old. He watched in fascination as Carter's face darkened, soft brown curls elongating into straight black locks, a wide nose shortening and curving down, a round face narrowing to a square jaw and pointed chin. Before long, Robin was looking at two identical Janyas.

"Wild," said the original.

Carter secured the capsule of Janya's blood to the tip of their finger and nodded.

Janya and Yara alone stayed on the Furtive, watching from the top of the loading ramp, as the rest of them stepped out into the brush that made up most of the landscape surrounding Kain's new base.

"Wait, shoot," said Janya-Carter, searching their pockets. "I can't find my Orb."

"It's up here," said Yara from the top of the loading ramp, looking over her shoulder. Carter ran back up and disappeared with the hyden before sprinting back down, clutching their ConvOrb.

"Got it," they said breathlessly.

The Guardians would go in two waves to the house. Carter, Ben, Orlando, and Elida would follow slightly behind and wait for Nayla, Ash, and Robin to cause enough of a diversion to allow them to get into the house undetected.

"Well," said Robin after a moment, "let's get this show on the road."

They made their way forward in silence, chain mail over their tunics, shrouded in white masks, cloaked in black. Their solenoids were safely attached to the backs of their armor, hidden beneath their robes and deactivated until summoned by their gauntlets.

It took them about ten minutes on foot to reach the house from where they landed with no path to speak of, the brush thick.

The mansion was enormous and had obviously once been elegant, almost regal. Now it was crumbling, peeling, and crawling with dried ivy. It had the distinct air of having been abandoned. But lights were on in some of the dusty windows. A low brick wall surrounded the grounds, topped with black iron spires, and a shimmer confirmed the forcefield Carter had encountered during their recon mission was active. The grounds within the perimeter were just as neglected as the mansion, overgrown with weeds and yellowed from the never-ending drought that gripped the region.

"Ugh," Ash whispered as they stopped short of the front gate. "I hate these uniforms."

"Would you rather do it naked?" said Robin.

"Yes. At least that way I wouldn't have to keep my human form."

"I can honestly say I've never thought of that," Robin conceded.

"Please don't spread," Nayla cut in as Ash stepped forward.

"I got this," said Ash. She didn't spare them a second look, taking confident strides toward the house, as her hair turned to fire. Her Guardian uniform—as much as Ash claimed she didn't want to wear it —was made specifically for her and was therefore fire resistant, allowing her to transform into a cloaked demon of flame under her mask. It was hard not to marvel at the strength and beauty of the

Vurwari. Robin was silently thankful that Ash was on their side. He wouldn't want to be on the receiving end of such a specter.

"Yeah," he said quietly, smirking. "She's got this."

The slight figure of Janya and her Guardians were crouched behind them, waiting for the coast to clear. First, Ash needed to take down the forcefield.

She walked up to the edge of the perimeter and, her hands aflame, gripped the edge of the invisible shield, which crackled to life under her touch. The faint blue was at odds with the burning of Ash's fire. Robin flinched at the sound of electricity as the two forces battled it out, but Ash did not relent.

The two guards at the front of the house had immediately noticed her and stood, dumbstruck, watching the scene. They didn't seem to think there was much of a chance of Ash breaking through.

Orange spread across the forcefield as Ash continued to pour her strength into it, and more of the barrier became visible as it fought against the onslaught of flame. The Shadow Men on the other side took a few cautious steps forward, raising their weapons, no longer as confident in the barrier. The forcefield continued to resist, but Ash was determined. Her face was barely visible, engulfed in flame. He heard a yell at the same time that Ash's fire exploded with a final thrust of force, and the field winked out, flashes of blue and green sparking angrily as it flickered into oblivion.

The Shadow Men didn't hesitate. They charged at Ash, but she was already shooting fireballs at them. The guards dodged them easily, but it was enough of a distraction to allow Robin and Nayla to fell them both with solenoidal stars across their chests. Not waiting for the others to follow, Ash moved over the threshold into the house. Robin didn't see so much as hear Ash take down more Shadow Men inside, feeling the heat from her fire burning with such intensity that by the time he and Nayla followed there was only the smell of scorched flesh, black burns still smoldering across three bodies.

"Where to now?" said Ash, her skin shiny with sweat as she returned to her human form, the flames subsiding like fading embers.

Robin looked around. The house was emptier than he'd anticipated. Perhaps he was expecting an army of Shadow Men who would be waiting for them, but the atrium was empty. He didn't know if that was good news or bad news.

He sent Carter a signal via ConvOrb, and shortly after, the form of Janya, flanked by her three Guardians, snuck in behind them.

"It's over there," came Janya's voice, pointing behind the grand staircase before them. They led Orlando, Ben, and Elida around pausing only long enough for Robin to mutter "good luck" as they went.

Orlando was focused, his attention narrowed like a laser beam, listening for any sound that could mean trouble. But the rest of the Guardians were also doing their jobs. Under the grand central staircase was a narrow set of stairs down which the spitting image of Janya went.

The stairs felt appropriate for this house. Wooden, creaky, worn. It was almost as though Kain had intentionally sought the creepiest mansion in which to build his new evil lair. The wood abruptly ended at the bottom of the staircase, though, where the landing was metal, as was the door the four of them stood in front of. No doubt several inches of solid steel now separated them from their goal. Janya's hand reached toward the biometric lock where a small finger pad was waiting for them. They hesitated a moment before placing their finger on it, and Orlando braced himself for the possibility that it wouldn't work. That it would set off alarms and they'd have to flee, empty handed. He watched nervously as his Ward's finger pressed down and a clicking sound indicated Janya's blood sample had been taken by the pad precisely as they'd planned. The locking mechanism released, and the door fell open an inch. Carter let Elida, Ben, and Orlando go in ahead of them. The stuffy quiet of the house above was replaced by a sterile silence, the smell of dust exchanged for the smell of chemicals, wood for steel.

Yara had told them all of her vision of Kain's old lab, of the pods he used to grow his clones. As they'd expected, there were at least five dozen of those pods lining the walls. Almost all of them were occupied by unconscious clones at various stages of development. Underdeveloped fetuses, pale and sickly and ill-defined; premature babies that were skinny and frail; fatter babies that looked to be about one year old; children...

Next to him, Elida made a sound of disgust mingled with horror. Ben cursed. Orlando looked away, revolted. The whole thing made him sick. But there didn't seem to be anyone alive. *Truly* alive. Nothing more than just a beating heart and comatose brain in a petri dish. Were these incomplete clones even 'alive'? What would happen if they were to drain the pods, break the glass, and free the bodies within? Would they live or die? Would they be people?

In any case, what Kain was keeping here was meant to be locked away from the world. The ceiling was low, and there was a simple, unreinforced door at the far wall in between two pods housing unconscious adults. Behind it was likely some sort of office or perhaps storage. Aside from the pods, the hall was empty except for several steel tables, upon which sat various lab equipment ranging from microscopes to pipettes. A centrifuge was whirring, spinning samples of what looked like blood plasma. They found more of the same as they rounded the stairs that led back upstairs: more pods, more tables, more equipment.

"Hey," whispered Elida next to an occupied pod. "Come here."

The three of them joined Elida at the pod she was peering into.

"Son of a..." said Ben, losing his voice halfway through.

Orlando's blood went cold. He recognized the sleeping face behind the glass.

"This one, too," called Janya's voice, looking in the next pod. There were at least six copies, all in a row, at various stages of development, the youngest looking around 5 years old, the oldest about 20 or so. But there was no mistaking that face, unconscious or otherwise.

They had to warn the others.

Yara was alone on the Furtive next to Carter's unconscious body. They were still in the shape of Janya.

That answers that, thought Yara to herself as she dragged their limp form into the co-pilot seat and strapping them down. *Shape shifters don't revert to their original form when they're asleep. Low level mystery solved.*

She felt a twinge of guilt for having lied to her Guardians. Janya had been very persuasive, though, so it was with only Carter's stupefied form as company that Yara set to work on her job.

As she worked, she kept trying to see what would happen, to get any hint or warning. Was Janya going to be OK? Was their plan going to work? But she was met over and over again with the same wall and a building headache.

Her upper lip was warm. Her nose was bleeding again. She wiped it away impatiently, sweat dripping down her neck and back and into her eyes. "Focus, Rivers," she muttered to herself.

It took less time than she anticipated to get everything set exactly as she'd been instructed. She was gripped with a moment of fear that perhaps she had missed something. After all, there were meant to be two of them doing it. But seeing as Janya and Carter were indisposed… well, Yara had to hope that she had done it all properly by herself.

She climbed back into the Furtive and sat gratefully, extending her legs, just as Carter started to regain consciousness.

"Wh—" they said, still groggy.

Yara knew that they would have a nasty headache from the dose of tranquilizer that she and Janya had injected into them, and she felt another pang of remorse. "Hi," she said apologetically.

Carter looked around, clutching their head. In a few moments, they seemed to recognize their surroundings and shot to their feet. "What's going on!" Just as quickly as they stood up, they lost their balance and Yara rushed over to ease them back down into the seat.

"Easy."

"What's going on?" they repeated.

Yara had a painkiller ready for them and handed it to them with a bottle of water. They accepted both without question. "Don't be mad."

"What are you talking about? What happened?"

"Janya decided she wanted to go," said Yara, happy that she had rehearsed what she was going to say beforehand. She didn't know if she could have found the words in the moment, so she recited her chosen story by wrote. "And I decided to help her. This is her fight, too. And we knew we wouldn't be able to convince any of you, so she took your place."

"What?" Carter exclaimed.

"I've done everything exactly as it's meant to be done, and the others will send word if there's any problem."

Carter gaped at her. After a moment, they slowly started to shift back into their usual form. In a few short seconds, Yara was looking again at the face she associated with her Guardian. There was no denying how much Yara loved watching Carter shift. She smiled at the transformation, but her smile faded at Carter's next words.

"You must not be serious."

Right. She was apologizing. She couldn't smile. "There's no undoing it. I'm sorry that we had to sedate you."

"How did—I mean, how—"

"I stole your ConvOrb," said Yara. "So you'd come back onto the ship and we could sedate you." She pointed to the used tranquilizer on the console.

Carter closed their eyes as if praying for patience. They didn't speak for a moment, and Yara wondered how long their ire would last. Evidently, they decided that there was no point in arguing now, because when they spoke again, it was not to scold her. She might have feared repercussions if the entire Society hadn't just collapsed, but as it was, Yara didn't have any regrets. Provided nothing bad happened to Janya.

"What's the status?" Carter said in a measured tone.

"Everything's been set according to your and Robin's directions. I just wish I knew why we were doing this."

"Well," said Carter, "we needed to test something. R and I think…" They trailed off.

"What?" said Yara.

Carter took a deep breath. "You weren't supposed to know this, but I suppose there's no going back now. We suspect N might be working for Kain. We determined that this would be the best way to smoke out a traitor."

Yara's heart skipped a beat. Nayla, a traitor? "Robin thinks this, too?" she asked, her mouth dry.

"He admits it may be a possibility."

Thoughts were racing through Yara's mind too fast for her to process. She vaguely remembered her aunt telling her that there were whispers of a mole within the Society back when she had first escaped Kain, but nothing had come of it and Yara had forgotten about it. She had been so caught up, first with training and then with Erik's return, that there was no part of her that spared any thought to the possibility of a White Mask betraying them in earnest. Secretly, a quiet, bitter part of her felt strangely… victorious. Yara's jealousy of Nayla now felt small mingled with the ugly satisfaction that Robin didn't truly trust her. Then just as quickly, she felt pity for her best friend that his own girlfriend might be a turncoat.

"So it wasn't Erik?" she said, feeling foolish that of all her thoughts this was the first one to be voiced.

"We don't know, Red. We don't know anything. We just… wanted to be sure it isn't N."

"And you're sure this will work?"

Carter looked at the console, staring fixedly at the screen between them showing the map of the area. "No," they said heavily. "I'm not."

"Not very reassuring," said Yara with a small laugh. A feeble attempt at a joke. It was unthinkable. She didn't want it to be true.

With any luck, she and Carter would sit in that Furtive, and nothing would happen until they got a call from the rest of the team saying they were ready for extraction.

"Whatever happens," said Carter, "we'll know soon enough." They were still rubbing their head, looking so beat down that guilt burned once again at Yara's stomach.

"Who else suspects?" she said.

"Just me and R."

"You didn't tell Ash? Or… anyone else?"

Carter shook their head. "They can't know. And I assume," they added, looking at Yara, "no one else knows that it's actually Janya down there instead of me?"

Yara looked down. "A correct assumption."

"They're never going to forgive me for this."

"You didn't know," said Yara.

"Maybe not. But it's not about me. It's about Janya, and the fact that she might die or else end up back with Kain."

"If Janya or I really thought that was a possibility," said Yara, "we wouldn't have done this. Don't forget that the two of us know better than anyone here what's at stake."

They were silent for a moment.

"For what it's worth," she said, "I'm sorry."

Carter didn't respond.

"So, what now?" said Yara, unable to take the silence.

"Now," said Carter, "we wait."

Hushed shadows moved through the brush, the crimson of their uniforms colorless in the darkness. There was no hesitation in the way they moved. No concern about being caught. Just two dozen figures marching obediently to the coordinates they had been given.

The Furtive waited exactly where they expected it to be, idle in the middle of the clearing. Without a word to each other, the figures spread out, circling the craft, weapons at the ready. They didn't expect many people to be on board. In fact, there were just meant to be two.

The two they wanted.

They crouched low and waited until they were sure they were all in position.

"Where is everyone?" whispered Nayla as the footsteps of fake-Janya and her three Guardians disappeared into the dark. "Shouldn't there be more Shadow Men?"

"Should we be worried that we haven't run into more?" said Ash.

Robin didn't answer. It was true, it felt ominous, like they were being lured into a false sense of security, a trap.

"This way," he whispered, ignoring the sense of foreboding. He led them around the central staircase, all three moving in near silence, barely more than ghosts. He signaled for Ash to check in the first room they passed and for Nayla to wait as he checked the next. Empty. Just the same as everywhere else.

He didn't want to believe what he knew this meant. A quiet voice in the back of his head reminded him where all the Shadow Men were. Where they had to be if not here. But he wasn't ready to believe it. Not yet. Not until he heard from Yara and could know for sure.

"It's weird to think of her as having grown up at Headquarters," Yara was saying, her chin in her hands. She was still looking at the screen, but Carter was sure her eyes were out of focus. "Janya, I mean."

"Why's that?"

"I don't know," said Yara. "She's a civilian. And she was a child. I don't really think of children at Headquarters, I guess."

"You were a child at Headquarters," Carter reminded her.

"Hardly. I don't even remember it." The part of Yara's life that had existed when her parents were alive was so distant, it felt in many ways irrelevant. She felt guilty for thinking that way, but without having any memories of them, how could they possibly have been a part of who she was? Carter said she'd been a child at Headquarters, but she had no more than their word it was true. The walls of the place she had learned to call home had never felt familiar. There was no twinge of recognition when she was first brought to the White Mask Society. No nagging voice in the back of her mind that told her she had ever been there before. No primal instinct calling her back.

In the time since Yara had joined the Society, she thought of it as her home and her place of work. It was easy to forget that Headquarters was so much more—had *always* been so much more than just a Society base. It housed Deviant civilians; children of White Masks grew up there; refugees were provided for there while the Society helped them integrate into a human world. It was not just a center of operations, but a whole community of Deviants. Most of Yara's life had been spent living as a civilian with no knowledge of the Society. So when she joined, she only ever saw what she needed to see. But Janya, whose mother had been a Researcher, had been a Deviant child who lived there with her mother. Erik had been the same, the child of a nymph. So many children called Headquarters their home. Yara never thought of them—despite having been one in a life long forgotten. She never saw the children, who were, understandably, kept far from the action.

She hoped the children were OK after the Fête. It hadn't occurred to her until now…

Carter was fiddling with their ConvOrb.

Yara's mind strayed to Janya, wondering how she was faring. Janya not only had to pretend to be Carter in disguise, but she would have to keep her head as she went back into the clutches of the man who had tortured her and killed her mother.

Perhaps this all *had* been a mistake. Tricking Carter and sending a civilian into danger… In the quiet, it was easy to think of how reckless this was.

We didn't have many options, she told herself. With Black dead, Glover unresponsive, and Headquarters out of commission, they'd had to act. Janya certainly indicated that she was planning on going after her mother with or without Yara's help. Sitting around and waiting for something to happen, for Kain either to come looking for them or potentially relocate as Robin and Carter feared he would, wasn't an option.

Yara hoped it wasn't reckless, wasn't a mistake. Hoped that it would go smoothly. She harkened back to Ash's words. *Recklessly entitled.* Was this just another example of that?

Janya would be safe. She was with her Guardians. Robin and Ash were more than capable. And Nayla…

Shifting in her seat, Yara leaned forward to look at the screen.

The silent figures, armed and in place, started to move toward the inactive Furtive. Their approach had gone unnoticed. Exactly as they'd expected.

The leader, flanked by two identical hulks, started to head toward the loading ramp, which was stowed away, but forcing it open with their superior weapons would be child's play.

Taking his glowing sword, he stabbed it into the seam where the door met the ship. But instead of the sound of metal on metal, he was met with an electric crackle. The door to the Furtive didn't yield but, instead, flickered out of existence, then in, then out again, before the whole craft disappeared.

They all stared at each other, flummoxed, looking straight across the clearing at the crimson figures opposite, a view now unobstructed.

The leader stepped forward, inspecting the place that had moments ago been filled by a flying machine. All that was left in its stead was a large, metallic egg-shaped device with a projection lens.

A simulation.

He stopped, at a loss. His orders had not accounted for the possibility of a trap. Before anyone could suggest going back, a fog started to rise from under the rocks and dry grass beneath their feet. It moved quickly, thick and black in the night, and the Shadow Men fell one by one, unconscious.

Carter and Yara watched on their screen from the real Furtive, which had been relocated to half a mile away.

"I don't believe it," Yara murmured as the scene unfolded. "I just don't believe it."

Neither could Carter. Nayla had betrayed them. Nayla, who was their friend, had sold them all out to Kain. One by one, the Shadow Men fell to the gas Yara had placed, booby trapped to be released by the pressure of their footsteps. They would be unconscious for at least six hours.

Carter's heart broke. *Nayla*, they thought. *How could you?*

There were much more pressing matters in the meantime.

They had to warn the others.

"We need to keep a clear getaway for the others," Robin whispered as the three of them approached the last few rooms at the end of the hallway.

"But Nayla's right. Where is everyone?" said Ash, her voice low.

A real sense of concern was starting to set in now that his adrenaline was fading. The buzz of energy that filled Robin's limbs at the prospect of a fight had nowhere to go and was leaving him antsy. He should have heard from Yara by now. Perhaps Kain had already cleared out of this location. Maybe he and his Shadow Men had taken over Headquarters now that the Society had evacuated.

"Wait." It was Ash. They all stopped, straining their ears. "I heard something."

Robin froze and looked at her, his gauntlet at the ready to summon the solenoid strapped to his back, dormant so as to avoid the telltale whirring sound they made when active.

"I think it's coming from upstairs," Ash whispered. Nayla and Robin followed her gaze up to the ceiling. He hadn't heard anything yet. It would have been easy to imagine it in a dark and unfamiliar house far from the beaten path, but Ash seemed certain.

"What do we do?" said Nayla.

"How many people?" said Robin.

Ash listened. "Not many. Two or three?"

Robin chewed his lip, weighing their options. "We should be fine if —" but he was cut off by a pulse from his ConvOrb. It was Yara.

It simply said, "Beware the ides."

His heart sank.

CHAPTER THIRTY-ONE

Traitor

"Fascinating," said Dyson, looking at Erik's most recent brain scan. She had been mapping his brain activity now that he was able to fight the conditioning, even if only a little. Her hope was to be able to find a more reliable way to activate the part of his mind that resisted. She had summoned her team of Researchers to work with her and Frankie, but it was slow going.

Wires were taped to Erik's forehead, meant to send pulses to stimulate the areas of his brain that were locked out when he was triggered now that they were able to identify them more effectively. He would periodically lose time as she flipped his metaphorical switch on and off as easily as if it were literal, and it was leaving him dizzy. He wanted to stop, but he knew that they were close. The sooner he was free, the sooner he could be with Yara—safely. It was unfathomable that he had been gone a year. A year that he could not remember, a year of Yara's life he'd missed while she developed stronger relationships with Carter and... Robin. Robin, who was in love with her. Robin, who had always been everything Erik wasn't and everything Erik wanted to be.

The music started.

The world around him lingered, still in the haze he came to associate with the paralysis of losing his body, but something was different this time.

There was a faint humming from the pulses of Dyson's machine. But it wasn't just that. He wasn't alone in his mind. It was as if someone else were living in his body. No... Not someone else... Not a new person… new memories. Erik was seeing himself in a place he'd never been. Yet, somehow, he was there, looking through liquid behind a panel of curved glass, beyond which was a room filled with 7-foot-tall tubes, each wide enough to fit a grown man.

A face peered from the other side of the glass: Kain.

There was another face reflected in the glass: his own. Green eyes under silver white hair.

Present-Erik started breathing heavily and after a moment he realized his body was responding to his emotional state. He was gaining control.

Just as quickly, he was snapped out of it by Dyson, who was saying something to someone Erik couldn't see.

Erik cut her off. "No! Put me back, hurry, while I still have it!"

And it was back. The same fog, but he was there and so was this other Erik. The one from his missing year. The Erik who was loyal to Kain and who had memories of his life as a clone. There were more flashes.

Kain ordering Shadow Men.

That same dark woman from the Fête. The Necromancer.

And someone else. Not a Shadow Man, not Kain, not the Necromancer…

Erik gasped and Dyson pulled him out.

"Incredible work, Erik, really—"

"You need to call R," he choked out between wretched gulps of air. "Call Robin now. It was her. I saw N. I saw Nayla."

"What's going on?" Nayla asked Robin. "Who was that?"

But Robin didn't wait for the words to leave her mouth. "A, get behind me," he said.

Ash moved quickly for someone who had no idea what was going on. She was at Robin's side, facing Nayla in less than a breath. He summoned his solenoidal star in one smooth movement and angled it at Nayla, his un-gauntleted hand at Nayla's throat as he slammed her into the wall behind her. In the quiet of the house, the solenoid was impossibly loud.

"Robin, what are you—" Nayla started.

"How could you?" said Robin, cutting her off, his voice trembling in anger.

"What's going on?" said Ash. "R, what the hell do you think you're doing?"

"What..." said Nayla. "Robin, I don't know what you're talking about." Her voice was weak, her hands clutching at Robin's arm, her eyes wide with fear and confusion. It was convincing, but then again, she had been fooling him this whole time. For how long, he wondered? How many times had the two of them been together? He thought of kissing her, of her hands on his heart, of nights spent wrapped in each other's arms, and all along, she'd been plotting against him and everything he cared about, allying herself with a madman who wanted to destroy the woman he loved.

"It was you. It's been you this whole time." His voice broke.

"R, what the hell is going on?" said Ash. An orange glow was coming over his left shoulder. Ash had started to burn again in the commotion.

"She's the one who betrayed us," he said through clenched teeth. "She's been working for Kain this whole time."

Ash cursed and let out a burst of heat as her fire expanded, causing Nayla to flinch. Robin could see Ash's fire reflected in Nayla's brown eyes. "I'll call Y," said Ash.

Their plan to draw Nayla out had worked. It explained why there were no Shadow Men in the house. If Nayla had called ahead to warn Kain, she would have told him that both hyden were left on board the Furtive. They were what Kain was after, but if Yara and Janya had done as Carter and Robin had instructed, the hyden were safe. Either way, they all needed to get out of there as fast as possible. Despite the urgency, Robin couldn't tear his eyes away from Nayla.

"All this time," Robin said. His eyes were burning.

"I don't know what you're talking about," said Nayla in a voice so quiet Robin could barely hear. He loosened his grip on her throat, but didn't answer. He so desperately wanted to believe her...

"The Furtive is coming," said Ash. "We have to get the others."

After a moment, Robin shook his head in disgust and released Nayla. She fell forward, relieved.

"Kill her," spat Ash, but before the words were out of her mouth, Robin had swung his solenoid at Nayla, slashing her leg. She fell to the ground with a scream of pain. He couldn't bring himself to kill her, but he couldn't let her follow them.

"Let's go," he said.

He turned his back on Nayla and led Ash away, with a only a few sobs to indicate Nayla was still there.

* * *

"I don't believe it," said Elida. "Nayla's a clone."

Orlando couldn't believe it either, but there was no denying what was in front of them. Kain was cloning Nayla.

"Do you think they're cloning more of us?" said Ben.

"We can't think about this right now," said the figure of their Ward. "We need to find my mother."

Orlando raised an eyebrow. It was strange for Carter to refer to Zenobia Varma as their "mother," though perhaps they were just taking on Janya's personality a little too wholeheartedly. Before they could tell the shape shifter that level of commitment was unnecessary, another voice spoke from behind them.

"Oh, but your mother isn't here."

The four of them spun around, Orlando, Ben, and Elida drawing weapons as they did, to find Kain standing in the doorway, flanked by seven Shadow Men, all identical to each other and all enormous.

"But I do want to thank you for coming to me." Kain's eyes fell on Carter. And in that moment, Orlando knew that it had never been Carter. Janya had somehow changed places with the shape shifter. His Ward was in extraordinary danger, and he had led her directly into the thick of it.

The Guardians didn't hesitate. Orlando swung his solenoid at Kain, while Ben and Elida attacked his guard. The Shadow Men made no move to stop the blades as they flew toward them, instead rushing forward to disarm the Guardians. By the time the gauntlets were wrestled off their hands, Orlando's solenoid had already cut clean through Kain and two of his Shadow Men, leaving their bodies crumpled on the floor.

Elida had sprung jaguar teeth, nails curving out of her fingertips as she fought two more with the ferocity of a cornered animal. She was doing as much damage to them as they did to her, the crucial difference being that the clones were impervious to pain. Ben and Orlando didn't have any Deviant blood, however, and without the advantage of claws and fangs, had a harder time fighting the hulking Shadow Men. Ben had taken one down and was embroiled in a hopeless fight, grappling for control of the Shadow Man's weapon, as Orlando had lost his own. Orlando kicked, bit, and heard several bones break in one of the Shadow Men, but his focus was Janya. She was holding her own against the Shadow Man who had launched at her. Janya was a hydan and, like her mother before her, had the ability to heal. Any damage done to her would repair itself just as quickly. The real Janya had been equipped with a taser back on the Furtive as a last resort, but when she reached for a weapon, that was not what she withdrew. Instead, clutched in her hands, was a gun.

Orlando blanched. *How did she get* that? He was unable to stop her as she shot a Shadow Man whose hands were shredded from his efforts to disable a solenoid. The bang was deafening. A flash of light and the Shadow Man stumbled back a few steps, but the armor under his uniform protected him. *Stupid. So stupid.* Putting Janya in danger like this, no matter the reason, should never have been on the table. If they lived through this, Orlando was going to kill whomever was responsible. Janya could not get captured. Orlando knew—as all Guardians of the hyden knew—that if it came to it, her fate was to die rather than end up back in Kain's possession.

"Run!" he yelled at Janya

She didn't need to be told twice. Ben was on his back, wrestling with one of the remaining Shadow Men, and Elida had freed herself to attack the one that Janya shot and failed to kill. Janya reached the door that led out of the basement and crashed to the floor, having run headlong into someone coming down the stairs.

"What was that?" said Ash.

Robin heard it, too. A crack that came from downstairs.

"Was that a gunshot?" she asked.

He chewed his lip, trying to decide what to do. More than anything, he wanted to get back to Yara, but she—in principle—was safe with Janya on the Furtive. The two of them were headed over to pick up the rest of the Guardians, including the four people in the basement. His urge to run to Yara would help no one. They had to get everyone out.

"R!" Ash said, snapping Robin back to reality.

"Right," he said. "Let's go."

As the two of them headed toward the basement, footsteps sounded above them. Robin had completely forgotten that Ash had heard people upstairs. Now whatever the mysterious people above them had been doing, whatever they'd been waiting for, it was over. They were coming.

"Go!" said Robin, and he pushed Ash ahead of him as they sprinted down the stairs. Once through the metal door at the base of the stairs, Robin slammed it shut behind them. Ash had crashed into someone. Carter, apparently, who still looked like Janya.

They were both picking themselves off the floor when people

slammed into the other side of the heavy door. There was no time to focus on that. They had just run from one crisis into another, and they needed to get the situation here under control first.

Bodies were on the floor. A quick glance told Robin that none of them were White Masks. Orlando was holding Ben up, who looked as though he had come close to losing his battle, while Elida tore into the throat of the one remaining Shadow Man, her teeth elongated into fangs. His body collapsed to join the other fallen, almost all of which were identical to him.

Except one: Kain.

Ash, who had flared up once more, coalesced back into her human form when she saw that the fight was over. Instead, she helped Orlando with Ben. One of his arms was held at an odd angle and his face was bloodied, but he was alive.

"Where's N?" said Elida over the pounding on the door, spitting blood out of her mouth. "She's a clone."

Robin, who had been primed to ignore her, not wanting to think about Nayla or face that he'd been completely bamboozled by his girlfriend, looked at Elida at these words. "Clone?" Could it be? Was the real Nayla somewhere else? Relief warred with fear in his gut. He knew she never could have betrayed them. Betrayed *him*. But for how long had she been replaced with a copy? If a mole had been within the Society for over a year, when could the last time he had seen the real Nayla have been? He felt sick. "You're sure?"

Elida pointed a bloody finger behind him at one of the many pods that lined the walls. Noticing them for the first time, Robin recoiled. Naked, gummy corpses hung in the viscous goo, from adult down to fetuses. Most horrifying of all were the several that were occupied by the unconscious body of Nayla Jackson, white blonde hair suspended around her face, ghostly in its gravity defying state.

"Oh Christ," said Robin.

"We've got bigger problems right now," said Ash.

The Guardians backed away from the door, picking up their fallen gauntlets and summoning their solenoids to hover menacingly at their sides, bracing themselves for another fight.

The biometric lock clicked as it was unlocked.

When the metal door was pushed open, Robin didn't know why he was surprised to see Kain standing on the other side. Despite all the resurrections they had been privy to in the last month, Robin still wasn't used to a world in which he could be staring at the living version of the man who lay dead at his feet. In a house full of clones, it should be expected that Kain would not let himself die so easily. After all, he did have a Necromancer on his side.

It was the same face Robin hated, as alive as ever. The only difference was the "Br" branded into this new Kain's neck.

"Won't you ever stay dead?" said Robin, lifting his solenoid to attack.

Kain laughed. "You're not impressed by my little trick?" He turned to Janya. "Hello, my dear. Nice to see you again so soon."

Ash ignited, filling the low-ceilinged room with heat, and placed herself between Kain and the hydan.

"Ah," said Kain, not only unconcerned but actually delighted by the display. "A Vurwari. I've been wanting to add one to my collection." He stepped aside to reveal the various Shadow Men behind him. There were at least fifteen people, including several copies of the model that now lay slain on the floor along with a couple other faces. "But nymphs are rather difficult to clone. That's one of the reasons it took me so long to make another Erik Carpenter. Of course, it helped that he's half human. But I would just love to try with *you*." His eyes flashed in Ash's direction, his expression hungry. "Who knows if it would even be possible. But how much fun would it be to try."

There was disturbance behind Kain, cutting him off. The Shadow Men in the back started moving, a few involuntary grunts, sounds that Robin associated with a dying clone. He frowned, straining to see, bracing himself. There was a struggle at the top of the stairs. A familiar yell. A roar. A few bodies fell down the stairs, and the rest of the Shadow Men parted to make way.

Robin's heart sank. "No!" he said, the word wrenched from him before he could stop himself.

"Robin!" It was Yara. Her gauntlet was in the hand of one of two Shadow Men who had her arms pinned behind her. They threw her down the rest of the stairs and she landed hard at Robin's feet. In a flash, he had his arms around her, pulling her up, inspecting her for damage. She had taken a beating. But from the bodies on the stairs, she'd taken more than just a few down before being disarmed.

"What are you doing here?" Robin hissed, but she was turning around, looking back.

Three more Shadow Men had a small, unconscious bear wearing chainmail in their clutches.

Carter.

"Wh—" Robin turned to Janya in disbelief. She at least had the decency to look ashamed, avoiding eye contact with anyone but Kain.

"How delightful!" said Kain. "A little reunion. I was wondering where the other hydan was. How kind of you both to deliver yourselves to me."

Yara spat at his feet.

A muscle in Kain's face twitched, but he never lost his smile. "Hmm," he said, considering her. "Put the shape shifter with them," he added, without turning to look at his clones.

Carter's unconscious ursine body was thrown at their feet and Ash rushed to them, cradling their head and inspecting them. "Knocked out," she said, looking up at Robin. The iron fist clutching his heart relaxed its grip just enough for him to catch his breath. Alive. Carter was alive.

"Oh, I don't want to *kill* any of you," said Kain, affronted. "Well. Maybe *some* of you." He looked at Yara. "I'm so happy you're here, my darling. I was just telling your friends here about how I couldn't get an exact copy of your beloved—the nymph, sweet little Erik." He said the name in a mocking, simpering tone. "I'm sure you noticed, given the differences he came out with. I did hope you would like the white hair. We just couldn't get any dyes to stick. But given what he's told us, you didn't seem to mind it, do you?"

Yara's face turned red beneath her mask. From anger or embarrassment, Robin couldn't tell.

Robin moved in front of her and, with a yell, swung his solenoid at Kain, but Kain was ready. Rather, his Shadow Men were. The one next to him, a tall, heavy man with gnarled fingers, swung a weapon in front of Kain to block Robin's solenoid. It looked like a cross between a bo staff and a sword, but the metal burned, giving it a sickly pink glow. The staff stopped the whirring star and knocked it away before it could get close to Kain. Robin swung again and again, the Shadow Man effortlessly parrying to block the solenoid. When the Shadow Man managed to knock the deadly star to the ground, Kain stepped on it, pinning it in place, his hands up placatingly. The solenoid screeched against the cement as Robin tried to summon it away, but Kain ground it deeper into the floor, his shoes getting torn by the razor sharp edges of the weapon.

"Tut tut, Robin. Don't you want to talk first? You know, we have a lot in common, young man."

"We have *nothing* in common," spat Robin.

"Don't we?" said Kain. "Human. Both of us. Utterly… unremarkable. And in love with a hydan." He looked back to Yara. Robin tensed, every sense heightened with adrenaline. If Kain made any move in her direction…

Why had she come inside? Of course, he knew why. Because *they* were there. She and Carter came to save the rest of them. To save him. "These women are above us, Robin," Kain continued. "We don't deserve them. After all, *Yara* chose the nymph, didn't she?" Yara shifted uncomfortably next to Robin, but he didn't take his eyes off of Kain. "They know, deep down, that meager humans such as ourselves will never be good enough.

"But I can help you. You'll never have to settle again." Kain's eyes stayed locked on Robin for a moment before he gestured behind him. The remaining Shadow Men made space once more for someone else to come forward. Nayla, no longer wearing her mask, was being held up on her damaged legs. Her face was tear streaked, her lips parted with sobs. Inside Robin, the version of himself who had loved her, who pitied this broken creature, was at war with the knowledge that if it weren't for her, none of this would be happening.

"Pathetic, isn't it?" said Kain. Looking at Nayla curiously, he held out a hand and a Shadow Man gave Kain his staff. Without so much as a flicker of hesitation, Kain swung the sharp edge across Nayla's throat.

"No!" Robin cried, unable to stop himself. Still, he didn't move, trying to shield Yara with his body, rooted to the spot as he helplessly watched blood spill across Nayla's neck. She gurgled for a few moments and fell to the floor, joining the carnage.

"Oh, don't be sad," said Kain, feigning concern. "This one was in pain. I simply put her out of her misery. It was a kindness. But mostly I wanted to show you my trick up close. Watch this part." He grinned wickedly and summoned another person to join him at the front, eliciting a cry of surprise from Janya.

The woman who stepped out from behind the door was, in many ways, the spitting image of Janya Varma, but she was not a clone. Her hair was graying, her nose more curved, her eyes dead.

"Mom?" said Janya.

The Necromancer didn't react, gave not so much as a flicker of recognition or even an indication that she'd heard her daughter.

The Guardians all tensed as two more Shadow Men came forward, but they made no move to attack. They merely walked to one of the pods that contained a Nayla clone. Robin watched with horror and fascination as the liquid was drained, the pod opened, and several injections in quick succession were used to wake the new copy of the woman who lay dead at their feet. The Necromancer placed her hands on the groggy Nayla's head and closed her eyes. For a moment, it felt like nothing was happening as the world held its breath.

Then, soft flashes of a blue-white light flickered beneath the Necromancer's fingers against Nayla's temple, like static. It was over in a minute, and when the new Nayla's eyes fluttered open, they were gentle and full of recognition. They were eyes Robin recognized.

It had looked so easy...

"Robin?" said Nayla, her voice hoarse from vocal chords that had never been used.

They had to get to the Furtive. Wherever Yara and Carter had left it, it was their only ticket out of here. The problem now was the army that stood in their way. Carter groaned on the floor, their bear head still in Ash's lap, as they slowly regained consciousness.

"So," said Kain, drawing Robin's attention back, "let's look at the situation you find yourselves in right now. You're outnumbered. Surrounded. And *we—*" he gestured at himself and his Shadow Men, "—cannot die. Can the same be said for you?"

"Mom!" said Janya, her voice breaking. Unable to help herself, she ran toward the Necromancer. Elida made a move to stop her, but she was too slow. Ben was in such terrible shape that he couldn't even lift a finger. Orlando grabbed her arm, but Janya shook him off vehemently. The Shadow Men easily restrained Janya, one of them punching her in the face to slow her down. Blood dripped down her cheek from a cut on her eyebrow that stitched itself shut almost instantaneously. "Mom, please," she begged, struggling against her captors. "Mom! Zenobia! It's me, it's Janya!"

But her words had no effect on the Necromancer.

"Shut her up," said Kain.

"No!" Orlando yelled, his voice cracking.

A Shadow Man stepped forward and swung his weapon—a short, flat blade—at Janya's head. Her neck lurched and she fell, her cheek knitting itself back together before she stumbled back to her feet, clutching at her face. Orlando managed to coax her behind him, still struggling as he was with Ben's nearly unconscious body.

Robin just couldn't see a way out.

* * *

The Furtive was close. Carter had tried to stop Yara from running into the house when the Guardians weren't outside waiting for them, but she had insisted. She felt stupid, now. Felt trapped. They *were* trapped.

If they could just fight their way past the Shadow Men, up the stairs, they could get to the Furtive. Robin seemed to sense that she wanted to charge. He squeezed her hand as a gentle warning.

"You know, Janya here isn't the only one who takes after her parent. Her mother, but..." He looked at Yara, "...it was your father, wasn't it?" He laughed. "I don't know why I bother asking. I know the answer already. Yes. You're so like him."

Yara's breath hitched.

"You both came in thinking you could defeat me, just because you were born with something I am without. And yet it was I who bested him. Bested your mother," he said to Janya. "Bested all of you. Does it hurt? Knowing you were defeated by a human?"

Every part of Yara hurt. But through the pain and through the fear she felt Kain's words penetrate her mind, slowly, delayed so that it was several seconds before she understood the words he had said. Her father. Kain had... *bested* her father?

"This has gone better than I could possibly have imagined!" he continued, clapping his hands and looking around the room. "I have not only one hydan, but *two*. And a shape shifter and a couple of nymphs here as well." He looked to Elida, her face torn, and Ash, who still had Carter in her lap. They were starting to stir as Ash stroked their furry head, whispering to them words Yara couldn't make out. An amber eye opened. "I haven't had enough of those to work with. So much to learn!"

Yara turned to Robin. This was it. The worst case scenario. And it was all her fault. If she had just listened to Carter... Her Guardians' orders were to kill her, to trigger the failsafe. Would they? Yara didn't believe them capable of it. The true question, the one she was afraid to ask herself was: did she want them to? She couldn't imagine going through it all again. Being back with Kain, him using her to become a Deviant, Yara nothing more than his tool. She would rather die than go through it a second time. She tried to tell Robin as much with her eyes, but he refused to look at her, his focus instead on Kain.

And there was Janya. She was in as much danger as Yara. Would her Guardians do what Robin would not, and kill Janya? Would they kill Yara?

Without looking, Kain held out his hand. The Necromancer

obediently came to stand next to him. "Do you recognize your daughter?" he asked her.

The Necromancer turned her dead eyes to Janya. After inspecting her for a moment, she said simply, "No."

"Of course not," said Kain sympathetically, stroking her cheek with his finger. "It's been so long. And she's grown so much. She's a woman now. But you'll have plenty of time to get acquainted. Something I'm sure *you're* looking forward to," he said, turning to Janya.

Janya shrugged. "Not particularly."

"What?" said Kain, taken aback.

"That's not my mother," said Janya, lowering her chin defiantly as she glared at Kain. "You killed my mother."

Kain chewed on the inside of his lip for a moment, considering this show of contempt as he debated how to respond. "I see," he said at last.

"She could bring herself back if you'd let her," Janya continued. "She's a necromancer, after all. She could resurrect herself. But you don't want to let her, do you?" She took a challenging step forward. "You know that she never loved you, and if you were to let her come back—if you were to *truly* let my mother come back, she would leave you. Just like she did before. When you killed her. She would hate everything that you've done, everything you've made her do."

The corners of Kain's mouth were curling, as though he were entertained by Janya's attempt at getting a rise out of him. But Yara, who had spent too long observing his mannerisms could recognize the flicker of anger behind his wild eyes. "My dear Janya," he said. "You never knew her like I did. You never saw her desire for progress. Her hunger for greatness."

"Maybe not," said Janya. "But I felt her love, which is more than I can say for you."

A twitch in his upper lip. She was getting under his skin. Distracting him.

Yara wanted so desperately to see into the future, get any hint as to how they might escape, that she tried one more time to see what they were facing, tried to sink into her mind and elicit a vision. Anything that could clue her in to what was going to happen.

And at last, unbelievably, it worked. The world disappeared and was replaced instead with a room... at Headquarters? That made no sense. She wasn't trying to see that far out into the future, though she supposed there was comfort in knowing that they made it back and

Headquarters wasn't gone forever after what happened. She was about to rewind the tape in her head, back to a time that was more immediate, when she noticed through the fog of her vision an unexpected scene. It was Robin and Nayla. Yara didn't recognize whose room it was. It must have been Nayla's. The scene that was unfolding in her head was not something Yara should be seeing. She had become an unintentional intruder of an intimate moment between the two Guardians. Yara abruptly jerked her hand out of Robin's, and the scene vanished.

He looked at her, confused.

She met his consternation with an equally dumbfounded expression. She was still trying to shake the image of Nayla's hand under Robin's tunic, faces so close they had shared breath. Yara shook her head and forced her attention back to Kain, hoping no one had noticed.

In trying to see the future, she had gotten instead a glimpse of Robin's past. Whatever barrier against her gift Kain had erected had not let up. She was still blind to their fate.

"Will you ever bring her back?" Janya was saying, tears of hatred in her eyes. "Or will you satisfy your lust with the hollow shell of a woman who never wanted you? Why should you bother yourself with little things like consent when you can craft walking puppets for your disposal? The death of one of your goons means nothing when you can grow another. So how much can she really be of value to you?"

Kain's anger came to a point. He raised his hand to strike Janya and stopped when Robin yelled, "Now!"

Yara fell to the ground and rolled away from the Shadow Men who had charged toward her, snatching a glowing blade from one as she did. She didn't have time to register what the rest of the Guardians were doing when Ash launched herself at Yara, encircling her completely as a shield of flame, just as she had done at the Fête. Yara started sweating instantly, the heat nearly unbearable.

"Move with me," came Ash's voice from somewhere within the inferno. "Go forward."

Through the crackling, Yara was barely aware of the fight around her. She let Ash's protective screen lead her blindly. "Wait! What's happening?" she yelled. "We have to get the others."

"Keep moving!" was Ash's only reply.

There was no time to think. Ash led Yara all the way up the stairs where the nymph collapsed on all fours in her human form, trembling.

Yara pulled her up. "You OK?"

Ash nodded. "It just takes a lot…" she managed. "Go."

"But—" said Yara, looking downstairs where the fight raged on.

"Go!" said Ash with a weak flare. She shoved Yara toward the front door. "Where did you park?" she said once they were outside.

"Just past the gate," said Yara, pointing to the dormant Furtive.

As they started to head in that direction, trees rustled from behind the house as though caught in a heavy wind. Without missing a beat, they changed directions and ran to the back, where a second Furtive was hovering within the perimeter of the grounds, black-clad figures rappelling down and running to meet them.

CHAPTER THIRTY-TWO
The Wall

"Yara!" Erik ran to Yara the moment his feet touched the ground. They crashed together. Her body trembled in his arms. He kissed her with relief, everywhere he could reach. She was crying. "Are you OK?" he said, his voice cracking.

"They're still inside!" said Ash.

More White Masks followed after Erik, including Zak Glover. Ash called to the others and led the charge toward the house, back into the fray now that Yara was safe with Erik.

Yara looked for Black for a moment, only to remember that she was dead and Glover was now in charge. She had no words to describe her relief at seeing them all. There was hope. They were saved.

"What's the status?" said Glover in his deep voice, still somehow collected even in the face of chaos.

"They're all still in the basement," said Yara.

"Where's N?" said Erik. "Nayla. It was her. Where is she? She's like me. A clone."

"We know," said Yara. "She's down there, too. We all know."

Erik sagged with relief and squeezed Yara again. "I'm so happy you're OK," he said, his voice muffled by her shoulder.

"How did you find out about Nayla?" she asked him.

"I remembered something. From the missing year."

Yara desperately wanted to know more, but she knew now wasn't the time. So instead she simply kissed him and said, "Thank god you're here."

"Thank you, Yara," said Glover. "We'll take it from here."

She felt less than a second of reassurance before confusion took over. Glover lifted a small device to Erik's ear.

"What're you—" Erik started, jerking away from Glover, his eyes flashing. But before he could finish speaking, his body froze, his gaze now dead and uncaring.

"Hey!" said Yara, unable to think. Glover turned to her and swung his fist. She barely had enough time to register what he was about to do, her hands reacting before her brain caught up, blocking him. "What—" she said, but he was already swinging again. He was moving impossibly fast, attacking her again even as she parried. He landed a blow, his fist connecting with her head. White and red filled her vision, rattling her brain.

By the time she got her bearings back, she was disarmed and being carried by Erik in a firefighter's lift.

"Put me down!" she screamed, struggling, but Erik was gone now. She knew what had been done—what *Glover* had done. Erik had been replaced by Kain's mindless puppet.

It was impossible to believe. How many White Masks were secretly working for Kain? Yara had assumed Nayla was the only one, but now she wasn't sure. Were there more? With Black dead, Glover was completely in charge. The Society was crumbling, decimated by Kain and his sympathizers.

Yara began to beat against Erik's back, squirming, trying frantically to escape his hold, but he was too strong, and thick branches had grown from his arms, twisting themselves around Yara's legs and torso. They wound toward her arms, pinning them down until she was completely immobilized. "Erik!" she cried, hopelessly trying to reach some dormant part of him that was still there. "Erik, please! It's me, Yara." She said it more quietly so Glover wouldn't hear, reminding herself of Janya, pleading to her uncaring mother then declaring that the Necromancer was no more her mother than any of the other Shadow Men.

That was what Kain did. He tore people apart. He stole Janya's childhood with her family, took Yara's innocence, exploited her love of Erik, violated Nayla by taking her body and copying it and making it something he owned and controlled...

And Yara's father...

What had Kain meant? Could he really be responsible for her father's death? It wasn't possible, or someone would have told her. She had asked about his death. Asked Glover about her parents... and

Glover had lied.

Of course. Of course he had lied. Glover had been working for Kain all this time. How could she be so stupid?

"Erik, don't do this," she tried again. "Erik, I love you."

His step faltered and Yara's heart skipped a beat, but her hope was quashed when he kept going. He must have just tripped.

"No!" Robin screamed. The Guardians had managed their way out of the basement and onto the ground floor, the weakened and outnumbered forces of the White Mask Society against the inferior but seemingly infinite Shadow Men, only to find Yara being marched right back into the enemy's clutches by none other than Erik. He wasn't alone either. A rock settled in Robin's gut.

It couldn't be.

Zak Glover.

He wore his uniform and mask just like the rest of them, a sea of anonymous black and white figures, but there was no mistaking his stature. There was no look of urgency, no surprise at the situation, no signs he had struggled. Glover was there because he meant to be, and everything was as he expected.

Nayla had never been the only spy.

The realization had stalled the Guardians, who now found themselves trapped. Glover and Erik were blocking the exit ahead of them, and the remaining Shadow Men, Kain, and the Necromancer were filling in from the basement behind.

The Guardians were too weak to keep fighting. The few seconds they had eked out for their attempted escape had been lost. They all but collapsed, clutching their various injuries. Ben was on death's door. Janya alone remained apparently unharmed.

Kain looked at Glover expectantly.

The new Head of the Society took off his white mask and said to Kain, "I have brought loyal sympathizers. They are outside securing the area from the other Guardians."

How many were on Kain's side?

"No..." Robin heard Yara cry, still draped carelessly over Erik's shoulder and bound by thick vines. She struggled, but Erik did not release her.

"What?" gasped Elida, torn and bloody, unable to comprehend the magnitude of the situation.

Real panic was gripping Robin now. Were they truly about to lose?

He couldn't let Yara die, nor could he let her get captured by Kain. Could not let her endure what the madman had done to her again.

"E!" yelled Robin, sweat mixing with blood on his jaw.

"Robin!" Yara cried, a plea in her voice. "Robin, please!"

Robin didn't waste time trying to understand what she was asking of him and called again to his comrade. "Erik! Don't do this!"

Those green eyes did not even flicker in Robin's direction. Instead, when Kain held out his hand, Erik brought him Yara, dropping her heavily onto her knees at Kain's feet. Still bound to her by the branches that grew from his arms, Erik held Yara before Kain, whose eyes gleamed victoriously.

Her back was turned to Robin, but even unable to see her eyes, he could sense her fear and anger. Kain touched her face, and his fingers came away bloody. Her nose must be bleeding again.

"You've lost," said Kain.

"I wouldn't be so sure of that."

It took a moment for Robin to know where the voice had come from. It was Erik.

By the look on Glover and Kain's faces, they were as stunned as Robin. But there was no mistaking it. Erik, who had moments before been as unresponsive as a Shadow Man, was now glaring at Kain, sweat falling down his temples from the apparent effort of fighting his conditioning.

In a swift movement, he whipped a blade from a hidden sheath in his pants and plunged it into Kain's neck.

Erik was trembling from the effort of resisting, his body telling him to stop, his mind telling him to go. The blade sank into Kain's neck, piercing through sinew and muscle and arteries. Hot blood gushed over Erik's fist and splashed onto his face, metallic and salty. He watched the man gurgle and splutter, shock filling those murky eyes. Erik knew it wasn't permanent. This shell was one of many, evidenced by the brand on his neck, now obscured by Erik's handiwork. The Necromancer would bring him back just as she had before. But it would buy them time. His grip on the handle was failing, his hand shaking too violently to keep hold. Before he could release the blade, Kain fell to the floor.

Somehow, Yara had untangled herself from the boughs that had grown from Erik. He felt a tug as she tore them from his arms and then her hands were on his face, shaking him, pulling him away. The world was muted as his fight for control weakened. He was barely aware of what was happening around him. He wanted to give in to the numbness that threatened to take over, but Yara's face in front of him was like an anchor, so he focused on holding onto it rather than let the tide take him.

"Erik!" she was saying. "Erik, can you hear me?"

"Yes," he heard himself say.

"We have to go!"

A blur of activity all around him was too difficult to discern through his narrow blinders. *Yara,* he thought. *Focus on Yara.*

So he did. She had an iron grip on his hand as she led him through a maze of havoc. She jerked around a few times, undoubtedly a result of trying to avoid a fight. Erik wanted to help, but he could barely focus. He would try to gain an understanding of what was happening and then his mind couldn't wrap itself around what he saw. There were periods in which he blacked out, losing time. And then he was in a different place than he remembered.

The dusty, still air was replaced by a cool breeze. Outside. They were outside.

Yara's hand disappeared and the world got foggy.

She was back. He was somewhere else. Time had passed but he didn't know how much.

"I got it!" came Yara's voice. And her face was in front of his. She was holding something in her other hand. Something small and silver. "I got it!" she said again. "What button is it?" He didn't know how to answer, couldn't understand what she was asking. But she wasn't asking him. Music started to play from the small device in her hand, the world cleared, and he was back.

"It worked!" Yara screamed as she saw the light return to Erik's eyes. He blinked a few times, taking in his surroundings. They were losing. The forces Glover had brought were all sympathizers and had joined Kain and his dwindling supply of Shadow Men. Even though there were only a handful of White Masks, they were fully armed and trained. Much more efficient fighters than the Shadow Men. Ash had caused significant damage, taking out more than half of them, before burning herself out. She was now fully human and trapped in NullBonds, locked in her corporal form.

Orlando had made it back to the Furtive and was firing cover from the ship, trying to clear a path for them. Carter was changing so quickly from shape to shape it was impossible to distinguish what they were but a flashing mess of fur and fangs and claws as they tore through the remaining Shadow Men.

"Let's go!" Yara cried, pulling Erik toward the Furtive. But Erik wasn't following her. Instead, his eyes were behind him, watching the battle. Robin had wrestled Ash away from the corrupt Guardians, but without the proper key he couldn't remove her bonds. Janya and Elida were trying to support the unconscious Ben between them, but they were being accosted by two more of Glover's people.

"I have to help," Erik said to Yara. "Go."

"No," she said. She wouldn't leave without him.

He turned to her and clutched her shoulders, her arms, her face, her neck. His hands moved frantically as though unable to decide where to hold her. "Listen to me," he said, his voice low. He kissed her, and she hadn't realized that she was crying until his face came away wet with her tears. His hands had settled on the back of her neck, and she was gripping his wrists so hard her knuckles were turning white. "I need you to make it out of here. Do you understand?"

"I won't—"

"You have to go. You have to trust me."

She stared at him mutely.

"Yara, I will not lose you. I can not lose you. Please."

She faltered for a moment. Did he not understand that he had never lost her? She had been the one to lose him. How could he ask her to go now? "Come with me," she said lamely. She couldn't think of anything else to say. Every word of love was lost in a sea of devotion; how could she find exactly the right drop of water amidst the flood? She was trembling.

He pressed his lips to hers. It was desperate and painful, but not as painful as when he pulled away. "I'll find you. I promise," he said.

Yara searched Erik's eyes. She wanted to believe him. But they had already lost one opportunity to say goodbye. Yara didn't want to risk it happening again. Anything could happen to either of them. "I love you," she whispered.

Whether he heard her through the din she didn't know, but he seemed to understand. He wiped a tear from her cheek with his thumb and kissed her again. "Go. Please."

Robin reached them, limping badly, a shackled Ash in tow. "You two," he said to Ash and Yara. "Get to the Furtive."

Yara didn't have time to protest any more when Carter, back in bear shape, swiped a huge paw at a corrupt Guardian's oncoming solenoid, knocking it out of the air and saving Yara, who was instead hit by nothing but a splash of Carter's blood. Carter couldn't speak in that form, but their burning gaze told Yara enough.

She and Ash ran toward the Furtive. They sprinted up the ramp onto the stealth ship. The silent engines ached to take off, but it stayed obediently on the disturbed grass, waiting for everyone else to join. Where they would go from there, Yara didn't know. Headquarters was lost. Everything had changed.

Ash took over from Elida in carrying Ben as they reached the edge of the clearing where the Furtive waited. Elida was on the verge of collapse herself.

"Where is Carter going?" Yara said, looking over her shoulder as the bear ran through the masses toward the opposite side of the house.

"They're disabling the other Furtive," said Ash.

"I have to go back and help them," said Janya once her Guardians were safe. "They can't hurt me."

"No," said Yara. "You can't risk—" She heard herself speak like someone else was saying the words. Janya was too valuable. Her capture by Kain could mean a second Necromancer. And Janya didn't know what Yara knew. About the failsafe. That her Guardians would not risk it. That it could mean forfeiting her life.

But Robin and Erik and Carter were back there. She could see them fighting. Another Kain had not yet been raised as far as Yara could see, but Glover was doing a fine job commanding the forces, including the Necromancer.

Janya was already sprinting back into the fray. Yara was impressed by Janya's fearlessness. It was true that Janya's healing was remarkable, and though she was impervious to lasting damage, she still had plenty to lose. She was not immune to being captured, not immune to pain, not immune to death. After all, Zenobia Varma had had the same ability to heal, and she had been killed.

Carter was limping toward the Furtive, but they were badly hurt. They staggered closer, transforming from a bear wearing armor back into a human, their right arm held gingerly against their chest.

They were too far. They weren't going to make it.

Back to back. It was just like old times. Though, admittedly, for Erik it felt like almost no time had passed. Even with the resurgence of lost memories of his year in Kain's custody, he had no real sense of having lived any of those experiences.

He and Robin still worked flawlessly as a team, together more powerful, more deadly than the sum of their skills. But they were tired and outnumbered. They just needed to hold the hoard back from the Furtive. It was becoming harder to do. Almost everyone was on board but them, yet every time they turned to run toward the stealth ship, the two of them were overtaken by White Masks who were fresh to battle. Erik knew the Furtive wouldn't leave without everyone on board, but they had no way of getting to it without the ship being overrun by the wrong people.

"I've got a bad feeling, E," said Robin with effort from behind him, having just kicked an assailant to the ground.

Erik didn't need to ask what Robin meant. He had the same bad feeling. "You go," he shouted over his shoulder. "I'll hold them back."

"No," said Robin.

Erik opened his mouth to protest, to insist that he be the one to stay behind. He was on his second chance at life already. This was borrowed time. But he never got the chance to say anything, cut off by Robin.

"Together."

They turned to look at each other. Robin's jaw was set. Erik knew better than to object. He nodded.

With an instinct that came from years of working and training together, Erik leapt past Robin and threw up his hands toward the wall that surrounded the house. He pulled from within himself, the often dormant nymph side of him summoned to the surface. In his old body, Erik's skills were mild and relatively useless. He barely used them. But Kain was in the business of amplifying, so now, the earth shook as branches sprang from Erik in an explosion of growth, and stemmed up from the ground at his feet, vines webbing in all directions around him. The earth around him quaked with such strength that several oncoming White Masks lost their footing as the dying lawn transformed into a tangle of bright green thickets.

The urge to stop was strong as energy leaked from him, manifesting as a wild forest. He resisted, instead redoubling his concentration and spreading his arms wider. The branches thickened as they grew, intertwining with one another, leaves overlapping and rustling as everything snaked around itself, until a barrier started to form from the growth. His reach was wide. He poured all that he had into the earth, demanding so much in return. Branches sprang up all around the property and started to latch onto the Furtive that he had arrived on with Glover, knitting it into the fabric of the blockade he was building.

Someone grabbed at his shoulder, a blade burning his arm, but just as quickly they were yanked away by Robin. He had Erik's back.

His shoulders and arms and legs were trembling with effort. His throat was raw from screaming. Boughs were growing around him, entangling him in their embrace. And still he surged them out from within, weaving a wall that would be solid enough to keep Kain's people in, to buy enough time for the others—for Yara—to escape.

He hoped she would forgive him. He was going to break his promise.

Janya started to run faster, struggling to keep her footing on the quaking earth as she saw what Erik was doing. A massive hedge was growing from his outstretched arms and out from under his feet, locking the bad guys in and her out, but she had to get to Carter and help the others. And her mother was still in there…

"No!" Robin yelled when he saw her running toward them. "Go back!"

She had taken a gauntlet from the Furtive and wanted to get it to him. She had no idea how to use it, but Robin did. And she *did* have an idea how to use the knife she'd swiped from Orlando. Her gun was long gone and had proved to be less useful than she'd hoped.

"Catch!" She chucked the metal glove at Robin, hoping he would be able to summon a solenoidal star. Her hopes were well-founded. The gauntlet was on his hand, swinging at an oncoming Guardian and stealing their solenoid.

Janya made it past the barrier and swung her knife wildly at another attacker who was making for Erik. She felt a deep cut on her shoulder that burned, pain radiating down her arm, before getting very itchy as it healed, all within the span of a few seconds. She reached for Carter and helped them up, losing her balance in the process as the ground jerked violently. Carter groaned in pain when she touched their arm, which was completely mangled, but there was no time for tenderness. She had to get them to the Furtive.

"Janya, go back," Carter said through clenched teeth.

"We're almost there," she said. The two of them staggered past Erik's growing hedge. She threw a look over her shoulder. She wouldn't be able to help Erik or Robin. She could scarcely believe they were still standing.

"No!" It was Carter who cried out. She turned to see what they were reacting to and just as soon they ran into something solid, falling back a step and eliciting another yell of pain from the shape shifter.

Janya gasped.

The Necromancer stood before them, having snuck away from the brawl to block their path.

It couldn't end like this. They were mere feet from freedom. Janya's bloodied and defeated Guardians were calling her name. Of all the people to stop her, it was her mother. Or rather, a body, a shell, a drone, nothing more than the carbon copy of the woman who had once held her in her arms, promising her the world. But the warm eyes Janya remembered were now as cold as the night air.

The Necromancer's grip on Janya's arm was solid, and Janya could feel, as though from premonition, the future that awaited her. Back in a cold room, nothing more than a vessel to be used by Kain and his Shadow Men. Panic was overwhelming her, but then something unexpected happened.

The hand holding her loosened.

In the span of three seconds, Janya looked up and saw her mother looking down at her. Not the Necromancer, not one of Kain's henchmen.

Her mother.

Tears filled Janya's eyes, and she was overcome by the urge to wrap her arms around her mother. But the Necromancer turned and walked away, back toward the people who had done this to her. To all of them.

"Janya!" It was Orlando who was running toward her from the Furtive. She started once again to move toward him, holding up Carter. Looking back, she saw the wall Erik was building, a massive blockade of growth, vines and branches weaving together to lock everyone else in, all to buy them time to get out.

Orlando was sprinting and stumbling down to help her with Carter. Erik and Robin couldn't hold the line much longer.

The world slowed. She was steps from freedom. But her mother...

Her mother was alive. Deep within the Necromancer was a part of Zenobia Varma. The proof was evident. She had let Janya go. She had been caught by the so-called Necromancer, and she had let her daughter go...

Carter and Orlando boarded the Furtive and Orlando took Janya's hand, but doubt—or rather *faith*—stayed her.

Their eyes met, and Orlando seemed to understand what she was thinking. "No!" he screamed, the sound guttural.

But Janya was already turning around and running back.

Back toward her mother.

Yara watched from the Furtive, the action small and removed through the view screen. She clutched at the controls to keep from falling over as the earth shook under them.

"What are they doing?" she said, panicking. Ben and Elida were in the back, Elida treating her unconscious partner as best she could despite her own grisly injuries. The badly wounded Carter had collapsed, and the rest of them were huddled around the bridge of the ship, watching Orlando, who was screaming outside, trying to call Janya back. Yara could see him despite the shadow of the Furtive. He was near the opening into the mansion grounds, but Robin and Erik were not only still on the wrong side of the gate, they no longer seemed to be trying to leave.

Ash strapped Carter to the seat next to Yara and followed her gaze.

"Carter, what are they doing?" Yara repeated.

Carter's eyes were bright with pain as they clutched their mangled arm to their chest.

"Oh shit," said Ash. She turned and started to head out of the Furtive when Carter stopped her.

"No," they said, soft yet firm.

"But—" said Ash.

"They understand."

The Guardians at her side had both understood something Yara was still trying to make sense of.

"They can't…" said Yara. "No… No!" As Ash had done, she made to run off the Furtive. This time it was Ash who made to stop her, but she was not fast enough. Yara evaded the Vurwari and ran back into the night, screaming, "Erik! Robin! No!" She stumbled as she moved toward them. The ground shuddered. Ash was already on Yara's heels, pulling her back. The nymph was stronger, so Yara's struggling was in vain. It didn't stop her from trying.

"Erik!" Her view of him was rapidly fading, obscured by the massive hedge growing from his outstretched hands.

Robin was still visible through the opening, however two Shadow Men were on him. And they were winning.

"Robin!" she cried, desperate, as Ash pulled her back to the ship.

His eyes snapped to her. She saw his lips moving, but heard nothing, his voice lost in the sea of sound.

"Yara, we need to go!" said Ash. "They're doing this to make sure we get out. Don't let it be for nothing."

Yara kept screaming, kept struggling, but it was no use. Before she knew it, she was back on the ship. She sprinted back up to the view screen, desperate to keep her eyes on Robin and Erik as long as she could. But Erik was already gone, hidden behind his own wall.

Something was happening with Orlando and Janya, but Yara no longer cared. Her focus was only on Robin.

Out of the corner of her eyes, she saw Orlando run back to them, heard him climb aboard without Janya and tell them to go, his face wet with sweat and tears. The engine started up, the floor vibrating softly under their feet, and they rose into the air. The shaking of the earthquake was replaced instead with the steady hum of the Furtive.

The last thing Yara saw as the hedge knitted together was Robin on his knees, his hands falling to his sides, the fight in him gone.

As he watched the Furtive lift up into the air, Robin knew he could stop. He could finally rest. He dropped his weapon in surrender and let himself fall, overcome with relief. Yara was safe. She'd made it out. Defeated, his arms were pulled painfully behind him by two treasonous White Masks.

Robin wanted to call out to Erik, but he had no voice. He was slammed into the ground, but he kept his eyes on his comrade. Erik was being consumed by his own power, the branches springing from the shaking ground and from his body, winding around him, caging him. If he didn't move, he would get trapped, and Robin had no idea how to get him out.

As the last few branches intertwined, closing them off completely, the ground finally fell still.

Janya lay face down to Robin's right, barely more than a silhouette in the dark. Her Guardians had made the impossible decision and sacrificed her to prevent Kain from being able to use her ability. A sacrifice Robin feared was made futilely, since her body was inside the barrier and being swarmed by Shadow Men. They would just be able to clone her, as they had done to her mother. The failsafe had been established without knowing the extent of Kain's power.

Robin's eyes were still on Erik—at least, where he thought Erik was within the hedge. Several people were hacking away at the growth, either trying to get through or to recover Erik or both. Robin almost didn't see Erik's body at first, his black clothes making him nearly invisible in the darkness, but his white hair was unmistakable.

A solenoid cut through one last branch and Erik fell backward into the awaiting arms. Panic swelled inside Robin's chest. Erik couldn't be dead. The traitors who had hold of Robin dragged him to his feet and Robin strained to get a better look at his partner, checking for any sign of life. Erik's limp body was being handled callously by the Shadow Man who carried him, and only marginally more carefully by one of Glover's Guardians.

"E!" Robin screamed, being dragged away. He struggled violently to get away and managed to jerk free of the two White Masks who held him. He staggered forward, weak and spent, but tried to get as close to his friend as possible. "E!" he shouted again. "Erik!" His hoarse voice broke when he was seized again, but there… Movement in Erik's chest. A breath. He was alive!

Robin started laughing, a joyless release of fear and tension as he let himself get pulled back, his eyes still glued to his partner.

"She made it out!" he croaked, hoping that Erik would hear, unsure if he would get another chance to tell him what they had sacrificed themselves for. "Yara made it out. She's gonna be OK."

They dragged him away, and Robin's head lolled forward, ready to succumb to whatever Kain would have in store for him, and smiled to himself.

"She's gonna be OK," he whispered.

CHAPTER THIRTY-THREE

Two Hours Later

A Furtive set down on the roof of a lesser White Mask Society outpost. Having retrieved everyone and everything left behind at the safe house, the seven people aboard were welcomed into the old winery that had been converted into a small base several decades ago. Only a dozen or so people occupied the outpost, and they showed the new arrivals around the kitchen, the old warehouse which had been converted to an office space, and the former tasting room which was now used as a commissary.

The shape shifter, the fauna nymph, and one of the humans were escorted to what had once been the bottling room, now a medical ward. The rest of the weary travelers could wait before having their injuries treated, instead falling to the cots set up in the erstwhile aging facility to get some rest. They were all asleep within minutes.

All except the hydan, who stared at the arched, rustic ceiling until the thin rays of the rising sun cast warm streaks of light across the wooden beams.

The woman's body was already starting to heal as she was carried back inside. The damage would have been enough to kill an ordinary human, even most Deviants, but it had not killed her instantly, and her natural ability to heal worked faster to keep her alive than her injuries worked to kill her.

Less work for me, thought the Necromancer as she followed the still limp form inside.

There was something about this young woman that intrigued the

Necromancer, though she couldn't put her finger directly on it. A familiarity she couldn't place. Perhaps it was nothing more than a physical resemblance. They did look strikingly similar to each other. Maybe that had been why she had let the young woman go…

Of course it didn't matter now.

For the moment, the Necromancer had only one job. Bringing Kain back into a new body. Again.

He would take it from there.

Epilogue

Yara Rivers had another headache.

After so long without any, she had forgotten how debilitating they could be. Her nose had not stopped bleeding since she had been trying to see what lay ahead for those who had been left behind. Just as before, she kept hitting a solid wall. Kain had figured out how to block her from seeing not only him, but all of his Shadow Men and everyone who was with him.

When she tried to look into her own future, it was barely more than a hazy mess of indecision.

Still, none of that explained the return of her headaches—which she had believed were gone once she'd learned to control her visions—or the nosebleeds—which were new.

She didn't care. She found herself returning to the same apathy, the same numbness that had consumed her after Erik's death. A feeling of such helplessness that she was paralyzed, her body and mind all but shut down from overload.

Three of the people she cared about most in the whole world, and she had no idea what would become of them. At that moment, Carter was in the infirmary, their arm badly mangled, the right side of their body shredded. Yara didn't know if they would be able to fully recover.

And Robin and Erik…

She could still see Erik's shock of white hair disappearing behind the massive hedges. Robin falling to his knees… Were they even still alive? She couldn't entertain the thought that they might be gone. It was suffocating.

Her cot sank near her feet, and Yara raised her head to see Ash

287

sitting down.

"How you doing?"

Yara's head flopped back down on the pillow. She didn't answer.

"Your nose is bleeding." Ash's voice was quiet. It was more a statement, simply informing Yara rather than a show of concern or beseeching that anything be done about it. They were all a mess. There was no need to draw any medical attention away from those who needed it more. There was doubt Ben would even make it through the night and Elida was in worse shape than Carter.

After several minutes of silence, Yara spoke, her voice rough after so much screaming. "What now?"

Ash placed her warm hand on Yara's knee and squeezed it before putting it back in her lap. The NullBonds had been removed, but she didn't fiddle with fire as she usually did, no doubt in an attempt to rekindle her spent energy after the events of the night. "I'm not sure," she said. It was the first time Yara had ever seen Ash so somber. "But I know we'll figure something out. Together."

Stay Tuned!

Keep an eye out for the epic conclusion of
The White Mask Society series, coming soon.

Acknowledgements

Storytelling is a compulsion. Over the years, I have found every outlet, every means of telling a story, or consuming one. As a child who loved to read (thanks to the coercion of maman and dad) I decided to start my own foray into the written word and I was bad at it. Like, desperately bad at it. But I enjoyed it and I never stopped.

"The White Mask Society" was a fantasy that started when I was in high school, and the story stayed with me and changed to become nearly unrecognizable from its first version to the book I eventually published. A few things never changed. Yara, Erik, Robin, and Carter. They were always with me from the beginning. It's strange to know them so intimately, and yet recognizing that I would be a complete stranger to them…

I digress.

I started sharing my story with friends, I tried sharing my story with masses. Friends were supportive, the masses weren't interested. And then I decided that it didn't matter if the masses wanted my story or not. If people wanted to find it, I wanted it to be there for them. Then something kind of magical happened.

I let go.

After working on this story—variations of it—for over a decade, as soon as I made the decision that it was finished, I felt empowered. I handed it off to more people to read and was met with enthusiasm and encouragement. All that gave me the motivation I needed to write a second book. And now a third and a fourth and even a fifth. Because it's not about how many people read your book or how much money you can make from it (although I admit it would be nice for those numbers to be higher). It's about telling a story that you want to tell.

Art is so necessary to the human experience that it is inevitable.

There is no time in human history in which we have existed without art. In times of joy or sadness, abundance or starvation, love or grief, we have always produced, shared, consumed art.

There have been people who were instrumental in my ability to let go of my book and send it out into the world, a fledgling, on its own, cast from the nest of my personal computer.

My parents, who were the ones who encouraged me to read; even if it involved bribery, it worked. The American Girl dolls are long gone, but my love of books remains.

My friend Lainie, who is the most outstandingly supportive friend I have ever had the fortune of knowing. She will brag about you and buy seven copies of your book—no matter how much you protest—and then ask you to sign them and give them to everyone in her family. Exceptional.

My friend and editor Sean. One month into our friendship I handed him a pile of smutty scenes and told him he would hate everything I'd written and still to this day I think he loves my books more than anyone I know, and is always the most reliably enthusiastic to read horrible, unfinished first drafts. And still be interested in reading slightly less horrible second drafts. Sean… I think you and I both know this book wouldn't be any good without your diligent notes. (And yes, that ellipsis is on purpose, just for you.)

My grandmother, who would absolutely hate this book. But I learned to write from her, as we drafted poems together when I was itty bitty. She was always patiently accepting my requests to write *another* ode to my cat, Spock.

And to my husband, my Danny J. I have no idea how I got lucky enough to deserve a man with the patience and support that he has, but boy am I glad I did. I doubt he would like this book, either, but he always encouraged me to write it.

And finally, a special shout out to my dogs, Lemon, Ender, and Sprout, and the cat who adopted us, Seven of Nine. None of them made it easier to write. In fact, they all made it harder by demanding attention. But I'm glad they did, and I'll never regret succumbing. 'Twas worth it. Life has been made so much richer by their presence and love.

Want to stay up to date with A.M. Colwell? Check

out her website:

ayliacolwell.com

Or follow her on social media!

 @AMColwellWrites

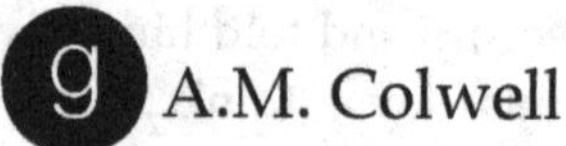 A.M. Colwell